CW01082017

The Collected Supernatural and Weird Fiction of John Kendrick Bangs Volume 2

The Collected Supernatural and Weird Fiction of John Kendrick Bangs Volume 2

Including Four Novellas
'A House-Boat on the Styx', 'The Pursuit of the House-Boat', 'The Enchanted Typewriter' and 'Mr. Munchausen' of the Strange and Unusual

John Kendrick Bangs

LEONAUR

The Collected
*Supernatural and Weird
Fiction of*
*John Kendrick Bangs
Volume 2
Including Four Novellas*
'*A House-Boat on the Styx*', '*The Pursuit of the House-Boat*',
'*The Enchanted Typewriter*'
*and 'Mr. Munchausen'
of the Strange and Unusual*
by John Kendrick Bangs

FIRST EDITION

Leonaur is an imprint
of Oakpast Ltd

Copyright in this form © 2010 Oakpast Ltd

ISBN: 978-0-85706-327-4 (hardcover)
ISBN: 978-0-85706-328-1 (softcover)

http://www.leonaur.com

Contents

A House-Boat on the Styx

1: CHARON MAKES A DISCOVERY

Charon, the Ferryman of renown, was cruising slowly along the Styx one pleasant Friday morning not long ago, and as he paddled idly on he chuckled mildly to himself as he thought of the monopoly in ferriage which in the course of years he had managed to build up.

"It's a great thing," he said, with a smirk of satisfaction—"it's a great thing to be the go-between between two states of being; to have the exclusive *franchise* to export and import shades from one state to the other, and withal to have had as clean a record as mine has been. Valuable as is my *franchise*, I never corrupted a public official in my life, and—"

Here Charon stopped his soliloquy and his boat simultaneously. As he rounded one of the many turns in the river a singular object met his gaze, and one, too, that filled him with misgiving. It was another craft, and that was a thing not to be tolerated. Had he, Charon, owned the exclusive right of way on the Styx all these years to have it disputed here in the closing decade of the Nineteenth Century? Had not he dealt satisfactorily with all, whether it was in the line of ferriage or in the providing of boats for pleasure-trips up the river? Had he not received expressions of satisfaction, indeed, from the most exclusive families of Hades with the very select series of picnics he had given at Charon's Glen Island? No wonder, then, that the queer-looking boat that met his gaze, moored in a shady nook on the dark side of the river, filled him with dismay.

"Blow me for a landlubber if I like that!" he said, in a hardly audible whisper. "And shiver my timbers if I don't find out what she's there for. If anybody thinks he can run an opposition line to mine on this river he's mightily mistaken. If it comes to competition, I can carry shades for nothing and still quaff the B. & G. yellow-label benzine three times a day without experiencing a financial panic. I'll show 'em a thing or two if they attempt to rival me. And what a boat! It looks for all the world like a Florentine barn on a canal-boat."

Charon paddled up to the side of the craft, and, standing up in the middle of his boat, cried out,

"Ship ahoy!"

There was no answer, and the Ferryman hailed her again. Receiving no response to his second call, he resolved to investigate for himself; so, fastening his own boat to the stern-post of the stranger, he clambered on board. If he was astonished as he sat in his ferry-boat, he was paralyzed when he cast his eye over the unwelcome vessel he had boarded. He stood for at least two minutes rooted to the spot. His eye swept over a long, broad deck, the polish of which resembled that of a ball-room floor. Amidships, running from three-quarters aft to three-quarters forward, stood a structure that in its lines resembled, as Charon had intimated, a barn, designed by an architect enamoured of Florentine simplicity; but in its construction the richest of woods had been used, and in its interior arrangement and adornment nothing more palatial could be conceived.

"What's the blooming thing for?" said Charon, more dismayed than ever. "If they start another line with a craft like this, I'm very much afraid I'm done for after all. I wouldn't take a boat like mine myself if there was a floating palace like this going the same way. I'll have to see the Commissioners about this, and find out what it all means. I suppose it'll cost me a pretty penny, too, confound them!"

A prey to these unhappy reflections, Charon investigated further, and the more he saw the less he liked it. He was about to encounter opposition, and an opposition which was apparently backed by persons of great wealth—perhaps the Commissioners themselves. It was a consoling thought that he had saved enough money in the course of his career to enable him to live in comfort all his days, but this was not really what Charon was after. He wished to acquire enough to retire and become one of the smart set. It had been done in that section of the universe which lay on the bright side of the Styx, why not, therefore, on the other, he asked.

"I'm pretty well connected even if I am a boatman," he had been known to say. "With Chaos for a grandfather, and Erebus and Nox for parents, I've just as good blood in my veins as anybody in Hades. The Noxes are a mighty fine family, not as bright as the Days, but older; and we're poor—that's it, poor—and it's money makes caste these days. If I had millions, and owned a railroad, they'd call me a yacht-owner. As I haven't, I'm only a boatman. Bah! Wait and see! I'll be giving swell functions myself some day, and these upstarts will be on their knees before me begging to be asked. Then I'll get up a little aristocracy of my own, and I won't let a soul into it whose name isn't mentioned in the Grecian mythologies. Mention in Burke's peerage and the *Élite* directories of America won't admit anybody to Commodore Charon's house unless there's some other mighty good reason for it."

Foreseeing an unhappy ending to all his hopes, the old man clambered sadly back into his ancient vessel and paddled off into the darkness. Some hours later, returning with a large company of new arrivals, while counting up the profits of the day Charon again caught sight of the new craft, and saw that it was brilliantly lighted and thronged with the most famous citizens of the Erebean country. Up in the bow was a spirit band discoursing music of the sweetest sort. Merry peals of laughter rang out over the dark waters of the Styx. The clink of glasses and the popping of corks punctuated the music with a frequency which would have delighted the soul of the most ardent lover of commas, all of which so overpowered the grand master boatman of the Stygian Ferry Company that he dropped three *oboli* and an American dime, which he carried as a pocket-piece, overboard. This, of course, added to his woe; but it was forgotten in an instant, for someone on the new boat had turned a search-light directly upon Charon himself, and simultaneously hailed the master of the ferry-boat.

"Charon!" cried the shade in charge of the light. "Charon, ahoy!"

"Ahoy yourself!" returned the old man, paddling his craft close up to the stranger. "What do you want?"

"You," said the shade. "The house committee want to see you right away."

"What for?" asked Charon, cautiously.

"I'm sure I don't know. I'm only a member of the club, and house committees never let mere members know anything about their plans. All I know is that you are wanted," said the other.

"Who are the house committee?" queried the Ferryman.

"Sir Walter Raleigh, Cassius, Demosthenes, Blackstone, Doctor Johnson, and Confucius," replied the shade.

"Tell 'em I'll be back in an hour," said Charon, pushing off. "I've got a cargo of shades on board consigned to various places up the river. I've promised to get 'em all through tonight, but I'll put on a couple of extra paddles—two of the new arrivals are working their passage this trip—and it won't take as long as usual. What boat is this, anyhow?"

"The *Nancy Nox*, of Erebus."

"Thunder!" cried Charon, as he pushed off and proceeded on his way up the river. "Named after my mother! Perhaps it'll come out all right yet."

More hopeful of mood, Charon, aided by the two dead-head passengers, soon got through with his evening's work, and in less than an hour was back seeking admittance, as requested, to the company of Sir Walter Raleigh and his fellow-members on the house committee. He was received by these worthies with considerable effusiveness, considering his position in society, and it warmed the cockles of his aged heart to note that Sir Walter, who had always been rather distant to him since he had carelessly upset that worthy and Queen Elizabeth in the middle of the Styx far back in the last century, permitted him to shake three fingers of his left hand when he entered the committee-room.

"How do you do, Charon?" said Sir Walter, affably. "We are very glad to see you."

"Thank you, kindly, Sir Walter," said the boatman. "I'm glad to hear those words, your honour, for I've been feeling very bad since I had the misfortune to drop your Excellency and her Majesty overboard. I never knew how it happened, sir, but happen it did, and but for her Majesty's kind assistance it might have been the worse for us. Eh, Sir Walter?"

The knight shook his head menacingly at Charon. Hitherto he had managed to keep it a secret that the Queen had rescued him from drowning upon that occasion by swimming ashore herself first and throwing Sir Walter her ruff as soon as she landed, which he had used as a life-preserver.

"'Sh!" he said, *sotto voce*. "Don't say anything about that, my man."

"Very well, Sir Walter, I won't," said the boatman; but he made a mental note of the knight's agitation, and perceived a means by which that illustrious courtier could be made useful to him in his scheming for social advancement.

"I understood you had something to say to me," said Charon, after he had greeted the others.

"We have," said Sir Walter. "We want you to assume command of this boat."

The old fellow's eyes lighted up with pleasure.

"You want a captain, eh?" he said.

"No," said Confucius, tapping the table with a diamond-studded chop-stick. "No. We want a—er—what the deuce is it they call the functionary, Cassius?"

"Senator, I think," said Cassius.

Demosthenes gave a loud laugh.

"Your mind is still running on Senatorships, my dear Cassius. That is quite evident," he said. "This is not one of them, however. The title we wish Charon to assume is neither Captain nor

Senator; it is Janitor."

"What's that?" asked Charon, a little disappointed. "What does a Janitor have to do?"

"He has to look after things in the house," explained Sir Walter. "He's a sort of proprietor by proxy. We want you to take charge of the house, and see to it that the boat is kept ship-shape."

"Where is the house?" queried the astonished boatman.

"This is it," said Sir Walter. "This is the house, and the boat too. In fact, it is a house-boat."

"Then it isn't a new-fangled scheme to drive me out of business?" said Charon, warily.

"Not at all," returned Sir Walter. "It's a new-fangled scheme to set you up in business. We'll pay you a large salary, and there won't be much to do. You are the best man for the place, because, while you don't know much about houses, you do know a great deal about boats, and the boat part is the most important part of a house-boat. If the boat sinks, you can't save the house; but if the house burns, you may be able to save the boat. See?"

"I think I do, sir," said Charon.

"Another reason why we want to employ you for Janitor," said Confucius, "is that our club wants to be in direct communication with both sides of the Styx; and we think you as Janitor would be able to make better arrangements for transportation with yourself as boatman, than some other man as Janitor could make with you."

"Spoken like a sage," said Demosthenes.

"Furthermore," said Cassius, "occasionally we shall want to have this boat towed up or down the river, according to the house committee's pleasure, and we think it would be well to have a Janitor who has some influence with the towing company which you represent."

"Can't this boat be moved without towing?" asked Charon.

"No," said Cassius.

"And I'm the only man who can tow it, eh?"

"You are," said Blackstone. "Worse luck."

"And you want me to be Janitor on a salary of what?"

"A hundred *oboli* a month," said Sir Walter, uneasily.

"Very well, gentlemen," said Charon. "I'll accept the office on a salary of two hundred *oboli* a month, with Saturdays off."

The committee went into executive session for five minutes, and on their return informed Charon that in behalf of the Associated Shades they accepted his offer.

"In behalf of what?" the old man asked.

"The Associated Shades," said Sir Walter. "The swellest organization in Hades, whose new house-boat you are now on board of. When shall you be ready to begin work?"

"Right away," said Charon, noting by the clock that it was the hour of midnight. "I'll start in right away, and as it is now Saturday morning, I'll begin by taking my day off."

2: A DISPUTED AUTHORSHIP

"How are you, Charon?" said Shakespeare, as the Janitor assisted him on board. "Anyone here tonight?"

"Yes, sir," said Charon. "Lord Bacon is up in the library, and Doctor Johnson is down in the billiard-room, playing pool with Nero."

"Ha-ha!" laughed Shakespeare. "Pool, eh? Does Nero play pool?"

"Not as well as he does the fiddle, sir," said the Janitor, with a twinkle in his eye.

Shakespeare entered the house and tossed up an *obolus*. "Heads—Bacon; tails—pool with Nero and Johnson," he said.

The coin came down with heads up, and Shakespeare went into the pool-room, just to show the Fates that he didn't care a tuppence for their verdict as registered through the *obolus*. It was a peculiar custom of Shakespeare's to toss up a coin to decide questions of little consequence, and then do the thing the coin decided he should not do. It showed, in Shakespeare's estimation, his entire independence of those dull persons who supposed that in them was centred the destiny of all mankind. The Fates, however, only smiled at these little acts of rebellion, and it was common gossip in Erebus that one of the trio had told the Furies that they had observed Shakespeare's tendency to kick over the traces, and always acted accordingly. They never let the coin fall so as to decide a question the way they wanted it, so that unwittingly the great dramatist did their will after all. It was a part of their plan that upon this occasion Shakespeare should play pool with Doctor Johnson and the Emperor Nero, and hence it was that the coin bade him repair to the library and chat with Lord Bacon.

"Hullo, William," said the Doctor, pocketing three balls on the break. "How's our little Swanlet of Avon this afternoon?"

"Worn out," Shakespeare replied. "I've been hard at work on a play this morning, and I'm tired."

"*All work and no play makes Jack a dull boy,*" said Nero, grinning broadly.

"You are a bright spirit," said Shakespeare, with a sigh. "I wish I had thought to work you up into a tragedy."

"I've often wondered why you didn't," said Doctor Johnson. "He'd have made a superb tragedy, Nero would. I don't believe there was any kind of a crime he left uncommitted. Was there, Emperor?"

"Yes. I never wrote an English dictionary," returned the Emperor, dryly. "I've murdered everything but English, though."

"I could have made a fine tragedy out of you," said Shakespeare. "Just think what a dreadful climax for a tragedy it would be, Johnson, to have Nero, as the curtain fell, playing a violin solo."

"Pretty good," returned the Doctor. "But what's the use of killing off your audience that way? It's better business to let 'em live, I say. Suppose Nero gave a London audience that little musicale he provided at Queen Elizabeth's Wednesday night. How many purely mortal beings, do you think, would have come out alive?"

"Not one," said Shakespeare. "I was mighty glad that night that we were an immortal band. If it had been possible to kill us we'd have died then and there."

"That's all right," said Nero, with a significant shake of his head. "As my friend Bacon makes Ingo say, '*Beware, my lord, of jealousy.*' You never could play a garden hose, much less a fiddle."

"What do you mean my attributing those words to Bacon?" demanded Shakespeare, getting red in the face.

"Oh, come now, William," remonstrated Nero. "It's all right to pull the wool over the eyes of the mortals. That's what they're there for; but as for us—we're all in the secret here. What's the use of putting on nonsense with us?"

"We'll see in a minute what the use is," retorted the Avonian. "We'll have Bacon down here." Here he touched an electric button, and Charon came in answer.

"Charon, bring Doctor Johnson the usual glass of ale. Get some ice for the Emperor, and ask Lord Bacon to step down here a minute."

"I don't want any ice," said Nero.

"Not now," retorted Shakespeare, "but you will in a few minutes. When we have finished with you, you'll want an iceberg. I'm getting tired of this idiotic talk about not having written my own works. There's one thing about Nero's music that I've never said, because I haven't wanted to hurt his feelings, but since he has chosen to cast aspersions upon my honesty I haven't any hesitation in saying it now. I believe it was one of his fiddlings that sent Nature into convulsions and caused the destruction of Pompeii—so there! Put that on your music rack and fiddle it, my little Emperor."

Nero's face grew purple with anger, and if Shakespeare had been anything but a shade he would have fared ill, for the enraged Roman, poising his cue on high as though it were a lance, hurled it at the impertinent dramatist with all his strength, and with such accuracy of aim withal that it pierced the spot beneath which in life the heart of Shakespeare used to beat.

"Good shot," said Doctor Johnson, nonchalantly. "If you had been a mortal, William, it would have been the end of you."

"You can't kill me," said Shakespeare, shrugging his shoulders.

"I know seven dozen actors in the United States who are trying to do it, but they can't. I wish they'd try to kill a critic once in a while instead of me, though," he added. "I went over to Boston one night last week, and, unknown to anybody, I waylaid a fellow who was to play Hamlet that night. I drugged him, and went to the theatre and played the part myself. It was the coldest house you ever saw in your life. When the audience did applaud, it sounded like an ice-man chopping up ice with a small pick. Several times I looked up at the galleries to see if there were not icicles growing on them, it was so cold. Well, I did the best could with the part, and next morning watched curiously for the criticisms."

"Favourable?" asked the Doctor.

"They all dismissed me with a line," said the dramatist. "Said my conception of the part was not Shakespearian. And that's criticism!"

"No," said the shade of Emerson, which had strolled in while Shakespeare was talking, "that isn't criticism; that's Boston."

"Who discovered Boston, anyhow?" asked Doctor Johnson. "It wasn't Columbus, was it?"

"Oh no," said Emerson. "Old Governor Winthrop is to blame for that. When he settled at Charlestown he saw the old Indian town of Shawmut across the Charles."

"And Shawmut was the Boston microbe, was it?" asked Johnson.

"Yes," said Emerson.

"Spelt with a P, I suppose?" said Shakespeare. "P-S-H-A-W, Pshaw, M-U-T, mut, Pshawmut, so called because the inhabitants are always muttering pshaw. Eh?"

"Pretty good," said Johnson. "I wish I'd said that."

"Well, tell Boswell," said Shakespeare. "He'll make you say it, and it'll be all the same in a hundred years."

Lord Bacon, accompanied by Charon and the ice for Nero and the ale for Doctor Johnson, appeared as Shakespeare spoke. The philosopher bowed stiffly at Doctor Johnson, as though he hardly approved of him, extended his left hand to Shakespeare, and stared coldly at Nero.

"Did you send for me, William?" he asked, languidly.

"I did," said Shakespeare. "I sent for you because this imperial violinist here says that you wrote *Othello*."

"What nonsense," said Bacon. "The only plays of yours I wrote were *Ham*—"

"Sh!" said Shakespeare, shaking his head madly. "Hush. Nobody's said anything about that. This is purely a discussion of *Othello*."

"The fiddling ex-Emperor Nero," said Bacon, loudly enough to be heard all about the room, "is mistaken when he attributes *Othello* to me."

"Aha, Master Nero!" cried Shakespeare triumphantly. "What did I tell you?"

"Then I erred, that is all," said Nero. "And I apologize. But really, my Lord," he added, addressing Bacon, "I fancied I detected your fine Italian hand in that."

"No. I had nothing to do with the *Othello*," said Bacon. "I never really knew who wrote it."

"Never mind about that," whispered Shakespeare. "You've said enough."

"That's good too," said Nero, with a chuckle. "Shakespeare here claims it as his own."

Bacon smiled and nodded approvingly at the blushing Avonian.

"Will always was having his little joke," he said. "Eh, Will? How we fooled 'em on *Hamlet*, eh, my boy? Ha-ha-ha! It was the greatest joke of the century."

"Well, the laugh is on you," said Doctor Johnson. "If you wrote *Hamlet* and didn't have the sense to acknowledge it, you present to my mind a closer resemblance to Simple Simon than to Socrates. For my part, I don't believe you did write it, and I do believe that Shakespeare did. I can tell that by the spelling in the original edition."

"Shakespeare was my stenographer, gentlemen," said Lord Bacon. "If you want to know the whole truth, he did write

17

Hamlet, literally. But it was at my dictation."

"I deny it," said Shakespeare. "I admit you gave me a suggestion now and then so as to keep it dull and heavy in spots, so that it would seem more like a real tragedy than a comedy punctuated with deaths, but beyond that you had nothing to do with it."

"I side with Shakespeare," put in Emerson. "I've seen his autographs, and no sane person would employ a man who wrote such a villanously bad hand as an amanuensis. It's no use, Bacon, we know a thing or two. I'm a New-Englander, I am."

"Well," said Bacon, shrugging his shoulders as though the results of the controversy were immaterial to him, "have it so if you please. There isn't any money in Shakespeare these days, so what's the use of quarrelling? I wrote *Hamlet*, and Shakespeare knows it. Others know it. Ah, here comes Sir Walter Raleigh. We'll leave it to him. He was cognizant of the whole affair."

"I leave it to nobody," said Shakespeare, sulkily.

"What's the trouble?" asked Raleigh, sauntering up and taking a chair under the cue-rack. "Talking politics?"

"Not we," said Bacon. "It's the old question about the authorship of *Hamlet*. Will, as usual, claims it for himself. He'll be saying he wrote Genesis next."

"Well, what if he does?" laughed Raleigh. "We all know Will and his droll ways."

"No doubt," put in Nero. "But the question of *Hamlet* always excites him so that we'd like to have it settled once and for all as to who wrote it. Bacon says you know."

"I do," said Raleigh.

"Then settle it once and for all," said Bacon. "I'm rather tired of the discussion myself."

"Shall I tell 'em, Shakespeare?" asked Raleigh.

"It's immaterial to me," said Shakespeare, airily. "If you wish—only tell the truth."

"Very well," said Raleigh, lighting a cigar. "I'm not ashamed of it. I wrote the thing myself."

There was a roar of laughter which, when it subsided, found

Shakespeare rapidly disappearing through the door, while all the others in the room ordered various beverages at the expense of Lord Bacon.

3: WASHINGTON GIVES A DINNER

It was Washington's Birthday, and the gentleman who had the pleasure of being Father of his Country decided to celebrate it at the Associated Shades' floating palace on the Styx, as the Elysium *Weekly Gossip*, "a Journal of Society," called it, by giving a dinner to a select number of friends. Among the invited guests were Baron Munchausen, Doctor Johnson, Confucius, Napoleon Bonaparte, Diogenes, and Ptolemy. Boswell was also present, but not as a guest. He had a table off to one side all to himself, and upon it there were no china plates, silver spoons, knives, forks, and dishes of fruit, but pads, pens, and ink in great quantity. It was evident that Boswell's reportorial duties did not end with his labours in the mundane sphere.

The dinner was set down to begin at seven o'clock, so that the guests, as was proper, sauntered slowly in between that hour and eight. The menu was particularly choice, the shades of countless canvas-back ducks, terrapin, and sheep having been called into requisition, and cooked by no less a person than Brillat-Savarin, in the hottest oven he could find in the famous cooking establishment superintended by the government. Washington was on hand early, sampling the olives and the celery and the wines, and giving to Charon final instructions as to the manner in which he wished things served.

The first guest to arrive was Confucius, and after him came Diogenes, the latter in great excitement over having discovered a comparatively honest man, whose name, however, he had not been able to ascertain, though he was under the impression that it was something like Burpin, or Turpin, he said.

At eight the brilliant company was arranged comfortably about the board. An orchestra of five, under the leadership of Mozart, discoursed sweet music behind a screen, and the feast of reason and flow of soul began.

"This is a great day," said Doctor Johnson, assisting himself copiously to the olives.

"Yes," said Columbus, who was also a guest—"yes, it is a great day, but it isn't a marker to a little day in October I wot of."

"Still sore on that point?" queried Confucius, trying the edge of his knife on the shade of a salted almond.

"Oh no," said Columbus, calmly. "I don't feel jealous of Washington. He is the Father of his Country and I am not. I only discovered the orphan. I knew the country before it had a father or a mother. There wasn't anybody who was willing to be even a sister to it when I knew it. But G. W. here took it in hand, groomed it down, spanked it when it needed it, and started it off on the career which has made it worthwhile for me to let my name be known in connection with it. Why should I be jealous of him?"

"I am sure I don't know why anybody anywhere should be jealous of anybody else anyhow," said Diogenes. "I never was and I never expect to be. Jealousy is a quality that is utterly foreign to the nature of an honest man. Take my own case, for instance. When I was what they call alive, how did I live?"

"I don't know," said Doctor Johnson, turning his head as he spoke so that Boswell could not fail to hear. "I wasn't there."

Boswell nodded approvingly, chuckled slightly, and put the Doctor's remark down for publication in *The Gossip*.

"You're doubtless right, there," retorted Diogenes. "What you don't know would fill a circulating library. Well—I lived in a tub. Now, if I believed in envy, I suppose you think I'd be envious of people who live in brownstone fronts with back yards and mortgages, eh?"

"I'd rather live under a mortgage than in a tub," said Bonaparte, contemptuously.

"I know you would," said Diogenes. "Mortgages never bothered you—but I wouldn't. In the first place, my tub was warm. I never saw a house with a brownstone front that was, except in summer, and then the owner cursed it because it was so. My tub had no plumbing in it to get out of order. It hadn't any flights

20

of stairs in it that had to be climbed after dinner, or late at night when I came home from the club. It had no front door with a wandering key-hole calculated to elude the key ninety-nine times out of every hundred efforts to bring the two together and reconcile their differences, in order that their owner may get into his own house late at night. It wasn't chained down to any particular neighbourhood, as are most brownstone fronts. If the neighbourhood ran down, I could move my tub off into a better neighbourhood, and it never lost value through the deterioration of its location. I never had to pay taxes on it, and no burglar was ever so hard up that he thought of breaking into my habitation to rob me. So why should I be jealous of the brownstone-house dwellers? I am a philosopher, gentlemen. I tell you, philosophy is the thief of jealousy, and I had the good-luck to find it out early in life."

"There is much in what you say," said Confucius. "But there's another side to the matter. If a man is an aristocrat by nature, as I was, his neighbourhood never could run down. Wherever he lived would be the swell section, so that really your last argument isn't worth a stewed icicle."

"Stewed icicles are pretty good, though," said Baron Munchausen, with an ecstatic smack of his lips. "I've eaten them many a time in the polar regions."

"I have no doubt of it," put in Doctor Johnson. "You've eaten fried pyramids in Africa, too, haven't you?"

"Only once," said the Baron, calmly. "And I can't say I enjoyed them. They are rather heavy for the digestion."

"That's so," said Ptolemy. "I've had experience with pyramids myself."

"You never ate one, did you, Ptolemy?" queried Bonaparte.

"Not raw," said Ptolemy, with a chuckle. "Though I've been tempted many a time to call for a second joint of the Sphinx."

There was a laugh at this, in which all but Baron Munchausen joined.

"I think it is too bad," said the Baron, as the laughter subsided—"I think it is very much too bad that you shades have brought mundane prejudice with you into this sphere. Just because some people with finite minds profess to disbelieve my stories, you think it well to be sceptical yourselves. I don't care, however, whether you believe me or not. The fact remains that I have eaten one fried pyramid and countless stewed icicles, and the stewed icicles were finer than any diamond-back rat Confucius ever had served at a state banquet."

"Where's Shakespeare tonight?" asked Confucius, seeing that the Baron was beginning to lose his temper, and wishing to avoid trouble by changing the subject. "Wasn't he invited, General?"

"Yes," said Washington, "he was invited, but he couldn't come. He had to go over the river to consult with an autograph syndicate they've formed in New York. You know, his autographs sell for about one thousand dollars apiece, and they're trying to get up a scheme whereby he shall contribute an autograph a week to the syndicate, to be sold to the public. It seems like a rich scheme, but there's one thing in the way. Posthumous autographs haven't very much of a market, because the mortals can't be made to believe that they are genuine; but the syndicate has got a man at work trying to get over that. These Yankees are a mighty inventive lot, and they think perhaps the scheme can be worked. The Yankee *is* an inventive genius."

"It was a Yankee invented that tale about your not being able to prevaricate, wasn't it, George?" asked Diogenes.

Washington smiled acquiescence, and Doctor Johnson returned to Shakespeare.

"I'd rather have a morning-glory vine than one of Shakespeare's autographs," said he. "They are far prettier, and quite as legible."

"Mortals wouldn't," said Bonaparte.

"What fools they be!" chuckled Johnson.

At this point the canvas-back ducks were served, one whole shade of a bird for each guest.

"Fall to, gentlemen," said Washington, gazing hungrily at his bird. "When canvas-back ducks are on the table conversation is not required of any one."

"It is fortunate for us that we have so considerate a host," said Confucius, unfastening his robe and preparing to do justice to the fare set before him. "I have dined often, but never before with one who was willing to let me eat a bird like this in silence. Washington, here's to you. May your life be chequered with birthdays, and may ours be equally well supplied with feasts like this at your expense!"

The toast was drained, and the diners fell to as requested.

"They're great, aren't they?" whispered Bonaparte to Munchausen.

"Well, rather," returned the Baron. "I don't see why the mortals don't erect a statue to the canvas-back."

"Did anybody at this board ever have as much canvas-back duck as he could eat?" asked Doctor Johnson.

"Yes," said the Baron. "I did. Once."

"Oh, you!" sneered Ptolemy. "You've had everything."

"Except the mumps," retorted Munchausen. "But, honestly, I did once have as much canvas-back duck as I could eat."

"It must have cost you a million," said Bonaparte. "But even then they'd be cheap, especially to a man like yourself who could perform miracles. If I could have performed miracles with the ease which was so characteristic of all your efforts, I'd never have died at St. Helena."

"What's the odds where you died?" said Doctor Johnson. "If it hadn't been at St. Helena it would have been somewhere else, and you'd have found death as stuffy in one place as in another."

"Don't let's talk of death," said Washington. "I am sure the Baron's tale of how he came to have enough canvas-back is more diverting."

"I've no doubt it is more perverting," said Johnson.

"It happened this way," said Munchausen. "I was out for sport, and I got it. I was alone, my servant having fallen ill, which was unfortunate, since I had always left the filling of my cartridge-box to him, and underestimated its capacity. I started at six in the

23

morning, and, not having hunted for several months, was not in very good form, so, no game appearing for a time, I took a few practice shots, trying to snip off the slender tops of the pine-trees that I encountered with my bullets, succeeding tolerably well for one who was a little rusty, bringing down ninety-nine out of the first one hundred and one, and missing the remaining two by such a close margin that they swayed to and fro as though fanned by a slight breeze. As I fired my one hundred and first shot what should I see before me but a flock of these delicate birds floating upon the placid waters of the bay!"

"Was this the Bay of Biscay, Baron?" queried Columbus, with a covert smile at Ptolemy.

"I counted them," said the Baron, ignoring the question, "and there were just sixty-eight. 'Here's a chance for the record, Baron,' said I to myself, and then I made ready to shoot them. Imagine my dismay, gentlemen, when I discovered that while I had plenty of powder left I had used up all my bullets. Now, as you may imagine, to a man with no bullets at hand, the sight of sixty-eight fat canvas-backs is hardly encouraging, but I was resolved to have every one of those birds; the question was, how shall I do it? I never can think on water, so I paddled quietly ashore and began to reflect. As I lay there deep in thought, I saw lying upon the beach before me a superb oyster, and as reflection makes me hungry I seized upon the bivalve and swallowed him. As he went down something stuck in my throat, and, extricating it, what should it prove to be but a pearl of surpassing beauty. My first thought was to be content with my day's find. A pearl worth thousands surely was enough to satisfy the most ardent lover of sport; but on looking up I saw those ducks still paddling contentedly about, and I could not bring myself to give them up. Suddenly the idea came, the pearl is as large as a bullet, and fully as round. Why not use it? Then, as thoughts come to me in shoals, I next reflected, 'Ah—but this is only one bullet as against sixty-eight birds:' immediately a third thought came, 'why not shoot them all with a single bullet? It is possible, though not probable.' I snatched out a pad of paper and a pencil, made a rapid calculation based on the doctrine of chances, and proved to my own satisfaction that at some time or another within the following two weeks those birds would doubtless be sitting in a straight line and paddling about, Indian file, for an instant. I resolved to await that instant. I loaded my gun with the pearl and a sufficient quantity of powder to send the charge through every one of the ducks if, perchance, the first duck were properly hit. To pass over wearisome details, let me say that it happened just as I expected. I had one week and six days to wait, but finally the critical moment came. It was at midnight, but fortunately the moon was at the full, and I could see as plainly as though it had been day. The moment the ducks were in line I aimed and fired. They every one squawked, turned over, and died. My pearl had pierced the whole sixty-eight."

Boswell blushed.

"Ahem!" said Doctor Johnson. "It was a pity to lose the pearl."

"That," said Munchausen, "was the most interesting part of the story. I had made a second calculation in order to save the pearl. I deduced the amount of powder necessary to send the gem through sixty-seven and a half birds, and my deduction was strictly accurate. It fulfilled its mission of death on sixty-seven and was found buried in the heart of the sixty-eighth, a trifle discoloured, but still a pearl, and worth a king's ransom."

Napoleon gave a derisive laugh, and the other guests sat with incredulity depicted upon every line of their faces.

"Do you believe that story yourself, Baron?" asked Confucius.

"Why not?" asked the Baron. "Is there anything improbable in it? Why should you disbelieve it? Look at our friend Washington here. Is there any one here who knows more about truth than he does? He doesn't disbelieve it. He's the only man at this table who treats me like a man of honour."

"He's host and has to," said Johnson, shrugging his shoulders.

"Well, Washington, let me put the direct question to you,"

said the Baron. "Say you aren't host and are under no obliga-
tion to be courteous. Do you believe I haven't been telling the
truth?"

"My dear Munchausen," said the General, "don't ask me. I'm
not an authority. I can't tell a lie—not even when I hear one. If
you say your story is true, I must believe it, of course; but—ah—
really, if I were you, I wouldn't tell it again unless I could produce the pearl and the wish-bone of one of the ducks at least."

Whereupon, as the discussion was beginning to grow acri-
monious, Washington hailed Charon, and, ordering a boat, invited his guests to accompany him over into the world of realities, where they passed the balance of the evening haunting a
vaudeville performance at one of the London music-halls.

4: Hamlet Makes a Suggestion

It was a beautiful night on the Styx, and the silvery surface
of that picturesque stream was dotted with gondolas, canoes,
and other craft to an extent that made Charon feel like a highly
prosperous savings-bank. Within the house-boat were gathered a
merry party, some of whom were on mere pleasure bent, others
of whom had come to listen to a debate, for which the entertainment committee had provided, between the venerable patriarch Noah and the late eminent showman P. T. Barnum. The
question to be debated was upon the resolution passed by the
committee, that "The Animals of the Antediluvian Period were
Far More Attractive for Show Purposes than those of Modern
Make," and, singular to relate, the affirmative was placed in the
hands of Mr. Barnum, while to Noah had fallen the task of up-
holding the virtues of the modern freak. It is with the party on
mere pleasure bent that we have to do upon this occasion. The
proceedings of the debating-party are as yet in the hands of the
official stenographer, but will be made public as soon as they are
ready.

The pleasure-seeking group were gathered in the smoking-
room of the club, which was, indeed, a smoking-room of a novel
sort, the invention of an unknown shade, who had sold all the

rights to the club through a third party, anonymously, preferring, it seemed, to remain in the Elysian world, as he had been in the mundane sphere, a mute inglorious Edison. It was a simple enough scheme, and, for a wonder, no one in the world of substantialities has thought to take it up. The smoke was stored in reservoirs, just as if it were so much gas or water, and was supplied on the hot-air furnace principle from a huge furnace in the hold of the house-boat, into which tobacco was shovelled by the hired man of the club night and day. The smoke from the furnace, carried through flues to the smoking-room, was there received and stored in the reservoirs, with each of which was connected one dozen rubber tubes, having at their ends amber mouth-pieces. Upon each of these mouth-pieces was arranged a small meter registering the amount of smoke consumed through it, and for this the consumer paid so much a foot. The value of the plan was threefold. It did away entirely with ashes, it saved to the consumers the value of the unconsumed tobacco that is represented by the unsmoked cigar ends, and it averted the possibility of cigarettes.

Enjoying the benefits of this arrangement upon the evening in question were Shakespeare, Cicero, Henry VIII., Doctor Johnson, and others. Of course Boswell was present too, for a moment, with his note-book, and this fact evoked some criticism from several of the smokers.

"You ought to be upstairs in the lecture-room, Boswell," said Shakespeare, as the great biographer took his seat behind his friend the Doctor. "Doesn't the *Gossip* want a report of the debate?"

"It does," said Boswell; "but the *Gossip* endeavours always to get the most interesting items of the day, and Doctor Johnson has informed me that he expects to be unusually witty this evening, so I have come here."

"Excuse me for saying it, Boswell," said the Doctor, getting red in the face over this unexpected confession, "but, really, you talk too much."

"That's good," said Cicero. "Stick that down, Boz, and print

27

it. It's the best thing Johnson has said this week."

Boswell smiled weakly, and said: "But, Doctor, you did say that, you know. I can prove it, too, for you told me some of the things you were going to say. Don't you remember, you were going to lead Shakespeare up to making the remark that he thought the English language was the greatest language in creation, whereupon you were going to ask him why he didn't learn it?"

"Get out of here, you idiot!" roared the Doctor. "You're enough to give a man apoplexy."

"You're not going back on the ladder by which you have climbed, are you, Samuel?" queried Boswell, earnestly.

"The wha-a-t?" cried the Doctor, angrily. "The ladder—on which I climbed? You? Great heavens! That it should come to this! . . . Leave the room—instantly! Ladder! By all that is beautiful—the ladder upon which I, Samuel Johnson, the tallest person in letters, have climbed! Go! Do you hear?"

Boswell rose meekly, and, with tears coursing down his cheeks, left the room.

"That's one on you, Doctor," said Cicero, wrapping his *toga* about him. "I think you ought to order up three baskets of champagne on that."

"I'll order up three baskets full of Boswell's remains if he ever dares speak like that again!" retorted the Doctor, shaking with anger. "He—my ladder—why, it's ridiculous."

"Yes," said Shakespeare, dryly. "That's why we laugh."

"You were a little hard on him, Doctor," said Henry VIII. "He was a valuable man to you. He had a great eye for your greatness."

"Yes. If there's any feature of Boswell that's greater than his nose and ears, it's his great I," said the Doctor.

"You'd rather have him change his I to a U, I presume," said Napoleon, quietly.

The Doctor waved his hand impatiently. "Let's drop him," he said. "Dropping one's biographer isn't without precedent. As soon as any man ever got to know Napoleon well enough to write him up he sent him to the front, where he could get a little lead in his system."

"I wish I had had a Boswell all the same," said Shakespeare. "Then the world would have known the truth about me."

"It wouldn't if he'd relied on your word for it," retorted the Doctor. "Hullo! here's Hamlet."

As the Doctor spoke, in very truth the melancholy Dane appeared in the doorway, more melancholy of aspect than ever.

"What's the matter with you?" asked Cicero, addressing the newcomer. "Haven't you got that poison out of your system yet?"

"Not entirely," said Hamlet, with a sigh; "but it isn't that that's bothering me. It's Fate."

"We'll get out an injunction against Fate if you like," said Blackstone. "Is it persecution, or have you deserved it?"

"I think it's persecution," said Hamlet. "I never wronged Fate in my life, and why she should pursue me like a demon through all eternity is a thing I can't understand."

"Maybe Ophelia is back of it," suggested Doctor Johnson. "These women have a great deal of sympathy for each other, and, candidly, I think you behaved pretty rudely to Ophelia. It's a poor way to show your love for a young woman, running a sword through her father every night for pay, and driving the girl to suicide with equal frequency, just to show theatre-goers what a smart little Dane you can be if you try."

"'Tisn't me does all that," returned Hamlet. "I only did it once, and even then it wasn't as bad as Shakespeare made it out to be."

"I put it down just as it was," said Shakespeare, hotly, "and you can't dispute it."

"Yes, he can," said Yorick. "You made him tell Horatio he knew me well, and he never met me in his life."

"I never told Horatio anything of the sort," said Hamlet. "I never entered the graveyard even, and I can prove an alibi."

"And, what's more, he couldn't have made the remark the way Shakespeare has it, anyhow," said Yorick, "and for a very good reason. I wasn't buried in that graveyard, and Hamlet and I can prove an alibi for the skull, too."

"It was a good play, just the same," said Cicero.

"Very," put in Doctor Johnson. "It cured me of insomnia."

"Well, if you don't talk in your sleep, the play did a Christian service to the world," retorted Shakespeare. "But, really, Hamlet, I thought I did the square thing by you in that play. I meant to, anyhow; and if it has made you unhappy, I'm honestly sorry."

"Spoken like a man," said Yorick.

"I don't mind the play so much," said Hamlet, "but the way I'm represented by these fellows who play it is the thing that rubs me the wrong way. Why, I even hear that there's a *troupe* out in the western part of the United States that puts the thing on with three Hamlets, two ghosts, and a pair of blood-hounds. It's called the Uncle-Tom-Hamlet Combination, and instead of my falling in love with one crazy Ophelia, I am made to woo three dusky maniacs named Topsy on a canvas ice-floe, while the blood-hounds bark behind the scenes. What sort of treatment is that for a man of royal lineage?"

"It's pretty rough," said Napoleon. "As the poet ought to have said, 'Oh, Hamlet, Hamlet, what crimes are committed in thy name!'"

"I feel as badly about the play as Hamlet does," said Shakespeare, after a moment of silent thought. "I don't bother much about this wild Western business, though, because I think the introduction of the bloodhounds and the Topsies makes us both more popular in that region than we should be otherwise. What I object to is the way we are treated by these so-called first-class intellectual actors in London and other great cities. I've seen Hamlet done before a highly cultivated audience, and, by Jove, it made me blush."

"Me too," sighed Hamlet. "I have seen a man who had a walk on him that suggested spring-halt and *locomotor ataxia* combined impersonating my graceful self in a manner that drove me almost crazy. I've heard my '*To be or not to be*' soliloquy uttered by a famous tragedian in tones that would make a graveyard yawn at mid-day, and if there was any way in which I could get even with that man I'd do it."

"It seems to me," said Blackstone, assuming for the moment a highly judicial manner—"it seems to me that Shakespeare, having got you into this trouble, ought to get you out of it."

"But how?" said Shakespeare, earnestly. "That's the point. Heaven knows I'm willing enough."

Hamlet's face suddenly brightened as though illuminated with an idea. Then he began to dance about the room with an expression of glee that annoyed Doctor Johnson exceedingly.

"I wish Darwin could see you now," the Doctor growled. "A kodak picture of you would prove his arguments conclusively."

"Rail on, O philosopher!" retorted Hamlet. "Rail on! I mind your railings not, for I the germ of an idea have got."

"Well, go quarantine yourself," said the Doctor. "I'd hate to have one of your idea microbes get hold of me."

"What's the scheme?" asked Shakespeare.

"You can write a play for *me!*" cried Hamlet. "Make it a farce-tragedy. Take the modern player for your hero, and let *me* play *him*. I'll bait him through four acts. I'll imitate his walk. I'll cultivate his voice. We'll have the first act a tank act, and drop the hero into the tank. The second act can be in a saw-mill, and we can cut his hair off on a buzz-saw. The third act can introduce a spile-driver with which to drive his hat over his eyes and knock his brains down into his lungs. The fourth act can be at Niagara Falls, and we'll send him over the falls; and for a grand climax we can have him guillotined just after he has swallowed a quart of prussic acid and a spoonful of powdered glass. Do that for me, William, and you are forgiven. I'll play it for six hundred nights in London, for two years in New York, and round up with a one-night stand in Boston."

"It sounds like a good scheme," said Shakespeare, meditatively. "What shall we call it?"

"Call it *Irving*," said Eugene Aram, who had entered. "I too have suffered."

"And let me be Hamlet's understudy," said Charles the First, earnestly.

"Done!" said Shakespeare, calling for a pad and pencil.

And as the sun rose upon the Styx the next morning the Bard of Avon was to be seen writing a comic chorus to be sung over the moribund tragedian by the shades of Charles, Aram, and other eminent deceased heroes of the stage, with which his new play of *Irving* was to be brought to an appropriate close.

This play has not as yet found its way upon the boards, but any enterprising manager who desires to consider it may address

Hamlet,
The House-Boat
Hades-on-the-Styx.

He is sure to get a reply by return mail, unless Mephistopheles interferes, which is not unlikely, since Mephistopheles is said to have been much pleased with the manner in which the eminent tragedian has put him before the British and American public.

5: THE HOUSE COMMITTEE DISCUSS THE POETS

"There's one thing this house-boat needs," wrote Homer in the complaint-book that adorned the centre-table in the reading-room, "and that is a Poets' Corner. There are smoking-rooms for those who smoke, billiard-rooms for those who play billiards, and a card-room for those who play cards. I do not smoke, I can't play billiards, and I do not know a trey of diamonds from a silver salver. All I can do is write poetry. Why discriminate against me? By all means let us have a Poets' Corner, where a man can be inspired in peace."

For four days this entry lay in the book apparently unnoticed. On the fifth day the following lines, signed by Samson, appeared:

"I approve of Homer's suggestion. There should be a Poets' Corner here. Then the rest of us could have some comfort. While playing *vingt-et-un* with Diogenes in the card-room on

Friday evening a poetic member of this club was taken with a most violent fancy, and it required the combined efforts of Diogenes and myself, assisted by the janitor, to remove the frenzied and objectionable member from the room. The habit some of our poets have acquired of giving way to their inspirations all over the club-house should be stopped, and I know of no better way to accomplish this desirable end than by the adoption of Homer's suggestion. Therefore I second the motion."

Of course the suggestion of two members so prominent as Homer and Samson could not well he ignored by the house committee, and it reluctantly took the subject in hand at an early meeting.

"I find here," said Demosthenes to the chairman, as the committee gathered, "a suggestion from Homer and Samson that this house-boat be provided with a Poets' Corner. I do not know that I approve of the suggestion myself, but in order to bring it before the committee for debate I am willing to make a motion that the request be granted."

"Excuse me," put in Doctor Johnson, "but where do you find that suggestion? 'Here' is not very definite. Where *is* 'here'?"

"In the complaint-book, which I hold in my hand," returned Demosthenes, putting a pebble in his mouth so that he might enunciate more clearly.

A frown ruffled the serenity of Doctor Johnson's brow.

"In the complaint-book, eh?" he said, slowly. "I thought house committees were not expected to pay any attention to complaints in complaint-books. I never heard of its being done before."

"Well, I can't say that I have either," replied Demosthenes, chewing thoughtfully on the pebble, "but I suppose complaint-books are the places for complaints. You don't expect people to write serial stories or dialect poems in them, do you?"

"That isn't the point, as the man said to the assassin who tried to stab him with the hilt of his dagger," retorted Doctor Johnson, with some asperity. "Of course, complaint-books are for the reception of complaints—nobody disputes that. What I want to have determined is whether it is necessary or proper for the complaints to go further."

"I fancy we have a legal right to take the matter up," said Blackstone, wearily; "though I don't know of any precedent for such action. In all the clubs I have known the house committees have invariably taken the ground that the complaint-book was established to guard them against the annoyance of hearing complaints. This one, however, has been forced upon us by our secretary, and in view of the age of the complainants I think we cannot well decline to give them a specific answer. Respect for age is *de rigueur* at all times, like clean hands. I'll second the motion."

"I think the Poets' Corner entirely unnecessary," said Confucius. "This isn't a class organization, and we should resist any effort to make it or any portion of it so. In fact, I will go further and state that it is my opinion that if we do any legislating in the matter at all, we ought to discourage rather than encourage these poets. They are always littering the club up with themselves. Only last Wednesday I came here with a guest—no less a person than a recently deceased Emperor of China—and what was the first sight that greeted our eyes?"

"I give it up," said Doctor Johnson. "It must have been a catacornered sight, whatever it was, if the Emperor's eyes slanted like yours."

"No personalities, please, Doctor," said Sir Walter Raleigh, the chairman, rapping the table vigorously with the shade of a handsome gavel that had once adorned the Roman Senate-chamber.

"He's only a Chinaman!" muttered Johnson.

"What was the sight that greeted your eyes, Confucius?" asked Cassius.

"Omar Khayyam stretched over five of the most comfortable chairs in the library," returned Confucius; "and when I ventured to remonstrate with him he lost his temper, and said I'd spoiled the whole second volume of the *Rubáiyát*. I told him he ought to do his *rubáiyátting* at home, and he made a scene, to

34

avoid which I hastened with my guest over to the billiard-room; and there, stretched at full length on the pool-table, was Robert Burns trying to write a sonnet on the cloth with chalk in less time than Villon could turn out another, with two lines start, on the billiard-table with the same writing materials. Now I ask you, gentlemen, if these things are to be tolerated? Are they not rather to be reprehended, whether I am a Chinaman or not?"

"What would you have us do, then?" asked Sir Walter Raleigh, a little nettled. "Exclude poets altogether? I was one, remember."

"Oh, but not much of one, Sir Walter," put in Doctor Johnson, deprecatingly.

"No," said Confucius. "I don't want them excluded, but they should be controlled. You don't let a shoemaker who has become a member of this club turn the library sofas into benches and go pegging away at boot-making, so why should you let the poets turn the place into a verse factory? That's what I'd like to know."

"I don't know but what your point is well taken," said Blackstone, "though I can't say I think your parallels are very parallel. A shoemaker, my dear Confucius, is somewhat different from a poet."

"Certainly," said Doctor Johnson. "Very different—in fact, different enough to make a conundrum of the question—what is the difference between a shoemaker and a poet? One makes the shoes and the other shakes the muse—all the difference in the world. Still, I don't see how we can exclude the poets. It is the very democracy of this club that gives it life. We take in everybody—peer, poet, or what not. To say that this man shall not enter because he is this or that or the other thing would result in our ultimately becoming a class organization, which, as Confucius himself says, we are not and must not be. If we put out the poet to please the sage, we'll soon have to put out the sage to please the fool, and so on. We'll keep it up, once the precedent is established, until finally it will become a class club entirely—a Plumbers' Club, for instance—and how absurd that

35

would be in Hades! No, gentlemen, it can't be done. The poets must and shall be preserved."

"What's the objection to class clubs, anyhow?" asked Cassius. "I don't object to them. If we could have had political organizations in my day I might not have had to fall on my sword to get out of keeping an engagement I had no fancy for. Class clubs have their uses."

"No doubt," said Demosthenes. "Have all the class clubs you want, but do not make one of this. An Authors' Club, where none but authors are admitted, is a good thing. The members learn there that there are other authors than themselves. Poets' Clubs are a good thing; they bring poets into contact with each other, and they learn what a bore it is to have to listen to a poet reading his own poem. Pugilists' Clubs are good; so are all other class clubs; but so also are clubs like our own, which takes in all who are worthy. Here a poet can talk poetry as much as he wants, but at the same time he hears something besides poetry. We must stick to our original idea."

"Then let us do something to abate the nuisance of which I complain," said Confucius. "Can't we adopt a house rule that poets must not be inspired between the hours of 11 a.m. and 5 p.m., or in the evening after eight; that any poet discovered using more than five arm-chairs in the composition of a quatrain will be charged two *oboli* an hour for each chair in excess of that number; and that the billiard-marker shall be required to charge a premium of three times the ordinary fee for tables used by versifiers in lieu of writing-pads?"

"That wouldn't be a bad idea," said Sir Walter Raleigh. "I, as a poet would not object to that. I do all my work at home, anyhow."

"There's another phase of this business that we haven't considered yet, and it's rather important," said Demosthenes, taking a fresh pebble out of his *bonbonnière*. "That's in the matter of stationery. This club, like all other well-regulated clubs, provides its members with a suitable supply of writing materials. Charon informs me that the waste-baskets last week turned out forty-two reams of our best correspondence paper on which these poets had scribbled the first draft of their verses. Now I don't think the club should furnish the poets with the raw material for their poems any more than, to go back to Confucius's shoemaker, it should supply leather for our cobblers."

"What do you mean by raw material for poems?" asked Sir Walter, with a frown.

"Pen, ink, and paper. What else?" said Demosthenes.

"Doesn't it take brains to write a poem?" said Raleigh.

"Doesn't it take brains to make a pair of shoes?" retorted Demosthenes, swallowing a pebble in his haste.

"They've got a right to the stationery, though," put in Blackstone. "A clear legal right to it. If they choose to write poems on the paper instead of boring people to death with letters, as most of us do, that's their own affair."

"Well, they're very wasteful," said Demosthenes.

"We can meet that easily enough," observed Cassius. "Furnish each writing-table with a slate. I should think they'd be pleased with that. It's so much easier to rub out the wrong word."

"Most poets prefer to rub out the right word," growled Confucius. "Besides, I shall never consent to slates in this house-boat. The squeaking of the pencils would be worse than the poems themselves."

"That's true," said Cassius. "I never thought of that. If a dozen poets got to work on those slates at once, a Fife corps wouldn't be a circumstance to them."

"Well, it all goes to prove what I have thought all along," said Doctor Johnson. "Homer's idea is a good one, and Samson was wise in backing it up. The poets need to be concentrated somewhere where they will not be a nuisance to other people, and where other people will not be a nuisance to them. Homer ought to have a place to compose in where the *vingt-et-un* players will not interrupt his frenzies, and, on the other hand, the *vingt-et-un* and other players should be protected from the wooers of the muse. I'll vote to have the Poets' Corner, and in it I move that Cassius's slate idea be carried out. It will be a great saving, and if the corner we select be far enough away from the other corners of the club, the squeaking of the slate-pencils need bother no one."

"I agree to that," said Blackstone. "Only I think it should be understood that, in granting the petition of the poets, we do not bind ourselves to yield to doctors and lawyers and shoemakers and plumbers in case they should each want a corner to themselves."

"A very wise idea," said Sir Walter. Whereupon the resolution was suitably worded, and passed unanimously.

Just where the Poets' Corner is to be located the members of the committee have not as yet decided, although Confucius is strongly in favour of having it placed in a dingy situated a quarter of a mile astern of the house-boat, and connected therewith by a slight cord, which can be easily cut in case the squeaking of the poets' slate-pencils becomes too much for the nervous system of the members who have no corner of their own.

6: SOME THEORIES, DARWINIAN AND OTHERWISE

"I observe," said Doctor Darwin, looking up from a perusal of an asbestos copy of the *London Times*—"I observe that an American professor has discovered that monkeys talk. I consider that a very interesting fact."

"It undoubtedly is," observed Doctor Livingstone, "though hardly new. I never said anything about it over in the other world, but I discovered years ago in Africa that monkeys were quite as well able to hold a sustained conversation with each other as most men are."

"And I, too," put in Baron Munchausen, "have frequently conversed with monkeys. I made myself a master of their idioms during my brief sojourn in—ah—in—well, never mind where. I never could remember the names of places. The interesting point is that at one period of my life I was a master of the monkey language. I have even gone so far as to write a sonnet in Simian, which was quite as intelligible to the uneducated as nine-tenths of the sonnets written in English or American."

"Do you mean to say that you could acquire the monkey accent?" asked Doctor Darwin, immediately interested.

"In most instances," returned the Baron, suavely, "though of course not in all. I found the same difficulty in some cases that the German or the Chinaman finds when he tries to speak French. A Chinaman can no more say *Trocadéro*, for instance, as the Frenchman says it, than he can fly. That peculiar throaty aspirate the Frenchman gives to the first syllable, as though it were spelled *trhoque*, is utterly beyond the Chinese—and beyond the American, too, whose idea of the tonsillar aspirate leads him to speak of the *trochedeero*, naturally falling back upon *troches* to help him out of his laryngeal difficulties."

"You ought to have been on the staff of *Punch*, Baron," said Thackeray, quietly. "That joke would have made you immortal."

"I *am* immortal," said the Baron. "But to return to our discussion of the Simian tongue: as I was saying, there were some little points about the accent that I could never get, and, as in the case of the German and Chinaman with the French language, the trouble was purely physical. When you consider that in polite Simian society most of the talkers converse while swinging by their tails from the limb of a tree, with a sort of droning accent, which results from their swaying to and fro, you will see at once why it was that I, deprived by nature of the necessary apparatus with which to suspend myself in mid-air, was unable to quite catch the quality which gives its chief charm to monkey-talk."

"I should hardly think that a man of your fertile resources would have let so small a thing as that stand in his way," said Doctor Livingstone. "When a man is able to make a reputation for himself like yours, in which material facts are never allowed to interfere with his doing what he sets out to do, he ought not to be daunted by the need of a tail. If you could make a cherry-tree grow out of a deer's head, I fail to see why you could not personally grow a tail, or anything else you might happen to need for the attainment of your ends."

"I was not so anxious to get the accent as all that," returned the Baron. "I don't think it is necessary for a man to make a monkey of himself just for the pleasure of mastering a language. Reasoning similarly, a man to master the art of braying in a fashion comprehensible to the jackass of average intellect should make a jackass of himself, cultivate his ears, and learn to kick, so as properly to punctuate his sentences after the manner of most conversational beasts of that kind."

"Then you believe that jackasses talk, too, do you?" asked Doctor Darwin.

"Why not?" said the Baron. "If monkeys, why not donkeys? Certainly they do. All creatures have some means of communicating their thoughts to each other. Why man in his conceit should think otherwise I don't know, unless it be that the birds and beasts in their conceit probably think that they alone of all the creatures in the world can talk."

"I haven't a doubt," said Doctor Livingstone, "that monkeys listening to men and women talking think they are only jabbering."

"They're not far from wrong in most cases if they do," said Doctor Johnson, who up to this time had been merely an interested listener. "I've thought that many a time myself."

"Which is perhaps, in a slight degree, a confirmation of my theory," put in Darwin. "If Doctor Johnson's mind runs in the same channels that the monkey's mind runs in, why may we not say that Doctor Johnson, being a man, has certain qualities of the monkey, and is therefore, in a sense, of the same strain?"

"You may say what you please," retorted Johnson, wrathfully, "but I'll make you prove what you say about me."

"I wouldn't if I were you," said Doctor Livingstone, in a peace-making spirit. "It would not be a pleasant task for you, compelling our friend to prove you descended from the ape. I should think you'd prefer to make him leave it unproved."

"Have monkeys Boswells?" queried Thackeray.

"I don't know anything about 'em," said Johnson, petulantly.

"No more do I," said Darwin, "and I didn't mean to be offensive, my dear Johnson. If I claim Simian ancestry for you, I claim it equally for myself."

"Well, I'm no snob," said Johnson, unmollified. "If you want to brag about your ancestors, do it. Leave mine alone. Stick to your own genealogical orchard."

"Well, I believe fully that we are all descended from the ape," said Munchausen. "There isn't any doubt in my mind that before the flood all men had tails. Noah had a tail. Shem, Ham, and Japheth had tails. It's perfectly reasonable to believe it. The Ark in a sense proved it. It would have been almost impossible for Noah and his sons to construct the Ark in the time they did with the assistance of only two hands apiece. Think, however, of how fast they could work with the assistance of that third arm. Noah could hammer a clapboard on to the Ark with two hands while grasping a saw and cutting a new board or planing it off with his tail. So with the others. We all know how much a third hand would help us at times."

"But how do you account for its disappearance?" put in Doctor Livingstone. "Is it likely they would dispense with such a useful adjunct?"

"No, it isn't; but there are various ways of accounting for its loss," said Munchausen. "They may have overworked it building the Ark; Shem, Ham, or Japheth may have had his caught in the door of the Ark and cut off in the hurry of the departure; plenty of things may have happened to eliminate it. Men lose their hair and their teeth; why might not a man lose a tail? Scientists say that coming generations far in the future will be toothless and bald. Why may it not be that through causes unknown to us we are similarly deprived of something our forefathers had?"

"The only reason for man's losing his hair is that he wears a hat all the time," said Livingstone. "The Derby hat is the enemy of hair. It is hot, and dries up the scalp. You might as well try to raise watermelons in the Desert of Sahara as to try to raise hair under the modern hat. In fact, the modern hat is a furnace."

"Well, it's a mighty good furnace," observed Munchausen. "You don't have to put coal on the modern hat."

41

"Perhaps," interposed Thackeray, "the ancients wore their hats on their tails."

"Well, I have a totally different theory," said Johnson.

"You always did have," observed Munchausen.

"Very likely," said Johnson. "To be commonplace never was my ambition."

"What is your theory?" queried Livingstone.

"Well—I don't know," said Johnson, "if it be worth expressing."

"It may be worth sending by freight," interrupted Thackeray. "Let us have it."

"Well, I believe," said Johnson—"I believe that Adam was a monkey."

"He behaved like one," ejaculated Thackeray.

"I believe that the forbidden tree was a tender one, and therefore the only one upon which Adam was forbidden to swing by his tail," said Johnson.

"Clear enough—so far," said Munchausen.

"But that the possession of tails by Adam and Eve entailed a love of swinging thereby, and that they could not resist the temptation to swing from every limb in Eden, and that therefore, while Adam was off swinging on other trees, Eve took a swing on the forbidden tree; that Adam, returning, caught her in the act, and immediately gave way himself and swung," said Johnson.

"Then you eliminate the serpent?" queried Darwin.

"Not a bit of it," Johnson answered. "The serpent was the tail. Look at most snakes today. What are they but unattached tails?"

"They do look it," said Darwin, thoughtfully.

"Why, it's clear as day," said Johnson. "As punishment Adam and Eve lost their tails, and the tail itself was compelled to work for a living and do its own walking."

"I never thought of that," said Darwin. "It seems reasonable."

"It is reasonable," said Johnson.

"And the snakes of the present day?" queried Thackeray.

"I believe to be the missing tails of men," said Johnson. "Somewhere in the world is a tail for every man and woman and child. Where one's tail is no one can ever say, but that it exists simultaneously with its owner I believe. The abhorrence man has for snakes is directly attributable to his abhorrence for all things which have deprived him of something that is good. If Adam's tail had not tempted him to swing on the forbidden tree, we should all of us have been able through life to relax from business cares after the manner of the monkey, who is happy from morning until night."

"Well, I can't see that it does us any good to sit here and discuss this matter," said Doctor Livingstone. "We can't reach any conclusion. The only way to settle the matter, it seems to me, is to go directly to Adam, who is a member of this club, and ask him how it was."

"That's a great idea," said Thackeray, scornfully. "You'd look well going up to a man and saying, 'Excuse me, sir, but—ah— were you ever a monkey?'"

"To say nothing of catechising a man on the subject of an old and dreadful scandal," put in Munchausen. "I'm surprised at you, Livingstone. African etiquette seems to have ruined your sense of propriety."

"I'd just as lief ask him," said Doctor Johnson. "Etiquette? Bah! What business has etiquette to stand in the way of human knowledge? Conventionality is the last thing men of brains should strive after, and I, for one, am not going to be bound by it."

Here Doctor Johnson touched the electric bell, and in an instant the shade of a buttons appeared.

"Boy, is Adam in the club-house today?" asked the sage.

"I'll go and see, sir," said the boy, and he immediately departed.

"Good boy that," said Thackeray.

"Yes; but the service in this club is dreadful, considering what we might have," said Darwin. "With Aladdin a member of this club, I don't see why we can't have his lamp with *genii* galore to respond. It certainly would be more economical."

"True; but I, for one, don't care to fool with genii," said Munchausen. "When one member can summon a servant who is strong enough to take another member and do him up in a bottle and cast him into the sea, I have no use for the system. Plain ordinary mortal shades are good enough for me."

As Munchausen spoke, the boy returned.

"Mr. Adam isn't here today, sir," he said, addressing Doctor Johnson. "And Charon says he's not likely to be here, sir, seeing as how his account is closed, not having been settled for three months."

"Good," said Thackeray. "I was afraid he was here. I don't want to have him asked about his Eden experiences in my behalf. That's personality."

"Well, then, there's only one other thing to do," said Darwin. "Munchausen claims to be able to speak Simian. He might seek out some of the prehistoric monkeys and put the question to them."

"No, thank you," said Munchausen. "I'm a little rusty in the language, and, besides, you talk like an idiot. You might as well speak of the human language as the Simian language. There are French monkeys who speak monkey French, African monkeys who talk the most barbarous kind of Zulu monkey patois, and Congo monkey slang, and so on. Let Johnson send his little Boswell out to drum up information. If there is anything to be found out he'll get it, and then he can tell it to us. Of course he may get it all wrong, but it will be entertaining, and we'll never know any difference."

Which seemed to the others a good idea, but whatever came of it I have not been informed.

7: A Discussion as to Ladies' Day

"I met Queen Elizabeth just now on the Row," said Raleigh, as he entered the house-boat and checked his cloak.

"Indeed?" said Confucius. "What if you did? Other people have met Queen Elizabeth. There's nothing original about that."

"True; but she made a suggestion to me about this house-boat which I think is a good one. She says the women are all crazy to see the inside of it," said Raleigh.

"Thus proving that immortal woman is no different from mortal woman," retorted Confucius. "They want to see the inside of everything. Curiosity, thy name is woman."

"Well, I am sure I don't see why men should arrogate to themselves the sole right to an investigating turn of mind," said Raleigh, impatiently. "Why shouldn't the ladies want to see the inside of this club-house? It is a compliment to us that they should, and I for one am in favour of letting them, and I am going to propose that in the Ides of March we give a ladies' day here."

"Then I shall go South for my health in the Ides of March," said Confucius, angrily. "What on earth is a club for if it isn't to enable men to get away from their wives once in a while? When do people go to clubs? When they are on their way home—that's when; and the more a man's at home in his club, the less he's at home when he's at home. I suppose you'll be suggesting a children's day next, and after that a parrot's or a canary-bird's day."

"I had no idea you were such a woman-hater," said Raleigh, in astonishment. "What's the matter? Were you ever disappointed in love?"

"I? How absurd!" retorted Confucius, reddening. "The idea of *my* ever being disappointed in love! I never met the woman who could bring me to my knees, although I was married in the other world. What became of Mrs. C. I never inquired. She may be in China yet, for aught I know. I regard death as a divorce."

"Your wife must be glad of it," said Raleigh, somewhat un-gallantly; for, to tell the truth, he was nettled by Confucius's demeanour. "I didn't know, however, but that since you escaped from China and came here to Hades you might have fallen in love with some spirit of an age subsequent to your own—Mary Queen of Scots, or Joan of Arc, or some other spook—who

45

rejected you. I can't account for your dislike of women otherwise."

"Not I," said Confucius. "Hades would have a less classic name than it has for me if I were hampered with a family. But go along and have your ladies' day here, and never mind my reasons for preferring my own society to that of the fair sex. I can at least stay at home that day. What do you propose to do—throw open the house to the wives of members, or to all ladies, irrespective of their husbands' membership here?"

"I think the latter plan would be the better," said Raleigh. "Otherwise Queen Elizabeth, to whom I am indebted for the suggestion, would be excluded. She never married, you know."

"Didn't she?" said Confucius. "No, I didn't know it; but that doesn't prove anything. When I went to school we didn't study the history of the Elizabethan period. She didn't have absolute sway over England, then?"

"She had; but what of that?" queried Raleigh.

"Do you mean to say that she lived and died an old maid from choice?" demanded Confucius.

"Certainly I do," said Raleigh. "And why should I not tell you that?"

"For a very good and sufficient reason," retorted Confucius, "which is, in brief, that I am not a marine. I may dislike women, my dear Raleigh, but I know them better than you do, gallant as you are; and when you tell me in one and the same moment that a woman holding absolute sway over men yet lived and died an old maid, you must not be indignant if I smile and bite the end of my thumb, which is the Chinese way of saying that's all in your eye, Betty Martin."

"Believe it or not, you poor old back number," retorted Raleigh, hotly. "It alters nothing. Queen Elizabeth could have married a hundred times over if she had wished. I know I lost my head there completely."

"That shows, Sir Walter," said Dryden, with a grin, "how wrong you are. You lost your head to King James. Hi! Shakespeare, here's a man doesn't know who chopped his head off."

Raleigh's face flushed scarlet. "'Tis better to have had a head and lost it," he cried, "than never to have had a head at all! Mark you, Dryden, my boy, it ill befits you to scoff at me for my misfortune, for dust thou art, and to dust thou hast returned, if word from t'other side about thy books and that which in and on them lies be true."

"Whate'er be said about my books," said Dryden, angrily, "be they read or be they not, 'tis mine they are, and none there be who dare dispute their authorship."

"Thus proving that men, thank Heaven, are still sane," ejaculated Doctor Johnson. "To assume the authorship of Dryden would be not so much a claim, my friend, as a confession."

"Shades of the mighty Chow!" cried Confucius. "An' will ye hear the poets squabble! Egad! A ladies' day could hardly introduce into our midst a more diverting disputation."

"We're all getting a little high-flown in our phraseology," put in Shakespeare at this point. "Let's quit talking in blank-verse and come down to business. *I* think a ladies' day would be great sport. I'll write a poem to read on the occasion."

"Then I oppose it with all my heart," said Doctor Johnson. "Why do you always want to make our entertainments commonplace? Leave occasional poems to mortals. I never knew an occasional poem yet that was worthy of an immortal."

"That's precisely why I want to write one occasional poem. I'd make it worthy," Shakespeare answered. "Like this, for instance:

Most fair, most sweet, most beauteous of ladies,
The greatest charm in all ye realm of Hades.

Why, my dear Doctor, such an opportunity for rhyming Hades with ladies should not be lost."

"That just proves what I said," said Johnson. "Any idiot can make ladies rhyme with Hades. It requires absolute genius to avoid the temptation. You are great enough to make Hades rhyme with bicycle if you choose to do it—but no, you succumb to the temptation to be commonplace. Bah! One of these modern drawing-room poets with three sections to his name couldn't do worse."

"On general principles," said Raleigh, "Johnson is right. We invite these people here to see our club-house, not to give them an exhibition of our metrical powers, and I think all exercises of a formal nature should be frowned upon."

"Very well," said Shakespeare. "Go ahead. Have your own way about it. Get out your brow and frown. I'm perfectly willing to save myself the trouble of writing a poem. Writing real poetry isn't easy, as you fellows would have discovered for yourselves if you'd ever tried it."

"To pass over the arrogant assumption of the gentleman who has just spoken, with the silence due to a proper expression of our contempt therefor," said Dryden, slowly, "I think in case we do have a ladies' day here we should exercise a most careful supervision over the invitation list. For instance, wouldn't it be awkward for our good friend Henry the Eighth to encounter the various Mrs. Henrys here? Would it not likewise be awkward for them to meet each other?"

"Your point is well taken," said Doctor Johnson. "I don't know whether the King's matrimonial ventures are on speaking terms with each other or not, but under any circumstances it would hardly be a pleasing spectacle for Katharine of Arragon to see Henry running his legs off getting cream and cakes for Anne Boleyn; nor would Anne like it much if, on the other hand, Henry chose to behave like a gentleman and a husband to Jane Seymour or Katharine Parr. I think, if the members themselves are to send out the invitations, they should each be limited to two cards, with the express understanding that no member shall be permitted to invite more than one wife."

"That's going to be awkward," said Raleigh, scratching his head thoughtfully. "Henry is such a hot-headed fellow that he might resent the stipulation."

"I think he would," said Confucius. "I think he'd be as mad as a hatter at your insinuation that he would invite any of his wives, if all I hear of him is true; and what I've heard, Wolsey has told me."

"He knew a thing or two about Henry," said Shakespeare. "If you don't believe it, just read that play of mine that Beaumont and Fletcher—er—ah—thought so much of."

"You came near giving your secret away that time, William," said Johnson, with a sly smile, and giving the Avonian a dig between the ribs.

"Secret! I haven't any secret," said Shakespeare, a little acridly. "It's the truth I'm telling you. Beaumont and Fletcher *did* admire *Henry the Eighth*."

"Thereby showing their conceit, eh?" said Johnson.

"Oh, of course, I didn't write anything, did I?" cried Shakespeare. "Everybody wrote my plays but me. I'm the only person that had no hand in Shakespeare. It seems to me that joke is about worn out, Doctor. I'm getting a little tired of it myself; but if it amuses you, why, keep it up. *I* know who wrote my plays, and whatever you may say cannot affect the facts. Next thing you fellows will be saying that I didn't write my own autographs?"

"I didn't say that," said Johnson, quietly. "Only there is no internal evidence in your autographs that you knew how to spell your name if you did. A man who signs his name Shixpur one day and Shikespeare the next needn't complain if the Bank of Posterity refuses to honour his check."

"They'd honour my check quick enough these days," retorted Shakespeare. "When a man's autograph brings five thousand dollars, or one thousand pounds, in the auction-room, there isn't a bank in the world fool enough to decline to honour any check he'll sign under a thousand dollars, or two hundred pounds."

"I fancy you're right," put in Raleigh. "But your checks or your plays have nothing to do with ladies' day. Let's get to some conclusion in this matter."

"Yes," said Confucius. "Let's. Ladies' day is becoming a dreadful bore, and if we don't hurry up the billiard-room will be full."

"Well, I move we get up a petition to the council to have it," said Dryden.

"I agree," said Confucius, "and I'll sign it. If there's one way to avoid having ladies' day in the future, it's to have one now and be done with it."

"All right," said Shakespeare. "I'll sign too."

"As—er—Shixpur or Shikespeare?" queried Johnson.

"Let him alone," said Raleigh. "He's getting sensitive about that; and what you need to learn more than anything else is that it isn't manners to twit a man on facts. What's bothering you, Dryden? You look like a man with an idea."

"It has just occurred to me," said Dryden, "that while we can safely leave the question of Henry the Eighth and his wives to the wisdom of the council, we ought to pay some attention to the advisability of inviting Lucretia Borgia. I'd hate to eat any supper if she came within a mile of the banqueting-hall. If she comes you'll have to appoint a tasting committee before I'll touch a drop of punch or eat a speck of salad."

"We might recommend the appointment of Raleigh to look after the fair Lucretia and see that she has no poison with her, or if she has, to keep her from dropping it into the salads," said Confucius, with a sidelong glance at Raleigh. "He's the especial champion of woman in this club, and no doubt would be proud of the distinction."

"I would with most women," said Raleigh. "But I draw the line at Lucretia Borgia."

And so a petition was drawn up, signed, and sent to the council, and they, after mature deliberation, decided to have the ladies' day, to which all the ladies in Hades, excepting Lucretia Borgia and Delilah, were to be duly invited, only the date was not specified. Delilah was excluded at the request of Samson, whose convincing muscles, rather than his arguments, completely won over all opposition to his proposition.

8: A Discontented Shade

"It seems to me," said Shakespeare, wearily, one afternoon at the club—"that this business of being immortal is pretty dull. Didn't somebody once say he'd rather ride fifty years on a trolley in Europe than on a bicycle in Cathay?"

"I never heard any such remark by any self-respecting person," said Johnson.

"I said something like it," observed Tennyson.

Doctor Johnson looked around to see who it was that spoke.

"You?" he cried. "And who, pray, may you be?"

"My name is Tennyson," replied the poet.

"And a very good name it is," said Shakespeare.

"I am not aware that I ever heard the name before," said Doctor Johnson. "Did you make it yourself?"

"I did," said the late *laureate*, proudly.

"In what pursuit?" asked Doctor Johnson.

"Poetry," said Tennyson. "I wrote *Locksley Hall* and *Come into the Garden, Maude.*"

"Humph!" said Doctor Johnson. "I never read 'em."

"Well, why should you have read them?" snarled Carlyle. "They were written after you moved over here, and they were good stuff. You needn't think because you quit, the whole world put up its shutters and went out of business. I did a few things myself which I fancy you never heard of."

"Oh, as for that," retorted Doctor Johnson, with a smile, "I've heard of you; you are the man who wrote the *Life of Frederick the Great* in nine hundred and two volumes—"

"Seven!" snapped Carlyle.

"Well, seven then," returned Johnson. "I never saw the work, but I heard Frederick speaking of it the other day. Bonaparte asked him if he had read it, and Frederick said no, he hadn't time. Bonaparte cried, 'Haven't time? Why, my dear king, you've got all eternity.' 'I know it,' replied Frederick, 'but that isn't enough. Read a page or two, my dear Napoleon, and you'll see why.'"

"Frederick will have his joke," said Shakespeare, with a wink at Tennyson and a smile for the two philosophers, intended, no doubt, to put them in a more agreeable frame of mind. "Why, he even asked me the other day why I never wrote a tragedy about him, completely ignoring the fact that he came along many years after I had departed. I spoke of that, and he said, 'Oh, I was only joking.' I apologized. 'I didn't know that,' said I. 'And why should you?' said he. 'You're English.'"

"A very rude remark," said Johnson. "As if we English were incapable of seeing a joke!"

"Exactly," put in Carlyle. "It strikes me as the absurdest notion that the Englishman can't see a joke. To the mind that is accustomed to snap judgments I have no doubt the Englishman appears to be dull of apprehension, but the philosophy of the whole matter is apparent to the mind that takes the trouble to investigate. The Briton weighs everything carefully before he commits himself, and even though a certain point may strike him as funny, he isn't going to laugh until he has fully made up his mind that it is funny. I remember once riding down Piccadilly with Froude in a hansom cab. Froude had a copy of *Punch* in his hand, and he began to laugh immoderately over something. I leaned over his shoulder to see what he was laughing at. 'That isn't so funny,' said I, as I read the paragraph on which his eye was resting. 'No,' said Froude. 'I wasn't laughing at that. I was enjoying the joke that appeared in the same relative position in last week's issue.' Now that's the point—the whole point. The Englishman always laughs over last week's *Punch*, not this week's, and that is why you will find a file of that interesting journal in the home of all well-to-do Britons. It is the back number that amuses him—which merely proves that he is a deliberative person who weighs even his humour carefully before giving way to his emotions."

"What is the average weight of a copy of *Punch*?" drawled Artemas Ward, who had strolled in during the latter part of the conversation.

Shakespeare snickered quietly, but Carlyle and Johnson looked upon the intruder severely.

"We will take that question into consideration," said Carlyle. "Perhaps tomorrow we shall have a definite answer ready for you."

"Never mind," returned the humorist. "You've proved your

point. Tennyson tells me you find life here dull, Shakespeare."

"Somewhat," said Shakespeare. "I don't know about the rest of you fellows, but I was not cut out for an eternity of ease. I must have occupation, and the stage isn't popular here. The trouble about putting on a play here is that our managers are afraid of libel suits. The chances are that if I should write a play with Cassius as the hero, Cassius would go to the first night's performance with a dagger concealed in his *toga*, with which to punctuate his objections to the lines put in his mouth. There is nothing I'd like better than to manage a theatre in this place, but think of the riots we'd have! Suppose, for an instant, that I wrote a play about Bonaparte! He'd have a box, and when the rest of you spooks called for the author at the end of the third act, if he didn't happen to like the play he'd greet me with a salvo of artillery instead of applause."

"He wouldn't if you made him out a great conqueror from start to finish," said Tennyson.

"No doubt," returned Shakespeare, sadly; "but in that event Wellington would be in the other stage-box, and I'd get the greeting from him."

"Why come out at all?" asked Johnson.

"Why come out at all?" echoed Shakespeare. "What fun is there in writing a play if you can't come out and show yourself at the first night? That's the author's reward. If it wasn't for the first-night business, though, all would be plain sailing."

"Then why don't you begin it the second night?" drawled Ward.

"How the deuce could you?" put in Carlyle.

"A most extraordinary proposition," sneered Johnson.

"Yes," said Ward; "but wait a week—you'll see the point then."

"There isn't any doubt in my mind," said Shakespeare, reverting to his original proposition, "that the only perfectly satisfactory life is under a system not yet adopted in either world—the one we have quitted or this. There we had hard work in which our mortal limitations hampered us grievously; here we have the freedom of the immortal with no hard work; in other words, now that we feel like fighting-cocks, there isn't any fighting to be done. The great life in my estimation, would be to return to earth and battle with mortal problems, but equipped mentally and physically with immortal weapons."

"Some people don't know when they are well off," said Beau Brummel. "This strikes me as being an ideal life. There are no tailors bills to pay—we are ourselves nothing but memories, and a memory can clothe himself in the shadow of his former grandeur—I clothe myself in the remembrance of my departed clothes, and as my memory is good I flatter myself I'm the best-dressed man here. The fact that there are ghosts of departed un-paid bills haunting my bedside at night doesn't bother me in the least, because the bailiffs that in the old life lent terror to an overdue account, thanks to our beneficent system here, are kept in the less agreeable sections of Hades. I used to regret that bailiffs were such low people, but now I rejoice at it. If they had been of a different order they might have proven unpleasant here."

"You are right, my dear Brummel," interposed Munchausen. "This life is far preferable to that in the other sphere. Any of you gentlemen who happen to have had the pleasure of reading my memoirs must have been struck with the tremendous difficulties that encumbered my progress. If I wished for a rare liqueur for my luncheon, a liqueur served only at the table of an Oriental potentate, more jealous of it than of his one thousand queens, I had to raise armies, charter ships, and wage warfare in which feats of incredible valor had to be performed by myself alone and unaided to secure the desired thimbleful. I have destroyed empires for a *bon-bon* at great expense of nervous energy."

"That's very likely true," said Carlyle. "I should think your feats of strength would have wrecked your imagination in time."

"Not so," said Munchausen. "On the contrary, continuous exercise served only to make it stronger. But, as I was going to say, in this life we have none of these fearful obstacles—it is a life of leisure; and if I want a bird and a cold bottle at any time, instead of placing my life in peril and jeopardizing the peace of all mankind to get it, I have only to summon before me the memory of some previous bird and cold bottle, dine thereon like a well-ordered citizen, and smoke the spirit of the best cigar my imagination can conjure up."

"You miss my point," said Shakespeare. "I don't say this life is worse or better than the other we used to live. What I do say is that a combination of both would suit me. In short, I'd like to live here and go to the other world every day to business, like a suburban resident who sleeps in the country and makes his living in the city. For instance, why shouldn't I dwell here and go to London every day, hire an office there, and put out a sign something like this:

WILLIAM SHAKESPEARE
DRAMATIST
Plays written while you wait
I guess I'd find plenty to do."

"Guess again," said Tennyson. "My dear boy, you forget one thing. *You are out of date.* People don't go to the theatres to hear *you*, they go to see the people who *do* you."

"That is true," said Ward. "And they do do you, my beloved William. It's a wonder to me you are not dizzy turning over in your grave the way they do you."

"Can it be that I can ever be out of date?" asked Shakespeare. "I know, of course, that I have to be adapted at times; but to be wholly out of date strikes me as a hard fate."

"You're not out of date," interposed Carlyle; "the date is out of you. There is a great demand for Shakespeare in these days, but there isn't any stuff."

"Then I should succeed," said Shakespeare.

"No, I don't think so," returned Carlyle. "You couldn't stand the pace. The world revolves faster today than it did in your time—men write three or four plays at once. This is what you might call a Type-writer Age, and to keep up with the procession you'd have to work as you never worked before."

"That is true," observed Tennyson. "You'd have to learn to be ambidextrous, so that you could keep two type-writing machines going at once; and, to be perfectly frank with you, I cannot even conjure up in my fancy a picture of you knocking out a tragedy with the right hand on one machine, while your left hand is fashioning a farce-comedy on another."

"He might do as a great many modern writers do," said Ward; "go in for the Paper-doll Drama. Cut the whole thing out with a pair of scissors. As the poet might have said if he'd been clever enough:

Oh, bring me the scissors,
And bring me the glue,
And a couple of dozen old plays.
I'll cut out and paste
A drama for you
That'll run for quite sixty-two days.

Oh, bring me a dress
Made of satin and lace,
And a book—say Joe Miller's—of wit;
And I'll make the old dramatists
Blue in the face
With the play that I'll turn out for it.

So bring me the scissors,
And bring me the paste,
And a dozen fine old comedies;
A fine line of dresses,
And popular taste
I'll make a strong effort to please.

"You draw a very blue picture, it seems to me," said Shakespeare, sadly.

"Well, it's true," said Carlyle. "The world isn't at all what it used to be in any one respect, and you fellows who made great reputations centuries ago wouldn't have even the ghost of a show now. I don't believe Homer could get a poem accepted by a modern magazine, and while the comic papers are still printing Diogenes' jokes the old gentleman couldn't make enough out of them in these days to pay taxes on his tub, let alone earning his bread."

"That is exactly so," said Tennyson. "I'd be willing to wager too that, in the line of personal prowess, even D'Artagnan and Athos and Porthos and Aramis couldn't stand London for one day."

"Or New York either," said Mr. Barnum, who had been an interested listener. "A New York policeman could have managed that quartet with one hand."

"Then," said Shakespeare, "in the opinion of you gentlemen, we old-time lions would appear to modern eyes to be more or less stuffed?"

"That's about the size of it," said Carlyle.

"But you'd draw," said Barnum, his face lighting up with pleasure. "You'd drive a five-legged calf to suicide from envy. If I could take you and Cæsar, and Napoleon Bonaparte and Nero over for one circus season we'd drive the mint out of business."

"There's your chance, William," said Ward. "You write a play for Bonaparte and Cæsar, and let Nero take his fiddle and be the orchestra. Under Barnum's management you'd get enough activity in one season to last you through all eternity."

"You can count on me," said Barnum, rising. "Let me know when you've got your plan laid out. I'd stay and make a contract with you now, but Adam has promised to give me points on the management of wild animals without cages, so I can't wait. By-by."

"Humph!" said Shakespeare, as the eminent showman passed out. "That's a gay proposition. When monkeys move in polite society William Shakespeare will make a side-show of himself for a circus."

"They do now," said Thackeray, quietly.

Which merely proved that Shakespeare did not mean what he said; for in spite of Thackeray's insinuation as to the monkeys and polite society, he has not yet accepted the Barnum proposition, though there can be no doubt of its value from the point of view of a circus manager.

CHAPTER 9: AS TO COOKERY AND SCULPTURE

Robert Burns and Homer were seated at a small table in the dining-room of the house-boat, discussing everything in general and the shade of a very excellent luncheon in particular.

"We are in great luck today," said Burns, as he cut a ruddy duck in twain. "This bird is done just right."

"I agree with you," returned Homer, drawing his chair a trifle closer to the table. "Compared to the one we had here last Thursday, this is a feast for the gods. I wonder who it was that cooked this fowl originally?"

"I give it up; but I suspect it was done by some man who knew his business," said Burns, with a smack of his lips. "It's a pity, I think, my dear Homer, that there is no means by which a cook may become immortal. Cooking is as much of an art as is the writing of poetry, and just as there are immortal poets so there should be immortal cooks. See what an advantage the poet has—he writes something, it goes out and reaches the inmost soul of the man who reads it, and it is signed. His work is known because he puts his name to it; but this poor devil of a cook—where is he? He has done his work as well as the poet ever did his, it has reached the inmost soul of the mortal who originally ate it, but he cannot get the glory of it because he cannot put his name to it. If the cook could sign his work it would be different."

"You have hit upon a great truth," said Homer, nodding, as he sometimes was wont to do. "And yet I fear that, ingenious as we are, we cannot devise a plan to remedy the matter. I do not know about you, but I should myself much object if my birds and my flapjacks, and other things, digestible and otherwise, that I eat here were served with the cook's name written upon them. An omelette is sometimes a picture—"

"I've seen omelettes that looked like one of Turner's sunsets," acquiesced Burns.

"Precisely; and when Turner puts down in one corner of his

canvas, 'Turner, *fecit*,' you do not object, but if the cook did that with the omelette you wouldn't like it."

"No," said Burns; "but he might fasten a tag to it, with his name written upon that."

"That is so," said Homer; "but the result in the end would be the same. The tags would get lost, or perhaps a careless waiter, dropping a tray full of dainties, would get the tags of a good and bad cook mixed in trying to restore the contents of the tray to their previous condition. The tag system would fail."

"There is but one other way that I can think of," said Burns, "and that would do no good now unless we can convey our ideas into the other world; that is, for a great poet to lend his genius to the great cook, and make the latter's name immortal by putting it into a poem. Say, for instance, that you had eaten a fine bit of terrapin, done to the most exquisite point—you could have asked the cook's name, and written an apostrophe to her. Something like this, for instance:

Oh, Dinah Rudd! oh, Dinah Rudd!
Thou art a cook of bluest blood!
Nowhere within
This world of sin
Have I e'er tasted better terrapin.
Do you see?"

"I do; but even then, my dear fellow, the cook would fall short of true fame. Her excellence would be a mere matter of hearsay evidence," said Homer.

"Not if you went on to describe, in a keenly analytical manner, the virtues of that particular bit of terrapin," said Burns. "Draw so vivid a picture of the dish that the reader himself would taste that terrapin even as you tasted it."

"You have hit it!" cried Homer, enthusiastically. "It is a grand plan; but how to introduce it—that is the question."

"We can haunt some modern poet, and give him the idea in that way," suggested Burns. "He will see the novelty of it, and will possibly disseminate the idea as we wish it to be disseminated."

"Done!" said Homer. "I'll begin right away. I feel like haunting tonight. I'm getting to be a pretty old ghost, but I'll never lose my love of haunting."

At this point, as Homer spoke, a fine-looking spirit entered the room, and took a seat at the head of the long table at which the regular club dinner was nightly served.

"Why, bless me!" said Homer, his face lighting up with pleasure. "Why, Phidias, is that you?"

"I think so," said the new-comer, wearily; "at any rate, it's all that's left of me."

"Come over here and lunch with us," said Homer. "You know Burns, don't you?"

"Haven't the pleasure," said Phidias.

The poet and the sculptor were introduced, after which Phidias seated himself at Homer's side.

"Are you any relation to Burns the poet?" the former asked, addressing the Scotchman.

"I *am* Burns the poet," replied the other.

"You don't look much like your statues," said Phidias, scanning his face critically.

"No, thank the Fates!" said Burns, warmly. "If I did, I'd commit suicide."

"Why don't you sue the sculptors for libel?" asked Phidias.

"You speak with a great deal of feeling, Phidias," said Homer, gravely. "Have they done anything to hurt you?"

"They have," said Phidias. "I have just returned from a tour of the world. I have seen the things they call sculpture in these degenerate days, and I must confess—who shouldn't, perhaps— that I could have done better work with a baseball-bat for a chisel and putty for the raw material."

"I think I could do good work with a baseball-bat too," said Burns; "but as for the raw material, give me the heads of the men who have sculped me to work on. I'd leave them so that they'd look like some of your Parthenon frieze figures with the noses gone."

"You are a vindictive creature," said Homer. "These men you

criticise, and whose heads you wish to sculp with a baseball-bat, have done more for you than you ever did for them. Every statue of you these men have made is a standing advertisement of your books, and it hasn't cost you a penny. There isn't a doubt in my mind that if it were not for those statues countless people would go to their graves supposing that the great Scottish Burns were little rivulets, and not a poet. What difference does it make to you if they haven't made an Adonis of you? You never set them an example by making one of yourself. If there's deception anywhere, it isn't you that is deceived; it is the mortals. And who cares about them or their opinions?"

"I never thought of it in that way," said Burns. "I hate caricatures—that is, caricatures of myself. I enjoy caricatures of other people, but—"

"You have a great deal of the mortal left in you, considering that you pose as an immortal," said Homer, interrupting the speaker.

"Well, so have I," said Phidias, resolved to stand by Burns in the argument, "and I'm sorry for the man who hasn't. I was a mortal once, and I'm glad of it. I had a good time, and I don't care who knows it. When I look about me and see Jupiter, the arch-snob of creation, and Mars, a little tin warrior who couldn't have fought a soldier like Napoleon, with all his alleged divinity, I thank the Fates that they enabled me to achieve immortality through mortal effort. Hang hereditary greatness, I say. These men were born immortals. You and I worked for it and got it. We know what it cost. It was ours because we earned it, and not because we were born to it. Eh, Burns?"

The Scotchman nodded assent, and the Greek sculptor went on.

"I am not vindictive myself, Homer," he said. "Nobody has hurt me, and, on the whole, I don't think sculpture is in such a bad way, after all. There's a shoemaker I wot of in the mortal realms who can turn the prettiest last you ever saw; and I encountered a carver in a London eating-house last month who turned out a slice of beef that was cut as artistically as I could have done it myself. What I object to chiefly is the tendency of the times. This is an electrical age, and men in my old profession aren't content to turn out one *chef-d'oeuvre* in a lifetime. They take orders by the gross. I waited upon inspiration. Today the sculptor waits upon custom, and an artist will make a bust of anybody in any material desired as long as he is sure of getting his pay afterwards. I saw a life-size statue of the inventor of a new kind of lard the other day, and what do you suppose the material was? Gold? Not by a great deal. Ivory? Marble, even? Not a bit of it. He was done in lard, sir. I have seen a woman's head done in butter, too, and it makes me distinctly weary to think that my art should be brought so low."

"You did your best work in Greece," chuckled Homer.

"A bad joke, my dear Homer," retorted Phidias. "I thought sculpture was getting down to a pretty low ebb when I had to fashion *friezes* out of marble; but marble is more precious than rubies alongside of butter and lard."

"Each has its uses," said Homer. "I'd rather have butter on my bread than marble, but I must confess that for sculpture it is very poor stuff, as you say."

"It is indeed," said Phidias. "For practice it's all right to use butter, but for exhibition purposes—bah!"

Here Phidias, to show his contempt for butter as raw material in sculpture, seized a wooden toothpick, and with it modelled a beautiful head of Minerva out of the pat that stood upon the small plate at his side, and before Burns could interfere had spread the chaste figure as thinly as he could upon a piece of bread, which he tossed to the shade of a hungry dog that stood yelping on the river-bank.

"Heavens!" cried Burns. "Imperious Cæsar dead and turned to bricks is as nothing to a Minerva carved by Phidias used to stay the hunger of a ravening cur."

"Well, it's the way I feel," said Phidias, savagely.

"I think you are a trifle foolish to be so eternally vexed about it," said Homer, soothingly. "Of course you feel badly, but, after all, what's the use? You must know that the mortals would pay more for one of your statues than they would for a specimen of any modern sculptor's art; yes, even if yours were modelled in wine-jelly and the other fellow's in pure gold. So why repine?"

"You'd feel the same way if poets did a similarly vulgar thing," retorted Phidias; "you know you would. If you should hear of a poet today writing a poem on a thin layer of lard or butter, you would yourself be the first to call a halt."

"No, I shouldn't," said Homer, quietly; "in fact, I wish the poets would do that. We'd have fewer bad poems to read; and that's the way you should look at it. I venture to say that if this modern plan of making busts and friezes in butter had been adopted at an earlier period, the public places in our great cities and our national Walhallas would seem less like repositories of comic art, since the first critical rays of a warm sun would have reduced the carven atrocities therein to a spot on the pavement. The butter school of sculpture has its advantages, my boy, and you should be crowning the inventor of the system with laurel, and not heaping coals of fire upon his brow."

"That," said Burns, "is, after all, the solid truth, Phidias. Take the brass caricatures of me, for instance. Where would they be now if they had been cast in lard instead of in bronze?"

Phidias was silent a moment.

"Well," he said, finally, as the value of the plan dawned upon his mind, "from that point of view I don't know but what you are right, after all; and, to show that I have spoken in no vindictive spirit, let me propose a toast. Here's to the Butter Sculptors. May their butter never give out."

The toast was drained to the dregs, and Phidias went home feeling a little better.

10: Story-Tellers' Night

It was Story-tellers' Night at the house-boat, and the best talkers of Hades were impressed into the service. Doctor Johnson was made chairman of the evening.

"Put him in the chair," said Raleigh. "That's the only way to keep him from telling a story himself. If he starts in on a tale he'll make it a serial sure as fate, but if you make him the medium through which other story-tellers are introduced to the club he'll be finely epigrammatic. He can be very short and sharp when he's talking about somebody else. Personality is his forte."

"Great scheme," said Diogenes, who was chairman of the entertainment committee. "The nights over here are long, but if Johnson started on a story they'd have to reach twice around eternity and halfway back to give him time to finish all he had to say."

"He's not very witty, in my judgment," said Carlyle, who since his arrival in the other world has manifested some jealousy of Solomon and Doctor Johnson.

"That's true enough," said Raleigh; "but he's strong, and he's bound to say something that will put the audience in sympathy with the man that he introduces, and that's half the success of a Story-tellers' Night. I've told stories myself. If your audience doesn't sympathize with you you'd be better off at home putting the baby to bed."

And so it happened. Doctor Johnson was made chairman, and the evening came. The Doctor was in great form. A list of the story-tellers had been sent him in advance, and he was prepared. The audience was about as select a one as can be found in Hades. The doors were thrown open to the friends of the members, and the smoke-furnace had been filled with a very superior quality of Arcadian mixture which Scott had brought back from a haunting-trip to the home of "The Little Minister," at Thrums.

"Friends and fellow-spooks," the Doctor began, when all were seated on the visionary camp-stools—which, by the way, are far superior to those in use in a world of realities, because they do not creak in the midst of a fine point demanding absolute silence for appreciation—"I do not know why I have been chosen to preside over this gathering of phantoms; it is the province of the presiding officer on occasions of this sort to say pleasant things, which he does not necessarily endorse, about the sundry persons who are to do the story-telling. Now, I suppose you all know me pretty well by this time. If there is anybody who doesn't, I'll be glad to have him presented after the formal work of the evening is over, and if I don't like him I'll tell him so. You know that if I can be counted upon for any one thing it is candour, and if I hurt the feelings of any of these individuals whom I introduce tonight, I want them distinctly to understand that it is not because I love them less, but that I love truth more. With this—ah—blanket apology, as it were, to cover all possible emergencies that may arise during the evening, I will begin. The first speaker on the programme, I regret to observe, is my friend Goldsmith. Affairs of this kind ought to begin with a snap, and while Oliver is a most excellent writer, as a speaker he is a pebbleless Demosthenes. If I had had the arrangement of the programme I should have had Goldsmith tell his story while the rest of us were down-stairs at supper. However, we must abide by our programme, which is unconscionably long, for otherwise we will never get through it. Those of you who agree with me as to the pleasure of listening to my friend Goldsmith will do well to join me in the grill-room while he is speaking, where, I understand, there is a very fine line of punches ready to be served. Modest Noll, will you kindly inflict yourself upon the gathering, and send me word when you get through, if you ever do, so that I may return and present number two to the assembly, whoever or whatever he may be?"

With these words the Doctor retired, and poor Goldsmith, pale with fear, rose up to speak. It was evident that he was quite as doubtful of his ability as a talker as was Johnson.

"I'm not much of a talker, or, as some say, speaker," he said. "Talking is not my forte, as Doctor Johnson has told you, and I am therefore not much at it. Speaking is not in my line. I cannot speak or talk, as it were, because I am not particularly ready at the making of a speech, due partly to the fact that I am not much of a talker anyhow, and seldom if ever speak. I will therefore not bore you by attempting to speak, since a speech by one who like myself is, as you are possibly aware, not a fluent nor indeed in any sense an eloquent speaker, is apt to be a bore to those who will be kind enough to listen to my remarks, but will read instead the first five chapters of the *Vicar of Wakefield*."

"Who suggested any such night as this, anyhow?" growled Carlyle. "Five chapters of the *Vicar of Wakefield* for a starter! Lord save us, we'll need a Vicar of Sleepfield if he's allowed to do this!"

"I move we adjourn," said Darwin.

"Can't something be done to keep these younger members quiet?" asked Solomon, frowning upon Carlyle and Darwin.

"Yes," said Douglas Jerrold. "Let Goldsmith go on. He'll have them asleep in ten minutes."

Meanwhile, Goldsmith was plodding earnestly through his stint, utterly and happily oblivious of the effect he was having upon his audience.

"This is awful," whispered Wellington to Bonaparte.

"Worse than Waterloo," replied the ex-Emperor, with a grin; "but we can stop it in a minute. Artemas Ward told me once how a camp-meeting he attended in the West broke up to go outside and see a dog-fight. Can't you and I pretend to quarrel? A personal assault by you on me will wake these people up and discombobulate Goldsmith. Say the word—only don't hit too hard."

"I'm with you," said Wellington. Whereupon, with a great show of heat, he roared out, "You? Never! I'm more afraid of a boy with a bean-snapper that I ever was of you!" and followed up his remark by pulling Bonaparte's camp-chair from under him, and letting the conqueror of Austerlitz fall to the floor with a thud which I have since heard described as dull and sickening.

The effect was instantaneous. Compared to a personal encounter between the two great figures of Waterloo, a reading from his own works by Goldsmith seemed lacking in the elements essential to the holding of an audience. Consequently, attention was centred in the belligerent warriors, and, by some odd mistake, when a peace-loving member of the assemblage, realizing the indecorousness of the incident, cried out, "Put him out! put him out!" the attendants rushed in, and, taking poor Goldsmith by his collar, hustled him out through the door, across the deck, and tossed him ashore without reference to the gang-plank. This accomplished, a personal explanation of their course was made by the quarrelling generals, and, peace having been restored, a committee was sent in search of Goldsmith with suitable apologies. The good and kindly soul returned, but having lost his book in the *mêlée*, much to his own gratification, as well as to that of the audience, he was permitted to rest in quiet the balance of the evening.

"Is he through?" said Johnson, poking his head in at the door when order was restored.

"Yes, sir," said Boswell; "that is to say, he has retired permanently from the field. He didn't finish, though."

"Fellow-spooks," began Johnson once more, "now that you have been delighted with the honeyed eloquence of the last speaker, it is my privilege to present to you that eminent fabulist Baron Munchausen, the greatest unrealist of all time, who will give you an exhibition of his paradoxical power of lying while standing."

The applause which greeted the Baron was deafening. He was, beyond all doubt, one of the most popular members of the club.

"Speaking of whales," said he, leaning gracefully against the table.

"Nobody has mentioned 'em," said Johnson.

"True," retorted the Baron; "but you always suggest them by your apparently unquenchable thirst for spouting—speaking of whales, my friend Jonah, as well as the rest of you, may be interested to know that I once had an experience similar to his own, and, strange to say, with the identical whale."

Jonah arose from his seat in the back of the room. "I do not wish to be unpleasant," he said, with a strong effort to be calm, "but I wish to ask if Judge Blackstone is in the room."

"I am," said the Judge, rising. "What can I do for you?"

"I desire to apply for an injunction restraining the Baron from using my whale in his story. That whale, your honour, is copyrighted," said Jonah. "If I had any other claim to the affection of mankind than the one which is based on my experience with that leviathan, I would willingly permit the Baron to introduce him into his story; but that whale, your honour, is my stock in trade—he is my all."

"I think Jonah's point is well taken," said Blackstone, turning to the Baron. "It would be a distinct hardship, I think, if the plaintiff in this action were to be deprived of the exclusive use of his sole accessory. The injunction prayed for is therefore granted. The court would suggest, however, that the Baron continue with his story, using another whale for the purpose."

"It is impossible," said Munchausen, gloomily. "The whole point of the story depends upon its having been Jonah's whale. Under the circumstances, the only thing I can do is to sit down. I regret the narrowness of mind exhibited by my friend Jonah, but I must respect the decision of the court."

"I must take exception to the Baron's allusion to my narrowness of mind," said Jonah, with some show of heat. "I am simply defending my rights, and I intend to continue to do so if the whole world unites in considering my mind a mere slot scarcely wide enough for the insertion of a nickel. That whale was my discovery, and the personal discomfort I endured in perfecting my experience was such that I resolved to rest my reputation upon his broad proportions only—to sink or swim with him— and I cannot at this late day permit another to crowd me out of his exclusive use."

Jonah sat down and fanned himself, and the Baron, with a look of disgust on his face, left the room.

"Up to his old tricks," he growled as he went. "He queers everything he goes into. If I'd known he was a member of this club I'd never have joined."

"We do not appear to be progressing very rapidly," said Doctor Johnson, rising. "So far we have made two efforts to have stories told, and have met with disaster each time. I don't know but what you are to be congratulated, however, on your escape. Very few of you, I observe, have as yet fallen asleep. The next number on the programme, I see, is Boswell, who was to have entertained you with a few reminiscences; I say was to have done so, because he is not to do so."

"I'm ready," said Boswell, rising.

"No doubt," retorted Johnson, severely, "but I am not. You are a man with one subject—myself. I admit it's a good subject, but you are not the man to treat of it—here. You may suffice for mortals, but here it is different. I can speak for myself. You can go out and sit on the banks of the Vitriol Reservoir and lecture to the imps if you want to, but when it comes to reminiscences of me I'm on deck myself, and I flatter myself I remember what I said and did more accurately than you do. Therefore, gentlemen, instead of listening to Boswell at this point, you will kindly excuse him and listen to me. Ahem! When I was a boy—"

"Excuse me," said Solomon, rising; "about how long is this—ah—this entertaining discourse of yours to continue?"

"Until I get through," returned Johnson, wrathfully.

"Are you aware, sir, that I am on the programme?" asked Solomon.

"I am," said the Doctor. "With that in mind, for the sake of our fellow-spooks who are present, I am very much inclined to keep on forever. When I was a boy—"

Carlyle rose up at this point.

"I should like to ask," he said, mildly, "if this is supposed to be an audience of children? I, for one, have no wish to listen to the juvenile stories of Doctor Johnson. Furthermore, I have come here particularly tonight to hear Boswell. I want to compare him with Froude. I therefore protest against—"

"There is a roof to this house-boat," said Doctor Johnson. "If Mr. Carlyle will retire to the roof with Boswell I have no doubt he can be accommodated. As for Solomon's interruption, I can afford to pass that over with the silent contempt it deserves, though I may add with propriety that I consider his most famous proverbs the most absurd bits of hack-work I ever en-

69

countered; and as for that story about dividing a baby between two mothers by splitting it in two, it was grossly inhuman unless the baby was twins. When I was a boy—"

As the Doctor proceeded, Carlyle and Solomon, accompanied by the now angry Boswell, left the room, and my account of the Story-tellers' Night must perforce stop; because, though I have never heretofore confessed it, all my information concerning the house-boat on the Styx has been derived from the memoranda of Boswell. It may be interesting to the reader to learn, however, that, according to Boswell's account, the Story-tellers' Night was never finished; but whether this means that it broke up immediately afterwards in a riot, or that Doctor Johnson is still at work detailing his reminiscences, I am not aware, and I cannot at the moment of writing ascertain, for Boswell, when I have the pleasure of meeting him, invariably avoids the subject.

11: As to Saurians and Others

It was Noah who spoke.

"I'm glad," he said, "that when I embarked at the time of the heavy rains that did so much damage in the old days, there weren't any dogs like that fellow Cerberus about. If I'd had to feed a lot of three-headed beasts like him the Ark would have run short of provisions inside of ten days."

"That's very likely true," observed Mr. Barnum; "but I must confess, my dear Noah, that you showed a lamentable lack of the showman's instinct when you selected the animals you did. A more commonplace lot of beasts were never gathered together, and while Adam is held responsible for the introduction of sin into the world, I attribute most of my offences to none other than yourself."

The members of the club drew their chairs a little closer. The conversation had opened a trifle spicily, and, furthermore, they had retained enough of their mortality to be interested in animal stories. Adam, who had managed to settle his back dues and delinquent house-charges, and once more acquired the privileges of the club, nodded his head gratefully at Mr. Barnum.

"I'm glad to find someone," said he, "who places the responsibility for trouble where it belongs. I'm round-shouldered with the blame I've had to bear. I didn't invent sin any more than I invented the telephone, and I think it's rather rough on a fellow who lived a quiet, retiring, pastoral life, minding his own business and staying home nights, to be held up to public reprobation for as long a time as I have."

"It'll be all right in time," said Raleigh; "just wait—be patient, and your vindication will come. Nobody thought much of the plays Bacon and I wrote for Shakespeare until Shakespeare 'd been dead a century."

"Humph!" said Adam, gloomily. "Wait! What have I been doing all this time? I've waited all the time there's been so far, and until Mr. Barnum spoke as he did I haven't observed the slightest inclination on the part of anybody to rehabilitate my lost reputation. Nor do I see exactly how it's to come about even if I do wait."

"You might apply for an investigating committee to look into the charges," suggested an American politician, just over. "Get your friends on it, and you'll be all right."

"Better let sleeping dogs lie," said Blackstone.

"I intend to," said Adam. "The fact is, I hate to give any further publicity to the matter. Even if I did bring the case into court and sue for libel, I've only got one witness to prove my innocence, and that's my wife. I'm not going to drag her into it. She's got nervous prostration over her position as it is, and this would make it worse. Queen Elizabeth and the rest of these snobs in society won't invite her to any of their functions because they say she hadn't any grandfather; and even if she were received by them, she'd be uncomfortable going about. It isn't pleasant for a woman to feel that everyone knows she's the oldest woman in the room."

"Well, take my word for it," said Raleigh, kindly. "It'll all come out all right. You know the old saying, 'History repeats itself.' Some day you will be living back in Eden again, and if you are only careful to make an exact record of all you do, and have a notary present, before whom you can make an affidavit as to the facts, you will be able to demonstrate your innocence."

"I was only condemned on hearsay evidence, anyhow," said Adam, ruefully.

"Nonsense; you were caught red-handed," said Noah; "my grandfather told me so. And now that I've got a chance to slip in a word edgewise, I'd like mightily to have you explain your statement, Mr. Barnum, that I am responsible for your errors. That is a serious charge to bring against a man of my reputation."

"I mean simply this: that to make a show interesting," said Mr. Barnum, "a man has got to provide interesting materials, that's all. I do not mean to say a word that is in any way derogatory to your morality. You were a surprisingly good man for a sea-captain, and with the exception of that one occasion when you—ah—you allowed yourself to be stranded on the bar, if I may so put it, I know of nothing to be said against you as a moral, temperate person."

"That was only an accident," said Noah, reddening. "You can't expect a man six hundred odd years of age—"

"Certainly not," said Raleigh, soothingly, "and nobody thinks less of you for it. Considering how you must have hated the sight of water, the wonder of it is that it didn't become a fixed habit. Let us hear what it is that Mr. Barnum does criticise in you."

"His taste, that's all," said Mr. Barnum. "I contend that, compared to the animals he might have had, the ones he did have were as ant-hills to Alps. There were more magnificent zoos allowed to die out through Noah's lack of judgment than one likes to think of. Take the *Proterosaurus*, for instance. Where on earth do we find his equal today?"

"You ought to be mighty glad you can't find one like him," put in Adam. "If you'd spent a week in the Garden of Eden with me, with lizards eight feet long dropping out of the trees on to your lap while you were trying to take a Sunday-afternoon nap, you'd be willing to dispense with things of that sort for the balance of your natural life. If you want to get an idea of that experience let somebody drop a calf on you some afternoon."

"I am not saying anything about that," returned Barnum. "It would be unpleasant to have an elephant drop on one after the fashion of which you speak, but I am glad the elephant was saved just the same. I haven't advocated the *Proterosaurus* as a Sunday-afternoon surprise, but as an attraction for a show. I still maintain that a lizard as big as a cow would prove a lodestone, the drawing powers of which the pocket-money of the small boy would be utterly unable to resist. Then there was the *Iguanadon*. He'd have brought a fortune to the box-office—"

"Which you'd have immediately lost," retorted Noah, "paying rent. When you get a reptile of his size, that reaches thirty feet up into the air when he stands on his hind-legs, the ordinary circus wagon of commerce can't be made to hold him, and your menagerie-room has to have ceilings so high that every penny he brought to the box-office would be spent storing him."

"Mischievous, too," said Adam, "that *Iguanadon*. You couldn't keep anything out of his reach. We used to forbid animals of his kind to enter the garden, but that didn't bother him; he'd stand up on his hind-legs and reach over and steal anything he'd happen to want."

"I could have used him for a fire-escape," said Mr. Barnum; "and as for my inability to provide him with quarters, I'd have met that problem after a short while. I've always lamented the absence, too, of the *Megalosaurus*—"

"Which simply shows how ignorant you are," retorted Noah. "Why, my dear fellow, it would have taken the whole of an ordinary zoo such as yours to give the *Megalosaurus* a lunch. Those fellows would eat a rhinoceros as easily as you'd crack a peanut. I did have a couple of *Megalosaurians* on my boat for just twenty-four hours, and then I chucked them both overboard. If I'd kept them ten days longer they'd have eaten every blessed beast I had with me, and your Zoo wouldn't have had anything else but *Megalosaurians*."

"Papa is right about that, Mr. Barnum," said Shem. "The whole Saurian tribe was a fearful nuisance. About four hundred years before the flood I had a pet *Creosaurus* that I kept in our barn. He was a cunning little devil—full of tricks, and all that; but we never could keep a cow or a horse on the place while he was about. They'd mysteriously disappear, and we never knew what became of 'em until one morning we surprised Fido in—"

"Surprised who?" asked Doctor Johnson, scornfully.

"Fido," returned Shem. "'That was my *Creosaurus's* name."

"Lord save us! Fido!" cried Johnson. "What a name for a *Creosaurus!*"

"Well, what of it?" asked Shem, angrily. "You wouldn't have us call a *mastodon* like that Fanny, would you, or Tatters?"

"Go on," said Johnson; "I've nothing to say."

"Shall I send for a physician?" put in Boswell, looking anxiously at his chief, the situation was so extraordinary.

Solomon and Carlyle giggled; and the Doctor having politely requested Boswell to go to a warmer section of the country, Shem resumed.

"I caught him in the act of swallowing five cows and Ham's favourite trotter, sulky and all."

Baron Munchausen rose up and left the room.

"If they're going to lie I'm going to get out," he said, as he passed through the room.

"What became of Fido?" asked Boswell.

"The sulky killed him," returned Shem, innocently. "He couldn't digest the wheels."

Noah looked approvingly at his son, and, turning to Barnum, observed, quietly:

"What he says is true, and I will go further and say that it is my belief that you would have found the show business impossible if I had taken that sort of creature aboard. You'd have got mightily discouraged after your *Antediluvians* had chewed up a few dozen steam *calliopes*, and eaten every other able-bodied exhibit you had managed to secure. I'd have tried to save a couple of *Discosaurians* if I hadn't supposed they were able to take care

74

of themselves. A combination of sea-serpent and dragon, with a neck twenty-two feet long, it seemed to me, ought to have been able to ride out any storm or fall of rain; but there I was wrong, and I am free to admit my error. It never occurred to me that the sea-serpents were in any danger, so I let them alone, with the result that I never saw but one other, and he was only an illusion due to that unhappy use of stimulants to which, with shocking bad taste, you have chosen to refer."

"I didn't mean to call up unpleasant memories," said Barnum. "I never believed you got half-seas over, anyhow; but, to return to our muttons, why didn't you hand down a few varieties of the *Therium* family to posterity? There were the *Dinotherium* and the *Megatherium*, either one of which would have knocked spots out of any leopard that ever was made, and along side of which even my woolly horse would have paled into insignificance. That's what I can't understand in your selections; with *Megatheriums* to burn, why save leopards and panthers and other such every-day creatures?"

"What kind of a boat do you suppose I had?" cried Noah. "Do you imagine for a moment that she was four miles on the water-line, with a mile and three-quarters beam? If I'd had a pair of *Dinotheriums* in the stern of that Ark, she'd have tipped up fore and aft, until she'd have looked like a telegraph-pole in the water, and if I'd put 'em amidships they'd have had to be wedged in so tightly they couldn't move to keep the vessel trim. I didn't go to sea, my friend, for the purpose of being tipped over in mid-ocean every time one of my cargo wanted to shift his weight from one leg to the other."

"It was bad enough with the elephants, wasn't it, papa?" said Shem.

"Yes, indeed, my son," returned the patriarch. "It was bad enough with the elephants. We had to shift our ballast half a dozen times a day to keep the boat from travelling on her beam ends, the elephants moved about so much; and when we came to the question of provender, it took up about nine-tenths of our hold to store hay and peanuts enough to keep them alive

75

and good-tempered. On the whole, I think it's rather late in the day, considering the trouble I took to save anything but myself and my family, to be criticised as I now am. You ought to be much obliged to me for saving any animals at all. Most people in my position would have built a yacht for themselves and family, and let everything else slide."

"That is quite true," observed Raleigh, with a pacificatory nod at Noah. "You were eminently unselfish, and while, with Mr. Barnum, I exceedingly regret that the Saurians and Therii and other tribes were left on the pier when you sailed, I nevertheless think that you showed most excellent judgment at the time."

"He was the only man who had any at all, for that matter," suggested Shem, "and it required all his courage to show it. Everybody was guying him. Sinners stood around the yard all day and every day, criticising the model; one scoffer pretended he thought her a canal-boat, and asked how deep the flood was likely to be on the tow-path, and whether we intended to use mules in shallow water and giraffes in deep; another asked what time allowance we expected to get in a fifteen-mile run, and hinted that a year and two months per mile struck him as being the proper thing—"

"It was far from pleasant," said Noah, tapping his fingers together reflectively. "I don't want to go through it again, and if, as Raleigh suggests, history is likely to repeat herself, I'll sublet the contract to Barnum here, and let him get the chaff."

"It was all right in the end, though, dad," said Shem. "We had the great laugh on 'hoi polloi' the second day out."

"We did, indeed," said Noah. "When we told 'em we only carried first-class passengers and had no room for emigrants, they began to see that the Ark wasn't such an old tub, after all; and a good ninety per cent. of them would have given ten dollars for a little of that time allowance they'd been talking to us about for several centuries."

Noah lapsed into a musing silence, and Barnum rose to leave.

"I still wish you'd saved a *Discosaurus*," he said. "A creature with a neck twenty-two feet long would have been a gold mine to me. He could have been trained to stand in the ring, and by stretching out his neck bite the little boys who sneak in under the tent and occupy seats on the top row."

"Well, for your sake," said Noah, with a smile, "I'm very sorry; but for my own, I'm quite satisfied with the general results."

And they all agreed that the patriarch had every reason to be pleased with himself.

12: THE HOUSE-BOAT DISAPPEARS

Queen Elizabeth, attended by Ophelia and Xanthippe, was walking along the river-bank. It was a beautiful autumn day, although, owing to certain climatic peculiarities of Hades, it seemed more like midsummer. The mercury in the club thermometer was nervously clicking against the top of the crystal tube, and poor Cerberus was having all he could do with his three mouths snapping up the pestiferous little shades of bygone gnats that seemed to take an almost unholy pleasure in alighting upon his various noses and ears.

Ophelia was doing most of the talking.

"I am sure I have never wished to ride one of them," she said, positively. "In the first place, I do not see where the pleasure of it comes in, and, in the second, it seems to me as if skirts must be dangerous. If they should catch in one of the pedals, where would I be?"

"In the hospital shortly, methinks," said Queen Elizabeth.

"Well, I shouldn't wear skirts," snapped Xanthippe. "If a man's wife can't borrow some of her husband's clothing to reduce her peril to a minimum, what is the use of having a husband? When I take to the bicycle, which, in spite of all Socrates can say, I fully intend to do, I shall have a man's wheel, and I shall wear Socrates' old dress-clothes. If Hades doesn't like it, Hades may suffer."

"I don't see how Socrates' clothes will help you," observed Ophelia. "He wore skirts himself, just like all the other old Greeks. His *toga* would be quite as apt to catch in the gear as your skirts."

Xanthippe looked puzzled for a moment. It was evident that she had not thought of the point which Ophelia had brought up—strong-minded ladies of her kind are apt sometimes to overlook important links in such chains of evidence as they feel called upon to use in binding themselves to their rights.

"The women of your day were relieved of that dress problem, at any rate," laughed Queen Elizabeth.

"The women of my day," retorted Xanthippe, "in matters of dress were the equals of their husbands—in my family particularly; now they have lost their rights, and are made to confine themselves still to garments like those of yore, while man has arrogated to himself the sole and exclusive use of sane habiliments. However, that is apart from the question. I was saying that I shall have a man's wheel, and shall wear Socrates' old dress-clothes to ride it in, if Socrates has to go out and buy an old dress-suit for the purpose."

The Queen arched her brows and looked inquiringly at Xanthippe for a moment.

"A magnificent old maid was lost to the world when you married," she said. "Feeling as you do about men, my dear Xanthippe, I don't see why you ever took a husband."

"Humph!" retorted Xanthippe. "Of course you don't. You didn't need a husband. You were born with something to govern. I wasn't."

"How about your temper?" suggested Ophelia, meekly.

Xanthippe sniffed frigidly at this remark.

"I never should have gone crazy over a man if I'd remained unmarried forty thousand years," she retorted, severely. "I married Socrates because I loved him and admired his sculpture; but when he gave up sculpture and became a thinker he simply tried me beyond all endurance, he was so thoughtless, with the result that, having ventured once or twice to show my natural resentment, I have been handed down to posterity as a shrew. I've never complained, and I don't complain now; but when a woman is married to a philosopher who is so taken up with his studies that when he rises in the morning he doesn't look what he is doing, and goes off to his business in his wife's clothes, I think she is entitled to a certain amount of sympathy."

"And yet you wish to wear his," persisted Ophelia.

"Turnabout is fair-play," said Xanthippe. "I've suffered so much on his account that on the principle of averages he deserves to have a little drop of bitters in his nectar."

"You are simply the victim of man's deceit," said Elizabeth, wishing to mollify the now angry Xanthippe, who was on the verge of tears. "I understood men, fortunately, and so never married. I knew my father, and even if I hadn't been a wise enough child to know him, I should not have wed, because he married enough to last one family for several years."

"You must have had a hard time refusing all those lovely men, though," sighed Ophelia. "Of course, Sir Walter wasn't as handsome as my dear Hamlet, but he was very fetching."

"I cannot deny that," said Elizabeth, "and I didn't really have the heart to say no when he asked me; but I did tell him that if he married me I should not become Mrs. Raleigh, but that he should become King Elizabeth. He fled to Virginia on the next steamer. My diplomacy rid me of a very unpleasant duty."

Chatting thus, the three famous spirits passed slowly along the path until they came to the sheltered nook in which the house-boat lay at anchor.

"There's a case in point," said Xanthippe, as the house-boat loomed up before them. "All that luxury is for men; we women are not permitted to cross the gangplank. Our husbands and brothers and friends go there; the door closes on them, and they are as completely lost to us as though they never existed. We don't know what goes on in there. Socrates tells me that their amusements are of a most innocent nature, but how do I know what he means by that? Furthermore, it keeps him from home, while I have to stay at home and be entertained by my sons, whom the *Encyclopædia Britannica* rightly calls dull and fatuous. In other words, club life for him, and dullness and fatuity for me."

"I think myself they're rather queer about letting women into that boat," said Queen Elizabeth. "But it isn't Sir Walter's fault. He told me he tried to have them establish a Ladies' Day, and that they agreed to do so, but have since resisted all his efforts to have a date set for the function."

"It would be great fun to steal in there now, wouldn't it," giggled Ophelia. "There doesn't seem to be anybody about to prevent our doing so."

"That's true," said Xanthippe. "All the windows are closed, as if there wasn't a soul there. I've half a mind to take a peep in at the house."

"I am with you," said Elizabeth, her face lighting up with pleasure. It was a great novelty, and an unpleasant one to her, to find someplace where she could not go. "Let's do it," she added.

So the three women tiptoed softly up the gang-plank, and, silently boarding the house-boat, peeped in at the windows. What they saw merely whetted their curiosity.

"I must see more," cried Elizabeth, rushing around to the door, which opened at her touch. Xanthippe and Ophelia followed close on her heels, and shortly they found themselves, open-mouthed in wondering admiration, in the billiard-room of the floating palace, and Richard, the ghost of the best billiard-room attendant in or out of Hades, stood before them.

"Excuse me," he said, very much upset by the sudden apparition of the ladies. "I'm very sorry, but ladies are not admitted here."

"We are equally sorry," retorted Elizabeth, assuming her most imperious manner, "that your masters have seen fit to prohibit our being here; but, now that we are here, we intend to make the most of the opportunity, particularly as there seem to be no members about. What has become of them all?"

Richard smiled broadly. "I don't know where they are," he replied; but it was evident that he was not telling the exact truth.

"Oh, come, my boy," said the Queen, kindly, "you do know. Sir Walter told me you knew everything. Where are they?"

"Well, if you must know, ma'am," returned Richard, captivated by the Queen's manner, "they've all gone down the river to see a prize-fight between Goliath and Samson."

"See there!" cried Xanthippe. "That's what this club makes possible. Socrates told me he was coming here to take luncheon with Carlyle, and they've both of 'em gone off to a disgusting prize-fight!"

"Yes, ma'am, they have," said Richard; "and if Goliath wins, I don't think Mr. Socrates will get home this evening."

"Betting, eh?" said Xanthippe, scornfully.

"Yes, ma'am," returned Richard.

"More club!" cried Xanthippe.

"Oh no, ma'am," said Richard. "Betting is not allowed in the club; they're very strict about that. But the shore is only ten feet off, ma'am, and the gentlemen always go ashore and make their bets."

During this little colloquy Elizabeth and Ophelia were wandering about, admiring everything they saw.

"I do wish Lucretia Borgia and Calpurnia could see this. I wonder if the Cæsars are on the telephone," Elizabeth said. Investigation showed that both the Borgias and the Cæsars were on the wire, and in short order the two ladies had been made acquainted with the state of affairs at the house-boat; and as they were both quite as anxious to see the interior of the much-talked-of club-house as the others, they were not long in arriving. Furthermore, they brought with them half a dozen more ladies, among whom were Desdemona and Cleopatra, and then began the most extraordinary session the house-boat ever knew.

A meeting was called, with Elizabeth in the chair, and all the best ladies of the Stygian realms were elected members. Xanthippe, amid the greatest applause, moved that every male member of the organization be expelled for conduct unworthy of a gentleman in attending a prize-fight, and encouraging two such horrible creatures as Goliath and Samson in their nefarious pursuits. Desdemona seconded the motion, and it was carried without a dissenting voice, although Mrs. Cæsar, with becoming dignity, merely smiled approval, not caring to take part too actively in the proceedings.

The men having thus been disposed of in a summary fashion, Richard was elected Janitor in Charon's place, and the club was entirely reorganized, with Cleopatra as permanent President. The meeting then adjourned, and the invaders set about enjoying their newly acquired privileges. The smoking-room was thronged for a few moments, but owing to the extraordinary strength of the tobacco which the faithful Richard shovelled into the furnace, it developed no enduring popularity, Xanthippe, with a suddenly acquired pallor, being the first to renounce the pastime as revolting.

So fast and furious was the enjoyment of these thirsty souls, so long deprived of their rights, that night came on without their observing it, and with the night was brought the great peril into which they were thrown, and from which at the moment of writing they had not been extricated, and which, to my regret, has cut me off for the present from any further information connected with the Associated Shades and their beautiful lounging-place.

Had they not been so intent upon the inner beauties of the House-boat on the Styx they might have observed approaching, under the shadow of the westerly shore, a long, rakish craft propelled by oars, which dipped softly and silently and with trained precision in the now jet-black waters of the Styx. Manning the oars were a dozen evil-visaged ruffians, while in the stern of the approaching vessel there sat a grim-faced, weather-beaten spirit, armed to the teeth, his coat sleeves bearing the skull and cross-bones, the insignia of piracy.

This boat, stealing up the river like a thief in the night, contained Captain Kidd and his pirate crew, and their mission was a mission of vengeance. To put the matter briefly and plainly, Captain Kidd was smarting under the indignity which the club had recently put upon him. He had been unanimously blackballed, even his proposer and seconder, who had been browbeaten into nominating him for membership, voting against him.

"I may be a pirate," he cried, when he heard what the club

had done, "but I have feelings, and the Associated Shades will repent their action. The time will come when they'll find that I have their club-house, and they have—its debts."

It was for this purpose that the great terror of the seas had come upon this, the first favourable opportunity. Kidd knew that the house-boat was unguarded; his spies had told him that the members had every one gone to the fight, and he resolved that the time had come to act. He did not know that the Fates had helped to make his vengeance all the more terrible and withering by putting the most attractive and fashionable ladies of the Stygian country likewise in his power; but so it was, and they, poor souls, while this fiend, relentless and cruel, was slowly approaching, sang on and danced on in blissful unconsciousness of their peril.

In less than five minutes from the time when his sinister-craft rounded the bend Kidd and his crew had boarded the house-boat, cut her loose from her moorings, and in ten minutes she had sailed away into the great unknown, and with her went some of the most precious gems in the social diadem of Hades.

The rest of my story is soon told. The whole country was aroused when the crime was discovered, but up to the date of this narrative no word has been received of the missing craft and her precious cargo. Raleigh and Cæsar have had the seas scoured in search of her, Hamlet has offered his kingdom for her return, but unavailingly; and the men of Hades were cast into a gloom from which there seems to be no relief.

Socrates alone was unaffected.

"They'll come back some day, my dear Raleigh," he said, as the knight buried his face, weeping, in his hands. "So why repine? I'll never lose my Xanthippe—permanently, that is. I know that, for I am a philosopher, and I know there is no such thing as luck. And we can start another club."

"Very likely," sighed Raleigh, wiping his eyes. "I don't mind the club so much, but to think of those poor women—"

"Oh, they're all right," returned Socrates, with a laugh. "Cæsar's wife is along, and you can't dispute the fact that she's a good chaperon. Give the ladies a chance. They've been after our club for years; now let 'em have it, and let us hope that they like it. Order me up a hemlock sour, and let's drink to their enjoyment of club life."

Which was done, and I, in spirit, drank with them, for I sincerely hope that the "New Women" of Hades are having a good time.

The Pursuit of the House-Boat

1
THE ASSOCIATED SHADES TAKE ACTION

The House-boat of the Associated Shades, formerly located upon the River Styx, as the reader may possibly remember, had been torn from its moorings and navigated out into unknown seas by that vengeful pirate Captain Kidd, aided and abetted by some of the most ruffianly inhabitants of Hades. Like a thief in the night had they come, and for no better reason than that the Captain had been unanimously voted a shade too shady to associate with self-respecting spirits had they made off with the happy floating club-house of their betters; and worst of all, with them, by force of circumstances over which they had no control, had sailed also the fair Queen Elizabeth, the spirited Xanthippe, and every other strong-minded and beautiful woman of Erebean society, whereby the men thereof were rendered desolate.

"I can't stand it!" cried Raleigh, desperately, as with his accustomed grace he presided over a special meeting of the club, called on the bank of the inky Stygian stream, at the point where the missing boat had been moored. "Think of it, gentlemen, Elizabeth of England, Calpurnia of Rome, Ophelia of Denmark, and every precious jewel in our social diadem gone, vanished completely; and with whom? Kidd, of all men in the universe! Kidd, the pirate, the ruffian—"

"Don't take on so, my dear Sir Walter," said Socrates, cheerfully. "What's the use of going into hysterics? You are not a woman, and should eschew that luxury. Xanthippe is with them, and I'll

85

warrant you that when that cherished spouse of mine has recovered from the effects of the sea, say the third day out, Kidd and his crew will be walking the plank, and voluntarily at that."

"But the House-boat itself," murmured Noah, sadly. "That was my delight. It reminded me in some respects of the Ark."

"The law of compensation enters in there, my dear Commodore," retorted Socrates. "For me, with Xanthippe abroad I do not need a club to go to; I can stay at home and take my hemlock in peace and straight. Xanthippe always compelled me to dilute it at the rate of one quart of water to the finger."

"Well, we didn't all marry Xanthippe," put in Cæsar, firmly, "therefore we are not all satisfied with the situation. I, for one, quite agree with Sir Walter that something must be done, and quickly. Are we to sit here and do nothing, allowing that fiend to kidnap our wives with impunity?"

"Not at all," interposed Bonaparte. "The time for action has arrived. All things considered he is welcome to Marie Louise, but the idea of Josephine going off on a cruise of that kind breaks my heart."

"No question about it," observed Dr. Johnson. "We've got to do something if it is only for the sake of appearances. The question really is, what shall be done first?"

"I am in favour of taking a drink as the first step, and considering the matter of further action afterwards," suggested Shakespeare, and it was this suggestion that made the members unanimous upon the necessity for immediate action, for when the assembled spirits called for their various favourite beverages it was found that there were none to be had, it being Sunday, and all the establishments wherein liquid refreshments were licensed to be sold being closed—for at the time of writing the local government of Hades was in the hands of the reform party.

"What!" cried Socrates. "Nothing but Styx water and vitriol, Sundays? Then the House-boat must be recovered whether Xanthippe comes with it or not. Sir Walter, I am for immediate action, after all. This ruffian should be captured at once and made an example of."

"Excuse me, Socrates," put in Lindley Murray, "but, ah—pray speak in Greek hereafter, will you, please? When you attempt English you have a beastly way of working up to climatic prepositions which are offensive to the ear of a purist."

"This is no time to discuss style, Murray," interposed Sir Walter. "Socrates may speak and spell like Chaucer if he pleases; he may even part his infinitives in the middle, for all I care. We have affairs of greater moment in hand."

"We must ransack the earth," cried Socrates, "until we find that boat. I'm dry as a fish."

"There he goes again!" growled Murray. "Dry as a fish! What fish I'd like to know is dry?"

"Red herrings," retorted Socrates; and there was a great laugh at the expense of the purist, in which even Hamlet, who had grown more and more melancholy and morbid since the abduction of Ophelia, joined.

"Then it is settled," said Raleigh; "something must be done. And now the point is, what?"

"Relief expeditions have a way of finding things," suggested Dr. Livingstone. "Or rather of being found by the things they go out to relieve. I propose that we send out a number of them. I will take Africa; Bonaparte can lead an expedition into Europe; General Washington may have North America; and—"

"I beg pardon," put in Dr. Johnson, "but have you any idea, Dr. Livingstone, that Captain Kidd has put wheels on this Houseboat of ours and is having it dragged across the Sahara by mules or camels?"

"No such absurd idea ever entered my head," retorted the Doctor.

"Do you then believe that he has put runners on it, and is engaged in the pleasurable pastime of taking the ladies tobogganing down the Alps?" persisted the philosopher.

"Not at all. Why do you ask?" queried the African explorer, irritably.

"Because I wish to know," said Johnson. "That is always my motive in asking questions. You propose to go looking for a house-boat in Central Africa; you suggest that Bonaparte lead an expedition in search of it through Europe—all of which strikes me as nonsense. This search is the work of sea-dogs, not of land-lubbers. You might as well ask Confucius to look for it in the heart of China. What earthly use there is in ransacking the earth I fail to see. What we need is a naval expedition to scour the sea, unless it is pretty well understood in advance that we believe Kidd has hauled the boat out of the water, and is now using it for a roller-skating rink or a bicycle academy in Ohio, or for some other purpose for which neither he nor it was designed."

"Dr. Johnson's point is well taken," said a stranger who had been sitting upon the string-piece of the pier, quietly, but with very evident interest, listening to the discussion. He was a tall and excessively slender shade, "like a spurt of steam out of a teapot," as Johnson put it afterwards, so slight he seemed. "I have not the honour of being a member of this association," the stranger continued, "but, like all well-ordered shades, I aspire to the distinction, and I hold myself and my talents at the disposal of this club. I fancy it will not take us long to establish our initial point, which is that the gross person who has so foully appropriated your property to his own base uses does not contemplate removing it from its keel and placing it somewhere inland.

"All the evidence in hand points to a radically different conclusion, which is my sole reason for doubting the value of that conclusion. Captain Kidd is a seafarer by instinct, not a landsman. The House-boat is not a house, but a boat; therefore the place to look for it is not, as Dr. Johnson so well says, in the Sahara Desert, or on the Alps, or in the State of Ohio, but upon the high sea, or upon the waterfront of some one of the world's great cities."

"And what, then, would be your plan?" asked Sir Walter, impressed by the stranger's manner as well as by the very manifest reason in all that he had said.

"The chartering of a suitable vessel, fully armed and equipped for the purpose of pursuit. Ascertain whither the House-boat has sailed, for what port, and start at once. Have you a model of the House-boat within reach?" returned the stranger.

"I think not; we have the architect's plans, however," said the chairman.

"We had, Mr. Chairman," said Demosthenes, who was secretary of the House Committee, rising, "but they are gone with the House-boat itself. They were kept in the safe in the hold."

A look of annoyance came into the face of the stranger.

"That's too bad," he said. "It was a most important part of my plan that we should know about how fast the House-boat was."

"Humph!" ejaculated Socrates, with ill-concealed sarcasm. "If you'll take Xanthippe's word for it, the House-boat was the fastest yacht afloat."

"I refer to the matter of speed in sailing," returned the stranger, quietly. "The question of its ethical speed has nothing to do with it."

"The designer of the craft is here," said Sir Walter, fixing his eyes upon Sir Christopher Wren. "It is possible that he may be of assistance in settling that point."

"What has all this got to do with the question, anyhow, Mr. Chairman?" asked Solomon, rising impatiently and addressing Sir Walter. "We aren't preparing for a yacht-race that I know of. Nobody's after a cup, or a championship of any kind. What we do want is to get our wives back. The Captain hasn't taken more than half of mine along with him, but I am interested none the less. The Queen of Sheba is on board, and I am somewhat interested in her fate. So I ask you what earthly or unearthly use there is in discussing this question of speed in the House-boat. It strikes me as a woeful waste of time, and rather unprecedented too, that we should suspend all rules and listen to the talk of an entire stranger."

"I do not venture to doubt the wisdom of Solomon," said Johnson, dryly, "but I must say that the gentleman's remarks rather interest me."

"Of course they do," ejaculated Solomon. "He agreed with you. That ought to make him interesting to everybody. Freaks usually are."

"That is not the reason at all," retorted Dr. Johnson. "Cold water agrees with me, but it doesn't interest me. What I do think, however, is that our unknown friend seems to have a grasp on the situation by which we are confronted, and he's going at the matter in hand in a very comprehensive fashion. I move, therefore, that Solomon be laid on the table, and that the privileges of the—ah—of the wharf be extended indefinitely to our friend on the string-piece."

The motion, having been seconded, was duly carried, and the stranger resumed.

"I will explain for the benefit of his Majesty King Solomon, whose wisdom I have always admired, and whose endurance as the husband of three hundred wives has filled me with wonder," he said, "that before starting in pursuit of the stolen vessel we must select a craft of some sort for the purpose, and that in selecting the pursuer it is quite essential that we should choose a vessel of greater speed than the one we desire to overtake. It would hardly be proper, I think, if the House-boat can sail four knots an hour, to attempt to overhaul her with a launch, or other nautical craft, with a maximum speed of two knots an hour."

"Hear! hear!" ejaculated Cæsar.

"That is my reason, your Majesty, for inquiring as to the speed of your late club-house," said the stranger, bowing courteously to Solomon. "Now if Sir Christopher Wren can give me her measurements, we can very soon determine at about what rate she is leaving us behind under favourable circumstances."

"'Tisn't necessary for Sir Christopher to do anything of the sort," said Noah, rising and manifesting somewhat more heat than the occasion seemed to require. "As long as we are discussing the question I will take the liberty of stating what I have never mentioned before, that the designer of the House-boat merely appropriated the lines of the Ark. Shem, Ham, and Japhet will bear testimony to the truth of that statement."

"There can be no quarrel on that score, Mr. Chairman," assented Sir Christopher, with cutting frigidity. "I am perfectly willing to admit that practically the two vessels were built on the same lines, but with modifications which would enable my boat to sail twenty miles to windward and back in six days less time than it would have taken the Ark to cover the same distance, and it could have taken all the wash of the excursion steamers into the bargain."

"Bosh!" ejaculated Noah, angrily. "Strip your old tub down to a flying balloon-jib and a marline-spike, and ballast the Ark with elephants until every inch of her reeked with ivory and peanuts, and she'd outfoot you on every leg, in a cyclone or a zephyr. Give me the Ark and a breeze, and your House-boat wouldn't be within hailing distance of her five minutes after the start if she had 40,000 square yards of canvas spread before a gale."

"This discussion is waxing very unprofitable," observed Confucius. "If these gentlemen cannot be made to confine themselves to the subject that is agitating this body, I move we call in the authorities and have them confined in the bottomless pit."

"I did not precipitate the quarrel," said Noah. "I was merely trying to assist our friend on the string-piece. I was going to say that as the Ark was probably a hundred times faster than Sir Christopher Wren's—tub, which he himself says can take care of all the wash of the excursion boats, thereby becoming on his own admission a wash-tub—"

"Order! order!" cried Sir Christopher.

"I was going to say that this wash-tub could be overhauled by a launch or any other craft with a speed of thirty knots a month," continued Noah, ignoring the interruption.

"Took him forty days to get to Mount Ararat!" sneered Sir Christopher.

"Well, your boat would have got there two weeks sooner, I'll admit," retorted Noah, "if she'd sprung a leak at the right time."

"Granting the truth of Noah's statement," said Sir Walter, motioning to the angry architect to be quiet—"not that we take any side in the issue between the two gentlemen, but merely for the sake of argument—I wish to ask the stranger who has been good enough to interest himself in our trouble what he proposes to do—how can you establish your course in case a boat were provided?"

"Also vot vill be dher gost, if any?" put in Shylock.

A murmur of disapprobation greeted this remark.

"The cost need not trouble you, sir," said Sir Walter, indignantly, addressing the stranger; "you will have *carte blanche.*"

"Den ve are ruint!" cried Shylock, displaying his palms, and showing by that act a select assortment of diamond rings.

"Oh," laughed the stranger, "that is a simple matter. Captain Kidd has gone to London."

"To London!" cried several members at once. "How do you know that?"

"By this," said the stranger, holding up the tiny stub end of a cigar.

"Tut-tut!" ejaculated Solomon. "What child's play this is!"

"No, your Majesty," observed the stranger, "it is not child's play; it is fact. That cigar end was thrown aside here on the wharf by Captain Kidd just before he stepped on board the Houseboat."

"How do you know that?" demanded Raleigh. "And granting the truth of the assertion, what does it prove?"

"I will tell you," said the stranger. And he at once proceeded as follows.

2

The Stranger Unravels a Mystery
and Reveals Himself

"I have made a hobby of the study of cigar ends," said the stranger, as the Associated Shades settled back to hear his account of himself. "From my earliest youth, when I used surreptitiously to remove the unsmoked ends of my father's cigars and break them up, and, in hiding, smoke them in an old clay pipe which I had presented to me by an ancient sea-captain of my acquaintance, I have been interested in tobacco in all forms, even including these self-same despised unsmoked ends; for they convey to my mind messages, sentiments, farces, comedies, and tragedies which to your minds would never become manifest through their agency."

The company drew closer together and formed themselves in a more compact mass about the speaker. It was evident that they were beginning to feel an unusual interest in this extraordinary person, who had come among them unheralded and unknown. Even Shylock stopped calculating percentages for an instant to listen.

"Do you mean to tell us," demanded Shakespeare, "that the unsmoked stub of a cigar will suggest the story of him who smoked it to your mind?"

"I do," replied the stranger, with a confident smile. "Take this one, for instance, that I have picked up here upon the wharf; it tells me the whole story of the intentions of Captain Kidd at the moment when, in utter disregard of your rights, he stepped aboard your House-boat, and, in his usual piratical fashion, made off with it into unknown seas."

"But how do you know he smoked it?" asked Solomon, who deemed it the part of wisdom to be suspicious of the stranger.

"There are two curious indentations in it which prove that. The marks of two teeth, with a *hiatus* between, which you will see if you look closely," said the stranger, handing the small bit of tobacco to Sir Walter, "make that point evident beyond peradventure. The Captain lost an eye-tooth in one of his later raids; it was knocked out by a marline-spike which had been hurled at him by one of the crew of the treasure-ship he and his followers had attacked. The adjacent teeth were broken, but not removed. The cigar end bears the marks of those two jagged molars, with the hiatus, which, as I have indicated, is due to the destruction of the eye-tooth between them. It is not likely that there was another man in the pirate's crew with teeth exactly like the commander's, therefore I say there can be no doubt that the cigar end was that of the Captain himself."

"Very interesting indeed," observed Blackstone, removing his wig and fanning himself with it; "but I must confess, Mr. Chairman, that in any properly constituted law court this evidence would long since have been ruled out as irrelevant and absurd. The idea of two or three hundred dignified spirits like ourselves, gathered together to devise a means for the recovery of our property and the rescue of our wives, yielding the floor to the delivering of a lecture by an entire stranger on 'Cigar Ends He Has Met,' strikes me as ridiculous in the extreme. Of what earthly interest is it to us to know that this or that cigar was smoked by Captain Kidd?"

"Merely that it will help us on, your honour, to discover the whereabouts of the said Kidd," interposed the stranger. "It is by trifles, seeming trifles, that the greatest detective work is done. My friends Le Coq, Hawkshaw, and Old Sleuth will bear me out in this, I think, however much in other respects our methods may have differed. They left no stone unturned in the pursuit of a criminal; no detail, however trifling, uncared for. No more should we in the present instance overlook the minutest bit of evidence, however irrelevant and absurd at first blush it may appear to be.

"The truth of what I say was very effectually proven in the strange case of the Brokedale tiara, in which I figured somewhat conspicuously, but which I have never made public, because it involves a secret affecting the integrity of one of the noblest families in the British Empire. I really believe that mystery was solved easily and at once because I happened to remember that the number of my watch was 86507B. How trivial a thing, and yet how important it was, as the event transpired, you will realize when I tell you the incident."

The stranger's manner was so impressive that there was a unanimous and simultaneous movement upon the part of all present to get up closer, so as the more readily to hear what he said, as a result of which poor old Boswell was pushed overboard, and fell with a loud splash into the Styx. Fortunately, however, one of Charon's pleasure-boats was close at hand, and in a short while the dripping, sputtering spirit was drawn into it, wrung out, and sent home to dry. The excitement attending this diversion having subsided, Solomon asked:

"What was the incident of the lost tiara?"

"I am about to tell you," returned the stranger; "and it must be understood that you are told in the strictest confidence, for, as I say, the incident involves a state secret of great magnitude. In life—in the mortal life—gentlemen, I was a detective by profession, and, if I do say it, who perhaps should not, I was one of the most interesting for purely literary purposes that has ever been known. I did not find it necessary to go about saying 'Ha! ha!' as M. Le Coq was accustomed to do to advertise his cleverness; neither did I disguise myself as a drum-major and hide under a kitchen-table for the purpose of solving a mystery involving the abduction of a parlor stove, after the manner of the talented Hawkshaw.

"By mental concentration alone, without fireworks or orchestral accompaniment of any sort whatsoever, did I go about my business, and for that very reason many of my fellow-sleuths were forced to go out of real detective work into that line of the business with which the stage has familiarized the most of us—a line in which nothing but stupidity, luck, and a yellow wig is required of him who pursues it."

"This man is an impostor," whispered Le Coq to Hawkshaw.

"I've known that all along by the mole on his left wrist," returned Hawkshaw, contemptuously.

"I suspected it the minute I saw he was not disguised," returned Le Coq, knowingly. "I have observed that the greatest villains latterly have discarded disguises, as being too easily penetrated, and therefore of no avail, and merely a useless expense."

"Silence!" cried Confucius, impatiently. "How can the gentleman proceed, with all this conversation going on in the rear?"

Hawkshaw and Le Coq immediately subsided, and the stranger went on.

"It was in this way that I treated the strange case of the lost tiara," resumed the stranger. "Mental concentration upon seemingly insignificant details alone enabled me to bring about the desired results in that instance. A brief outline of the case is as follows: It was late one evening in the early spring of 1894. The London season was at its height. Dances, *fêtes* of all kinds, opera, and the theatres were in full blast, when all of a sudden society was paralyzed by a most audacious robbery. A diamond tiara valued at £50,000 sterling had been stolen from the Duchess of Brokedale, and under circumstances which threw society itself and every individual in it under suspicion—even his Royal Highness the Prince himself, for he had danced frequently with the Duchess, and was known to be a great admirer of her tiara.

"It was at half-past eleven o'clock at night that the news of the robbery first came to my ears. I had been spending the evening alone in my library making notes for a second volume of my memoirs, and, feeling somewhat depressed, I was on the point of going out for my usual midnight walk on Hampstead Heath, when one of my servants, hastily entering, informed me of the robbery. I changed my mind in respect to my midnight walk immediately upon receipt of the news, for I knew that before one o'clock someone would call upon me at my lodgings with reference to this robbery. It could not be otherwise. Any mystery of such magnitude could no more be taken to another bureau than elephants could fly—"

"They used to," said Adam. "I once had a whole aviary full of winged elephants. They flew from flower to flower, and thrusting their probabilities deep into—"

"Their what?" queried Johnson, with a frown.

"Probabilities—isn't that the word? Their trunks," said Adam.

"Proboscis, I imagine you mean," suggested Johnson.

"Yes—that was it. Their proboscis," said Adam. "They were great honey-gatherers, those elephants—far better than the bees, because they could make so much more of it in a given time."

Munchausen shook his head sadly. "I'm afraid I'm outclassed by these *antediluvians*," he said.

"Gentlemen! gentlemen!" cried Sir Walter. "These interruptions are inexcusable!"

"That's what I think," said the stranger, with some asperity. "I'm having about as hard a time getting this story out as I would if it were a serial. Of course, if you gentlemen do not wish to hear it, I can stop; but it must be understood that when I do stop I stop finally, once and for all, because the tale has not a sufficiency of dramatic climaxes to warrant its prolongation over the usual magazine period of twelve months."

"Go on! go on!" cried some.

"Shut up!" cried others—addressing the interrupting members, of course.

"As I was saying," resumed the stranger, "I felt confident that within an hour, in some way or other, that case would be placed in my hands. It would be mine either positively or negatively— that is to say, either the person robbed would employ me to ferret out the mystery and recover the diamonds, or the robber himself, actuated by motives of self-preservation, would endeavour to direct my energies into other channels until he should have the time to dispose of his ill-gotten booty. A mental discussion of the probabilities inclined me to believe that the latter would be the case. I reasoned in this fashion: The person robbed is of exalted rank. She cannot move rapidly because she is so. Great bodies move slowly.

"It is probable that it will be a week before, according to the etiquette by which she is hedged about, she can communicate with me. In the first place, she must inform one of her attendants that she has been robbed. He must communicate the news to the functionary in charge of her residence, who will communicate with the Home Secretary, and from him will issue the orders to the police, who, baffled at every step, will finally address themselves to me. 'I'll give that side two weeks,' I said. On the other hand, the robber: will he allow himself to be lulled into a false sense of security by counting on this delay, or will he not, noting my habit of occasionally entering upon detective enterprises of this nature of my own volition, come to me at once and set me to work ferreting out some crime that has never been committed?

"My feeling was that this would happen, and I pulled out my watch to see if it were not nearly time for him to arrive. The robbery had taken place at a state ball at the Buckingham Palace. 'H'm!' I mused. 'He has had an hour and forty minutes to get here. It is now twelve twenty. He should be here by twelve forty-five. I will wait.' And hastily swallowing a cocaine tablet to nerve myself up for the meeting, I sat down and began to read my *Schopenhauer*. Hardly had I perused a page when there came a tap upon my door. I rose with a smile, for I thought I knew what was to happen, opened the door, and there stood, much to my surprise, the husband of the lady whose tiara was missing. It was the Duke of Brokedale himself. It is true he was disguised. His beard was powdered until it looked like snow, and he wore a wig and a pair of green goggles; but I recognized him at once by his lack of manners, which is an unmistakable sign of nobility. As I opened the door, he began:

"'You are Mr.——'

"'I am,' I replied. 'Come in. You have come to see me about your stolen watch. It is a gold hunting-case watch with a Swiss movement; loses five minutes a day; stem-winder; and the back cover, which does not bear any inscription, has upon it the indentations made by the molars of your son Willie when that interesting youth was cutting his teeth upon it.'"

"Wonderful!" cried Johnson.

"May I ask how you knew all that?" asked Solomon, deeply impressed. "Such penetration strikes me as marvellous."

"I didn't know it," replied the stranger, with a smile. "What I said was intended to be jocular, and to put Brokedale at his ease. The Americans present, with their usual astuteness, would term it bluff. It was. I merely rattled on. I simply did not wish to offend the gentleman by letting him know that I had penetrated his disguise. Imagine my surprise, however, when his eye brightened as I spoke, and he entered my room with such alacrity that half the powder which he thought disguised his beard was shaken off on to the floor. Sitting down in the chair I had just vacated, he quietly remarked:

"'You are a wonderful man, sir. How did you know that I had lost my watch?'

"For a moment I was nonplussed; more than that, I was completely staggered. I had expected him to say at once that he had not lost his watch, but had come to see me about the tiara; and to have him take my words seriously was entirely unexpected and overwhelmingly surprising. However, in view of his rank, I deemed it well to fall in with his humour. 'Oh, as for that,' I replied, 'that is a part of my business. It is the detective's place to know everything; and generally, if he reveals the machinery by means of which he reaches his conclusions, he is a fool, since his method is his secret, and his secret his stock in trade.

"I do not mind telling you, however, that I knew your watch was stolen by your anxious glance at my clock, which showed that you wished to know the time. Now most rich Americans have watches for that purpose, and have no hesitation about showing them. If you'd had a watch, you'd have looked at it, not at my clock.'

"My visitor laughed, and repeated what he had said about my being a wonderful man.

"'And the dents which my son made cutting his teeth?' he added.

"'Invariably go with an American's watch. Rubber or ivory rings aren't good enough for American babies to chew on,' said I. 'They must have gold watches or nothing.'

"'And finally, how did you know I was a rich American?' he asked.

"'Because no other can afford to stop at hotels like the Savoy in the height of the season,' I replied, thinking that the jest would end there, and that he would now reveal his identity and speak of the tiara. To my surprise, however, he did nothing of the sort.

"'You have an almost supernatural gift,' he said. 'My name is Bunker. I *am* stopping at the Savoy. I *am* an American. I *was* rich when I arrived here, but I'm not quite so bloated with wealth as I was, now that I have paid my first week's bill. I *have* lost my watch; such a watch, too, as you describe, even to the dents. Your only mistake was that the dents were made by my son John, and not Willie; but even there I cannot but wonder at you, for John and Willie are twins, and so much alike that it sometimes baffles even their mother to tell them apart. The watch has no very great value intrinsically, but the associations are such that I want it back, and I will pay £200 for its recovery. I have no clew as to who took it. It was numbered—'

"Here a happy thought struck me. In all my description of the watch I had merely described my own, a very cheap affair which I had won at a raffle. My visitor was deceiving me, though for what purpose I did not on the instant divine. No one would like to suspect him of having purloined his wife's tiara. Why should I not deceive him, and at the same time get rid of my poor chronometer for a sum that exceeded its value a hundredfold?"

"Good business!" cried Shylock.

The stranger smiled and bowed.

"Excellent," he said. "I took the words right out of his mouth. 'It was numbered 86507B!' I cried, giving, of course, the number of my own watch.

"He gazed at me narrowly for a moment, and then he smiled. 'You grow more marvellous at every step. That was indeed the number. Are you a demon?'

"'No,' I replied. 'Only something of a mind-reader.'

"Well, to be brief, the bargain was struck. I was to look for a watch that I knew he hadn't lost, and was to receive £200 if I found it. It seemed to him to be a very good bargain, as, indeed, it was, from his point of view, feeling, as he did, that there never having been any such watch, it could not be recovered, and little suspecting that two could play at his little game of deception, and that under any circumstances I could foist a ten-shilling watch upon him for two hundred pounds. This business concluded, he started to go.

"'Won't you have a little Scotch?' I asked, as he started, feeling, with all that prospective profit in view, I could well afford the expense. 'It is a stormy night.'

"'Thanks, I will,' said he, returning and seating himself by my table—still, to my surprise, keeping his hat on.

"'Let me take your hat,' I said, little thinking that my courtesy would reveal the true state of affairs. The mere mention of the word hat brought about a terrible change in my visitor; his knees trembled, his face grew ghastly, and he clutched the brim of his beaver until it cracked. He then nervously removed it, and I noticed a dull red mark running about his forehead, just as there would be on the forehead of a man whose hat fitted too tightly; and that mark, gentlemen, had the undulating outline of nothing more nor less than a tiara, and on the apex of the uppermost extremity was a deep indentation about the size of a shilling, that could have been made only by some adamantine substance! The mystery was solved! The robber of the Duchess of Brokedale stood before me."

A suppressed murmur of excitement went through the assembled spirits, and even Messrs. Hawkshaw and Le Coq were silent in the presence of such genius.

"My plan of action was immediately formulated. The man was completely at my mercy. He had stolen the tiara, and had it concealed in the lining of his hat. I rose and locked the door. My visitor sank with a groan into my chair.

"'Why did you do that?' he stammered, as I turned the key in the lock.

"'To keep my Scotch whiskey from evaporating,' I said, dryly. 'Now, my lord,' I added, 'it will pay your Grace to let me have your hat. I know who you are. You are the Duke of Brokedale. The Duchess of Brokedale has lost a valuable tiara of diamonds, and you have not lost your watch. Somebody has stolen the diamonds, and it may be that somewhere there is a Bunker who has lost such a watch as I have described. The queer part of it all is,' I continued, handing him the decanter, and taking a couple of loaded six-shooters out of my *escritoire*—'the queer part of it all is that I have the watch and you have the tiara. We'll swap the swag. Hand over the bauble, please.'

"'But—' he began.

"'We won't have any butting, your Grace,' said I. 'I'll give you the watch, and you needn't mind the £200; and you must give me the tiara, or I'll accompany you forthwith to the police, and have a search made of your hat. It won't pay you to defy me. Give it up.'

"He gave up the hat at once, and, as I suspected, there lay the tiara, snugly stowed away behind the head-band.

"'You are a great fellow,' said I, as I held the tiara up to the light and watched with pleasure the flashing brilliance of its gems.

"'I beg you'll not expose me,' he moaned. 'I was driven to it by necessity.'

"'Not I,' I replied. 'As long as you play fair it will be all right. I'm not going to keep this thing. I'm not married, and so have no use for such a trifle; but what I do intend is simply to wait until your wife retains me to find it, and then I'll find it and get the reward. If you keep perfectly still, I'll have it found in such a fashion that you'll never be suspected. If, on the other hand, you say a word about tonight's events, I'll hand you over to the police.'

"'Humph!' he said. 'You couldn't prove a case against me.'

"'I can prove any case against anybody,' I retorted. 'If you don't believe it, read my book,' I added, and I handed him a copy of my memoirs.

"'I've read it,' he answered, 'and I ought to have known better than to come here. I thought you were only a literary success.' And with a deep-drawn sigh he took the watch and went out. Ten days later I was retained by the Duchess, and after a pretended search of ten days more I found the tiara, restored it to the noble lady, and received the £5000 reward. The Duke kept perfectly quiet about our little encounter, and afterwards we became stanch friends; for he was a good fellow, and was driven to his desperate deed only by the demands of his creditors, and the following Christmas he sent me the watch I had given him, with the best wishes of the season.

"So, you see, gentlemen, in a moment, by quick wit and a mental concentration of no mean order, combined with strict observance of the pettiest details, I ferreted out what bade fair to become a great diamond mystery; and when I say that this cigar end proves certain things to my mind, it does not become you to doubt the value of my conclusions."

"Hear! hear!" cried Raleigh, growing tumultuous with enthusiasm.

"Your name? your name?" came from all parts of the wharf.

The stranger, putting his hand into the folds of his coat, drew forth a bundle of business cards, which he tossed, as the prestidigitator tosses playing-cards, out among the audience, and on each of them was found printed the words:

SHERLOCK HOLMES,
DETECTIVE.

——

Ferreting Done Here.

——

Plots for Sale.

"I think he made a mistake in not taking the £200 for the watch. Such carelessness destroys my confidence in him," said Shylock, who was the first to recover from the surprise of the revelation.

3

THE SEARCH-PARTY IS ORGANIZED

"Well, Mr. Holmes," said Sir Walter Raleigh, after three rousing cheers, led by Hamlet, had been given with a will by the assembled spirits, "after this demonstration in your honour I think it is hardly necessary for me to assure you of our hearty co-operation in anything you may venture to suggest. There is still manifest, however, some desire on the part of the ever-wise King Solomon and my friend Confucius to know how you deduce that Kidd has sailed for London, from the cigar end which you hold in your hand."

"I can easily satisfy their curiosity," said Sherlock Holmes, genially. "I believe I have already proven that it is the end of Kidd's cigar. The marks of the teeth have shown that. Now observe how closely it is smoked—there is barely enough of it left for one to insert between his teeth. Now Captain Kidd would hardly have risked the edges of his moustache and the comfort of his lips by smoking a cigar down to the very light if he had had another; nor would he under any circumstances have smoked it that far unless he were passionately addicted to this particular brand of the weed. Therefore I say to you, first, this was his cigar; second, it was the last one he had; third, he is a confirmed smoker.

"The result, he has gone to the one place in the world where these Connecticut hand-rolled Havana cigars—for I recognize this as one of them—have a real popularity, and are therefore more certainly obtainable, and that is at London. You cannot get so vile a cigar as that outside of a London hotel. If I could have seen a quarter-inch more of it, I should have been able definitely to locate the hotel itself. The wrappers unroll to a degree that varies perceptibly as between the different hotels. The Metropole cigar can be smoked a quarter through before its wrapper gives way; the Grand wrapper goes as soon as you light the cigar; whereas the Savoy, fronting on the Thames, is surrounded by a moister atmosphere than the others, and, as a consequence, the wrapper will hold really until most people are willing to throw the whole thing away."

"It is really a wonderful art!" said Solomon.

"The making of a Connecticut Havana cigar?" laughed Holmes. "Not at all. Give me a head of lettuce and a straw, and I'll make you a box."

"I referred to your art—that of detection," said Solomon. "Your logic is perfect; step by step we have been led to the irresistible conclusion that Kidd has made for London, and can be found at one of these hotels."

"And only until next Tuesday, when he will take a house in the neighbourhood of Scotland Yard," put in Holmes, quickly, observing a sneer on Hawkshaw's lips, and hastening to overwhelm him by further evidence of his ingenuity. "When he gets his bill he will open his piratical eyes so wide that he will be seized with jealousy to think of how much more refined his profession has become since he left it, and out of mere pique he will leave the hotel, and, to show himself still cleverer than his modern prototypes, he will leave his account unpaid, with the result that the affair will be put in the hands of the police, under which circumstances a house in the immediate vicinity of the famous police headquarters will be the safest hiding-place he can find, as was instanced by the remarkable case of the famous Penstock bond robbery.

"A certain church-warden named Hinkley, having been appointed cashier thereof, robbed the Penstock Imperial Bank of £1,000,000 in bonds, and, fleeing to London, actually joined the detective force at Scotland Yard, and was detailed to find himself, which of course he never did, nor would he ever have been found had he not crossed my path."

Hawkshaw gazed mournfully off into space, and Le Coq muttered profane words under his breath.

"We're not in the same class with this fellow, Hawkshaw," said Le Coq. "You could tap your forehead knowingly eight hours a day through all eternity with a sledge-hammer without loosening an idea like that."

"Nevertheless I'll confound him yet," growled the jealous detective. "I shall myself go to London, and, disguised as Captain Kidd, will lead this visionary on until he comes there to arrest me, and when these club members discover that it is Hawkshaw and not Kidd he has run to earth, we'll have a great laugh on Sherlock Holmes."

"I am anxious to hear how you solved the bond-robbery mystery," said Socrates, wrapping his *toga* closely about him and settling back against one of the spiles of the wharf.

"So are we all," said Sir Walter. "But meantime the Houseboat is getting farther away."

"Not unless she's sailing backwards," sneered Noah, who was still nursing his resentment against Sir Christopher Wren for his reflections upon the speed of the Ark.

"What's the hurry?" asked Socrates. "I believe in making haste slowly; and on the admission of our two eminent naval architects, Sir Christopher and Noah, neither of their vessels can travel more than a mile a week, and if we charter the *Flying Dutchman* to go in pursuit of her we can catch her before she gets out of the Styx into the Atlantic."

"Jonah might lend us his whale, if the beast is in commission," suggested Munchausen, dryly. "I for one would rather take a state-room in Jonah's whale than go aboard the *Flying Dutchman* again. I made one trip on the *Dutchman*, and she's worse than a dory for comfort; furthermore, I don't see what good it would do us to charter a boat that can't land oftener than once in seven years, and spends most of her time trying to double the Cape of Good Hope."

"My whale is in commission," said Jonah, with dignity. "But Baron Munchausen need not consider the question of taking a state-room aboard of her. She doesn't carry second-class passengers. And if I took any stock in the idea of a trip on the *Flying Dutchman* amounting to a seven years' exile, I would cheerfully pay the Baron's expenses for a round trip."

"We are losing time, gentlemen," suggested Sherlock Holmes. "This is a moment, I think, when you should lay aside personal differences and personal preferences for immediate action. I have examined the wake of the House-boat, and I judge from the condition of what, for want of a better term, I may call the suds, when she left us the House-boat was making ten knots a day. Almost any craft we can find suitably manned ought to be able to do better than that; and if you could summon Charon and ascertain what boats he has at hand, it would be for the good of all concerned."

"That's a good plan," said Johnson. "Boswell, see if you can find Charon."

"I am here already, sir," returned the ferryman, rising. "Most of my boats have gone into winter quarters, your Honour. The *Mayflower* went into dry dock last week to be calked up; the *Pin-*

ta and the *Santa Maria* are slow and cranky; the *Monitor* and the *Merrimac* I haven't really had time to patch up; and the *Valkyrie* is two months overdue. I cannot make up my mind whether she is lost or kept back by excursion steamers. Hence I really don't know what I can lend you. Any of these boats I have named you could have had for nothing; but my others are actively employed, and I couldn't let them go without a serious interference with my business."

The old man blinked sorrowfully across the waters at the opposite shore. It was quite evident that he realized what a dreadful expense the club was about to be put to, and while of course there would be profit in it for him, he was sincerely sorry for them.

"I repeat," he added, "those boats you could have had for nothing, but the others I'd have to charge you for, though of course I'll give you a discount."

And he blinked again, as he meditated upon whether that discount should be an eighth or one-quarter of one per cent.

"The *Flying Dutchman*," he pursued, "ain't no good for your purposes. She's too fast. She's built to fly by, not to stop. You'd catch up with the House-boat in a minute with her, but you'd go right on and disappear like a visionary; and as for the Ark, she'd never do—with all respect to Mr. Noah. She's just about as suitable as any other waterlogged cattle-steamer'd be, and no more—first-rate for elephants and kangaroos, but no good for cruiser-work, and so slow she wouldn't make a ripple high enough to drown a gnat going at the top of her speed. Furthermore, she's got a great big hole in her bottom, where she was stove in by running afoul of—Mount Arrus-root, I believe it was called when Captain Noah went cruising with that menagerie of his."

"That's an unmitigated falsehood!" cried Noah, angrily. "This man talks like a professional amateur yachtsman. He has no regard for facts, but simply goes ahead and makes statements with an utter disregard of the truth. The Ark was not stove in. We beached her very successfully. I say this in defence of my seamanship, which was top-notch for my day."

"Couldn't sail six weeks without fouling a mountain-peak!" sneered Wren, perceiving a chance to get even.

"The hole's there, just the same," said Charon. "Maybe she was a centreboard, and that's where you kept the board."

"The hole is there because it was worn there by one of the elephants," retorted Noah. "You get a beast like the elephant shuffling one of his fore-feet up and down, up and down, a plank for twenty-four hours a day for forty days in one of your boats, and see where your boat would be."

"Thanks," said Charon, calmly. "But the elephants don't patronize my line. All the elephants I've ever seen in Hades waded over, except Jumbo, and he reached his trunk across, fastened on to a tree limb with it, and swung himself over. However, the Ark isn't at all what you want, unless you are going to man her with a lot of *centaurs*. If that's your intention, I'd charter her; the accommodations are just the thing for a crew of that kind."

"Well, what do you suggest?" asked Raleigh, somewhat impatiently. "You've told us what we can't do. Now tell us what we can do."

"I'd stay right here," said Charon, "and let the ladies rescue themselves. That's what I'd do. I've had the honour of bringing 'em over here, and I think I know 'em pretty well. I've watched 'em close, and it's my private opinion that before many days you'll see your club-house sailing back here, with Queen Elizabeth at the hellum, and the other ladies on the for'ard deck knittin' and crochetin', and tearin' each other to pieces in a conversational way, as happy as if there never had been any Captain Kidd and his pirate crew."

"That suggestion is impossible," said Blackstone, rising. "Whether the relief expedition amounts to anything or not, it's good to be set going. The ladies would never forgive us if we sat here inactive, even if they were capable of rescuing themselves. It is an accepted principle of law that this climate hath no fury like a woman left to herself, and we've got enough professional furies hereabouts without our aiding in augmenting the ranks.

We must have a boat."

"It'll cost you a thousand dollars a week," said Charon.

"I'll subscribe fifty," cried Hamlet.

"I'll consult my secretary," said Solomon, "and find out how many of my wives have been abducted, and I'll pay ten dollars apiece for their recovery."

"That's liberal," said Hawkshaw. "There are sixty-three of 'em on board, together with eighty of his *fiancées*. What's the quotation on *fiancées*, King Solomon?"

"Nothing," said Solomon. "They're not mine yet, and it's their fathers' business to get 'em back. Not mine."

Other subscriptions came pouring in, and it was not long before everybody save Shylock had put his name down for something. This some one of the more quick-witted of the spirits soon observed, and, with reckless disregard of the feelings of the Merchant of Venice, began to call: "Shylock! Shylock! How much?"

The Merchant tried to leave the pier, but his path was blocked.

"Subscribe, subscribe!" was the cry. "How much?"

"Order, gentlemen, order!" said Sir Walter, rising and holding a bottle aloft. "A black person by the name of Friday, a valet of our friend Mr. Crusoe, has just handed me this bottle, which he picked up ten minutes ago on the bank of the river a few miles distant. It contains a bit of paper, and may perhaps give us a clew based upon something more substantial than even the wonderful theories of our new brother Holmes."

A deathly silence followed the chairman's words, as Sir Walter drew a cork-screw from his pocket and opened the bottle. He extracted the paper, and, as he had surmised, it proved to be a message from the missing vessel. His face brightening with a smile of relief, Sir Walter read, aloud:

"Have just emerged into the Atlantic. Club in hands of Kidd and forty ruffians. One hundred and eighty-three ladies on board. Headed for the Azores. Send aid at once. All well except Xanthippe, who is seasick in the billiard-room. (Signed) Portia."

"Aha!" cried Hawkshaw. "That shows how valuable the Holmes theory is."

"Precisely," said Holmes. "No woman knows anything about seafaring, but Portia is right. The ship is headed for the Azores, which is the first tack needed in a windward sail for London under the present conditions."

The reply was greeted with cheers, and when they subsided the cry for Shylock's subscription began again, but he declined.

"I had intended to put up a thousand *ducats*," he said, defiantly, "but with that woman Portia on board I won't give a red *obolus!*" and with that he wrapped his cloak about him and stalked off into the gathering shadows of the wood.

And so the funds were raised without the aid of Shylock, and the shapely twin-screw steamer the *Gehenna* was chartered of Charon, and put under the command of Mr. Sherlock Holmes, who, after he had thanked the company for their confidence, walked abstractedly away, observing in strictest confidence to himself that he had done well to prepare that bottle beforehand and bribe Crusoe's man to find it.

"For now," he said, with a chuckle, "I can get back to earth again free of cost on my own hook, whether my eminent inventor wants me there or not. I never approved of his killing me off as he did at the very height of my popularity."

4
ON BOARD THE HOUSE-BOAT

Meanwhile the ladies were not having such a bad time, after all. Once having gained possession of the House-boat, they were loath to think of ever having to give it up again, and it is an open question in my mind if they would not have made off with it themselves had Captain Kidd and his men not done it for them.

"I'll never forgive these men for their selfishness in monopolizing all this," said Elizabeth, with a vicious stroke of a billiard-cue, which missed the cue-ball and tore a right angle in the cloth. "It is not right."

"No," said Portia. "It is all wrong; and when we get back home I'm going to give my beloved Bassanio a piece of my mind; and if he doesn't give in to me, I'll reverse my decision in the famous case of Shylock *versus* Antonio."

"Then I sincerely hope he doesn't give in," retorted Cleopatra, "for I swear by all my auburn locks that that was the very worst bit of injustice ever perpetrated. Mr. Shakespeare confided to me one night, at one of Mrs. Cæsar's card-parties, that he regarded that as the biggest joke he ever wrote, and Judge Blackstone observed to Antony that the decision wouldn't have held in any court of equity outside of Venice. If you owe a man a thousand *ducats*, and it costs you three thousand to get them, that's your affair, not his. If it cost Antonio every drop of his bluest blood to pay the pound of flesh, it was Antonio's affair, not Shylock's. However, the world applauds you as a great jurist, when you have nothing more than a woman's keen instinct for sentimental technicalities."

"It would have made a horrid play, though, if it had gone on," shuddered Elizabeth.

"That may be, but, carried out realistically, it would have done away with a raft of bad actors," said Cleopatra. "I'm half sorry it didn't go on, and I'm sure it wouldn't have been any worse than compelling Brutus to fall on his sword until he resembles a chicken liver *en brochette*, as is done in that Julius Cæsar play."

"Well, I'm very glad I did it," snapped Portia.

"I should think you would be," said Cleopatra. "If you hadn't done it, you'd never have been known. What was that?"

The boat had given a slight lurch.

"Didn't you hear a shuffling noise up on deck, Portia?" asked the Egyptian Queen.

"I thought I did, and it seemed as if the vessel had moved a bit," returned Portia, nervously; for, like most women in an advanced state of development, she had become a martyr to her nerves.

"It was merely the wash from one of Charon's new ferry-boats, I fancy," said Elizabeth, calmly. "It's disgusting, the way that old fellow allows these modern innovations to be brought in here! As if the old paddle-boats he used to carry shades in weren't good enough for the immigrants of this age! Really this Styx River is losing a great deal of its charm. Sir Walter and I were upset, while out rowing one day last summer, by the waves kicked up by one of Charon's excursion steamers going up the river with a party of picnickers from the city—the Greater Gehenna Chowder Club, I believe it was—on board of her.

"One might just as well live in the midst of the turmoil of a great city as try to get uninterrupted quiet here in the suburbs in these days. Charon isn't content to get rich slowly; he must make money by the barrelful, if he has to sacrifice all the comfort of everybody living on this river. Anybody'd think he was an American, the way he goes on; and everybody else here is the same way. The Erebeans are getting to be a race of shopkeepers."

"I think myself," sighed Cleopatra, "that Hades is being spoiled by the introduction of American ideas—it is getting by far too democratic for my tastes; and if it isn't stopped, it's my belief that the best people will stop coming here. Take Madame Récamier's salon as it is now and compare it with what it used to be! In the early days, after her arrival here, everybody went because it was the swell thing, and you'd be sure of meeting the intellectually elect. On the one hand you'd find Sophocles; on the other, Cicero; across the room would be Horace chatting gaily with some such person as myself. Great warriors, from Alexander to Bonaparte, were there, and glad of the opportunity to be there, too; statesmen like Macchiavelli; artists like Cellini or Tintoretto. You couldn't move without stepping on the toes of genius.

"But now all is different. The money-getting instinct has been aroused within them all, with the result that when I invited Mozart to meet a few friends at dinner at my place last autumn, he sent me a card stating his terms for dinners. Let me see, I think I have it with me; I've kept it by me for fear of losing it, it is such a complete revelation of the actual condition of affairs in this locality. Ah! this is it," she added, taking a small bit of paste-board from her card-case. "Read that."

The card was passed about, and all the ladies were much astonished—and naturally so, for it ran this wise:

Notice to Hostesses.

Owing to the very great, constantly growing, and at times vexatious demands upon his time socially,

Herr Wolfgang Amadeus Mozart

takes this method of announcing to his friends that on and after January 1, 1897, his terms for functions will be as follows:

Marks.

Dinners with conversation on the Theory of Music

500

Dinners with conversation on the Theory of Music, illustrated 750

Dinners without any conversation

300

Receptions, public, with music

1000

Receptions, private, with music

750

Encores (single)

100

Three encores for

150

Autographs

10

Positively no Invitations for Five-o'Clock Teas or Morning Musicales considered.

"Well, I declare!" tittered Elizabeth, as she read. "Isn't that extraordinary? He's got the three-name craze, too!"

"It's perfectly ridiculous," said Cleopatra. "But it's fairer than Artemus Ward's plan. Mozart gives notice of his intentions to charge you; but with Ward it's different. He comes, and afterwards sends a bill for his fun. Why, only last week I got a 'quarterly statement' from him showing a charge against me of thirty-eight dollars for humorous remarks made to my guests at a little chafing-dish party I gave in honour of Balzac, and, worst of all, he had marked it 'Please remit.' Even Antony, when he wrote a sonnet to my eyebrow, wouldn't let me have it until he had heard whether or not Boswell wanted it for publication in the *Gossip*. With Rubens giving chalk-talks for pay, Phidias doing 'Five-minute Masterpieces in Putty' for suburban lyceums, and all the illustrious in other lines turning their genius to account through the entertainment *bureaus*, it's impossible to have a *salon* now."

"You are indeed right," said Madame Récamier, sadly. "Those were palmy days when genius was satisfied with chicken salad and lemonade. I shall never forget those nights when the wit and wisdom of all time were—ah—were on tap at my house, if I may so speak, at a cost to me of lights and supper. Now the only people who will come for nothing are those we used to think of paying to stay away. Boswell is always ready, but you can't run a salon on Boswell."

"Well," said Portia, "I sincerely hope that you won't give up the functions altogether, because I have always found them most delightful. It is still possible to have lights and supper."

"I have a plan for next winter," said Madame Récamier, "but I suppose I shall be accused of going into the commercial side of it if I adopt it. The plan is, briefly, to incorporate my salon. That's an idea worthy of an American, I admit; but if I don't do it I'll have to give it up entirely, which, as you intimate, would be too bad. An incorporated salon, however, would be a grand thing, if only because it would perpetuate the salon. 'The Récamier Salon (Limited)' would be a most excellent title, and, suitably capitalized, would enable us to pay our lions sufficiently. Private enterprise is powerless under modern conditions. It's as much as I can afford to pay for a dinner, without running up an expense account for guests; and unless we get up a salon trust, as it were, the whole affair must go to the wall."

"How would you make it pay?" asked Portia. "I can't see where your dividends would come from."

"That is simple enough," said Madame Récamier. "We could put up a large reception-hall with a portion of our capital, and advertise a series of nights—say one a week throughout the season. These would be Warriors' Night, Story-tellers' Night, Poets' Night, Chafing-dish Night under the charge of Brillat-Savarin, and so on. It would be understood that on these particular evenings the most interesting people in certain lines would be present, and would mix with outsiders, who should be admitted only on payment of a certain sum of money. The commonplace inhabitants of this country could thus meet the truly great; and if I know them well, as I think I do, they'll pay readily for the privilege. The obscure love to rub up against the famous here as well as they do on earth."

"You'd run a sort of Social Zoo?" suggested Elizabeth.

"Precisely; and provide entertainment for private residences too. An advertisement in Boswell's paper, which everybody buys—"

"And which nobody reads," said Portia.

"They read the advertisements," retorted Madame Récamier. "As I was saying, an advertisement could be placed in Boswell's paper as follows: 'Are you giving a Function? Do you want Talent? Get your Genius at the Récamier Salon (Limited).' It would be simply magnificent as a business enterprise. The common herd would be tickled to death if they could get great people at their homes, even if they had to pay roundly for them."

"It would look well in the society notes, wouldn't it, if Mr. John Boggs gave a reception, and at the close of the account it said, 'The supper was furnished by Calizetti, and the genius by the Récamier Salon (Limited)'?" suggested Elizabeth, scornfully.

"I must admit," replied the French lady, "that you call up an unpleasant possibility, but I don't really see what else we can do if we want to preserve the salon idea. Somebody has told these talented people that they have a commercial value, and they are availing themselves of the demand."

"It is a sad age!" sighed Elizabeth.

"Well, all I've got to say is just this," put in Xanthippe: "You people who get up functions have brought this condition of affairs on yourselves. You were not satisfied to go ahead and indulge your passion for lions in a moderate fashion. Take the case of Demosthenes last winter, for instance. His wife told me that he dined at home three times during the winter. The rest of the time he was out, here, there, and everywhere, making after-dinner speeches. The saving on his dinner bills didn't pay his pebble account, much less remunerate him for his time, and the fearful expense of nervous energy to which he was subjected. It was as much as she could do, she said, to keep him from shaving one side of his head, so that he couldn't go out, the way he used to do in Athens when he was afraid he would be invited out and couldn't scare up a decent excuse for refusing."

"Did he do that?" cried Elizabeth, with a roar of laughter.

"So the cyclopædias say. It's a good plan, too," said Xanthippe. "Though Socrates never had to do it. When I got the notion Socrates was going out too much, I used to hide his dress clothes. Then there was the case of Rubens. He gave a Carbon Talk at the Sforza's Thursday Night Club, merely to oblige Madame Sforza, and three weeks later discovered that she had sold his pictures to pay for her gown! You people simply run it into the ground. You kill the goose that when taken at the flood leads on to fortune. It advertises you, does the lion no good, and he is expected to be satisfied with confectionery, material and theoretical. If they are getting tired of candy and compliments, it's because you have forced too much of it upon them."

"They like it, just the same," retorted Récamier. "A genius likes nothing better than the sound of his own voice, when he feels that it is falling on aristocratic ears. The social laurel rests pleasantly on many a noble brow."

"True," said Xanthippe. "But when a man gets a pile of Christmas wreaths a mile high on his head, he begins to wonder what they will bring on the market. An occasional wreath is very nice, but by the ton they are apt to weigh on his mind. Up to a certain point notoriety is like a woman, and a man is apt to love it; but when it becomes exacting, demanding instead of permitting itself to be courted, it loses its charm."

"That is Socratic in its wisdom," smiled Portia.

"But Xanthippic in its origin," returned Xanthippe. "No man ever gave me my ideas."

As Xanthippe spoke, Lucretia Borgia burst into the room.

"Hurry and save yourselves!" she cried. "The boat has broken loose from her moorings, and is floating down the stream. If we don't hurry up and do something, we'll drift out to sea!"

"What!" cried Cleopatra, dropping her cue in terror, and rushing for the stairs. "I was certain I felt a slight motion. You said it was the wash from one of Charon's barges, Elizabeth."

"I thought it was," said Elizabeth, following closely after.

"Well, it wasn't," moaned Lucretia Borgia. "Calpurnia just looked out of the window and discovered that we were in mid-stream."

The ladies crowded anxiously about the stair and attempted to ascend, Cleopatra in the van; but as the Egyptian Queen reached the doorway to the upper deck, the door opened, and the hard features of Captain Kidd were thrust roughly through, and his strident voice rang out through the gathering gloom. "Pipe my eye for a sardine if we haven't captured a female seminary!" he cried.

And one by one the ladies, in terror, shrank back into the billiard-room, while Kidd, overcome by surprise, slammed the door to, and retreated into the darkness of the forward deck to consult with his followers as to "what next."

6

A Conference on Deck

"Here's a kettle of fish!" said Kidd, pulling his chin whisker in perplexity as he and his fellow-pirates gathered about the capstan to discuss the situation. "I'm blessed if in all my experience

I ever sailed athwart anything like it afore! Pirating with a lot of low-down ruffians like you gentlemen is bad enough, but on a craft loaded to the water's edge with advanced women—I've half a mind to turn back."

"If you do, you swim—we'll not turn back with you," retorted Abeuchapeta, whom, in honour of his prowess, Kidd had appointed executive officer of the House-boat. "I have no desire to be mutinous, Captain Kidd, but I have not embarked upon this enterprise for a pleasure sail down the Styx. I am out for business. If you had thirty thousand women on board, still should I not turn back."

"But what shall we do with 'em?" pleaded Kidd. "Where can we go without attracting attention? Who's going to feed 'em? Who's going to dress 'em? Who's going to keep 'em in bonnets? You don't know anything about these creatures, my dear Abeuchapeta; and, by-the-way, can't we arbitrate that name of yours? It would be fearful to remember in the excitement of a fight."

"Call him Ab," suggested Sir Henry Morgan, with an ill-concealed sneer, for he was deeply jealous of Abeuchapeta's preferral.

"If you do I'll call you Morgue, and change your appearance to fit," retorted Abeuchapeta, angrily.

"By the beards of all my sainted Buccaneers," began Morgan, springing angrily to his feet, "I'll have your life!"

"Gentlemen! Gentlemen—my noble ruffians!" expostulated Kidd. "Come, come; this will never do! I must have no quarrelling among my aides. This is no time for divisions in our councils. An entirely unexpected element has entered into our affairs, and it behooveth us to act in concert. It is no light matter—"

"Excuse me, captain," said Abeuchapeta, "but that is where you and I do not agree. We've got our ship and we've got our crew, and in addition we find that the Fates have thrown in a hundred or more women to act as ballast. Now I, for one, do not fear a woman. We can set them to work. There is plenty for them to do keeping things tidy; and if we get into a very hard fight,

118

and come out of the *mêlée* somewhat the worse for wear, it will be a blessing to have 'em along to mend our *togas*, sew buttons on our uniforms, and darn our hosiery."

Morgan laughed sarcastically. "When did you flourish, if ever, colonel?" he asked.

"Do you refer to me?" queried Abeuchapeta, with a frown.

"You have guessed correctly," replied Morgan, icily. "I have quite forgotten your date; were you a success in the year one, or when?"

"Admiral Abeuchapeta, Sir Henry," interposed Kidd, fearing a further outbreak of hostilities—"Admiral Abeuchapeta was the terror of the seas in the seventh century, and what he undertook to do he did, and his piratical enterprises were carried on on a scale of magnificence which is without parallel off the comic-opera stage. He never went forth without at least seventy galleys and a hundred other vessels."

Abeuchapeta drew himself up proudly.

"Six-ninety-eight was my great year," he said.

"That's what I thought," said Morgan. "That is to say, you got your ideas of women twelve hundred years ago, and the ladies have changed somewhat since that time. I have great respect for you, sir, as a ruffian. I have no doubt that as a ruffian you are a complete success, but when it comes to 'feminology' you are sailing in unknown waters. The study of women, my dear Abeuchadnezzar—"

"Peta," retorted Abeuchapeta, irritably.

"I stand corrected. The study of women, my dear Peter," said Morgan, with a wink at Conrad, which fortunately the seventh-century pirate did not see, else there would have been an open break—"the study of women is more difficult than that of astronomy; there may be two stars alike, but all women are unique. Because she was this, that, or the other thing in your day does not prove that she is any one of those things in our day—in fact, it proves the contrary. Why, I venture even to say that no individual woman is alike."

"That's rather a hazy thought," said Kidd, scratching his head in a puzzled sort of way.

"I mean that she's different from herself at different times," said Morgan. "What is it the poet called her?—'an infinite variety show,' or something of that sort; a perpetual vaudeville—a continuous performance, as it were, from twelve to twelve."

"Morgan is right, admiral!" put in Conrad the corsair, acting temporarily as bo'sun. "The times are sadly changed, and woman is no longer what she was. She is hardly what she is, much less what she was. The Roman Gynæceum would be an impossibility today. You might as well expect Delilah to open a barbershop on board this boat as ask any of these advanced females below-stairs to sew buttons on a pirate's uniform after a fray, or to keep the fringe on his epaulets curled.

"They're no longer sewing-machines—they are Keeley motors for mystery and perpetual motion. Women have views now—they are no longer content to be looked at merely; they must see for themselves; and the more they see, the more they wish to domesticate man and emancipate woman. It's my private opinion that if we are to get along with them at all the best thing to do is to let 'em alone.

"I have always found I was better off in the abstract, and if this question is going to be settled in a purely democratic fashion by submitting it to a vote, I'll vote for any measure which involves leaving them strictly to themselves. They're nothing but a lot of ghosts anyhow, like ourselves, and we can pretend we don't see them."

"If that could be, it would be excellent," said Morgan; "but it is impossible. For a pirate of the Byronic order, my dear Conrad, you are strangely unversed in the ways of the sex which cheers but not inebriates. We can no more ignore their presence upon this boat than we can expect whales to spout kerosene. In the first place, it would be excessively impolite of us to cut them—to decline to speak to them if they should address us. We may be pirates, ruffians, cutthroats, but I hope we shall never forget that we are gentlemen."

"The whole situation is rather contrary to etiquette, don't

you think?" suggested Conrad. "There's nobody to introduce us, and I can't really see how we can do otherwise than ignore them. I certainly am not going to stand on deck and make eyes at them, to try and pick up an acquaintance with them, even if I am of a Byronic strain."

"You forget," said Kidd, "two essential features of the situation. These women are at present—or shortly will be, when they realize their situation—in distress, and a true gentleman may always fly to the rescue of a distressed female; and, the second point, we shall soon be on the seas, and I understand that on the fashionable transatlantic lines it is now considered *de rigueur* to speak to anybody you choose to. The introduction business isn't going to stand in my way."

"Well, may I ask," put in Abeuchapeta, "just what it is that is worrying you? You said something about feeding them, and dressing them, and keeping them in bonnets. I fancy there's fish enough in the sea to feed 'em; and as for their gowns and hats, they can make 'em themselves. Every woman is a milliner at heart."

"Exactly, and we'll have to pay the milliners. That is what bothers me. I was going to lead this expedition to London, Paris, and New York, admiral. That is where the money is, and to get it you've got to go ashore, to headquarters. You cannot nowadays find it on the high seas. Modern civilization," said Kidd, "has ruined the pirate's business.

"The latest news from the other world has really opened my eyes to certain facts that I never dreamed of. The conditions of the day of which I speak are interestingly shown in the experience of our friend Hawkins here. Captain Hawkins, would you have any objection to stating to these gentlemen the condition of affairs which led you to give up piracy on the high seas?"

"Not the slightest, Captain Kidd," returned Captain Hawkins, who was a recent arrival in Hades. "It is a sad little story, and it gives me a pain for to think on it, but none the less I'll tell it, since you ask me. When I were a mere boy, fellow-pirates, I had but one ambition, due to my readin', which was confined to

121

stories of a Sunday-school nater—to become somethin' different from the little Willies an' the clever Tommies what I read about therein.

"They was all good, an' they went to their reward too soon in life for me, who even in them days regarded death as a stuffy an' unpleasant diversion. Learnin' at an early period that virtue was its only reward, an' a-wish-in' others, I says to myself: 'Jim,' says I, 'if you wishes to become a magnet in this village, be sinful. If so be as you are a good boy, an' kind to your sister an' all other animals, you'll end up as a prosperous father with fifteen hundred a year sure, with never no hope for no public preferment beyond bein' made the superintendent of the Sunday-school; but if so be as how you're bad, you may become famous, an' go to Congress, an' have your picture in the Sunday noospapers.'

"So I looks around for books tellin' how to get 'Famous in Fifty Ways,' an' after due reflection I settles in my mind that to be a pirate's just the thing for me, seein' as how it's both profitable an' healthy. Passin' over details, let me tell you that I became a pirate. I ran away to sea, an' by dint of perseverance, as the Sunday-school books useter say, in my badness I soon became the centre of a evil lot; an' when I says to 'em, 'Boys, I wants to be a pirate chief,' they hollers back, loud like, 'Jim, we're with you,' an' they was. For years I was the terror of the Venezuelan Gulf, the Spanish Main, an' the Pacific seas, but there was precious little money into it.

"The best pay I got was from a Sunday noospaper, which paid me well to sign an article on 'Modern Piracy' which I didn't write. Finally business got so bad the crew began to murmur, an' I was at my wits' ends to please 'em; when one mornin', havin' passed a restless night, I picks up a noospaper and sees in it that 'Next Saturday's steamer is a weritable treasure-ship, takin' out twelve million dollars, and the jewels of a certain *prima donna* valued at five hundred thousand.'

"'Here's my chance,' says I, an' I goes to sea and lies in wait for the steamer. I captures her easy, my crew bein' hungry, an' fightin' according like. We steals the box a-hold-in' the jewels an' the bag containin' the millions, hustles back to our own ship, an' makes for our rondyvoo, me with two bullets in my leg, four o' my crew killed, and one engin' of my ship disabled by a shot—but happy. Twelve an' a half millions at one break is enough to make anybody happy."

"I should say so," said Abeuchapeta, with an ecstatic shake of his head. "I didn't get that in all my career."

"Nor I," sighed Kidd. "But go on, Hawkins."

"Well, as I says," continued Captain Hawkins, "we goes to the rondyvoo to look over our booty. 'Captain 'Awkins,' says my valet—for I was a swell pirate, gents, an' never travelled nowhere without a man to keep my clothes brushed and the proper wrinkles in my trousers—'this 'ere twelve millions,' says he, 'is werry light,' says he, carryin' the bag ashore. 'I don't care how light it is, so long as it's twelve millions, Henderson,' says I; but my heart sinks inside o' me at his words, an' the minute we lands I sits down to investigate right there on the beach. I opens the bag, an' it's the one I was after—but the twelve millions!"

"Weren't there?" cried Conrad.

"Yes, they was there," sighed Hawkins, "but every bloomin' million was represented by a certified check, an' payable in London!"

"By Jingo!" cried Morgan. "What fearful luck! But you had the *prima donna's* jewels."

"Yes," said Hawkins, with a moan. "But they was like all other *prima donna's* jewels—for advertisin' purposes only, an' made o' gum-arabic!"

"Horrible!" said Abeuchapeta. "And the crew, what did they say?"

"They was a crew of a few words," sighed Hawkins. "Werry few words, an' not a civil word in the lot—mostly adjectives of a profane kind. When I told 'em what had happened, they got mad at Fortune for a-jiltin' of 'em, an'—well, I came here. I was 'sas'inated that werry night!"

"They killed you?" cried Morgan.

"A dozen times," nodded Hawkins. "They always was a lavish

123

lot. I met death in all its most horrid forms. First they stabbed me, then they shot me, then they clubbed me, and so on, endin' up with a lynchin'—but I didn't mind much after the first, which hurt a bit. But now that I'm here I'm glad it happened. This life is sort of less responsible than that other. You can't hurt a ghost by shooting him, because there ain't nothing to hurt, an' I must say I like bein' a mere vision what everybody can see through."

"All of which interesting tale proves what?" queried Abeuchapeta.

"That piracy on the sea is not profitable in these days of the check banking system," said Kidd. "If you can get a chance at real gold it's all right, but it's of no earthly use to steal checks that people can stop payment on. Therefore it was my plan to visit the cities and do a little freebooting there, where solid material wealth is to be found."

"Well? Can't we do it now?" asked Abeuchapeta.

"Not with these women tagging after us," returned Kidd. "If we went to London and lifted the whole Bank of England, these women would have it spent on Regent Street inside of twenty-four hours."

"Then leave them on board," said Abeuchapeta.

"And have them steal the ship!" retorted Kidd. "No. There are but two things to do. Take 'em back, or land them in Paris. Tell them to spend a week on shore while we are provisioning. Tell 'em to shop to their hearts' content, and while they are doing it we can sneak off and leave them stranded."

"Splendid!" cried Morgan.

"But will they consent?" asked Abeuchapeta.

"Consent! To shop? In Paris? For a week?" cried Morgan.

"Ha, ha!" laughed Hawkins. "Will they consent! Will a duck swim?"

And so it was decided, which was the first incident in the career of the House-boat upon which the astute Mr. Sherlock Holmes had failed to count.

6
A Conference Below-Stairs

When, with a resounding slam, the door to the upper deck of the House-boat was shut in the faces of queens Elizabeth and Cleopatra by the unmannerly Kidd, these ladies turned and gazed at those who thronged the stairs behind them in blank amazement, and the heart of Xanthippe, had one chosen to gaze through that diaphanous person's ribs, could have been seen to beat angrily.

Queen Elizabeth was so excited at this wholly novel attitude towards her regal self that, having turned, she sat down plump upon the floor in the most unroyal fashion.

"Well!" she ejaculated. "If this does not surpass everything! The idea of it! Oh for one hour of my olden power, one hour of the axe, one hour of the block!"

"Get up," retorted Cleopatra, "and let us all return to the billiard-room and discuss this matter calmly. It is quite evident that something has happened of which we wotted little when we came aboard this craft."

"That is a good idea," said Calpurnia, retreating below. "I can see through the window that we are in motion. The vessel has left her moorings, and is making considerable headway down the stream, and the distinctly masculine voices we have heard are indications to my mind that the ship is manned, and that this is the result of design rather than of accident. Let us below."

Elizabeth rose up and readjusted her ruff, which in the excitement of the moment had been forced to assume a position about her forehead which gave one the impression that its royal wearer had suddenly donned a *sombrero*.

"Very well," she said. "Let us below; but oh, for the axe!"

"Bring the lady an axe," cried Xanthippe, sarcastically. "She wants to cut somebody."

The sally was not greeted with applause. The situation was regarded as being too serious to admit of humour, and in silence they filed back into the billiard-room, and, arranging themselves in groups, stood about anxiously discussing the situation.

"It's getting rougher every minute," sobbed Ophelia. "Look at those pool-balls!" These were in very truth chasing each other about the table in an extraordinary fashion. "And I wish I'd never followed you horrid new creatures on board!" the poor girl added, in an agony of despair.

"I believe we've crossed the bar already!" said Cleopatra, gazing out of the window at a nasty choppy sea that was adding somewhat to the disquietude of the fair gathering. "If this is merely a joke on the part of the Associated Shades, it is a mighty poor one, and I think it is time it should cease."

"Oh, for an axe!" moaned Elizabeth, again.

"Excuse me, your Majesty," put in Xanthippe. "You said that before, and I must say it is getting tiresome. You couldn't do anything with an axe. Suppose you had one. What earthly good would it do you, who were accustomed to doing all your killing by proxy? I don't believe, if you had the unmannerly person who slammed the door in your face lying prostrate upon the billiard-table here, you could hit him a square blow in the neck if you had a hundred axes.

"Delilah might as well cry for her scissors, for all the good it would do us in our predicament. If Cleopatra had her asp with her it might be more to the purpose. One deadly little snake like that let loose on the upper deck would doubtless drive these boors into the sea, and even then our condition would not be bettered, for there isn't any of us that can sail a boat. There isn't an old salt among us."

"Too bad Mrs. Lot isn't along," giggled Marguerite de Valois, whose Gallic spirits were by no means overshadowed by the unhappy predicament in which she found herself.

"I'm here," piped up Mrs. Lot. "But I'm not that kind of a salt."

"I am present," said Mrs. Noah. "Though why I ever came I don't know, for I vowed the minute I set my foot on Ararat that dry land was good enough for me, and that I'd never step aboard another boat as long as I lived. If, however, now that I am here, I can give you the benefit of my nautical experience, you are all

126

perfectly welcome to it."

"I'm sure we're very much obliged for the offer," said Portia, "but in the emergency which has arisen we cannot say how much obliged we are until we know what your experience amounted to. Before relying upon you we ought to know how far that reliance can go—not that I lack confidence in you, my dear madam, but that in an hour of peril one must take care to rely upon the oak, not upon the reed."

"The point is properly taken," said Elizabeth, "and I wish to say here that I am easier in my mind when I realize that we have with us so level-headed a person as the lady who has just spoken. She has spoken truly and to the point. If I were to become queen again, I should make her my attorney-general. We must not go ahead impulsively, but look at all things in a calm, judicial manner."

"Which is pretty hard work with a sea like this on," remarked Ophelia, faintly, for she was getting a trifle sallow, as indeed she might, for the House-boat was beginning to roll tremendously, with no alleviation save an occasional pitch, which was an alleviation only in the sense that it gave variety to their discomfort. "I don't believe a chief-justice could look at things calmly and in a judicial manner if he felt as I do."

"Poor dear!" said the matronly Mrs. Noah, sympathetically. "I know exactly how you feel. I have been there myself. The fourth day out I and my whole family were in the same condition, except that Noah, my husband, was so very far gone that I could not afford to yield. I nursed him for six days before he got his sea-legs on, and then succumbed myself."

"But," gasped Ophelia, "that doesn't help me—"

"It did my husband," said Mrs. Noah. "When he heard that the boys were sea-sick too, he actually laughed and began to get better right away. There is really only one cure for the *mal de mer*, and that is the fun of knowing that somebody else is suffering too. If some of you ladies would kindly yield to the seductions of the sea, I think we could get this poor girl on her feet in an instant."

Unfortunately for poor Ophelia, there was no immediate response to this appeal, and the unhappy young woman was forced to suffer in solitude.

"We have no time for untimely diversions of this sort," snapped Xanthippe, with a scornful glance at the suffering Ophelia, who, having retired to a comfortable lounge at an end of the room, was evidently improving. "I have no sympathy with this habit some of my sex seem to have acquired of succumbing to an immediate sensation of this nature."

"I hope to be pardoned for interrupting," said Mrs. Noah, with a great deal of firmness, "but I wish Mrs. Socrates to understand that it is rather early in the voyage for her to lay down any such broad principle as that, and for her own sake tomorrow, I think it would be well if she withdrew the sentiment. There are certain things about a sea-voyage that are more or less beyond the control of man or woman, and anyone who chides that poor suffering child on yonder sofa ought to be more confident than Mrs. Socrates can possibly be that within an hour she will not be as badly off. People who live in glass houses should not throw dice."

"I shall never yield to anything so undignified as seasickness, let me tell you that," retorted Xanthippe. "Furthermore, the proverb is not as the lady has quoted it. '*People who live in glass houses should not throw stones*' is the proper version."

"I was not quoting," returned Mrs. Noah, calmly. "When I said that people who live in glass houses should not throw dice, I meant precisely what I said. People who live in glass houses should not take chances. In assuming with such vainglorious positiveness that she will not be seasick, the lady who has just spoken is giving tremendous odds, as the boys used to say on the Ark when we gathered about the table at night and began to make small wagers on the day's run."

"I think we had better suspend this discussion," suggested Cleopatra. "It is of no immediate interest to anyone but Ophelia, and I fancy she does not care to dwell upon it at any great length. It is more important that we should decide upon our future course of action. In the first place, the question is who these people up on deck are. If they are the members of the club, we are all right. They will give us our scare, and land us safely again at the pier. In that event it is our womanly duty to manifest no concern, and to seem to be aware of nothing unusual in the proceeding. It would never do to let them think that their joke has been a good one.

"If, on the other hand, as I fear, we are the victims of some horde of ruffians, who have pounced upon us unawares, and are going into the business of abduction on a wholesale basis, we must meet treachery with treachery, strategy with strategy. I, for one, am perfectly willing to make every man on board walk the plank, having confidence in the seawomanship of Mrs. Noah and her ability to steer us into port."

"I am quite in accord with these views," put in Madame Récamier, "and I move you, Mrs. President, that we organize a series of subcommittees—one on treachery, with Lucretia Borgia and Delilah as members; one on strategy, consisting of Portia and Queen Elizabeth; one on navigation, headed by Mrs. Noah; with a final subcommittee on reconnoitre, with Cassandra to look forward, and Mrs. Lot to look aft—all of these subordinated to a central committee of safety headed by Cleopatra and Calpurnia. The rest of us can then commit ourselves and our interests unreservedly to these ladies, and proceed to enjoy ourselves without thought of the morrow."

"I second the motion," said Ophelia, "with the amendment that Madame Récamier be appointed chairlady of another subcommittee, on entertainment."

The amendment was accepted, and the motion put. It was carried with an enthusiastic aye, and the organization was complete.

The various committees retired to the several corners of the room to discuss their individual lines of action, when a shadow was observed to obscure the moonlight which had been streaming in through the window. The faces of Calpurnia and Cleopatra blanched for an instant, as, immediately following upon this apparition, a large bundle was hurled through the open port into the middle of the room, and the shadow vanished.

"Is it a bomb?" cried several of the ladies at once.

"Nonsense!" said Madame Récamier, jumping lightly forward. "A man doesn't mind blowing a woman up, but he'll never blow himself up. We're safe enough in that respect. The thing looks to me like a bundle of illustrated papers."

"That's what it is," said Cleopatra, who had been investigating. "It's rather a discourteous bit of courtesy, tossing them in through the window that way, I think, but I presume they mean well. Dear me," she added, as, having untied the bundle, she held one of the open papers up before her, "how interesting! All the latest Paris fashions. Humph! Look at those sleeves, Elizabeth. What an impregnable fortress you would have been with those sleeves added to your ruffs!"

"I should think they'd be very becoming," put in Cassandra, standing on her tiptoes and looking over Cleopatra's shoulder. "That Watteau isn't bad, either, is it, now?"

"No," remarked Calpurnia. "I wonder how a Watteau back like that would go on my blue alpaca?"

"Very nicely," said Elizabeth. "How many gores has it?"

"Five," observed Calpurnia. "One more than Cæsar's *toga*. We had to have our costumes distinct in some way."

"A remarkable hat, that," nodded Mrs. Lot, her eye catching sight of a Virot creation at the top of the page.

"Reminds me of Eve's description of an autumn scene in the garden," smiled Mrs. Noah. "Gorgeous in its foliage, beautiful thing; though I shouldn't have dared wear one in the Ark, with all those hungry animals browsing about the upper and lower decks."

"I wonder," remarked Cleopatra, as she cocked her head to one side to take in the full effect of an attractive summer gown— "I wonder how that waist would make up in blue *crépon*, with a yoke of lace and a stylishly contrasting stock of satin ribbon?"

"It would depend upon how you finished the sleeves," remarked Madame Récamier. "If you had a few puffs of rich brocaded satin set in with deeply folded pleats it wouldn't be bad."

"I think it would be very effective," observed Mrs. Noah, "but a trifle too light for general wear. I should want some kind of a wrap with it."

"It does need that," assented Elizabeth. "A wrap made of *passementerie* and jet, with a *mousseline de soie* ruche about the neck held by a *chou*, would make it fascinating."

"The committee on treachery is ready to report," said Delilah, rising from her corner, where she and Lucretia Borgia had been having so animated a discussion that they had failed to observe the others crowding about Cleopatra and the papers.

"A little sombre," said Cleopatra. "The corsage is effective, but I don't like those *basque* terminations. I've never approved of those full godets—"

"The committee on treachery," remarked Delilah again, raising her voice, "has a suggestion to make."

"I can't get over those sleeves, though," laughed Helen of Troy. "What is the use of them?"

"They might be used to get Greeks into Troy," suggested Madame Récamier.

"The committee on treachery," roared Delilah, thoroughly angered by the absorption of the chairman and others, "has a suggestion to make. This is the third and last call."

"Oh, I beg pardon," cried Cleopatra, rapping for order. "I had forgotten all about our committees. Excuse me, Delilah. I—ah—was absorbed in other matters. Will you kindly lay your pattern—I should say your plan—before us?"

"It is briefly this," said Delilah. "It has been suggested that we invite the crew of this vessel to a chafing-dish party, under the supervision of Lucretia Borgia, and that she—"

The balance of the plan was not outlined, for at this point the speaker was interrupted by a loud knocking at the door, its instant opening, and the appearance in the doorway of that ill-visaged ruffian Captain Kidd.

"Ladies," he began, "I have come here to explain to you the situation in which you find yourselves. Have I your permission

131

to speak?"

The ladies started back, but the chairman was equal to the occasion.

"Go on," said Cleopatra, with queenly dignity, turning to the interloper; and the pirate proceeded to take the second step in the nefarious plan upon which he and his brother ruffians had agreed, of which the tossing in through the window of the bundle of fashion papers was the first.

7

THE "GEHENNA" IS CHARTERED

It was about twenty-four hours after the events narrated in the preceding chapters that Mr. Sherlock Holmes assumed command of the *Gehenna*, which was nothing more nor less than the shadow of the ill-starred ocean steamship *City of Chicago*, which tried some years ago to reach Liverpool by taking the overland route through Ireland, fortunately without detriment to her passengers or crew, who had the pleasure of the experience of shipwreck without any of the discomforts of drowning.

As will be remembered, the obstructionist nature of the Irish soil prevented the *City of Chicago* from proceeding farther inland than was necessary to keep her well balanced amidships upon a convenient and not too stony bed; and that after a brief sojourn on the rocks she was finally disposed of to the Styx Navigation Company, under which title Charon had had himself incorporated, is a matter of nautical history. The change of name to the *Gehenna* was the act of Charon himself, and was prompted, no doubt, by a desire to soften the jealous prejudices of the residents of the Stygian capital against the flourishing and ever-growing metropolis of Illinois.

The Associated Shades had had some trouble in getting this craft. Charon, through his constant association with life on both sides of the dark river, had gained a knowledge, more or less intimate, of modern business methods, and while as janitor of the club he was subject to the will of the House Committee, and sympathized deeply with the members of the association in their trouble, as president of the Styx Navigation Company he was bound up in certain newly attained commercial ideas which were embarrassing to those members of the association to whose hands the chartering of a vessel had been committed.

"See here, Charon," Sir Walter Raleigh had said, after Charon had expressed himself as deeply sympathetic, but unable to shave the terms upon which the vessel could be had, "you are an infernal old hypocrite. You go about wringing your hands over our misfortunes until they've got as dry and flabby as a pair of kid gloves, and yet when we ask you for a ship of suitable size and speed to go out after those pirates, you become a sort of twin brother to Shylock, without his excuse. His instincts are accidents of birth. Yours are cultivated, and you know it."

"You are very much mistaken, Sir Walter," Charon had answered to this. "You don't understand my position. It is a very hard one. As janitor of your club I am really prostrated over the events of the past twenty-four hours. My occupation is gone, and my despair over your loss is correspondingly greater, for I have time on my hands to brood over it. I was hysterical as a woman yesterday afternoon—so hysterical that I came near upsetting one of the Furies who engaged me to row her down to Madame Medusa's villa last evening; and right at the sluice of the vitriol reservoir at that."

"Then why the deuce don't you do something to help us?" pleaded Hamlet.

"How can I do any more than I have done? I've offered you the *Gehenna*," retorted Charon.

"But on what terms?" expostulated Raleigh. "If we had all the wealth of the Indies we'd have difficulty in paying you the sums you demand."

"But I am only president of the company," explained Charon. "I'd like, as president, to show you some courtesy, and I'm perfectly willing to do so; but when it comes down to giving you a vessel like that, I'm bound by my official oath to consider the interest of the stockholders. It isn't as it used to be when I had boats to hire in my own behalf alone. In those days I had nobody's interest but my own to look after. Now the ships all belong to the Styx Navigation Company. Can't you see the difference?"

"You own all the stock, don't you?" insisted Raleigh.

"I don't know," Charon answered, blandly. "I haven't seen the transfer-books lately."

"But you know that you did own every share of it, and that you haven't sold any, don't you?" put in Hamlet.

Charon was puzzled for a moment, but shortly his face cleared, and Sir Walter's heart sank, for it was evident that the old fellow could not be cornered.

"Well, it's this way, Sir Walter, and your Highness," he said, "I—I can't say whether any of that stock has been transferred or not. The fact is, I've been speculating a little on margin, and I've put up that stock as security, and, for all I know, I may have been sold out by my brokers. I've been so upset by this unfortunate occurrence that I haven't seen the market reports for two days. Really you'll have to be content with my offer or go without the *Gehenna*. There's too much suspicion attached to high corporate officials lately for me to yield a jot in the position I have taken.

"It would never do to get you all ready to start, and then have an injunction clapped on you by some unforeseen stockholder who was not satisfied with the terms offered you; nor can I ever let it be said of me that to retain my position as janitor of your organization I sacrificed a trust committed to my charge. I'll gladly lend you my private launch, though I don't think it will aid you much, because the naphtha-tank has exploded, and the screw slipped off and went to the bottom two weeks ago. Still, it is at your service, and I've no doubt that either Phidias or Benvenuto Cellini will carve out a paddle for you if you ask him to."

"Bah!" retorted Raleigh. "You might as well offer us a pair of skates."

"I would, if I thought the river'd freeze," retorted Charon, blandly.

Raleigh and Hamlet turned away impatiently and left Charon to his own devices, which for the time being consisted largely of winking his other eye quietly and outwardly making a great show of grief.

"He's too canny for us, I am afraid," said Sir Walter. "We'll have to pay him his money."

"Let us first consult Sherlock Holmes," suggested Hamlet, and this they proceeded at once to do.

"There is but one thing to be done," observed the astute detective after he had heard Sir Walter's statement of the case. "It is an old saying that one should fight fire with fire. We must meet modern business methods with modern commercial ideas. Charter his vessel at his own price."

"But we'd never be able to pay," said Hamlet.

"Ha-ha!" laughed Holmes. "It is evident that you know nothing of the laws of trade nowadays. Don't pay!"

"But how can we?" asked Raleigh.

"The method is simple. You haven't anything to pay with," returned Holmes. "Let him sue. Suppose he gets a verdict. You haven't anything he can attach—if you have, make it over to your wives or your *fiancées*."

"Is that honest?" asked Hamlet, shaking his head doubtfully.

"It's business," said Holmes.

"But suppose he wants an advance payment?" queried Hamlet.

"Give him a check drawn to his own order. He'll have to endorse it when he deposits it, and that will make him responsible," laughed Holmes.

"What a simple thing when you understand it!" commented Raleigh.

"Very," said Holmes. "Business is getting by slow degrees to be an exact science. It reminds me of the Brighton mystery, in which I played a modest part some ten years ago, when I first took up ferreting as a profession. I was sitting one night in my room at one of the Brighton hotels, which shall be nameless. I never give the name of any of the hotels at which I stop, because

135

it might give offence to the proprietors of other hotels, with the result that my books would be excluded from sale therein. Suffice it to say that I was spending an early summer Sunday at Brighton with my friend Watson. We had dined well, and were enjoying our evening smoke together upon a small balcony overlooking the water, when there came a timid knock on the door of my room.

"'Watson,' said I, 'here comes someone for advice. Do you wish to wager a small bottle upon it?'

"'Yes,' he answered, with a smile. 'I am thirsty and I'd like a small bottle; and while I do not expect to win, I'll take the bet. I should like to know, though, how you know.'

"'It is quite simple,' said I. 'The timidity of the knock shows that my visitor is one of two classes of persons—an autograph-hunter or a client, one of the two. You see I give you a chance to win. It may be an autograph-hunter, but I think it is a client. If it were a creditor, he would knock boldly, even ostentatiously; if it were the maid, she would not knock at all; if it were the hall-boy, he would not come until I had rung five times for him. None of these things has occurred; the knock is the half-hearted knock which betokens either that the person who knocked is in trouble, or is uncertain as to his reception. I am willing, however, considering the heat and my desire to quench my thirst, to wager that it is a client.'

"'Done,' said Watson; and I immediately remarked, 'Come in.'

"The door opened, and a man of about thirty-five years of age, in a bathing-suit, entered the room, and I saw at a glance what had happened.

"'Your name is Burgess,' I said. 'You came here from London this morning, expecting to return tonight. You brought no luggage with you. After luncheon you went in bathing. You had machine No. 35, and when you came out of the water you found that No. 35 had disappeared, with your clothes and the silver watch your uncle gave you on the day you succeeded to his business.'

"Of course, gentlemen," observed the detective, with a smile at Sir Walter and Hamlet—"of course the man fairly gasped, and I continued: 'You have been lying face downward in the sand ever since, waiting for nightfall, so that you could come to me for assistance, not considering it good form to make an afternoon call upon a stranger at his hotel, clad in a bathing-suit. Am I correct?'

"'Sir,' he replied, with a look of wonder, 'you have narrated my story exactly as it happened, and I find I have made no mistake in coming to you. Would you mind telling me what is your course of reasoning?'

"'It is plain as day,' said I. 'I am the person with the red beard with whom you came down third class from London this morning, and you told me your name was Burgess and that you were a butcher. When you looked to see the time, I remarked upon the oddness of your watch, which led to your telling me that it was the gift of your uncle.'

"'True,' said Burgess, 'but I did not tell you I had no luggage.'

"'No,' said I, 'but that you hadn't is plain; for if you had brought any other clothing besides that you had on with you, you would have put it on to come here. That you have been robbed I deduce also from your costume.'

"'But the number of the machine?' asked Watson.

"'Is on the tag on the key hanging about his neck,' said I.

"'One more question,' queried Burgess. 'How do you know I have been lying face downward on the beach ever since?'

"'By the sand in your eyebrows,' I replied; and Watson ordered up the small bottle."

"I fail to see what it was in our conversation, however," observed Hamlet, somewhat impatient over the delay caused by the narration of this tale, "that suggested this train of thought to you."

"The sequel will show," returned Holmes.

"Oh, Lord!" put in Raleigh. "Can't we put off the sequel until a later issue? Remember, Mr. Holmes, that we are constantly losing time."

"The sequel is brief, and I can narrate it on our way to the office of the Navigation Company," observed the detective. "When the bottle came I invited Mr. Burgess to join us, which he did, and as the hour was late when we came to separate, I offered him the use of my parlour overnight. This he accepted, and we retired.

"The next morning when I arose to dress, the mystery was cleared."

"You had dreamed its solution?" asked Raleigh.

"No," replied Holmes. "Burgess had disappeared with all my clothing, my false-beard, my suit-case, and my watch. The only thing he had left me was the bathing-suit and a few empty small bottles."

"And why, may I ask," put in Hamlet, as they drew near to Charon's office—"why does that case remind you of business as it is conducted today?"

"In this, that it is a good thing to stay out of unless you know it all," explained Holmes. "I omitted in the case of Burgess to observe one thing about him. Had I observed that his nose was rectilinear, incurved, and with a lifted base, and that his auricular temporal angle was between 96 and 97 degrees, I should have known at once that he was an impostor. *Vide* Ottolenghui on *Ears and Noses I Have Met*, pp. 631-640."

"Do you mean to say that you can tell a criminal by his ears?" demanded Hamlet.

"If he has any—yes; but I did not know that at the time of the Brighton mystery. Therefore I should have stayed out of the case. But here we are. Good-morning, Charon."

By this time the trio had entered the private office of the president of the Styx Navigation Company, and in a few moments the vessel was chartered at a fabulous price.

On the return to the wharf, Sir Walter somewhat nervously asked Holmes if he thought the plan they had settled upon would work.

"Charon is a very shrewd old fellow," said he. "He may outwit us yet."

"The chances are just two and one-eighth degrees in your favour," observed Holmes, quietly, with a glance at Raleigh's ears. "The temporal angle of your ears is 93-1/8 degrees, whereas Charon's stand out at 91, by my otometer. To that extent your criminal instincts are superior to his. If criminology is an exact science, reasoning by your respective ears, you ought to beat him out by a perceptible though possibly narrow margin."

With which assurance Raleigh went ahead with his preparations, and within twelve hours the *Gehenna* was under way, carrying a full complement of crew and officers, with every stateroom on board occupied by some spirit of the more illustrious kind.

Even Shylock was on board, though no one knew it, for in the dead of night he had stolen quietly up the gang-plank and had hidden himself in an empty water-cask in the forecastle.

"'Tisn't Venice," he said, as he sat down and breathed heavily through the bung of the barrel, "but it's musty and damp enough, and, considering the cost, I can't complain. You can't get something for nothing, even in Hades."

8
ON BOARD THE "GEHENNA"

When the *Gehenna* had passed down the Styx and out through the beautiful Cimmerian Harbour into the broad waters of the ocean, and everything was comparatively safe for a while at least, Sherlock Holmes came down from the bridge, where he had taken his place as the commander of the expedition at the moment of departure. His brow was furrowed with anxiety, and through his massive forehead his brain could be seen to be throbbing violently, and the corrugations of his gray matter were not pleasant to witness as he tried vainly to squeeze an idea out of them.

"What is the matter?" asked Demosthenes, anxiously. "We are not in any danger, are we?"

"No," replied Holmes. "But I am somewhat puzzled at the

bubbles on the surface of the ocean, and the ripples which we passed over an hour or two ago, barely perceptible through the most powerful microscope, indicate to my mind that for some reason at present unknown to me the House-boat has changed her course. Take that bubble floating by. It is the last expiring bit of aerial agitation of the House-boat's wake. Observe whence it comes. Not from the Azores quarter, but as if instead of steering a straight course thither the House-boat had taken a sharp turn to the northeast, and was making for Havre; or, in other words, Paris instead of London seems to have become their destination."

Demosthenes looked at Holmes with blank amazement, and, to keep from stammering out the exclamation of wonder that rose to his lips, he opened his *bonbonnière* and swallowed a pebble.

"You don't happen to have a cocaine tablet in your box, do you?" queried Holmes.

"No," returned the Greek. "Cocaine makes me flighty and nervous, but these pebbles sort of ballast me and hold me down. How on earth do you know that that bubble comes from the wake of the House-boat?"

"By my chemical knowledge, merely," replied Holmes. "A merely worldly vessel leaves a phosphorescent bubble in its wake. That one we have just discovered is not so, but sulphurescent, if I may coin a word which it seems to me the English language is very much in need of. It proves, then, that the bubble is a portion of the wake of a Stygian craft, and the only Stygian craft that has cleared the Cimmerian Harbour for years is the House-boat—Q.E.D."

"We can go back until we find the ripple again, and follow that, I presume," sneered Le Coq, who did not take much stock in the theories of his great rival, largely because he was a detective by intuition rather than by study of the science.

"You can if you want to, but it is better not to," rejoined Holmes, simply, as though not observing the sneer, "because the ripple represents the outer lines of the angle of disturbance in the water; and as any one of the sides to an angle is greater than the perpendicular from the hypothenuse to the apex, you'd merely be going the long way. This is especially important when you consider the formation of the bow of the House-boat, which is rounded like the stern of most vessels, and comes near to making a pair of ripples at an angle of ninety degrees."

"Then," observed Sir Walter, with a sigh of disappointment, "we must change our course and sail for Paris?"

"I am afraid so," said Holmes; "but of course it's by no means certain as yet. I think if Columbus would go up into the mizzen-top and look about him, he might discover something either in confirmation or refutation of the theory."

"He couldn't discover anything," put in Pinzon. "He never did."

"Well, I like that!" retorted Columbus. "I'd like to know who discovered America."

"So should I," observed Leif Ericson, with a wink at Vespucci.

"Tut!" retorted Columbus. "I did it, and the world knows it, whether you claim it or not."

"Yes, just as Noah discovered Ararat," replied Pinzon. "You sat upon the deck until we ran plumb into an island, after floating about for three months, and then you couldn't tell it from a continent, even when you had it right before your eyes. Noah might just as well have told his family that he discovered a roof garden as for you to go back to Spain telling 'em all that San Salvador was the United States."

"Well, I don't care," said Columbus, with a short laugh. "I'm the one they celebrate, so what's the odds? I'd rather stay down here in the smoking-room enjoying a small game, anyhow, than climb up that mast and strain my eyes for ten or a dozen hours looking for evidence to prove or disprove the correctness of another man's theory. I wouldn't know evidence when I saw it, anyhow. Send Judge Blackstone."

"I draw the line at the mizzentop," observed Blackstone. "The dignity of the bench must and shall be preserved, and I'll never consent to climb up that rigging, getting pitch and paint on my ermine, no matter who asks me to go."

"Whomsoever I tell to go, shall go," put in Holmes, firmly. "I am commander of this ship. It will pay you to remember that, Judge Blackstone."

"And I am the Court of Appeals," retorted Blackstone, hotly. "Bear that in mind, captain, when you try to send me up. I'll issue a writ of *habeas corpus* on my own body, and commit you for contempt."

"There's no use of sending the Judge, anyhow," said Raleigh, fearing by the glitter that came into the eye of the commander that trouble might ensue unless pacificatory measures were resorted to. "He's accustomed to weighing everything carefully, and cannot be rushed into a decision. If he saw any evidence, he'd have to sit on it a week before reaching a conclusion. What we need here more than anything else is an expert seaman, a lookout, and I nominate Shem. He has sailed under his father, and I have it on good authority that he is a nautical expert."

Holmes hesitated for an instant. He was considering the necessity of disciplining the recalcitrant Blackstone, but he finally yielded.

"Very well," he said. "Shem be it. Bo'sun, pipe Shem on deck, and tell him that general order number one requires him to report at the mizzentop right away, and that immediately he sees anything he shall come below and make it known to me. As for the rest of us, having a very considerable appetite, I do now decree that it is dinner-time. Shall we go below?"

"I don't think I care for any, thank you," said Raleigh. "Fact is—ah—I dined last week, and am not hungry."

Noah laughed. "Oh, come below and watch us eat, then," he said. "It'll do you good."

But there was no reply. Raleigh had plunged head first into his state-room, which fortunately happened to be on the upper deck. The rest of the spirits repaired below to the saloon, where they were soon engaged in an animated discussion of such viands as the larder provided.

"This," said Dr. Johnson, from the head of the table, "is what I call comfort. I don't know that I am so anxious to recover the House-boat, after all."

"Nor I," said Socrates, "with a ship like this to go off cruising on, and with such a larder. Look at the thickness of that puree, Doctor—"

"Excuse me," said Boswell, faintly, "but I—I've left my note-bub-book upstairs, Doctor, and I'd like to go up and get it."

"Certainly," said Dr. Johnson. "I judge from your colour, which is highly suggestive of a modern magazine poster, that it might be well too if you stayed on deck for a little while and made a few entries in your commonplace book."

"Thank you," said Boswell, gratefully. "Shall you say anything clever during dinner, sir? If so, I might be putting it down while I'm up—"

"Get out!" roared the Doctor. "Get up as high as you can—get up with Shem on the mizzentop—"

"Very good, sir," replied Boswell, and he was off.

"You ought to be more lenient with him, Doctor," said Bonaparte; "he means well."

"I know it," observed Johnson; "but he's so very previous. Last winter, at Chaucer's dinner to Burns, I made a speech, which Boswell printed a week before it was delivered, with the words 'laughter' and 'uproarious applause' interspersed through it. It placed me in a false position."

"How did he know what you were going to say?" queried Demosthenes.

"Don't know," replied Johnson. "Kind of mind-reader, I fancy," he added, blushing a trifle. "But, Captain Holmes, what do you deduce from your observation of the wake of the House-boat? If she's going to Paris, why the change?"

"I have two theories," replied the detective.

"Which is always safe," said Le Coq.

"Always; it doubles your chances of success," acquiesced Holmes. "Anyhow, it gives you a choice, which makes it more interesting. The change of her course from Londonward to Parisward proves to me either that Kidd is not satisfied with the extent of the revenge he has already taken, and wishes to ruin you gentlemen financially by turning your wives, daughters, and sisters loose on the Parisian shops, or that the pirates have themselves been overthrown by the ladies, who have decided to prolong their cruise and get some fun out of their misfortune."

"And where else than to Paris would anyone in search of pleasure go?" asked Bonaparte.

"I had more fun a few miles outside of Brussels," said Wellington, with a sly wink at Washington.

"Oh, let up on that!" retorted Bonaparte. "It wasn't you beat me at Waterloo. You couldn't have beaten me at a plain ordinary game of old-maid with a stacked pack of cards, much less in the game of war, if you hadn't had the elements with you."

"Tut!" snapped Wellington. "It was clear science laid you out, Boney."

"*Taisey-voo!*" shouted the irate Corsican. "Clear science be hanged! Wet science was what did it. If it hadn't been for the rain, my little Duke, I should have been in London within a week, my grenadiers would have been camping in your Rue Peekadeely, and the Old Guard all over everywhere else."

"You must have had a gay army, then," laughed Cæsar. "What are French soldiers made of, that they can't stand the wet—unshrunk linen or flannel?"

"Bah!" observed Napoleon, shrugging his shoulders and walking a few paces away. "You do not understand the French. The Frenchman is not a pell-mell soldier like you Romans; he is the poet of arms; he does not go in for glory at the expense of his dignity; style, form, is dearer to him than honour, and he has no use for fighting in the wet and coming out of the fight conspicuous as a victor with the curl out of his feathers and his epaulets rusted with the damp. There is no glory in water. But if we had had umbrellas and mackintoshes, as every Englishman who comes to the Continent always has, and a bath-tub for everybody, then would your Waterloo have been different again, and the great democracy of Europe with a Bonaparte for emperor would have been founded for what the Americans call the keeps; and as for your little Great Britain, ha! she would have become the Blackwell's Island of the Greater France."

"You're almost as funny as *Punch* isn't," drawled Wellington, with an angry gesture at Bonaparte. "You weren't within telephoning distance of victory all day. We simply played with you, my boy. It was a regular game of golf for us. We let you keep up pretty close and win a few holes, but on the home drive we had you beaten in one stroke. Go to, my dear Bonaparte, and stop talking about the flood."

"It's a lucky thing for us that Noah wasn't a Frenchman, eh?" said Frederick the Great. "How that rain would have fazed him if he had been! The human race would have been wiped out."

"Oh, pshaw!" ejaculated Noah, deprecating the unseemliness of the quarrel, and putting his arm affectionately about Bonaparte's shoulder. "When you come down to that, I was French—as French as one could be in those days—and these Gallic subjects of my friend here were, every one of 'em, my lineal descendants, and their hatred of rain was inherited directly from me, their ancestor."

"Are not we English as much your descendants?" queried Wellington, arching his eyebrows.

"You are," said Noah, "but you take after Mrs. Noah more than after me. Water never fazes a woman, and your delight in tubs is an essentially feminine trait. The first thing Mrs. Noah carried aboard was a laundry outfit, and then she went back for rugs and coats and all sorts of hand-baggage. Gad, it makes me laugh to this day when I think of it! She looked for all the world like an Englishman travelling on the Continent as she walked up the gang-plank behind the elephants, each elephant with a Gladstone bag in his trunk and a hat-box tied to his tail." Here the venerable old weather-prophet winked at Munchausen, and the little quarrel which had been imminent passed off in a general laugh.

"Where's Boswell? He ought to get that anecdote," said Johnson.

145

"I've locked him up in the library," said Holmes. "He's in charge of the log, and as I have a pretty good general idea as to what is about to happen, I have mapped out a skeleton of the plot and set him to work writing it up." Here the detective gave a sudden start, placed his hand to his ear, listened intently for an instant, and, taking out his watch and glancing at it, added, quietly, "In three minutes Shem will be in here to announce a discovery, and one of great importance, I judge, from the squeak."

The assemblage gazed earnestly at Holmes for a moment.

"The squeak?" queried Raleigh.

"Precisely," said Holmes. "The squeak is what I said, and as I always say what I mean, it follows logically that I meant what I said."

"I heard no squeak," observed Dr. Johnson; "and, furthermore, I fail to see how a squeak, if I had heard it, would have portended a discovery of importance."

"It would not—to you," said Holmes; "but with me it is different. My hearing is unusually acute. I can hear the dropping of a pin through a stone wall ten feet thick; any sound within a mile of my eardrum vibrates thereon with an intensity which would surprise you, and it is by the use of cocaine that I have acquired this wonderfully acute sense. A property which dulls the senses of most people renders mine doubly apprehensive; therefore, gentlemen, while to you there was no auricular disturbance, to me there was. I heard Shem sliding down the mast a minute since. The fact that he slid down the mast instead of climbing down the rigging showed that he was in great haste, therefore he must have something to communicate of great importance."

"Why isn't he here already, then? It wouldn't take him two minutes to get from the deck here," asked the ever-suspicious Le Coq.

"It is simple," returned Holmes, calmly. "If you will go yourself and slide down that mast you will see. Shem has stopped for a little witch-hazel to soothe his burns. It is no cool matter sliding down a mast two hundred feet in height."

As Sherlock Holmes spoke the door burst open and Shem rushed in.

"A signal of distress, captain!" he cried.

"From what quarter—to larboard?" asked Holmes.

"No," returned Shem, breathless.

"Then it must be dead ahead," said Holmes.

"Why not to starboard?" asked Le Coq, dryly.

"Because," answered Holmes, confidently, "it never happens so. If you had ever read a truly exciting sea-tale, my dear Le Coq, you would have known that interesting things, and particularly signals of distress, are never seen except to larboard or dead ahead."

A murmur of applause greeted this retort, and Le Coq subsided.

"The nature of the signal?" demanded Holmes.

"A black flag, skull and cross-bones down, at half-mast!" cried Shem, "and on a rock-bound coast!"

"They're marooned, by heavens!" shouted Holmes, springing to his feet and rushing to the deck, where he was joined immediately by Sir Walter, Dr. Johnson, Bonaparte, and the others.

"Isn't he a daisy?" whispered Demosthenes to Diogenes as they climbed the stairs.

"He is more than that; he's a blooming orchid," said Diogenes, with intense enthusiasm. "I think I'll get my X-ray lantern and see if he's honest."

9

Captain Kidd Meets with an Obstacle

"Excuse me, Your Majesty," remarked Helen of Troy as Cleopatra accorded permission to Captain Kidd to speak, "I have not been introduced to this gentleman nor has he been presented to me, and I really cannot consent to any proceeding so irregular as this. I do not speak to gentlemen I have not met, nor do I permit them to address me."

"Hear, hear!" cried Xanthippe. "I quite agree with the principle of my young friend from Troy. It may be that when we claimed for ourselves all the rights of men that the right to speak and be spoken to by other men without an introduction was included in the list, but I for one have no desire to avail myself of the privilege, especially when it's a horrid-looking man like this."

Kidd bowed politely, and smiled so terribly that several of the ladies fainted.

"I will withdraw," he said, turning to Cleopatra; and it must be said that his suggestion was prompted by his heartfelt wish, for now that he found himself thus conspicuously brought before so many women, with falsehood on his lips, his courage began to ooze.

"Not yet, please," answered the chair-lady. "I imagine we can get about this difficulty without much trouble."

"I think it a perfectly proper objection too," observed Delilah, rising. "If we ever needed etiquette we need it now. But I have a plan which will obviate any further difficulty. If there is no one among us who is sufficiently well acquainted with the gentleman to present him formally to us, I will for the time being take upon myself the office of ship's barber and cut his hair. I understand that it is quite the proper thing for barbers to talk, while cutting their hair, to persons to whom they have not been introduced. And, besides, he really needs a hair-cut badly. Thus I shall establish an acquaintance with the captain, after which I can with propriety introduce him to the rest of you."

"Perhaps the gentleman himself might object to that," put in Queen Elizabeth. "If I remember rightly, your last customer was very much dissatisfied with the trim you gave him."

"It will be unnecessary to do what Delilah proposes," said Mrs. Noah, with a kindly smile, as she rose up from the corner in which she had been sitting, an interested listener. "I can introduce the gentleman to you all with perfect propriety. He's a member of my family. His grandfather was the great-grandson a thousand and eight times removed of my son Shem's great-grandnephew on his father's side. His relationship to me is therefore obvious, though from what I know of his reputation I think he takes more after my husband's ancestors than my own. Willie, dear, these ladies are friends of mine. Ladies, this young man is one of my most famous descendants. He has been a man of many adventures, and he has been hanged once, which, far from making him undesirable as an acquaintance, has served merely to render him harmless, and therefore a safe person to know. Now, my son, go ahead and speak your piece."

The good old spirit sat down, and the scruples of the objectors having thus been satisfied, Captain Kidd began.

"Now that I know you all," he remarked, as pleasantly as he could under the circumstances, "I feel that I can speak more freely, and certainly with a great deal less embarrassment than if I were addressing a gathering of entire strangers. I am not much of a hand at speaking, and have always felt somewhat nonplussed at finding myself in a position of this nature. In my whole career I never experienced but one irresistible impulse to make a public address of any length, and that was upon that unhappy occasion to which the greatest and grandest of my great-grandmothers has alluded, and that only as the chain by which I was suspended in mid-air tightened about my vocal chords. At that moment I could have talked impromptu for a year, so fast and numerously did thoughts of the uttermost import surge upward into my brain; but circumstances over which I had no control prevented the utterance of those thoughts, and that speech is therefore lost to the world."

"He has the gift of continuity," observed Madame Récamier.

"Ought to be in the United States Senate," smiled Elizabeth.

"I wish I could make up my mind as to whether he is outrageously handsome or desperately ugly," remarked Helen of Troy. "He fascinates me, but whether it is the fascination of liking or of horror I can't tell, and it's quite important."

"Ladies," resumed the captain, his uneasiness increasing as he came to the point, "I am but the agent of your respective husbands, *fiancés*, and other masculine guardians. The gentlemen who were previously the tenants of this club-house have delegated to me the important, and I may add highly agreeable, task of showing you the world. They have noted of late years the growth of that feeling of unrest which is becoming every day more and more conspicuous in feminine circles in all parts of the universe—on the earth, where women are clamouring to vote, and to be allowed to go out late at night without an escort; in Hades, where, as you are no doubt aware, the management of the government has fallen almost wholly into the hands of the Furies; and even in the halls of Jupiter himself, where, I am credibly informed, Juno has been taking private lessons in the art of hurling thunderbolts—information which the extraordinary quality of recent electrical storms on the earth would seem to confirm.

"Thunderbolts of late years have been cast hither and yon in a most erratic fashion, striking where they were least expected, as those of you who keep in touch with the outer world must be fully aware. Now, actuated by their usual broad and liberal motives, the men of Hades wish to meet the views of you ladies to just that extent that your views are based upon a wise selection, in turn based upon experience, and they have come to me and in so many words have said, 'Mr. Kidd, we wish the women of Hades to see the world. We want them to be satisfied. We do not like this constantly increasing spirit of unrest. We, who have seen all the life that we care to see, do not ourselves feel equal to the task of showing them about. We will pay you liberally if you will take our House-boat, which they have always been anxious to enter, and personally conduct our beloved ones to Paris, London, and elsewhere. Let them see as much of life as they can stand.

"Accord them every privilege. Spare no expense; only bring them back again to us safe and sound.' These were their words, ladies. I asked them why they didn't come along themselves, saying that even if they were tired of it all, they should make some personal sacrifice to your comfort; and they answered, reasonably and well, that they would be only too glad to do so, but that they feared they might unconsciously seem to exert a repressing influence upon you. 'We want them to feel absolutely free, Captain Kidd,' said they, 'and if we are along they may not feel so.' The answer was convincing, ladies, and I accepted the commission."

"But we knew nothing of all this," interposed Elizabeth. "The subject was not broached to us by our husbands, brothers, *fiancés*, or fathers. My brother, Sir Walter Raleigh—"

Cleopatra chuckled. "Brother! Brother's good," she said.

"Well, that's what he is," retorted Elizabeth, quickly. "I promised to be a sister to him, and I'm going to keep my word. That's the kind of a queen I am. I was about to remark," Elizabeth added, turning to the captain, "that my brother, Sir Walter Raleigh, never even hinted at any such plan, and usually he asked my advice in matters of so great importance."

"That is easily accounted for, *madame*," retorted Kidd. "Sir Walter intended this as a little surprise for you, that is all. The arrangements were all placed in his hands, and it was he who bound us all to secrecy. None of the ladies were to be informed of it."

"It does not sound altogether plausible," interposed Portia. "If you ladies do not object, I should like to cross-examine this— ah—gentleman."

Kidd paled visibly. He was not prepared for any such trial; however, he put as good a face on the matter as he could, and announced his willingness to answer any questions that he might be asked.

"Shall we put him under oath?" asked Cleopatra.

"As you please, ladies," said the pirate. "A pirate's word is as good as his bond; but I'll take an oath if you choose—a half-dozen of 'em, if need be."

"I fancy we can get along without that," said Portia. "Now, Captain Kidd, who first proposed this plan?"

"Socrates," said Kidd, unblushingly, with a sly glance at Xanthippe.

"What?" cried Xanthippe. "My husband propose anything that would contribute to my pleasure or intellectual advancement? Bah! Your story is transparently false at the outset."

"Nevertheless," said Kidd, "the scheme was proposed by Socrates. He said a trip of that kind for Xanthippe would be very restful and health-giving."

"For me?" cried Xanthippe, sceptically.

"No, *madame*, for him," retorted Kidd.

"Ah—ho-ho! That's the way of it, eh?" said Xanthippe, flushing to the roots of her hair. "Very likely. You—ah—you will excuse my doubting your word, Captain Kidd, a moment since. I withdraw my remark, and in order to make fullest reparation, I beg to assure these ladies that I am now perfectly convinced that you are telling the truth. That last observation is just like my husband, and when I get back home again, if I ever do, well—ha, ha!—we'll have a merry time, that's all."

"And what was—ah—Bassanio's connection with this affair?" added Portia, hesitatingly.

"He was not informed of it," said Kidd, archly. "I am not acquainted with Bassanio, my lady, but I overheard Sir Walter enjoining upon the others the absolute necessity of keeping the whole affair from Bassanio, because he was afraid he would not consent to it. 'Bassanio has a most beautiful wife, gentlemen,' said Sir Walter, 'and he wouldn't think of parting with her under any circumstances; therefore let us keep our intentions a secret from him.' I did not hear whom the gentleman married, *madame*; but the others, Prince Hamlet, the Duke of Buckingham, and Louis the Fourteenth, all agreed that Mrs. Bassanio was too beautiful a person to be separated from, and that it was better, therefore, to keep Bassanio in the dark as to their little enterprise until it was too late for him to interfere."

A pink glow of pleasure suffused the lovely countenance of the cross-examiner, and it did not require a very sharp eye to see that the wily Kidd had completely won her over to his side. On the other hand, Elizabeth's brow became as corrugated as her ruff, and the spirit of the pirate shivered to the core as he turned and gazed upon that glowering face.

"Sir Walter agreed to that, did he?" snapped Elizabeth. "And yet he was willing to part with—ah—his sister."

"Well, your Majesty," began Kidd, hesitatingly, "you see it was this way: Sir Walter—er—did say that, but—ah—he—ah—but he added that he of course merely judged—er—this man Bassanio's feelings by his own in parting from his sister—"

"Did he say sister?" cried Elizabeth.

"Well—no—not in those words," shuffled Kidd, perceiving quickly wherein his error lay, "but—ah—I jumped at the conclusion, seeing his intense enthusiasm for the lady's beauty and—er—intellectual qualities, that he referred to you, and it is from yourself that I have gained my knowledge as to the fraternal, not to say sororal, relationship that exists between you."

"That man's a diplomat from Diplomaville!" muttered Sir Henry Morgan, who, with Abeuchapeta and Conrad, was listening at the port without.

"He is that," said Abeuchapeta, "but he can't last much longer. He's perspiring like a pitcher of ice-water on a hot day, and a spirit of his size and volatile nature can't stand much of that without evaporating. If you will observe him closely you will see that his left arm already has vanished into thin air."

"By Jove!" whispered Conrad, "that's a fact! If they don't let up on him he'll vanish. He's getting excessively tenuous about the top of his head."

All of which was only too true. Subjected to a scrutiny which he had little expected, the deceitful ambassador of the thieving band was rapidly dissipating, and, as those without had so fearsomely noted, was in imminent danger of complete sublimation, which, in the case of one possessed of so little elementary purity, meant nothing short of annihilation. Fortunately for Kidd, however, his wonderful tact had stemmed the tide of suspicion. Elizabeth was satisfied with his explanation, and in the minds of at least three of the most influential ladies on board, Portia, Xanthippe, and Elizabeth, he had become a creature worthy of credence, which meant that he had nothing more to fear.

"I am prepared, your Majesty," said Elizabeth, addressing Cleopatra, "to accept from this time on the gentleman's word.

The little that he has already told us is hall-marked with truth. I should like to ask, however, one more question, and that is how our gentleman friends expected to embark us upon this voyage without letting us into the secret?"

"Oh, as for that," replied Kidd, with a deep-drawn sigh of relief, for he too had noticed the gradual evaporation of his arm and the incipient etherisation of his cranium—"as for that, it was simple enough. There was to have been a day set apart for ladies' day at the club, and when you were all on board we were quietly to weigh anchor and start. The fact that you had anticipated the day, of your own volition, was telephoned by my scouts to me at my headquarters, and that news was by me transmitted by messenger to Sir Walter at Charon's Glen Island, where the long-talked-of fight between Samson and Goliath was taking place.

"Raleigh immediately replied, '*Good! Start at once. Paris first. Unlimited credit. Love to Elizabeth.*' Wherefore, ladies," he added, rising from his chair and walking to the door—"wherefore you are here and in my care. Make yourselves comfortable, and with the aid of the fashion papers which you have already received prepare yourselves for the joys that await you. With the aid of Madame Récamier and Baedeker's *Paris*, which you will find in the library, it will be your own fault if when you arrive there you resemble a great many less fortunate women who don't know what they want."

With these words Kidd disappeared through the door, and fainted in the arms of Sir Henry Morgan. The strain upon him had been too great.

"A charming fellow," said Portia, as the pirate disappeared.

"Most attractive," said Elizabeth.

"Handsome, too, don't you think?" asked Helen of Troy.

"And truthful beyond peradventure," observed Xanthippe, as she reflected upon the words the captain had attributed to Socrates. "I didn't believe him at first, but when he told me what my sweet-tempered philosopher had said, I was convinced."

"He's a sweet child," interposed Mrs. Noah, fondly. "One of

my favourite grandchildren."

"Which makes it embarrassing for me to say," cried Cassandra, starting up angrily, "that he is a base caitiff!"

Had a bomb been dropped in the middle of the room, it could not have created a greater sensation than the words of Cassandra.

"What?" cried several voices at once. "A caitiff?"

"A caitiff with a capital K," retorted Cassandra. "I know that, because while he was telling his story I was listening to it with one ear and looking forward into the middle of next week with the other—I mean the other eye—and I saw—"

"Yes, you saw?" cried Cleopatra.

"I saw that he was deceiving us. Mark my words, ladies, he is a base caitiff," replied Cassandra—"a base caitiff."

"What did you see?" cried Elizabeth, excitedly.

"This," said Cassandra, and she began a narration of future events which I must defer to the next chapter. Meanwhile his associates were endeavouring to restore the evaporated portions of the prostrated Kidd's spirit anatomy by the use of a steam-atomizer, but with indifferent success. Kidd's training had not fitted him for an intellectual combat with superior women, and he suffered accordingly.

10
A WARNING ACCEPTED

"It is with no desire to interrupt my friend Cassandra unnecessarily," said Mrs. Noah, as the prophetess was about to narrate her story, "that I rise to beg her to remember that, as an ancestress of Captain Kidd, I hope she will spare a grandmother's feelings, if anything in the story she is about to tell is improper to be placed before the young. I have been so shocked by the stories of perfidy and baseness generally that have been published of late years, that I would interpose a protest while there is yet time if there is a line in Cassandra's story which ought to be withheld from the public; a protest based upon my affection for posterity, and in the interests of morality everywhere."

"You may rest easy upon that score, my dear Mrs. Noah," said the prophetess. "What I have to say would commend itself, I am sure, even to the ears of a British matron; and while it is as complete a demonstration of man's perfidy as ever was, it is none the less as harmless a little tale as the Dottie Dimple books or any other more recent study of New England character."

"Thank you for the load your words have lifted from my mind," said Mrs. Noah, settling back in her chair, a satisfied expression upon her gentle countenance. "I hope you will understand why I spoke, and withal why modern literature generally has been so distressful to me. When you reflect that the world is satisfied that most of man's criminal instincts are the result of heredity, and that Mr. Noah and I are unable to shift the responsibility for posterity to other shoulders than our own, you will understand my position. We were about the most domestic old couple that ever lived, and when we see the long and varied assortment of crimes that are cropping out everywhere in our descendants it is painful to us to realize what a pair of unconsciously wicked old fogies we must have been."

"We all understand that," said Cleopatra, kindly; "and we are all prepared to acquit you of any responsibility for the advanced condition of wickedness today. Man has progressed since your time, my dear grandma, and the modern improvements in the science of crime are no more attributable to you than the invention of the telephone or the oyster cocktail is attributable to your lord and master."

"Thank you kindly," murmured the old lady, and she resumed her knitting upon a phantom tam-o'-shanter, which she was making as a Christmas surprise for her husband.

"When Captain Kidd began his story," said Cassandra, "he made one very bad mistake, and yet one which was prompted by that courtesy which all men instinctively adopt when addressing women. When he entered the room he removed his hat, and therein lay his fatal error, if he wished to convince me of the truth of his story, for with his hat removed I could see the workings of his mind. While you ladies were watching his lips or his

156

eyes, some of you taking in the gorgeous details of his dress, all of you hanging upon his every word, I kept my eye fixed firmly upon his imagination, and I saw, what you did not, *that he was drawing wholly upon that!*"

"How extraordinary!" cried Elizabeth.

"Yes—and fortunate," said Cassandra. "Had I not done so, a week hence we should, every one of us, have been lost in the surging wickedness of the city of Paris."

"But, Cassandra," said Trilby, who was anxious to return once more to the beautiful city by the Seine, "he told us we were going to Paris."

"Of course he did," said Madame Récamier, "and in so many words. Certainly he was not drawing upon his imagination there."

"And one might be lost in a very much worse place," put in Marguerite de Valois, "if, indeed, it were possible to lose us in Paris at all. I fancy that I know enough about Paris to find my way about."

"Humph!" ejaculated Cassandra. "What a foolish little thing you are! You don't imagine that the Paris of today is the Paris of your time, or even the Paris of that sweet child Trilby's time, do you? If you do you are very much mistaken. I almost wish I had not warned you of your danger and had let you go, just to see those eyes of yours open with amazement at the change. You'd find your Louvre a very different sort of a place from what it used to be, my dear lady. Those pleasing little windows through which your relations were wont in olden times to indulge in target practice at people who didn't go to their church are now kept closed; the galleries which used to swarm with people, many of whom ought to have been hanged, now swarm with pictures, many of which ought not to have been hung; the romance which clung about its walls is as much a part of the dead past as yourselves, and were you to materialize suddenly therein you would find yourselves jostled and hustled and trodden upon by the curious from other lands, with Argus eyes taking in five hundred pictures a minute, and traversing those halls at a rate of speed at which Mercury himself would stand aghast."

"But my beloved Tuileries?" cried Marie Antoinette.

"Has been swallowed up by a play-ground for the people, my dear," said Cassandra, gently. "Paris is no place for us, and it is the intention of these men, in whose hands we are, to take us there and then desert us. Can you imagine anything worse than ourselves, the phantoms of a glorious romantic past, basely deserted in the streets of a wholly strange, superficial, material city of today? What do you think, Elizabeth, would be your fate if, faint and famished, you begged for sustenance at an English door today, and when asked your name and profession were to reply, 'Elizabeth, Queen of England'?"

"Insane asylum," said Elizabeth, shortly.

"Precisely. So in Paris with the rest of us," said Cassandra.

"How do you know all this?" asked Trilby, still unconvinced.

"I know it just as you knew how to become a *prima donna,*" said Cassandra. "I am, however, my own Svengali, which is rather preferable to the patent detachable hypnotizer you had. I hypnotize myself, and direct my mind into the future. I was a professional forecaster in the days of ancient Troy, and if my revelations had been heeded the Priam family would, I doubt not, still be doing business at the old stand, and Mr. Æneas would not have grown round-shouldered giving his poor father a pickyback ride on the opening night of the horse-show, so graphically depicted by Virgil."

"I never heard about that," said Trilby. "It sounds like a very funny story, though."

"Well, it wasn't so humorous for some as it was for others," said Cassandra, with a sly glance at Helen. "The fact is, until you mentioned it yourself, it never occurred to me that there was much fun in any portion of the Trojan incident, excepting perhaps the *delirium tremens* of old Laocoon, who got no more than he deserved for stealing my thunder. I had warned Troy against the Greeks, and they all laughed at me, and said my eye to the future was *strabismatic*; that the Greeks couldn't get into Troy at all, even if they wanted to. And then the Greeks made a great wooden horse as a gift for the Trojans, and when I turned my X-ray gaze upon it I saw that it contained about six brigades of infantry, three artillery regiments, and sharp-shooters by the score.

"It was a sort of military Noah's Ark; but I knew that the prejudice against me was so strong that nobody would believe what I told them. So I said nothing. My prophecies never came true, they said, failing to observe that my warning as to what would be was in itself the cause of their non-fulfilment. But desiring to save Troy, I sent for Laocoon and told him all about it, and he went out and announced it as his own private prophecy; and then, having tried to drown his conscience in strong waters, he fell a victim to the usual serpentine hallucination, and everybody said he wasn't sober, and therefore unworthy of belief. The horse was accepted, hauled into the city, and that night orders came from hindquarters to the regiments concealed inside to march.

"They marched, and next morning Troy had been removed from the map; ninety *per cent.* of the Trojans died suddenly, and Æneas, grabbing up his family in one hand and his gods in the other, went yachting for several seasons, ultimately settling down in Italy. All of this could have been avoided if the Trojans would have taken the hint from my prophecies. They preferred, however, not to do it, with the result that today no one but Helen and myself knows even where Troy was, and we'll never tell."

"It is all true," said Helen, proudly. "I was the woman who was at the bottom of it all, and I can testify that Cassandra always told the truth, which is why she was always so unpopular. When anything that was unpleasant happened, after it was all over she would turn and say, sweetly, 'I told you so.' She was the original 'I told you so' nuisance, and of course she had the *newspapy-nuses* down on her, because she never left them any sensation to spring upon the public. If she had only told a fib once in a while, the public would have had more confidence in her."

"Thank you for your endorsement," said Cassandra, with a nod at Helen. "With such testimony I cannot see how you can refrain from taking my advice in this matter; and I tell you, ladies, that this man Kidd has made his story up out of whole cloth; the men of Hades had no more to do with our being here than we had; they were as much surprised as we are to find us gone. Kidd himself was not aware of our presence, and his object in taking us to Paris is to leave us stranded there, disembodied spirits, vagrant souls with no familiar haunts to haunt, no place to rest, and nothing before us save perpetual exile in a world that would have no sympathy for us in our misfortune, and no belief in our continued existence."

"But what, then, shall we do?" cried Ophelia, wringing her hands in despair.

"It is a terrible problem," said Cleopatra, anxiously; "and yet it does seem as if our woman's instinct ought to show us some way out of our trouble."

"The Committee on Treachery," said Delilah, "has already suggested a chafing-dish party, with Lucretia Borgia in charge of the lobster Newberg."

"That is true," said Lucretia; "but I find, in going through my reticule, that my maid, for some reason unknown to me, has failed to renew my supply of poisons. I shall discharge her on my return home, for she knows that I never go anywhere without them; but that does not help matters at this juncture. The sad fact remains that I could prepare a thousand delicacies for these pirates without fatal results."

"You mean immediately fatal, do you not?" suggested Xanthippe. "I could myself prepare a cake which would in time reduce our captors to a state of absolute dependence, but of course the effect is not immediate."

"We might give a *musicale*, and let Trilby sing 'Ben Bolt' to them," suggested Marguerite de Valois, with a giggle.

"Don't be flippant, please," said Portia. "We haven't time to waste on flippant suggestions. Perhaps a court-martial of these pirates, supplemented by a yard-arm, wouldn't be a bad thing. I'll prosecute the case."

"You forget that you are dealing with immortal spirits," observed Cleopatra. "If these creatures were mortals, hanging them would be all right, and comparatively easy, considering that we outnumber them ten to one, and have many resources for getting them, more or less, in our power, but they are not. They have gone through the refining process of dissolution once, and there's an end to that. Our only resource is in the line of deception, and if we cannot deceive them, then we have ceased to be women."

"That is truly said," observed Elizabeth. "And inasmuch as we have already provided ourselves with a suitable committee for the preparation of our plans of a deceptive nature, I move, as the easiest possible solution of the difficulty for the rest of us, that the Committee on Treachery be requested to go at once into executive session, with orders not to come out of it until they have suggested a plausible plan of campaign against our abductors. We must be rid of them. Let the Committee on Treachery say how."

"Second the motion," said Mrs. Noah. "You are a very clear-headed young woman, Lizzie, and your grandmother is proud of you."

The Committee on Treachery were about to protest, but the chair refused to entertain any debate upon the question, which was put and carried with a storm of approval.

Five minutes later a note was handed through the port, addressed to Cleopatra, which read as follows:

"Dear *Madame*,—Six bells has just struck, and the officers and crew are hungry. Will you and your fair companions co-operate with us in our enterprise by having a hearty dinner ready within two hours? A speck has appeared on the horizon which betokens a coming storm, else we would prepare our supper ourselves. As it is, we feel that your safety depends on our remaining on deck. If there is any beer on the ice, we prefer it to tea. Two cases will suffice.

"Yours respectfully,

"Henry Morgan, Bart., First Mate."

"Hurrah!" cried Cleopatra, as she read this communication.

161

"I have an idea. Tell the Committee on Treachery to appear before the full meeting at once."

The committee was summoned, and Cleopatra announced her plan of operation, and it was unanimously adopted; but what it was we shall have to wait for another chapter to learn.

11
Marooned

When Captain Holmes arrived upon deck he seized his glass, and, gazing intently through it for a moment, perceived that the faithful Shem had not deceived him. Flying at half-mast from a rude, roughly hewn pole set upon a rocky height was the black flag, emblem of piracy, and, as Artemus Ward put it, "with the second joints reversed." It was in very truth a signal of distress.

"I make it a point never to be surprised," observed Holmes, as he peered through the glass, "but this beats me. I didn't know there was an island of this nature in these latitudes. Blackstone, go below and pipe Captain Cook on deck. Perhaps he knows what island that is."

"You'll have to excuse me, Captain Holmes," replied the Judge. "I didn't ship on this voyage as a cabin-boy or a messenger-boy. Therefore I—"

"Bonaparte, put the Judge in irons," interrupted Holmes, sternly. "I expect to be obeyed, Judge Blackstone, whether you shipped as a Lord Chief-Justice or a state-room steward. When I issue an order it must be obeyed. Step lively there, Bonaparte. Get his honour ironed and summon your marines. We may have work to do before night. Hamlet, pipe Captain Cook on deck."

"Aye, aye, sir," replied Hamlet, with alacrity, as he made off.

"That's the way to obey orders," said Holmes, with a scornful glance at Blackstone.

"I was only jesting, Captain," said the latter, paling somewhat.

"That's all right," said Holmes, taking up his glass again. "So was I when I ordered you in irons, and in order that you may appreciate the full force of the joke I repeat it. Bonaparte, do your duty."

In an instant the order was obeyed, and the unhappy Judge shortly found himself manacled and alone in the forecastle. Meanwhile Captain Cook, in response to the commander's order, repaired to the deck and scanned the distant coast.

"I can't place it," he said. "It can't be Monte Cristo, can it?"

"No, it can't," said the Count, who stood hard by. "My island was in the Mediterranean, and even if it dragged anchor it couldn't have got out through the Strait of Gibraltar."

"Perhaps it's Robinson Crusoe's island," suggested Doctor Johnson.

"Not it," observed De Foe. "If it is, the rest of you will please keep off. It's mine, and I may want to use it again. I've been having a number of interviews with Crusoe latterly, and he's given me a lot of new points, which I intend incorporating in a sequel for the *Cimmerian Magazine.*"

"Well, in the name of Atlas, what island is it, then?" roared Holmes, angrily. "What is the matter with all you learned lubbers that I have brought along on this trip? Do you suppose I've brought you to whistle up favourable winds? Not by the beard of the Prophet! I brought you to give me information, and now when I ask for the name of a simple little island like that in plain sight there's not one of you able so much as to guess at it reasonably. The next man I ask for information goes into irons with Judge Blackstone if he doesn't answer me instantly with the information I want. Munchausen, what island is that?"

"Ahem! that?" replied Munchausen, trembling, as he reflected upon the Captain's threat. "What? Nobody knows what island that is? Why, you surprise me—"

"See here, Baron," retorted Holmes, menacingly, "I ask you a plain question, and I want a plain answer, with no evasions to gain time. Now it's irons or an answer. What island is that?"

"It's an island that doesn't appear on any chart, Captain," Munchausen responded instantly, pulling himself together for a mighty effort, "and it has never been given a name; but as you insist upon having one, we'll call it Holmes Island, in your honour. It is not stationary. It is a floating island of lava formation, and is a menace to every craft that goes to sea. I spent a year of my life upon it once, and it is more barren than the desert of Sahara, because you cannot raise even sand upon it, and it is devoid of water of any sort, salt or fresh."

"What did you live on during that year?" asked Holmes, eying him narrowly.

"Canned food from wrecks," replied the Baron, feeling much easier now that he had got a fair start—"canned food from wrecks, commander. There is a magnetic property in the upper stratum of this piece of derelict real estate, sir, which attracts to it every bit of canned substance that is lost overboard in all parts of the world. A ship is wrecked, say, in the Pacific Ocean, and ultimately all the loose metal upon her will succumb to the irresistible attraction of this magnetic upper stratum, and will find its way to its shores. So in any other part of the earth. Everything metallic turns up here sooner or later; and when you consider that thousands of vessels go down every year, vessels which are provisioned with tinned foods only, you will begin to comprehend how many millions of pounds of preserved salmon, sardines, *pâté de foie gras*, peaches, and so on, can be found strewn along its coast."

"Munchausen," said Holmes, smiling, "by the blush upon your cheek, coupled with an occasional uneasy glance of the eye, I know that for once you are standing upon the, to you, unfamiliar ground of truth, and I admire you for it. There is nothing to be ashamed of in telling the truth occasionally. You are a man after my own heart. Come below and have a cocktail. Captain Cook, take command of the *Gehenna* during my absence; head her straight for Holmes Island, and when you discover anything new let me know. Bonaparte, in honor of Munchausen's remarkable genius I proclaim general amnesty to our prisoners, and you may release Blackstone from his dilemma; and if you have any tin soldiers among your marines, see that they are lashed to the rigging. I don't want this electric island of the Baron's to get a grip upon my military force at this juncture."

With this Holmes, followed by Munchausen, went below, and the two worthies were soon deep in the mysteries of a phantom cocktail, while Doctor Johnson and De Foe gazed mournfully out over the ocean at the floating island.

"De Foe," said Johnson, "that ought to be a lesson to you. This realism that you tie up to is all right when you are alone with your conscience; but when there are great things afoot, an imagination and a broad view as to the limitations of truth aren't at all bad. You or I might now be drinking that cocktail with Holmes if we'd only risen to the opportunity the way Munchausen did."

"That is true," said De Foe, sadly. "But I didn't suppose he wanted that kind of information. I could have spun a better yarn than that of Munchausen's with my eyes shut. I supposed he wanted truth, and I gave it."

"I'd like to know what has become of the House-boat," said Raleigh, anxiously gazing through the glass at the island. "I can see old Henry Morgan sitting down there on the rocks with his elbows on his knees and his chin in his hands, and Kidd and Abeuchapeta are standing back of him, yelling like mad, but there isn't a boat in sight."

"Who is that man, off to the right, dancing a *fandango?*" asked Johnson.

"It looks like Conrad, but I can't tell. He appears to have gone crazy. He's got that wild look on his face which betokens insanity. We'll have to be careful in our parleyings with these people," said Raleigh.

"Anything new?" asked Holmes, returning to the deck, smacking his lips in enjoyment of the cocktail.

"No—except that we are almost within hailing distance," said Cook.

"Then give orders to cast anchor," observed Holmes. "Bonaparte, take a crew of picked men ashore and bring those pirates aboard. Take the three musketeers with you, and don't let Kidd or Morgan give you any back talk. If they try any funny business, exorcise them."

"Aye, aye, sir," replied Bonaparte, and in a moment a boat had been lowered and a sturdy crew of sailors were pulling for the shore. As they came within ten feet of it the pirates made a mad dash down the rough, rocky hillside and clamoured to be saved.

"What's happened to you?" cried Bonaparte, ordering the sailors to back water, lest the pirates should too hastily board the boat and swamp her.

"We are marooned," replied Kidd, "and on an island of a volcanic nature. There isn't a square inch of it that isn't heated up to 125 degrees, and seventeen of us have already evaporated. Conrad has lost his reason; Abeuchapeta has become so tenuous that a child can see through him. As for myself, I am growing iridescent with anxiety, and unless I get off this infernal furnace I'll disappear like a soap-bubble. For Heaven's sake, then, General, take us off, on your own terms. We'll accept anything."

As if in confirmation of Kidd's words, six of the pirate crew collapsed and disappeared into thin air, and a glance at Abeuchapeta was proof enough of his condition. He had become as clear as crystal, and had it not been for his rugged outlines he would hardly have been visible even to his fellow-spirits. As for Kidd, he had taken on the aspect of a rainbow, and it was patent that his fears for himself were all too well founded.

Bonaparte embarked the leaders of the band first, returning subsequently for the others, and repaired with them at once to the *Gehenna*, where they were ushered into the presence of Sherlock Holmes. The first question he asked was as to the whereabouts of the House-boat.

"That we do not know," replied Kidd, mournfully, gazing downward at the wreck of his former self. "We came ashore, sir, early yesterday morning, in search of food. It appears that when—acting in a wholly inexcusable fashion, and influenced, I confess it, by motives of revenge—I made off with your clubhouse, I neglected to ascertain if it were well stocked with provisions, a fatal error; for when we endeavoured to get supper we discovered that the larder contained but half a bottle of *farcie* olives, two salted almonds, and a soda cracker—not a luxurious feast for sixty-nine pirates and a hundred and eighty-three women to sit down to."

"That's all nonsense," said Demosthenes. "The House Committee had provided enough supper for six hundred people, in anticipation of the appetite of the members on their return from the fight."

"Of course they did," said Confucius; "and it was a good one, too—salads, *salmon glacé*, lobsters—every blessed thing a man can't get at home we had; and what is more, they'd been delivered on board. I saw to that before I went up the river."

"Then," moaned Kidd, "it is as I suspected. We were the victims of base treachery on the part of those women."

"Treachery? Well, I like that. Call it reciprocity," said Hamlet, dryly.

"We were informed by the ladies that there was nothing for supper save the items I have already referred to," said Kidd. "I see it all now. We had tried to make them comfortable, and I put myself to some considerable personal inconvenience to make them easy in their minds, but they were ungrateful."

"Whatever induced you to take 'em along with you?" asked Socrates.

"We didn't want them," said Kidd. "We didn't know they were on board until it was too late to turn back. They'd broken in, and were having the club all to themselves in your absence."

"It served you good and right," said Socrates, with a laugh. "Next time you try to take things that don't belong to you, maybe you'll be a trifle more careful as to whose property you confiscate."

"But the House-boat—you haven't told us how you lost her," put in Raleigh, impatiently.

"Well, it was this way," said Kidd. "When, in response to our polite request for supper, the ladies said there was nothing to eat on board, something had to be done, for we were all as hungry as bears, and we decided to go ashore at the first port and provision. Unfortunately the crew got restive, and when this floating frying-pan loomed into view, to keep them good-natured we decided to land and see if we could beg, borrow, or steal some supplies. We had to. Observations taken with the sextant showed that there was no port within five hundred miles; the island looked as if it might be inhabited at least by goats, and ashore we went, every man of us, leaving the House-boat safely anchored in the harbour. At first we didn't mind the heat, and we hunted and hunted and hunted; but after three or four hours I began to notice that three of my sailors were shrivelling up, and Conrad began to act as if he were daft.

"Hawkins burst right before my eyes. Then Abeuchapeta got *prismatic* around the eyes and began to fade, and I noticed a slight iridescence about myself; and as for Morgan, he had the misfortune to lie down to take a nap in the sun, and when he waked up, his whole right side had evaporated. Then we saw what the trouble was. We'd struck this lava island, and were gradually succumbing to its intense heat. We rushed madly back to the harbour to embark; and our ship, gentlemen, and your House-boat, was slowly but surely disappearing over the horizon, and flying from the flag-staff at the fore were signals of farewell, with an unfeeling P.S. below to this effect: '*Don't wait up for us. We may not be back until late.*'"

There was a pause, during which Socrates laughed quietly to himself, while Abeuchapeta and the one-sided Morgan wept silently.

"That, gentlemen of the Associated Shades, is all I know of the whereabouts of the House-boat," continued Captain Kidd. "I have no doubt that the ladies practised a deception, to our discomfiture, and I must say that I think it was exceedingly clever—granting that it was desirable to be rid of us, which I don't, for we meant well by them, and they would have enjoyed themselves."

"But," cried Hamlet, "may they not now be in peril? They cannot navigate that ship."

"They got her out of the harbour all right," said Kidd. "And I judged from the figure at the helm that Mrs. Noah had taken charge. What kind of a seaman she is I don't know."

"Almighty bad," ejaculated Shem, turning pale. "It was she who ran us ashore on Ararat."

"Well, wasn't that what you wanted?" queried Munchausen.

"What we wanted!" cried Shem. "Well, I guess not. You don't want your yacht stranded on a mountain-top, do you? She was a dead loss there, whereas if mother hadn't been in such a hurry to get ashore, we could have waited a month and landed on the seaboard."

"You might have turned her into a summer hotel," suggested Munchausen.

"Well, we must up anchor and away," said Holmes. "Our pursuit has merely begun, apparently. We must overtake this vessel, and the question to be answered is—where?"

"That's easy," said Artemus Ward. "From what Shem says, I think we'd better look for her in the Himalayas."

"And, meanwhile, what shall be done with Kidd?" asked Holmes.

"He ought to be expelled from the club," said Johnson.

"We can't expel him, because he's not a member," replied Raleigh.

"Then elect him," suggested Ward.

"What on earth for?" growled Johnson.

"So that we can expel him," said Ward.

And while Boswell's hero was trying to get the value of this notion through his head, the others repaired to the deck, and the *Gehenna* was soon under way once more. Meanwhile Captain Kidd and his fellows were put in irons and stowed away in the forecastle, alongside of the water-cask in which Shylock lay in hiding.

12

THE ESCAPE AND THE END

If there was anxiety on board of the *Gehenna* as to the condition and whereabouts of the House-boat, there was by no means less uneasiness upon that vessel itself. Cleopatra's scheme for ridding herself and her abducted sisters of the pirates had worked to a charm, but, having worked thus, a new and hitherto undreamed-of problem, full of perplexities bearing upon their immediate safety, now confronted them. The sole representative of a sea-faring family on board was Mrs. Noah, and it did not require much time to see that her knowledge as to navigation was of an extremely primitive order, limited indeed to the science of floating.

When the last pirate had disappeared behind the rocks of Holmes Island, and all was in readiness for action, the good old lady, who had hitherto been as calm and unruffled as a child, began to get red in the face and to bustle about in a manner which betrayed considerable perturbation of spirit.

"Now, Mrs. Noah," said Cleopatra, as, peeping out from the billiard-room window, she saw Morgan disappearing in the distance, "the coast is clear, and I resign my position of chairman to you. We place the vessel in your hands, and ourselves subject to your orders. You are in command. What do you wish us to do?"

"Very well," replied Mrs. Noah, putting down her knitting and starting for the deck. "I'm not certain, but I think the first thing to do is to get her moving. Do you know, I've never discovered whether this boat is a steamboat or a sailing-vessel? Does anybody know?"

"I think it has a naphtha tank and a propeller," said Elizabeth, "although I don't know. It seems to me my brother Raleigh told me they'd had a naphtha engine put in last winter after the freshet, when the House-boat was carried ten miles down the river, and had to be towed back at enormous expense. They put it in so that if she were carried away again she could get back of her own power."

"That's unfortunate," said Mrs. Noah, "because I don't know anything about these new fangled notions. If there's any one here who knows anything about naphtha engines, I wish they'd speak."

"I'm of the opinion," said Portia, "that I can study out the theory of it in a short while."

"Very well, then," said Mrs. Noah, "you can do it. I'll appoint you engineer, and give you all your orders now, right away, in advance. Set her going and keep her going, and don't stop without a written order signed by me. We might as well be very careful, and have everything done properly, and it might happen that in the excitement of our trip you would misunderstand my spoken orders and make a fatal error. Therefore, pay no attention to unwritten orders.

"That will do for you for the present. Xanthippe, you may take Ophelia and Madame Récamier, and ten other ladies, and, every morning before breakfast, swab the larboard deck. Cassandra, Tuesdays you will devote to polishing the brasses in the dining-room, and the balance of your time I wish you to expend in dusting the bric-a-brac. Dido, you always were strong at building fires. I'll make you chief stoker. You will also assist Lucretia Borgia in the kitchen. Inasmuch as the latter's maid has neglected to supply her with the usual line of poisons, I think we can safely entrust to Lucretia's hands the responsibilities of the culinary department."

"I'm perfectly willing to do anything I can," said Lucretia, "but I must confess that I don't approve of your methods of commanding a ship. A ship's captain isn't a domestic martinet, as you are setting out to be. We didn't appoint you housekeeper."

"Now, my child," said Mrs. Noah, firmly, "I do not wish any words. If I hear any more impudence from you, I'll put you ashore without a reference; and the rest of you I would warn in all kindness that I will not tolerate insubordination. You may, all of you, have one night of the week and alternate Sundays off, but your work must be done. The regimen I am adopting is precisely that in vogue on the Ark, only I didn't have the help I have now, and things got into very bad shape. We were out forty days, and, while the food was poor and the service execrable, we never lost a life."

The boat gave a slight tremor.

"Hurrah," cried Elizabeth, clapping her hands with glee, "we are off!"

"I will repair to the deck and get our bearings," said Mrs.

Noah, putting her shawl over her shoulders. "Meantime, Cleopatra, I appoint you first mate. See that things are tidied up a bit here before I return. Have the windows washed, and tomorrow I want all the rugs and carpets taken up and shaken."

Portia meanwhile had discovered the naphtha engine, and, after experimenting several times with the various levers and stop-cocks, had finally managed to move one of them in such a way as to set the engine going, and the wheel began to revolve.

"Are we going all right?" she cried, from below.

"I am afraid not," said the gallant commander. "The wheel is roiling up the water at a great rate, but we don't seem to be going ahead very fast—in fact, we're simply moving round and round as though we were on a pivot."

"I'm afraid we're aground amidships," said Xanthippe, gazing over the side of the House-boat anxiously. "She certainly acts that way—like a merry-go-round."

"Well, there's something wrong," said Mrs. Noah; "and we've got to hurry and find out what it is, or those men will be back and we shall be as badly off as ever."

"Maybe this has something to do with it," observed Mrs. Lot, pointing to the anchor rope. "It looks to me as if those horrid men had tied us fast."

"That's just what it is," snapped Mrs. Noah. "They guessed our plan, and have fastened us to a pole or something, but I imagine we can untie it."

Portia, who had come on deck, gave a short little laugh.

"Why, of course we don't move," she said—"we are anchored!"

"What's that?" queried Mrs. Noah. "We never had an experience like that on the Ark."

Portia explained the science of the anchor.

"What nonsense!" ejaculated Mrs. Noah. "How can we get away from it?"

"We've got to pull it up," said Portia. "Order all hands on deck and have it pulled up."

"It can't be done, and, if it could, I wouldn't have it!" said

172

Mrs. Noah, indignantly. "The idea! Lifting heavy pieces of iron, my dear Portia, is not a woman's work. Send for Delilah, and let her cut the rope with her scissors."

"It would take her a week to cut a hawser like that," said Elizabeth, who had been investigating. "It would be more to the purpose, I think, to chop it in two with an axe."

"Very well," replied Mrs. Noah, satisfied. "I don't care how it is done as long as it is done quickly. It would never do for us to be recaptured now."

The suggestion of Elizabeth was carried out, and the queen herself cut the hawser with six well-directed strokes of the axe.

"You *are* an expert with it, aren't you?" smiled Cleopatra.

"I am, indeed," replied Elizabeth, grimly. "I had it suspended over my head for so long a time before I got to the throne that I couldn't help familiarizing myself with some of its possibilities."

"Ah!" cried Mrs. Noah, as the vessel began to move. "I begin to feel easier. It looks now as if we were really off."

"It seems to me, though," said Cleopatra, gazing forward, "that we are going backward."

"Oh, well, what if we are!" said Mrs. Noah. "We did that on the Ark half the time. It doesn't make any difference which way we are going as long as we go, does it?"

"Why, of course it does!" cried Elizabeth. "What can you be thinking of? People who walk backward are in great danger of running into other people. Why not the same with ships? It seems to me, it's a very dangerous piece of business, sailing backward."

"Oh, nonsense," snapped Mrs. Noah. "You are as timid as a zebra. During the Flood, we sailed days and days and days, going backward. It didn't make a particle of difference how we went— it was as safe one way as another, and we got just as far away in the end. Our main object now is to get away from the pirates, and that's what we are doing. Don't get emotional, Lizzie, and remember, too, that I am in charge. If I think the boat ought to go sideways, sideways she shall go. If you don't like it, it is still not too late to put you ashore."

The threat calmed Elizabeth somewhat, and she was satisfied, and all went well with them, even if Portia had started the propeller revolving reverse fashion; so that the House-boat was, as Elizabeth had said, backing her way through the ocean.

The day passed, and by slow degrees the island and the marooned pirates faded from view, and the night came on, and with it a dense fog.

"We're going to have a nasty night, I am afraid," said Xanthippe, looking anxiously out of the port.

"No doubt," said Mrs. Noah, pleasantly. "I'm sorry for those who have to be out in it."

"That's what I was thinking about," observed Xanthippe. "It's going to be very hard on us keeping watch."

"Watch for what?" demanded Mrs. Noah, looking over the tops of her glasses at Xanthippe.

"Why, surely you are going to have lookouts stationed on deck?" said Elizabeth.

"Not at all," said Mrs. Noah. "Perfectly absurd. We never did it on the Ark, and it isn't necessary now. I want you all to go to bed at ten o'clock. I don't think the night air is good for you. Besides, it isn't proper for a woman to be out after dark, whether she's new or not."

"But, my dear Mrs. Noah," expostulated Cleopatra, "what will become of the ship?"

"I guess she'll float through the night whether we are on deck or not," said the commander. "The Ark did, why not this? Now, girls, these new-fangled yachting notions are all nonsense. It's night, and there's a fog as thick as a stone-wall all about us. If there were a hundred of you upon deck with ten eyes apiece, you couldn't see anything. You might much better be in bed. As your captain, chaperon, and grandmother, I command you to stay below."

"But—who is to steer?" queried Xanthippe.

"What's the use of steering until we can see where to steer to?" demanded Mrs. Noah. "I certainly don't intend to bother with that tiller until some reason for doing it arises. We haven't any place to steer to yet; we don't know where we are going. Now, my dear children, be reasonable, and don't worry me. I've had a very hard day of it, and I feel my responsibilities keenly. Just let me manage, and we'll come out all right. I've had more experience than any of you, and if—"

A terrible crash interrupted the old lady's remarks. The House-boat shivered and shook, careened way to one side, and as quickly righted and stood still. A mad rush up the gangway followed, and in a moment a hundred and eighty-three pale-faced, trembling women stood upon the deck, gazing with horror at a great helpless hulk ten feet to the rear, fastened by broken ropes and odd pieces of rigging to the stern-posts of the House-boat, sinking slowly but surely into the sea.

It was the *Gehenna!*

The House-boat had run her down and her last hour had come, but, thanks to the stanchness of her build and wonderful beam, the floating club-house had withstood the shock of the impact and now rode the waters as gracefully as ever.

Portia was the first to realize the extent of the catastrophe, and in a short while chairs and life-preservers and tables—everything that could float—had been tossed into the sea to the struggling immortals therein. On board the *Gehenna*, those who had not cast themselves into the waters, under the cool direction of Holmes and Bonaparte, calmly lowered the boats, and in a short while were not only able to felicitate themselves upon their safety, but had likewise the good fortune to rescue their more impetuous brethren who had preferred to swim for it. Ultimately, all were brought aboard the House-boat in safety, and the men in Hades were once more reunited to their wives, daughters, sisters, and *fiancées*, and Elizabeth had the satisfaction of once more saving the life of Raleigh by throwing him her ruff as she had done a year or so previously, when she and her brother had been upset in the swift current of the river Styx.

Order and happiness being restored, Holmes took command of the House-boat and soon navigated her safely back into her old-time berth. The *Gehenna* went to the bottom and was never seen again, and when the roll was called it was found that all who had set out upon her had returned in safety save Shylock, Kidd, Sir Henry Morgan, and Abeuchapeta; but even they were not lost, for, five weeks later, these four worthies were found early one morning drifting slowly up the River Styx, gazing anxiously out from the top of a water-cask and yelling lustily for help.

And here endeth the chronicle of the pursuit of the good old House-boat. Back to her moorings, the even tenor of her ways was once more resumed, but with one slight difference.

The ladies became eligible for membership, and, availing themselves of the privilege, began to think less and less of the advantages of being men and to rejoice that, after all, they were women; and even Xanthippe and Socrates, after that night of peril, reconciled their differences, and no longer quarrel as to which is the more entitled to wear the *toga* of authority. It has become for them a divided skirt.

As for Kidd and his fellows, they have never recovered from the effects of their fearful, though short, exile upon Holmes Island, and are but shadows of their former shades; whereas Mr. Sherlock Holmes has so endeared himself to his new-found friends that he is quite as popular with them as he is with us, who have yet to cross the dark river and be subjected to the scrutiny of the Committee on Membership at the House-boat on the Styx.

Even Hawkshaw has been able to detect his genius.

The Enchanted Typewriter

1: THE DISCOVERY

It is a strange fact, for which I do not expect ever satisfactorily to account, and which will receive little credence even among those who know that I am not given to romancing—it is a strange fact, I say, that the substance of the following pages has evolved itself during a period of six months, more or less, between the hours of midnight and four o'clock in the morning, proceeding directly from a typewriting machine standing in the corner of my library, manipulated by unseen hands. The machine is not of recent make. It is, in fact, a relic of the early seventies, which I discovered one morning when, suffering from a slight attack of the grip, I had remained at home and devoted my time to pottering about in the attic, unearthing old books, bringing to the light long-forgotten correspondences, my boyhood collections of "stuff," and other memory-inducing things

Whence the machine came originally I do not recall. My impression is that it belonged to a stenographer once in the employ of my father, who used frequently to come to our house to take down dictations. However this may be, the machine had lain hidden by dust and the flotsam and jetsam of the house for twenty years, when, as I have said, I came upon it unexpectedly. Old man as I am—I shall soon be thirty—the fascination of a machine has lost none of its potency. I am as pleased today watching the wheels of my watch "go round" as ever I was, and to "monkey" with a typewriting apparatus has always brought great joy into my heart—though for composing give me the

177

pen.

Perhaps I should apologize for the use here of the verb monkey, which savours of what a friend of mine calls the "English slanguage," to differentiate it from what he also calls the "Andrew Language." But I shall not do so, because, to whatever branch of our tongue the word may belong, it is exactly descriptive, and descriptive as no other word can be, of what a boy does with things that click and "go," and is therefore not at all out of place in a tale which I trust will be regarded as a polite one.

The discovery of the machine put an end to my attic potterings. I cared little for finding old bill-files and collections of Atlantic cable-ends when, with a whole morning, a typewriting machine, and a screwdriver before me I could penetrate the mysteries of that useful mechanism. I shall not endeavour to describe the delightful sensations of that hour of screwing and unscrewing; they surpass the powers of my pen. Suffice it to say that I took the whole apparatus apart, cleaned it well, oiled every joint, and then put it together again. I do not suppose a seven-year-old boy could have derived more satisfaction from taking a piano to pieces.

It was exhilarating, and I resolved that as a reward for the pleasure it had given me the machine should have a brand-new ribbon and as much ink as it could consume. And that, in brief, is how it came to be that this machine of antiquated pattern was added to the library bric-a-brac. To say the truth, it was of no more practical use than Barye's dancing bear, a plaster cast of which adorns my mantel-shelf, so that when I classify it with the bric-a-brac I do so advisedly. I frequently tried to write a jest or two upon it, but the results were extraordinarily like Sir Arthur Sullivan's experience with the organ into whose depths the lost chord sank, never to return. I dashed off the jests well enough, but somewhere between the keys and the types they were lost, and the results, when I came to scan the paper, were depressing.

And once I tried a sonnet on the keys. Exactly how to classify the jumble that came out of it I do not know, but it was curious enough to have appealed strongly to D'Israeli or any other collector of the literary oddity. More singular than the sonnet, though, was the fact that when I tried to write my name upon this strange machine, instead of finding it in all its glorious length written upon the paper, I did find "William Shakespeare" printed there in its stead. Of course you will say that in putting the machine together I mixed up the keys and the letters. I have no doubt that I did, but when I tell you that there have been times when, looking at myself in the glass, I have fancied that I saw in my mirrored face the lineaments of the great bard; that the contour of my head is precisely the same as was his; that when visiting Stratford for the first time every foot of it was pregnant with clearly defined recollections to me, you will perhaps more easily picture to yourself my sensations at the moment.

However, enough of describing the machine in its relation to myself. I have said sufficient, I think, to convince you that whatever its make, its age, and its limitations, it was an extraordinary affair; and, once convinced of that, you may the more readily believe me when I tell you that it has gone into business apparently for itself—and incidentally for me.

It was on the morning of the 26th of March last that I discovered the curious condition of affairs concerning which I have essayed to write. My family do not agree with me as to the date. They say that it was on the evening of the 25th of March that the episode had its beginning; but they are not aware, for I have not told them, that it was not evening, but morning, when I reached home after the dinner at the Aldus Club. It was at a quarter of three a.m. precisely that I entered my house and proceeded to remove my hat and coat, in which operation I was interrupted, and in a startling manner, by a click from the dark recesses of the library.

A man does not like to hear a click which he cannot comprehend, even before he has dined. After he has dined, however, and feels a satisfaction with life which cannot come to him before dinner, to hear a mysterious click, and from a dark corner, at an hour when the world is at rest, is not pleasing. To say that my heart jumped into my mouth is mild. I believe it jumped out of my mouth and rebounded against the wall opposite back though my system into my boots. All the sins of my past life, and they are many—I once stepped upon a caterpillar, and I have coveted my neighbour both his man-servant and his maid-servant, though not his wife nor his ass, because I don't like his wife and he keeps no live-stock—all my sins, I say, rose up before me, for I expected every moment that a bullet would penetrate my brain, or my heart if perchance the burglar whom I suspected of levelling a clicking revolver at me aimed at my feet.

"Who is there?" I cried, making a vocal display of bravery I did not feel, hiding behind our hair sofa.

The only answer was another click.

"This is serious," I whispered softly to myself. "There are two of 'em; I am in the light, unarmed. They are concealed by the darkness and have revolvers. There is only one way out of this, and that is by strategy. I'll pretend I think I've made a mistake." So I addressed myself aloud.

"What an idiot you are," I said, so that my words could be heard by the burglars. "If this is the effect of Aldus Club dinners you'd better give them up. That click wasn't a click at all, but the ticking of our new eight-day clock."

I paused, and from the corner there came a dozen more clicks in quick succession, like the cocking of as many revolvers.

"Great Heavens!" I murmured, under my breath. "It must be Ali Baba with his forty thieves."

As I spoke, the mystery cleared itself, for following close upon a thirteenth click came the gentle ringing of a bell, and I knew then that the typewriting machine was in action; but this was by no means a reassuring discovery. Who or what could it be that was engaged upon the typewriter at that unholy hour, 3 a.m.? If a mortal being, why was my coming no interruption? If a supernatural being, what infernal complication might not the immediate future have in store for me?

My first impulse was to flee the house, to go out into the night and pace the fields—possibly to rush out to the golf links and play a few holes in the dark in order to cool my brow, which was rapidly becoming fevered. Fortunately, however, I am not a man of impulse. I never yield to a mere nerve suggestion, and so, instead of going out into the storm and certainly contracting pneumonia, I walked boldly into the library to investigate the causes of the very extraordinary incident. You may rest well assured, however, that I took care to go armed, fortifying myself with a stout stick, with a long, ugly steel blade concealed within it—a cowardly weapon, by-the-way, which I permit to rest in my house merely because it forms a part of a collection of weapons acquired through the failure of a comic paper to which I had contributed several articles.

The editor, when the crash came, sent me the collection as part payment of what was owed me, which I think was very good of him, because a great many people said that it was my stuff that killed the paper. But to return to the story. Fortifying myself with the sword-cane, I walked boldly into the library, and, touching the electric button, soon had every gas-jet in the room giving forth a brilliant flame; but these, brilliant as they were, disclosed nothing in the chair before the machine.

The latter, apparently oblivious of my presence, went clicking merrily and as rapidly along as though some expert young woman were in charge. Imagine the situation if you can. A typewriting machine of ancient make, its letters clear, but out of accord with the keys, confronted by an empty chair, three hours after midnight, rattling off page after page of something which might or might not be readable, I could not at the moment determine. For two or three minutes I gazed in open-mouthed wonder. I was not frightened, but I did experience a sensation which comes from contact with the uncanny. As I gradually grasped the situation and became used, somewhat, to what was going on, I ventured a remark.

"This beats the deuce!" I observed.

The machine stopped for an instant. The sheet of paper upon which the impressions of letters were being made flew out from under the cylinder, a pure white sheet was as quickly substituted, and the keys clicked off the line:

181

"What does?"

I presumed the line was in response to my assertion, so I replied:

"You do. What uncanny freak has taken possession of you to-night that you start in to write on your own hook, having resolutely declined to do any writing for me ever since I rescued you from the dust and dirt and cobwebs of the attic?"

"You never rescued me from any attic," the machine replied. "You'd better go to bed; you've dined too well, I imagine. When did you rescue me from the dust and dirt and the cobwebs of any attic?"

"What an ungrateful machine you are!" I cried. "If you have sense enough to go into writing on your own account, you ought to have mind enough to remember the years you spent up-stairs under the roof neglected, and covered with hammocks, awnings, family portraits, and receipted bills."

"Really, my dear fellow," the machine tapped back, "I must repeat it. Bed is the place for you. You're not coherent. I'm not a machine, and upon my honour, I've never seen your darned old attic."

"Not a machine!" I cried. "Then what in Heaven's name are you?—a sofa-cushion?"

"Don't be sarcastic, my dear fellow," replied the machine. "Of course I'm not a machine; I'm Jim—Jim Boswell."

"What?" I roared. "You? A thing with keys and type and a bell—"

"I haven't got any keys or any type or a bell. What on earth are you talking about?" replied the machine. "What have you been eating?"

"What's that?" I asked, putting my hand on the keys.

"That's keys," was the answer.

"And these, and that?" I added, indicating the type and the bell.

"Type and bell," replied the machine.

"And yet you say you haven't got them," I persisted.

"No, I haven't. The machine has got them, not I," was the

response. "I'm not the machine. I'm the man that's using it—Jim—Jim Boswell. What good would a bell do me? I'm not a cow or a bicycle. I'm the editor of the *Stygian Gazette,* and I've come here to copy off my notes of what I see and hear, and besides all this I do typewriting for various people in Hades, and as this machine of yours seemed to be of no use to you I thought I'd try it. But if you object, I'll go."

As I read these lines upon the paper I stood amazed and delighted.

"Go!" I cried, as the full value of his patronage of my machine dawned upon me, for I could sell his copy and he would be none the worse off, for, as I understand the copyright laws, they are not designed to benefit authors, but for the protection of type-setters. "Why, my dear fellow, it would break my heart if, having found my machine to your taste, you should ever think of using another. I'll lend you my bicycle, too, if you'd like it—in fact, anything I have is at your command."

"Thank you very much," returned Boswell through the medium of the keys, as usual. "I shall not need your bicycle, but this machine is of great value to me. It has several very remarkable qualities which I have never found in any other machine. For instance, singular to relate, Mendelssohn and I were fooling about here the other night, and when he saw this machine he thought it was a spinet of some new pattern; so what does he do but sit down and play me one of his songs without words on it, and, by Jove! when he got through, there was the theme of the whole thing printed on a sheet of paper before him."

"You don't really mean to say—" I began.

"I'm telling you precisely what happened," said Boswell. "Mendelssohn was tickled to death with it, and he played every song without words that he ever wrote, and every one of 'em was fitted with words which he said absolutely conveyed the ideas he meant to bring out with the music. Then I tried the machine, and discovered another curious thing about it. It's intensely American. I had a story of Alexander Dumas' about his Musketeers that he wanted translated from French into American, which is the language we speak below, in preference to German, French, Volapuk, or English. I thought I'd copy off a few lines of the French original, and as true as I'm sitting here before your eyes, where you can't see me, the copy I got was a good, though rather free, translation. Think of it! That's an advanced machine for you!"

I looked at the machine wistfully. "I wish I could make it work," I said; and I tried as before to tap off my name, and got instead only a confused jumble of letters. It wouldn't even pay me the compliment of transforming my name into that of Shakespeare, as it had previously done.

It was thus that the magic qualities of the machine were made known to me, and out of it the following papers have grown. I have set them down without much editing or alteration, and now submit them to your inspection, hoping that in perusing them you will derive as much satisfaction and delight as I have in being the possessor of so wonderful a machine, manipulated by so interesting a person as "Jim—Jim Boswell"—as he always calls himself—and others, who, as you will note, if perchance you have the patience to read further, have upon occasions honoured my machine by using it.

I must add in behalf of my own reputation for honesty that Mr. Boswell has given me all right, title, and interest in these papers in this world as a return for my permission to him to use my machine.

"What if they make a hit and bring in barrels of gold in royalties," he said. "I can't take it back with me where I live, so keep it yourself."

2: Mr. Boswell Imparts Some Late News of Hades

Boswell was a little late in arriving the next night. He had agreed to be on hand exactly at midnight, but it was after one o'clock before the machine began to click and the bell to ring. I had fallen asleep in the soft upholstered depths of my armchair, feeling pretty thoroughly worn out by the experiences of the night before, which, in spite of their pleasant issue, were nevertheless somewhat disturbing to a nervous organization like mine. Suddenly I waked, and with the awakening there entered into my mind the notion that the whole thing was merely a dream, and that in the end it would be the better for me if I were to give up Aldus and other club dinners with nightmare inducing menus. But I was soon convinced that the real state of affairs was quite otherwise, and that everything really had happened as I have already related it to you, for I had hardly gotten my eyes free from what my poetic son calls "the seeds of sleep" when I heard the typewriter tap forth:

"Hello, old man!"

Incidentally let me say that this had become another interesting feature of the machine. Since my first interview with Boswell the taps seemed to speak, and if someone were sitting before it and writing a line the mere differentiation of sounds of the various keys would convey to the mind the ideas conveyed to it by the printed words. So, as I say, my ears were greeted with a clicking "Hello, old man!" followed immediately by the bell.

"You are late," said I, looking at my watch.

"I know it," was the response. "But I can't help it. During the campaign I am kept so infernally busy I hardly know where I am."

"Campaign, eh?" I put in. "Do you have campaigns in Hades?"

"Yes," replied Boswell, "and we are having a—well, to be polite, a regular Gehenna of a time. Things have changed much in Hades latterly. There has been a great growth in the democratic spirit below, and his Majesty is having a deuce of a time running his kingdom. Washington and Cromwell and Caesar have had the nerve to demand a constitution from the venerable Nicholas—"

"From whom?" I queried, perplexed somewhat, for I was not yet fully awake.

"Old Nick," replied Boswell; "and I can tell you there's a pretty fight on between the supporters of the administration and the opposition. Secure in his power, the Grand Master of Hades has been somewhat arbitrary, and he has made the mistake of doing some of his subjects a little too brown. Take the case of Bonaparte, for instance: the government has ruled that he was personally responsible for all the wars of Europe from 1800 up to Waterloo, and it was proposed to hang him once for every man killed on either side throughout that period.

Bonaparte naturally resisted. He said he had a good neck, which he did not object to have broken three or four times, because he admitted he deserved it; but when it came to hanging him five or six million times, once a month, for, say, five million months, or twelve times a year for 415,000 years, he didn't like it, and wouldn't stand it, and wanted to submit the question to arbitration.

"Nicholas observed that the word arbitration was not in his especially expurgated dictionary, whereupon Bonaparte remarked that he wasn't responsible for that; that he thought it a good word and worthy of incorporation in any dictionary and in all vocabularies.

"'I don't care what you think,' retorted his Majesty. 'It's what I don't think that goes;' and he commanded his imps to prepare the gallows on the third Thursday of each month for Bonaparte's expiation; ordered his secretary to send Bonaparte a type-written notice that his presence on each occasion was expected, and gave orders to the police to see that he was there willy-nilly. Naturally Bonaparte resisted, and appealed to the courts. Blackstone sustained his appeal, and Nicholas overruled him. The first Thursday came, and the police went for the Emperor, but he was surrounded by a good half of the men who had fought under him, and the minions of the law could do nothing against them.

"In consequence, Bonaparte's brother, Joseph, a quiet, inoffensive citizen, was dragged from his home and hanged in his place, Nicholas contending that when a soldier could not, or would not, serve, the government had a right to expect a substitute. Well," said Boswell, at this point, "that set all Hades on fire. We were divided as to Bonaparte's deserts, but the hanging of other people as substitutes was too much. We didn't know who'd be substituted next. The English backed up Blackstone, of course. The French army backed up Bonaparte. The inoffensive citizens were aroused in behalf of Joseph, for they saw at once whither they were drifting if the substitute idea was carried out to its logical conclusion; and in half an hour the administration was on the defensive, which, as you know, is a very, very, very bad thing for an administration."

"It is, if it desires to be returned to office," said I.

"It is anyhow," replied Boswell through the medium of the keys. "It's in exactly the same position as that of a humorist who has to print explanatory diagrams with all of his jokes. The administration papers were hot over the situation. The king can do no wrong idea was worked for all it was worth, but beyond this they drew pathetic pictures of the result of all these deplorable tendencies. What was Hades for, they asked, if a man, after leading a life of crime in the other world, was not to receive his punishment there? The attitude of the opposition was a radical and vicious blow at the vital principles of the sphere itself. The opposition papers coolly and calmly took the position that the vital principles of Hades were all right; that it was the extreme view as to the power of the Emperor taken by that person himself that wouldn't go in these democratic days.

"Punishment for Bonaparte was the correct thing, and Bonaparte expected some, but was not grasping enough to want it all. They added that recent fully settled ideas as to a humane application of the laws required the bunching of the indictments or the selection of one and a fair trial based upon that, and that anyhow, under no circumstances, should a wholly innocent person be made to suffer for the crimes of another. These journals were suppressed, but the next day a set of new papers were started to promulgate the same theories as to individual rights. The province of Cimmeria declared itself independent of the throne, and set up in the business of government for itself.

"Gehenna declared for the Emperor, but insisted upon home rule for cities of its own class, and finally, as I informed you at the beginning, Washington, Cromwell, and Caesar went in person to Apollyon and demanded a constitution. That was the day before yesterday, and just what will come of it we don't as yet know, because Washington and Cromwell and Caesar have not been seen since, but we have great fears for them, because seventeen car-loads of vitriol and a thousand extra tons of coal were ordered by the Lord High Steward of the palace to be delivered to the Minister of Justice last night."

"Quite a complication," said I. "The Americanization of Hades has begun at last. How does society regard the affair?"

"Variously," observed Boswell. "Society hates the government as much as anybody, and really believes in curtailing the Emperor's powers, but, on the other hand, it desires to maintain all of its own aristocratic privileges. The main trouble in Hades at present is the gradual disintegration of society; that is to say, its former component parts are beginning to differentiate themselves the one from the other."

"Like capital and labour here?" I queried.

"In a sense, yes—possibly more like your Colonial Dames, and Daughters of the Revolution. For instance, great organizations are in process of formation—people are beginning to flock together for purposes of protection. Charles the First and Henry the Eighth and Louis the Fourteenth have established Ye Ancient and Honourable Order of Kings, to which only those who have actually worn crowns shall be eligible. The painters have gotten together with a Society of Fine Arts, the sculptors have formed a Society of Chisellers, and all the authors from Homer down to myself have got up an Authors' Club where we have a lovely time talking about ourselves, no man to be eligible who hasn't written something that has lasted a hundred years. Perhaps, if you are thinking of coming over soon, you'll let me put you on our waiting-list?"

I smiled at his seeming inconsistency and let myself into his snare.

"I haven't written anything that has lasted a hundred years yet," said I.

"Oh, yes, I think you have," replied Boswell, and the machine seemed to laugh as he wrote out his answer. "I saw a joke of yours the other day that's two hundred centuries old. Diogenes showed it to me and said that it was a great favourite with his grandfather, who had inherited it from one of his remote ancestors."

A hot retort was on my lips, but I had no wish to offend my guest, so I smiled and observed that I had frequently indulged in unconscious plagiarism of that sort.

"I should imagine," I hastened to add, "that to men like Charles the First this uncertainty as to the safety of Cromwell would be great joy."

"I hardly know," returned Boswell. "That very question has been discussed among us. Charles made a great outward show of grief when he heard of the coal being delivered at the office of the Minister of Justice, and we all thought him quite magnanimous, but it leaked out, just before I left to come here, that he sent his private secretary to the palace with a Panama hat and a palm-leaf fan for Cromwell, with his congratulations."

"That seems to savour somewhat of sarcasm."

"Oh, ultimately Hades is bound to be a republic," replied Boswell. "There are too many clever and ambitious politicians among us for the place to go along as a despotism much longer. If the place were filled up with poets and society people, and things like that, it might go on as an autocracy forever, but you see it isn't. To men of the calibre of Alexander the Great and Bonaparte and Caesar, and a thousand other warriors who never were used to taking orders from anybody, but were themselves headquarters, the despotic sway of Apollyon is intolerable, and he hasn't made any effort to conciliate any of them.

"If he had appointed Bonaparte commander-in-chief of his army and made a friend of him, instead of ordering him to be hanged every month for 415,000 years, or put Caesar in as Secretary of State, instead of having him roasted three times a month for seventy or eighty centuries, he would have strengthened his hold. As it is, he has ignored all these people officially, treats them like criminals personally; makes friends with Mazarin and Powhatan, awards the office of Tax Assessor to Dick Turpin, and makes old Falstaff commander of his Imperial Guard. And just because poor Ben Jonson scribbled off a rhyme for my paper, *The Gazette*—a rhyme running:

Mazarin And Powhatan,
Turpin and Falstaff,
Form, you bet, A cabinet
To make a donkey laugh.

Mazarin And Powhatan
Run Apollyon's state.
The Dick and Jacks Collect the tax—
The people pay the freight.

—just because Jonson wrote that and I published it, my paper was confiscated, Jonson was boiled in oil for ten weeks, and I was seized and thrown into a dungeon where a lot of savages from the South Sea Islands tattooed the darned old jingle between my shoulder blades in green letters, and not satisfied with this barbaric act, right under the jingle they added the line, in red letters, 'This edition strictly limited to one copy, for private circulation only,' and they every one of 'em, Apollyon, Mazarin, and the rest, signed the guarantee personally with red-hot pens dipped in sulphuric acid. It makes a valuable collection of autographs, no doubt, but I prefer my back as nature made it. Talk about enlightened government under a man who'll permit things like that to be done!"

I ought not to have done it, but I couldn't help smiling.

"I must say," I observed, apologetically, "that the treatment was barbarous, but really I do think it showed a sense of humour on the part of the government."

"No doubt," replied Boswell, with a sigh; "but when the joke is on me I don't enjoy it very much. I'm only human, and should prefer to observe that the government had some sense of justice."

The apparently empty chair before the machine gave a slight

hitch forward, and the typewriter began to tap again.

"You'll have to excuse me now," observed Boswell through the usual medium. "I have work to do, and if you'll go to bed like a good fellow, while I copy off the minutes of the last meeting of the Authors' Club, I'll see that you don't lose anything by it. After I get the minutes done I have an interesting story for my Sunday paper from the advance sheets of *Munchausen's Further Recollections,* which I shall take great pleasure in leaving for you when I depart. If you will take the bundle of manuscript I leave with you and boil it in alcohol for ten minutes, you will be able to read it, and, no doubt, if you copy it off, sell it for a goodly sum. It is guaranteed absolutely genuine."

"Very well," said I, rising, "I'll go; but I should think you would put in most of your time whacking at the government editorially, instead of going in for minutes and abstract stories of adventure."

"You do, eh?" said Boswell. "Well, if you were in my place you'd change your mind. After my unexpected endorsement by the Emperor and his cabinet, I've decided to keep out of politics for a little while. I can stand having a poem tattooed on my back, but if it came to having a three-column editorial expressing my emotions etched alongside of my spine, I'm afraid I'd disappear into thin air."

So I left him at work and retired. The next morning I found the promised bundle of manuscripts, and, after boiling the pages as instructed, discovered the following tale.

3: FROM ADVANCE SHEETS OF BARON MUNCHAUSEN'S FURTHER RECOLLECTIONS

It is with some very considerable hesitation that I come to this portion of my personal recollections, and yet I feel that I owe it to my fellow-citizens in this delightful Stygian country, where we are all enjoying our well-earned rest, to lay before them the exact truth concerning certain incidents which have now passed into history, and for participation in which a number of familiar figures are improperly gaining all the credit, or discredit, as the case may be. It is not a pleasant task to expose an impostor; much less is it agreeable to expose four impostors; but to one who from the earliest times—and when I say earliest times I speak advisedly, as you will see as you read on—to one, I say, who from the earliest times has been actuated by no other motive than the promulgation of truth, the task of exposing fraud becomes a duty which cannot be ignored.

Therefore, with regret I set down this chapter of my memoirs, regardless of its consequences to certain figures which have been of no inconsiderable importance in our community for many years—figures which in my own favourite club, the Associated Shades, have been most welcome, but which, as I and they alone know, have been nothing more than impostures.

In previous volumes I have confined my attention to my memoirs as Baron Munchausen—but, dear reader, there are others. *I was not always Baron Munchausen; I have been others!* I am not aware that it has fallen to the lot of any but myself in the whole span of universal existence to live more than one life upon that curious, compact little ball of land and water called the Earth, but, in any event, to me has fallen that privilege or distinction, or whatever it may be, and upon the record made by me in four separate existences, placed centuries apart, four residents of this sphere are basing their claims to notice, securing election to our clubs, and even venturing so far at times as to make themselves personally obnoxious to me, who with a word could expose their wicked deceit in all its naked villainy to an astounded community.

And in taking this course they have gone too far. There is a limit beyond which no man shall dare go with me. Satisfied with the ultimate embodiment of my virtues in the Baron Munchausen, I have been disposed to allow the impostors to pursue their deception in peace so long as they otherwise behave themselves, but when Adam chooses to allude to my writings as frothy lies, when Jonah attacks my right as a literary person to tell tales of *leviathans*, when Noah states that my ignorance in yachting matters is colossal, and when William Shakespeare publicly brands me as a person unworthy of belief who should be expelled from the Associated Shades, then do I consider it time to speak out and expose four of the greatest frauds that have ever been inflicted upon a long-suffering public.

To begin at the beginning then, let me state that my first recollection dates back to a beautiful summer morning, when in a lovely garden I opened my eyes and became conscious of two very material facts: first, a charming woman arranging her hair in the mirror-like waters of a silver lake directly before me; and, second, a poignant pain in my side, as though I had been operated upon for appendicitis, but which in reality resulted from the loss of a rib which had in turn evoluted into the charming and very human being I now saw before me. That woman was Eve; that mirror-like lake was set in the midst of the Garden of Eden; I was Adam, and not this watery-eyed *antediluvian* calling himself by my name, who is a familiar figure in the Anthropological Society, an authority on evolution, and a blot upon civilization.

I have little to say about this first existence of mine. It was full of delights. Speech not having been invented, Eve was an attractive companion to a man burdened as I was with responsibilities, and until our children were born we went our way in happiness and silence. It is not in the nature of things, however, that children should not wish to talk, and it was through the irrepressible efforts of Cain and Abel to be heard as well as seen that first called the attention of Eve and myself to the desirability of expressing our thoughts in words rather than by Masonic signs.

I shall not burden my readers with further recollections of this period. It was excessively primitive, of necessity, but before leaving it I must ask the reader to put one or two questions to himself in this matter.

1st. How is it that this bearded patriarch, who now poses as the only original Adam, has never been able, with any degree of positiveness, to answer the question as to whether or not he was provided with a caudal appendage—a question which I am prepared to answer definitely, at any moment, if called upon by the proper authorities, and, if need be, to produce not only the tail itself, but the fierce and untamed pterodactyl that bit it off upon that unfortunate autumn afternoon when he and I had our first and last conflict.

2nd. Why is it that when describing a period concerning which he is supposed to know all, he seems to have given voice to sentiments in phrases which would have delighted Sheridan and shed added glory upon the eloquence of Webster, *at a time when, as I have already shown, there was no such thing as speech?*

Upon these two points alone I rest my case against Adam: the first is the reticence of guilt—he doesn't know, and he knows he doesn't know; the second is a deliberate and offensive prevarication, which shows again that he doesn't know, and assumes that we are all equally ignorant.

So much for Adam. Now for the cheap and year-ridden person who has taken unto himself my second personality, Noah; and that other strange combination of woe and wickedness, Jonah, who has chosen to pre-empt my third. I shall deal with both at one and the same time, for, taken separately, they are not worthy of notice.

Noah asserts that I know nothing of yachting. I will accept the charge with the qualification that I know a great sight more about Arking than he does; and as for Jonah, I can give Jonah points on whaling, and I hereby challenge them both to a Memoir Match for $2000 a side, in gold, to see which can give to the world the most interesting reminiscences concerning the cruises of the two craft in question, the Ark and the Whale, upon neither of which did either of these two anachronisms ever set foot, and of both of which I, in my two respective existences, was commander-in-chief. The fact is that, as in the case of the fictitious Adam, these two impersonators are frauds.

The man now masquerading as Noah was my hired man in the latter part of the *antediluvian* period; was discharged three years before the flood; was left on shore at the hour of departure, and when last seen by me was sitting on the top of an apple-tree, begging to do two men's work for nothing if we'd only let him out of the wet. If he will at any time submit to a cross-examination at my hands as to the principal events of that memorable voyage, I will show to any fair-minded judge how impossible is his claim that he was in command, or even afloat, after the first week. I have hitherto kept silent in this matter, in spite of many and repeated outrageous flings, for the sake of his—or rather my—family, who have been deceived, as have all the rest of us, barring, of course, myself.

References to portraits of leading citizens of that period will easily show how this can be. We were all alike as two peas in the olden days, and at a time when men reached to an advanced age which is not known now, it frequently became almost impossible to distinguish one old man from another. I will say, finally, in regard to this person Noah that if he can give to the public a statement telling the essential differences between a pterodactyl and a double spondee that will not prove utterly absurd to an educated person, I will withdraw my accusation and resign from the club. *But I know well he cannot do it,* and he does too, and that is about the extent of his knowledge.

Now as to Jonah. I really dislike very much to tread upon this worthy's toes, and I should not do it had he not chosen to clap an injunction upon a volume of *Tales of the Whales,* which I wrote for children last summer, claiming that I was infringing upon his copyright, and feeling that I as a self-respecting man would never claim the discredit of having myself been the person he claims to have been. I will candidly confess that I am not proud of my achievements as Jonah. I was a very oily person even before I embarked upon the seas as Lord High Admiral of H.M.S. *Leviathan.*

I was not a pleasant person to know. If I spent the night with a friend, his roof would fall in or his house would burn down. If I bet on a horse, he would lead up to the home-stretch and fall down dead an inch from the finish. If I went into a stock speculation, I was invariably caught on a rising or a falling market. In my youth I spoiled every yachting-party I went on by attracting a gale. When I came out the moon went behind a cloud, and people who began by endorsing my paper ended up in the poor-house. Commerce wouldn't have me.

Boards of Trade everywhere repudiated me, and I gradually sank into that state of despair which finds no solace anywhere but on the sea or in politics, and as politics was then unknown I went to sea. The result is known to the world. I was cast overboard, ingulfed by a whale, which, in his defence let me be generous enough to say, swallowed me inadvertently and with the usual result. I came back, and life went on. Finally I came here, and when it got to the ears of the authorities that I was in Hades, they sent me back for the fourth time to earth in the person of William Shakespeare.

That is the whole of the Jonah story. It is a sad story, and I regret it; and I am sorry for the impostor when I reflect that the character he has assumed possesses attractions for him. His real life must have been a fearful thing if he is happy in his impersonation, and for his punishment let us leave him where he is. Having told the truth, I have done my duty. I cheerfully resign my claim to the personality he claims—I relinquish from this time on all right, title, and interest in the name; but if he ever dares to interfere with me again in the use of my personal recollections concerning the inside of whales I shall hale him before the authorities.

And now, finally, I come to Shakespeare, whom I have kept for the last, not because he was the last chronologically, but because I like to work up to a climax.

Previous to my existence as Baron Munchausen I lived for a term of years on earth as William Shakespeare, and what I have to say now is more in the line of confession than otherwise.

In my boyhood I was wild and I poached. If I were not afraid of having it set down as a joke, I should say that I poached everything from eggs to deer. I was not a great joy to my parents. There was no deviltry in Stratford in which I did not take a leading part, and finally, for the good of Warwickshire, I was sent to London, where a person of my talents was more likely to find congenial and appreciative surroundings.

A glance at such of my autographs as are now extant will

demonstrate the fact that I never learned to write; a glance at the first folios of the plays attributed to me will likewise show that I never learned to spell; and yet I walked into London with one of the most exquisite poems in the English language in my pocket. I am still filled with merriment over it. How was it, the critics of the years since have asked—how was it that this untutored little savage from leafy Warwickshire, with no training and little education, came into London with *Venus and Adonis* in manuscript in his pocket?

It is quite evident that the critic fraternity have no Sherlock Holmes in their midst. It would not take much of an eye, a true detective's eye, to see the milk in that cocoanut, for it is but a simple tale after all. The way of it was this: On my way from Stratford to London I walked through Coventry, and I remained in Coventry overnight. I was ill-clad and hungry, and, having no money with which to pay for my supper, I went to the Royal Arms Hotel and offered my services as porter for the night, having noted that a rich cavalcade from London, *en route* to Kenilworth, had arrived unexpectedly at the Royal Arms.

Taken by surprise, and, therefore, unprepared to accommodate so many guests, the landlord was glad to avail himself of my services, and I was assigned to the position of boots. Among others whom I served was Walter Raleigh, who, noting my ragged condition and hearing what a roisterer and roustabout I had been, immediately took pity upon me, and gave me a plum-coloured court-suit with which he was through, and which I accepted, put upon my back, and next day wore off to London.

It was in the pocket of this that I found the poem of *Venus and Adonis.*" That poem, to keep myself from starving, I published when I reached London, sending a complimentary copy of course to my benefactor. When Raleigh saw it he was naturally surprised but gratified, and on his return to London he sought me out, and suggested the publication of his sonnets. I was the first man he'd met, he said, who was willing to publish his stuff on his own responsibility. I immediately put out some of the sonnets, and in time was making a comfortable living, publishing the anonymous works of most of the young bucks about town, who paid well for my imprint.

That the public chose to think the works were mine was none of my fault. I never claimed them, and the line on the title-page, "By William Shakespeare," had reference to the publisher only, and not, as many have chosen to believe, to the author. Thus were published Lord Bacon's *Hamlet*, Raleigh's poems, several plays of Messrs. Beaumont and Fletcher—who were themselves among the cleverest adapters of the times—and the rest of that glorious monument to human credulity and memorial to an impossible, wholly apocryphal genius, known as the works of William Shakespeare.

The extent of my writing during this incarnation was ten autographs for collectors, and one attempt at a comic opera called *A Midsummer's Nightmare*, which was never produced, because no one would write the music for it, and which was ultimately destroyed with three of my quatrains and all of Bacon's evidence against my authorship of *Hamlet*, in the fire at the Globe Theatre in the year 1613.

These, then, dear reader, are the revelations which I have to make. In my next incarnation I was the man I am now known to be, Baron Munchausen. As I have said, I make the exposure with regret, but the arrogance of these impudent impersonators of my various personalities has grown too great to be longer borne. I lay the simple story of their villany before you for what it is worth. I have done my duty. If after this exposure the public of Hades choose to receive them in their homes and at their clubs, and as guests at their functions, they will do it with a full knowledge of their duplicity.

In conclusion, fearing lest there be some doubters among the readers of this paper, I have allowed my friend, the editor of this esteemed journal, which is to publish this story exclusively on Sunday next, free access to my archives, and he has selected as exhibits of evidence, to which I earnestly call your attention, the originals of the cuts which illustrate this chapter—*viz*:

1 A full-length portrait of Eve as she appeared at our first

meeting.

2. Portraits of Cain and Abel at the ages of two, five, and seven.

3. The original plans and specifications of the Ark.

4. Facsimile of her commission.

5. Portrait-sketch of myself and the false Noah, made at the time, and showing how difficult it would have been for any member of my family, save myself, to tell us apart.

6. A cathode-ray photograph of the whale, showing myself, the original Jonah, seated inside.

7. Facsimiles of the Shakespeare autographs, proving that he knew neither how to write nor to spell, and so of course proving effectually that I was not the author of his works.

It must be confessed that I read this article of Munchausen's with amazement, and I awaited with much excited curiosity the coming again of the manipulator of my typewriting machine. Surely a revelation of this nature should create a sensation in Hades, and I was anxious to learn how it was received. Boswell did not materialize, however, and for five nights I fairly raged with the fever of curiosity, but on the sixth night the familiar tinkle of the bell announced an arrival, and I flew to the machine and breathlessly cried:

"Hullo, old chap, how did it come out?"

The reply was as great a surprise as I have yet had, for it was not Boswell, Jim Boswell, who answered my question.

4: A Chat With Xanthippe

The machine stopped its clicking the moment I spoke, and the words, "Hullo, old chap!" were no sooner uttered than my face grew red as a carnation pink. I felt as if I had committed some dreadful *faux-pas*, and instead of gazing steadfastly into the vacant chair, as I had been wont to do in my conversation with Boswell, my eyes fell, as though the invisible occupant of the chair were regarding me with a look of indignant scorn.

"I beg your pardon," I said.

"I should think you might," returned the types. "Hullo, old

chap! is no way to address a woman you've never had the honour of meeting, even if she is of the most advanced sort. No amount of newness in a woman gives a man the right to be disrespectful to her."

"I didn't know," I explained. "Really, miss, I—"

"*Madame*," interrupted the machine, "not miss. I am a married woman, sir, which makes of your rudeness an even more reprehensible act. It is well enough to affect a good-fellowship with young unmarried females, but when you attempt to be flippant with a married woman—"

"But I didn't know, I tell you," I appealed. "How should I? I supposed it was Boswell I was talking to, and he and I have become very good friends."

"Humph!" said the machine. "You're a chum of Boswell's, eh?"

"Well, not exactly a chum, but—" I began.

"But you go with him?" interrupted the lady.

"To an extent, yes," I confessed.

"And does he GO with you?" was the query. "If he does, permit me to depart at once. I should not feel quite in my element in a house where the editor of a Sunday newspaper was an attractive guest. If you like that sort of thing, your tastes—"

"I do not, *madame*," I replied, quickly. "I prefer the opium habit to the Sunday-newspaper habit, and if I thought Boswell was merely a purveyor of what is known as Sunday literature, which depends on the goodness of the day to offset its shortcomings, I should forbid him the house."

A distinct sigh of relief emanated from the chair.

"Then I may remain," was the remark rapidly clicked off on the machine.

"I am glad," said I. "And may I ask whom I have the honour of addressing?"

"Certainly," was the immediate response. "My name is Socrates, nee Xanthippe."

I instinctively cowered. Candidly, I was afraid. Never in my life before had I met a woman whom I feared. Never in my life have I wavered in the presence of the sex which cheers, but I have always felt that while I could hold my own with Elizabeth, withstand the wiles of Cleopatra, and manage the recalcitrant Katherine even as did Petruchio, Xanthippe was another story altogether, and I wished I had gone to the club. My first impulse was to call upstairs to my wife and have her come down.

She knows how to handle the new woman far better than I do. She has never wanted to vote, and my collars are safe in her hands. She has frequently observed that while she had many things to be thankful for, her greatest blessing was that she was born a woman and not a man, and the new women of her native town never leave her presence without wondering in their own minds whether or not they are mere humorous contributions of the Almighty to a too serious world. I pulled myself together as best I could, and feeling that my better-half would perhaps decline the proffered invitation to meet with one of the most illustrious of her sex, I decided to fight my own battle. So I merely said:

"Really? How delightful! I have always felt that I should like to meet you, and here is one of my devoutest wishes gratified."

I felt cheap after the remark, for Mrs. Socrates, nee Xanthippe, covered five sheets of paper with laughter, with an occasional bracketing of the word "derisively," such as we find in the daily newspapers interspersed throughout the after-dinner speeches of a candidate of another party. Finally, to my relief, the oft-repeated "Ha-ha-ha!" ceased, and the line, "I never should have guessed it," closed her immediate contribution to our interchange of ideas.

"May I ask why you laugh?" I observed, when she had at length finished.

"Certainly," she replied. "Far be it from me to dispute the right of a man to ask any question he sees fit to ask. Is he not the lord of creation? Is not woman his abject slave? I not the whole difference between them purely economic? Is it not the law of supply and demand that rules them both, he by nature demanding and she supplying?"

Dear reader, did you ever encounter a machine, man-made, merely a mechanism of ivory, iron, and ink, that could sniff contemptuously? I never did before this encounter, but the infernal power of either this type-writer or this woman who manipulated its keys imparted to the atmosphere I was breathing a sniffing contemptuousness which I have never experienced anywhere outside of a London hotel, and then only when I ventured, as few Americans have dared, to complain of the ducal personage who presided over the dining-room, but who, I must confess, was conquered subsequently by a tip of ten shillings.

At any rate, there was a sniff of contempt imparted, as I have said, to the atmosphere I was breathing as Xanthippe answered my question, and the sniff saved me, just as it did in the London hotel, when I complained of the lordly lack of manners on the part of the head waiter. I asserted my independence.

"Don't trouble yourself," I put in. "Of course I shall be interested in anything you may choose to say, but as a gentleman I do not care to put a woman to any inconvenience and I do not press the question."

And then I tried to crush her by adding, "What a lovely day we have had," as if any subject other than the most commonplace was not demanded by the situation.

"If you contemplate discussing the weather," was the retort, "I wish you would kindly seek out someone else with whom to do it. I am not one of your latter-day sit-out-on-the-stairs-while-the-others-dance girls. I am, as I have always been, an ardent admirer of principles, of great problems. For small talk I have no use."

"Very well, *madame*—" I began.

"You asked me a moment ago why I laughed," clicked the machine.

"I know it," said I. "But I withdraw the question. There is no great principle involved in a woman's laughter. I have known women who have laughed at a broken heart, as well as at jokes, which shows that there is no principle involved there; and as a problem, I have never cared enough about why women laugh to inquire deeply into it. If she'll just consent to laugh, I'm satisfied without inquiring into the causes thereof. Let us get down to an agreeable basis for yourself. What problem do you wish to discuss? Servants, baby-food, floor-polish, or the number of godets proper to the skirt of a well-dressed woman?"

I was regaining confidence in myself, and as I talked I ceased to fear her. Thought I to myself, "This attitude of supreme patronage is man's safest weapon against a woman. Keep cool, assume that there is no doubt of your superiority, and that she knows it. Appear to patronize her, and her own indignation will defeat her ends." It is a good principle generally. Among mortal women I have never known it to fail, and when I find myself worsted in an argument with one of man's greatest blessings, I always fall back upon it and am saved the ignominy of defeat. But this time I counted without my antagonist.

"Will you repeat that list of problems?" she asked, coldly.

"Servants, baby-food, floor-polish, and godets," I repeated, somewhat sheepishly, she took it so coolly.

"Very well," said Xanthippe, with a note of amusement in her manipulation of the keys. "If those are your subjects, let us discuss them. I am surprised to find an able-bodied man like yourself bothering with such problems, but I'll help you out of your difficulties if I can. No needy man shall ever say that I ignored his cry for help. What do you want to know about baby-food?"

This turning of the tables nonplussed me, and I didn't really know what to say, and so wisely said nothing, and the machine grew sharp in its clicking.

"You men!" it cried. "You don't know how fearfully shallow you are. I can see through you in a minute."

"Well," I said, modestly, "I suppose you can." Then calling my feeble wit to my rescue, I added, "It's only natural, since I've made a spectacle of myself."

"Not you!" cried Xanthippe. "You haven't even made a monocle of yourself."

And here we both laughed, and the ice was broken.

"What has become of Boswell?" I asked.

"He's been sent to the ovens for ten days for libelling Shakespeare and Adam and Noah and old Jonah," replied Xanthippe. "He printed an article alleged to have been written by Baron Munchausen, in which those four gentlemen were held up to ridicule and libelled grossly."

"And Munchausen?" I cried.

"Oh, the Baron got out of it by confessing that he wrote the article," replied the lady. "And as he swore to his confession the jury were convinced he was telling another one of his lies and acquitted him, so Boswell was sent up alone. That's why I am here. There isn't a man in all Hades that dared take charge of Boswell's paper—they're all so deadly afraid of the government, so I stepped in, and while Boswell is baking I'm attending to his editorial duties."

"But you spoke contemptuously of the Sunday newspapers awhile ago, Mrs. Socrates," said I.

"I know that," said Xanthippe, "but I've fixed that. I get out the Sunday edition on Saturdays."

"Oh—I see. And you like it?" I queried.

"First rate," she replied. "I'm in love with the work. I almost wish poor old Bos had been sentenced for ten years. I have enough of the woman in me to love minding other people's business, and, as far as I can find out, that's about all journalism amounts to. Sewing societies aren't to be mentioned in the same day with a newspaper for scandal and gossip, and, besides, I'm an ardent advocate of men's rights—have been for centuries—and I've got my first chance now to promulgate a few of my ideas. I'm really a man in all my views of life—that's the inevitable end of an advanced woman who persists in following her 'newness' to its logical conclusion. Her habits of thought gradually come to be those of a man. Even I have a great deal more sympathy with Socrates than I used to have. I used to think I was the one that should be emancipated, but I'm really reaching that stage in my manhood where I begin to believe that he needs emancipation."

"Then you admit, do you," I cried, with great glee, "that this new-woman business is all Tommy-rot?"

"Not by a great deal," snapped the machine. "Far from it. It's the salvation of the happy life. It is perfectly logical to say that the more manny a woman becomes, the more she is likely to sympathize with the troubles and trials which beset men."

I scratched my head and pulled the lobe of my ear in the hope of loosening an argument to confront her with, not that I disagreed with her entirely, but because I instinctively desired to oppose her as pleasantly disagreeably as I could. But the result was nil.

"I'm afraid you are right," I said.

"You're a truthful man," clicked the machine, laughingly. "You are afraid I'm right. And why are you afraid? Because you are one of those men who take a cynical view of woman. You want woman to be a mere lump of sugar, content to be left in a bowl until it pleases you in your high-and-mightiness to take her in the tongs and drop her into the coffee of your existence, to sweeten what would otherwise not please your taste—and like most men you prefer two or three lumps to one."

I could only cough. The lady was more or less right. I am very fond of sugar, though one lump is my allowance, and I never exceed it, whatever the temptation. Xanthippe continued.

"You criticise her because she doesn't understand you and your needs, forgetting that out of twenty-four hours of your daily existence your wife enjoys personally about twelve hours of your society, during eight of which you are lying flat on your back, snoring as though your life depended on it; but when she asks to be allowed to share your responsibilities as well as what, in her poor little soul, she thinks are your joys, you flare up and call her 'new' and 'advanced,' as if advancement were a crime. You ride off on your wheel for forty miles on your days of rest, and she is glad to have you do it, but when she wants a bicycle to ride, you think it's all wrong, immoral, and conducive to a weak heart. Bah!"

"I—ah—" I began.

"Yes you do," she interrupted. "You ah and you hem and you

haw, but in the end you're a poor miserable social mugwump, conscious of your own magnificence and virtue, but nobody else ever can attain to your lofty plane. Now what I want to see among women is more good fellows. Suppose you regarded your wife as good a fellow as you think your friend Jones. Do you think you'd be running off to the club every night to play billiards with Jones, leaving your wife to enjoy her own society?"

"Perhaps not," I replied, "but that's just the point. My wife isn't a good fellow."

"Exactly, and for that reason you seek out Jones. You have a right to the companionship of the good fellow—that's what I'm going to advocate. I've advanced far enough to see that on the average in the present state of woman she is not a suitable companion for man—she has none of the qualities of a chum to which he is entitled. I'm not so blind but that I can see the faults of my own sex, particularly now that I have become so very masculine myself. Both sexes should have their rights, and that is the great policy I'm going to hammer at as long as I have Boswell's paper in charge. I wish you might see my editorial page for tomorrow; it is simply fine.

"I urge upon woman the necessity of joining in with her husband in all his pleasures whether she enjoys them or not. When he lights a cigar, let her do the same; when he calls for a cocktail, let her call for another. In time she will begin to understand him. He understands her pleasures, and often he joins in with them—opera, dances, lectures; she ought to do the same, and join in with him in his pleasures, and after a while they'll get upon a common basis, have their clubs together, and when that happy time comes, when either one goes out the other will also go, and their companionship will be perfect."

"But you objected to my calling you old chap when we first met," said I. "Is that quite consistent?"

"Of course," retorted the lady. "We had never met before, and, besides, doctors do not always take their own medicine."

"But that women ought to become good fellows is what

you're going to advocate, eh?" said I.

"Yes," replied Xanthippe. "It's excellent, don't you think?"

"Superb," I answered, "for Hades. It's just my idea of how things ought to be in Hades. I think, however, that we mortals will stick to the old plan for a little while yet; most of us prefer to marry wives rather than old chaps."

The remark seemed so to affect my visitor that I suddenly became conscious of a sense of loneliness.

"I don't wish to offend you," I said, "but I rather like to keep the two separate. Aren't you man enough yet to see the value of variety?"

But there was no answer. The lady had gone. It was evident that she considered me unworthy of further attention.

5: THE EDITING OF XANTHIPPE

After my interview with Xanthippe, I hesitated to approach the typewriter for a week or two. It did a great deal of clicking after the midnight hour had struck, and I was consumed with curiosity to know what was going on, but I did not wish to meet Mrs. Socrates again, so I held aloof until Boswell should have served his sentence. I was no longer afraid of the woman, but I do fear the good fellow of the weaker sex, and I deemed it just as well to keep out of any and all disputes that might arise from a casual conversation with a creature of that sort.

An agreement with a real good fellow, even when it ends in a row, is more or less diverting; but a disputation with a female good fellow places a man at a disadvantage. The *argumentum ad hominem* is not an easy thing with men, but with women it is impossible. Hence, I let the typewriter click and ring for a fort-night.

Finally, to my relief, I recognized Boswell's touch upon the keys and sauntered up to the side of the machine.

"Is this Boswell—Jim Boswell?" I inquired.

"All that's left of him," was the answer. "How have you been?"

"Very well," said I. And then it seemed to me that tact required that I should not seem to know that he had been in the superheated jail of the Stygian country. So I observed, "You've been off on a vacation, eh?"

"How do you know that?" was the immediate response.

"Well," I put in, "you've been absent for a fortnight, and you look more or less—ah—burned."

"Yes, I am," replied the deceitful editor. "Very much burned, in fact. I've been—er—I've been playing golf with a friend down in Cimmeria."

"I envy you," I observed, with an inward chuckle.

"You wouldn't if you knew the links," replied Boswell, sadly. "They're awfully hard. I don't know any harder course than the Cimmerian."

And then I became conscious of a mistrustful gaze fastened upon me.

"See here," clicked the machine. "I thought I was invisible to you? If so, how do you know I look burned?"

I was cornered, and there was only one way out of it, and that was by telling the truth. "Well, you are invisible, old chap," I said. "The fact is, I've been told of your trouble, and I know what you have undergone."

"And who told you?" queried Boswell.

"Your successor on the *Gazette*, Madame Socrates, nee Xanthippe," I replied.

"Oh, that woman—that woman!" moaned Boswell, through the medium of the keys. "Has she been here, using this machine too? Why didn't you stop her before she ruined me completely?"

"Ruined you?" I cried.

"Well, next thing to it," replied Boswell. "She's run my paper so far into the ground that it will take an almighty powerful grip to pull it out again. Why, my dear boy, when I went to—to the ovens, I had a circulation of a million, and when I came back that woman had brought it down to eight copies, seven of which have already been returned. All in ten days, too."

"How do you account for it?" I asked.

"*Side Talks with Men* helped, and *The Man's Corner* did a little, but the editorial page did the most of it. It was given over wholly to the advancement of certain Xanthippian ideas, which were very offensive to my women readers, and which found no favour among the men. She wants to change the whole social structure. She thinks men and women are the same kind of animal, and that both need to be educated on precisely the same lines—the girls to be taught business, the boys to go through a course of domestic training. She called for subscriptions for a cooking-school for boys, and demanded the endowment of a commercial college for girls, and wound up by insisting upon a uniform dress for both sexes.

"I tell you, if you'd worked for years to establish a dignified newspaper the way I have, it would have broken your heart to see the suggested fashion-plates that woman printed. The uniform dress was a holy terror. It was a combination of all the worst features of modern garb. Trousers were to be universal and compulsory; sensible masculine coats were discarded entirely, and puffed-sleeved dress-coats were substituted. Stiff collars were abolished in favour of ribbons, and rosettes cropped up everywhere. Imagine it if you can—and everybody in all Hades was to be forced into garments of that sort!"

"I should enjoy seeing it," I said.

"Possibly—but you wouldn't enjoy wearing it," retorted the machine. "And then that woman's funny column—it was frightful. You never saw such jokes in your life; every one of them contained a covert attack upon man. There was only one good thing in it, and that was a bit of verse called *Fair Play for the Little Girls*. It went like this:

If little boys, when they are young,
Can go about in skirts,
And wear upon their little backs
Small broidered girlish shirts,
Pray why cannot the little girls,
When infants, have a chance
To toddle on their little ways

In little pairs of pants?

"That isn't at all bad," said I, smiling in spite of poor Boswell's woe. "If the rest of the paper was on a par with that I don't see why the circulation fell off."

"Well, she took liberties, that's all," said Boswell. "For instance, in her 'Side Talks with Men' she had something like this: 'Napoleon—It is rather difficult to say just what you can do with your last season's cocked-hat. If you were to purchase five yards of one-inch blue ribbon, cut it into three strips of equal length, and fasten one end to each of the three corners of the hat, tying the other ends into a *choux*, it would make a very acceptable work-basket to send to your grandmother at Christmas.'

"Now Napoleon never asked that woman for advice on the subject. Then there was an answer to a purely fictitious inquiry from Solomon which read: 'It all depends on local custom. In Salt Lake City, and in London at the time of Henry the Eighth, it was not considered necessary to be off with the old love before being on with the new, but latterly the growth of monopolistic ideas tends towards the uniform rate of one at a time.' A purely gratuitous fling, that was, at one of my most eminent patrons, or rather two of them, for latterly both Solomon and Henry the Eighth have yielded to the tendency of the times and gone into business, which they have paid me well to advertise.

"Solomon has established an 'Information Bureau,' where advice can always be had from the 'Wise-man,' as he calls himself, on payment of a small fee; while Henry, taking advantage of his superior equipment over any English king that ever lived, has founded and liberally advertised his 'Chaperon Company (Limited).' It's a great thing even in Hades for young people to be chaperoned by an English queen, and Henry has been smart enough to see it, and having seven or eight queens, all in good standing, he has been doing a great business. Just look at it from a business point of view.

"There are seven nights in every week, and something going on somewhere all the time, and queens in demand. With a queen quoted so low as $100 a night, Henry can make nearly

$5000 a week, or $260,000 a year, out of evening chaperonage alone; and when, in addition to this, yachting-parties up the Styx and slumming-parties throughout the country are being constantly given, the man's opportunity to make half a million a year is in plain sight. I'm told that he netted over $500,000 last year; and of course he had to advertise to get it, and this Xanthippe woman goes out of her way to get in a nasty little fling at one of my mainstays for his matrimonial propensities."

"Failing utterly to see," said I, "that, in marrying so many times, Henry really paid a compliment to her sex which is without parallel in royal circles."

"Well, nearly so," said Boswell. "There have been other kings who were quite as complimentary to the ladies, but Henry was the only man among them who insisted on marrying them all."

"True," said I. "Henry was eminently proper—but then he had to be."

"Yes," said Boswell, with a meditative tap on the letter Y. "Yes—he had to be. He was the head of the Church, you know."

"I know it," I put in. "I've always had a great deal of sympathy for Henry. He has been very much misjudged by posterity. He was the father of the really first new woman, Elizabeth, and his other daughter, Mary, was such a vindictive person."

"You are a very fair man, for an American," said Boswell. "Not only fair, but rare. You think about things."

"I try to," said I, modestly. "And I've really thought a great deal about Henry, and I've truly seen a valid reason for his continuous matrimonial performances. He set himself up against the Pope, and he had to be consistent in his antagonism."

"He did, indeed," said Boswell. "A religious discussion is a hard one."

"And Henry was consistent in his opposition," said I. "He didn't yield a jot on any point, and while a great many people criticise him on the score of his wives—particularly on their number—I feel that I have in very truth discovered his principle."

"Which was?" queried Boswell.

"That the Pope was wrong in all things," said I.

"So he said," commented Boswell.

"And being wrong in all things, celibacy was wrong," said I.

"Exactly," ejaculated Boswell.

"Well, then," said I, "if celibacy is wrong, the surest way to protest against it is to marry as many times as you can."

"By Jove!" said Boswell, tapping the keys yearningly, as though he wished he might spare his hand to shake mine, "you are a man after my own heart."

"Thanks, old chap," said I, reaching out my hand and shaking it in the air with my visionary friend—"thanks. I've studied these things with some care, and I've tried to find a reason for everything in life as I know it. I have always regarded Henry as a moral man—as is natural, since in spite of all you can say he is the real head of the English Church. He wasn't willing to be married a second or a seventh time unless he was really a widower. He wasn't as long in taking notice again as some modern widowers that I have met, but I do not criticise him on that score. I merely attribute his record to his kingly nature, which involves necessarily a quickness of decision and a decided perception of the necessities which is sadly lacking in people who are born to a lesser station in life.

"England demanded a queen, and he invariably met the demand, which shows that he knew something of political economy as well as of matrimony; and as I see it, being an American, a man needs to know something of political economy to be a good ruler. So many of our statesmen have acquired a merely kindergarten knowledge of the science, that we have had many object-lessons of the disadvantages of a merely elementary knowledge of the subject. To come right down to it, I am a great admirer of Henry. At any rate, he had the courage of his heart-convictions."

"You really surprise me," tapped Boswell. "I never expected to find an American so thoroughly in sympathy with kings and their needs."

"Oh, as for that," said I, "in America we are all kings and we are not without our needs, matrimonial and otherwise, only our courts are not quite so expeditious as Henry's little axe. But what was Henry's attitude towards this extraordinary flight of Xanthippe's?"

"Wrath," said Boswell. "He was very much enraged, and withdrew his advertisements, declined to give our society reporters the usual accounts of the functions his wives chaperoned, and, worst of all, has withdrawn himself and induced others to withdraw from the symposium I was preparing for my special Summer Girls' issue, which is to appear in August, on 'How Men Propose.' He and Brigham Young and Solomon and Bonaparte had agreed to dictate graphic accounts of how they had done it on various occasions, and Queen Elizabeth, who probably had more proposals to the square minute that any other woman on record, was to write the introduction. This little plan, which was really the idea of genius, is entirely shattered by Mrs. Socrates's infernal interference."

"Nonsense," said I. "Don't despair. Why don't you come out with a plain statement of the facts? Apologize."

"You forget, my dear sir," interposed Boswell, "that one of the fundamental principles of Hades as an institution is that excuses don't count. It isn't a place for repentance so much as for expiation, and I might apologize nine times a minute for forty years and would still have to suffer the penalty of the offence. No, there is nothing to be done but to begin my newspaper work again, build up again the institution that Xanthippe has destroyed, and bear my misfortunes like a true spirit."

"Spoken like a philosopher!" I cried. "And if I can help you, my dear Boswell, count upon me. In anything you may do, whether you start a monthly magazine, a sporting weekly, or a purely American Sunday newspaper, you are welcome to anything I can do for you."

"You are very kind," returned Boswell, appreciatively, "and if I need your services I shall be glad to avail myself of them.

Just at present, however, my plans are so fully prepared that I do not think I shall have to call upon you. With Sherlock Holmes engaged to write twelve new detective stories; Poe to look after my tales of horror; D'Artagnan dictating his personal memoirs; Lucretia Borgia running my Girls' Department; and others too numerous to mention, I have a sufficient supply of stuff to fill up; but if you feel like writing a few poems for me I may be able to use them as fillers, and they may help to make your name so well known in Hades that next year I shall be able to print a Worldly Letter from you every week with a good chance of its proving popular."

And with this promise Boswell left me to get out the first number of *The Cimmerian*: a Sunday Magazine for all. Taking him at his word, I sent him the following poem a few days later:

Locality
Whither do we drift,
Insensate souls, whose every breath
Foretells the doom of nothingness?
Yet onward, upward let it be
Through all the myriad circles
Of the ensuing years—
And then, pray what?
Alas! 'tis all, and never shall be stated.
Atoms, yet atomless we drift,
But whitherward?

I had intended this for one of our leading magazines, but it seemed so to lack the mystical quality, which is essential to a successful magazine poem in our sphere, that I deemed it best to try it on Boswell.

6: THE BOSWELL TOURS: PERSONALLY CONDUCTED

It was and will no doubt be considered, even by those who are not too friendly towards myself, a daring idea, and it was all my own. One night, several weeks after the interview with Boswell just narrated, the idea came to me simultaneously with the first tapping of the keys for the evening upon the Enchanted Typewriter. It was Boswell's touch that summoned me from my divan. My family were on the eve of departure for a month's rest from care and play in the mountains, and I was looking forward to a period of very great loneliness. But as Boswell materialized and began his work upon the machine, the great idea flashed across my mind, and I resolved to "play it" for all it was worth.

"Jim," said I, as I approached the vacant chair in which he sat—for by this time the great biographer and I had got upon terms of familiarity—"Jim," said I, "I've got a very gloomy prospect ahead of me."

"Well, why not?" he tapped off. "Where do you expect to have your gloomy prospects? They can't very well be behind you."

"Humph!" said I. "You are facetious this evening."

"Not at all," he replied. "I have been spending the day with my old-time boss, Samuel Johnson, and I am so saturated with purism that I hardly know where I am. From the Johnsonian point of view you have expressed yourself ill—"

"Well, I am ill," I retorted. "I don't know how far you are acquainted with home life, but I do know that there is no greater homesickness in the world than that of the man who is sick of home."

"I am not an imitator," said Boswell, "but I must imitate you to the extent of saying humph! I quote you, and, doing so, I honour you. But really, I never thought you could be sick of home, as you put it—you who are so happy at home and who so wildly hate being away from home."

"I'm not surprised at that, my dear Boswell," said I. "But you are, of course, familiar with the phrase 'Stone walls do not a prison make?'"

"I've heard it," said Boswell.

"Well, there's another equally valid phrase which I have not yet heard expressed by another, and it is this: 'Stone walls do not a home make.'"

"It isn't very musical, is it?" said he.

"Not very," I answered, "but we don't all live magazine lives, do we? We have occasionally a sentiment, a feeling, out of which we do not try 'to make copy.' It is undoubtedly a truth which I have not yet seen voiced by any modern poet of my acquaintance, not even by the dead-baby poets, that home is not always preferable to some other things. At any rate, it is my feeling, and is shortly to represent my condition. My home, you know. It has its walls and its pictures, and its thousand and one comforts, and its associations, but when my wife and my children are away, and the four walls do not re-echo the voices of the children, and my library lacks the presence of *madame*, it ceases truly to be home, and if I've got to stay here during the month of August alone I must have diversion, else I shall find myself as badly off as the butterfly man, to whom a vaudeville exhibition is the greatest joy in life."

"I think you are queer," said Boswell.

"Well, I am not," said I. "However low we may set the standard of man, Mr. B."—and I called him Mr. B. instead of Jim, because I wished to be severe and yet retain the basis of familiarity—"however low we may set the standard of man, I think man as a rule prefers his home to the most seductive roof-garden life in existence."

"Wherefore?" said he, coldly.

"Wherefore my home about to become unattractive through the absence of my boys and their mother, I shall need some extraordinary diversion to accomplish my happiness. Now if you can come here, why can't others? Suppose tonight you dash off on the machine a lot of invitations to the pleasantest people in Hades to come up here with you and have an evening on earth, which isn't all bad."

"It's a scheme and a half," said Boswell, with more enthusiasm than I had expected. "I'll do it, only instead of trying to get these people to make a pilgrimage to your shrine, which I think they would decline to do—Shakespeare, for instance, wouldn't give a tuppence to inspect your birthplace as you have inspected his—I'll institute a series of 'Boswell's Personally Conducted

Pleasure Parties,' and make you my agent here. That, you see, will naturally make your home our headquarters, and I think the scheme would work a charm, because there are a great many well-known Stygians who are curious to revisit the scenes of their earlier state, but who are timid about coming on their own responsibility."

"I see," said I. "Immortals are but mortal after all, with all the timidity and weaknesses of mortality. But I agree to the proposition, and if you wish it I'll prepare to give them a rousing old time."

"And be sure to show them something characteristic," said Boswell.

"I will," I replied; "I may even get up a trolley-party for them."

"I don't know what a trolley-party is, but it sounds well," said Boswell, "and I'll advertise the enterprise at once. 'Boswell's Personally Conducted Pleasure Parties. First Series, No. 1. Trolleying Through Hoboken. For the Round Trip, Four Dollars. Supper and All Expenses Included. No Tips. Extra Lady's Ticket, One Dollar.'"

"Hold on!" I cried. "That can't be. These affairs will really have to be stag-parties—with my wife away, you know."

"Not if we secure a suitable chaperon," said Boswell.

"Anyhow!" said I, with great positiveness. "You don't suppose that in the absence of my family I'm going to have my neighbours see me cavorting about the country on a trolley-car full of queens and duchesses and other females of all ages? Not a bit of it, my dear James. I'm not a strictly conventional person, but there are some points between which I draw lines. I've got to live on this earth for a little while yet, and until I leave it I must be guided more or less in what I do by what the world approves or disapproves."

"Very well," Boswell answered. "I suppose you are right, but in the autumn, when your family has returned—"

"We can discuss the matter again," said I, resolved to put off the question for as long a time as I could, for I candidly confess that I had no wish to make myself responsible for the welfare of such Stygian ladies as might avail themselves of the opportunity to go off on one of Boswell's tours. "Show the value and beauties of your plan to the influential men of Hades first, my dear Boswell," I added, "and then if they choose they can come again and bring their wives with them on their own responsibility."

"I fancy that is the best plan, but we ought to have some variety in these tours," he replied. "A trolley-party, however successful, would not make a great season for an entertainment bureau, would it?"

"No, indeed," said I. "You are perfectly right about that. What you want is one function a week during the summer season. Open with the trolley-party as No. 1 of your first series. Follow this with 'An Evening of Vaudeville: The Grand Tour of the Roof Gardens.' After that have a 'Sunday at the Sea-side—Surf Bathing, Summer Girls and Sand.' That would make a mighty attractive line for your advertisement."

"Magnificent. I don't see why you don't give up poetry and magazine work and get a position as poster-writer for a circus. You are only a mediocre magazinist, but in the poster business you'd be a genius."

This was tapped off with such manifest sincerity that I could not take offence, so I thanked him and resumed.

"The grand finale of your first series might be 'A Tandem Scorch: A Century Run on a Bicycle Built for Two Hundred!'"

"Magnificent!" cried Boswell, with such enthusiasm that I feared he would smash the machine. "I'll devote a whole page of my Sunday issue to the prospectus—but, to return to the woman question, we ought really to have something to announce for them. Hades hath no fury like a woman scorned, and I can't afford to scorn the sex. You needn't have anything to do with them if you don't want to—only tell me something I can announce, and I'll make Henry the Eighth solid again by putting that branch of the enterprise in his wives' hands. In that way I'll kill two birds with one stone."

"That's all very well, Boswell, but I'm afraid I can't," said I. "It's hard enough to know how to please a mortal woman without attempting to get up a series of picnics for the rather miscellaneous assortment of ladies who form your social structure below. All men are alike, and man's pleasures in all times have been generally the same, but every woman is unique. I never knew two who were alike, and if it's all the same to you I'd rather you left me out of your ladies' tours altogether. Of course I know that even the Queen of Sheba would enjoy a visit to a Monday sale at one of our big department stores, and I am quite as well aware that nine out of ten women in Hades or out of it would enjoy the millinery exhibition at the opera matinee—and if these two ideas impress you at all you are welcome to them—but beyond this I have nothing to suggest."

"Well, I'm sure those two ideas are worth a great deal," returned Boswell, making a note of them; "I shall announce four trips to Monday sales—"

"Call 'em 'To Bargaindale and Back: The Great Markeddown Tour,' and be sure you add, 'For Able-bodied Women Only. No Tickets Issued Except on Recommendation of your Family Physician.' This is especially important, for next to a war or a football match there's nothing that I know of that is quite so dangerous to the participants as a bargain day."

"I'll bear what you say in mind," quoth Boswell, and he made a note of my injunction. "And immediately upon my return to Hades I will request an audience with Henry's queens, and ask them to devise a number of other tours likely to prove profitable and popular."

Shortly after my visitor departed and I retired. The next day my family deserted me and went to the mountains, and all my fears as to the inordinate sense of loneliness which was to be my lot were realized. Even Boswell neglected me apparently for a week. I went to my desk daily and returned at night hoping that my type-writer would bring forth something of an interesting nature, but naught other than disappointment awaited me. For a whole blessed week I was thrown back upon the society of my neighbours for diversion. The typewriter gave no sign of being.

Little did I guess that Boswell was busy working up my scheme in his Stygian home!

But it came to pass finally that I was roused up. Walking one morning to my desk to find a bit of memoranda I needed, I discovered a typewritten slip marked, "No time for small talk. Boswell's tours grand success. Trolley-party tonight. Ten cars wanted. Jim."

It was a large order for a town like mine, where forty thousand people have to get along with five cars—two open ones for winter and two closed for summer, and one, which we have never seen, which is kept for use in the repair-shop. I was in despair. Ten car-loads of immortals coming to my house for a trolley-party under such conditions! It was frightful! I did the best I could, however.

I ordered one trolley-car to be ready at eight, and a large variety of good things edible and drinkable, the latter to be held subject to the demand-notes of our guests.

As may be imagined, I did little real work that day, and when I returned home at night I was on tenter-hooks lest something should go wrong; but fortunately Boswell himself came early and relieved me of my worry—in fact, he was at the machine when I entered the house.

"Well," he said, "have you the ten cars?"

"What do you take me for," said I, "a trolley-car trust? Of course I haven't. There are only five cars in town, one of which is kept in the repair-shop for effect. I've hired one."

"Humph!" he cried. "What will the kings do?"

"Kings!" I cried. "What kings?"

"I have nine kings and one car-load of common souls besides for this affair," he explained. "Each king wants a special car."

"Kings be jiggered!" said I. "A trolley-party, my much beloved James, is an essentially democratic institution, and private cars are not de rigueur. If your kings choose to come, let 'em hang on by the straps."

"But I've charged 'em extra!" cried Boswell.

"That's all right," said I, "they receive extra. They have the ride plus the straps, with the privilege of standing out on the platform and ringing the gong if they want to. The great thing about the trolley-party is that there's no private car business about it."

"Well, I don't know," Boswell murmured, reflectively. "If Charles the First and Louis Fourteenth don't kick about being crowded in with all the rest, I can stand anything that Frederick the Great or Nero might say; but those two fellows are great sticklers for the royal prerogative."

"There isn't any such thing as royal prerogative on a trolley-car," I retorted, "and if they don't like what they get they can sit down in the waiting-room and wait until we get back."

But Boswell's fears were not realized. Charles and Louis were perfectly delighted with the trolley-party, and long before we reached home the former had rung up the fare-register to its full capacity, while the latter, a half-a-dozen times, delightedly occupied himself in mastering the intricacies of the overhead wire. The trolley-party was an undoubted success. The same remains to be said of the vaudeville expedition of the following week. The same guests and potentates attended this, to the number of twenty, and the Boswell tours were accounted a great enterprise, and bade fair to redeem the losses of the eminent journalist incurred during Xanthippe's administration of his affairs; but after the bicycle night I had to withdraw from the combination to save my reputation.

The fact upon which I had not counted was that my neighbours began to think me insane. I had failed to remember that none of these visiting spirits was visible to us in this material world, and while my fellow-townsmen were disposed to lay up my hiring of a special trolley-car for my own private and particular use against the eccentricity of genius, they marvelled greatly that I should purchase twenty of the best seats at a vaudeville show seemingly for my own exclusive use. When, besides this, they saw me start off apparently alone on one tandem bicycle, followed by twenty-eight other empty wheels, which they could not know were manipulated by some of the most famous legs in the history of the world, from Noah's down to those of Henry Fielding the novelist, they began to regard me as something uncanny.

Nor can I blame them. It seems to me that if I saw one man scorching along a road alone on a tandem bicycle chatting to an empty front-seat, I should think him queer, but if following in his wake I perceived twenty-eight other wheels, scorching up hill and down dale without any visible motive power, I should regard him as one who was in league with the devil himself.

Nevertheless, I judge from what Boswell has told me that I am regarded in Hades as a great benefactor of the people there, for having established a series of excursions from that world into this, a service which has done much to convince the Stygians that after all, if only by contrast, the life below has its redeeming features.

7: An Important Decision

For some time after the organization of the Pleasure Tours, the Enchanted Typewriter appeared to be deserted. Night after night I watched over it with great care lest I should lose any item of interest that might come to me from below, but, much to my sorrow, things in Hades appeared to be dull—so dull that the machine was not called into requisition at all. I little guessed what important matters were transpiring in that wonderful country. Had I done so, I doubt I should have waited so patiently, although my only method of getting there was suicide, for which diversion I have very little liking. On the twenty-fourth night of waiting, however, the welcome sound of the bell dragged me forth from my comfortable couch, whither, expecting nothing, I had retired early.

"Glad to hear your pleasant tinkle again," I said. "I've missed you."

"I'm glad to get back," returned Boswell, for it was he who was manipulating the keys. "I've been so infernally busy, however, over the court news, that I haven't had a minute to spare."

"Court news, eh?" I said. "You are going to open up a society column, are you?"

"Not I," he replied. "It's the other kind of a court. We've been having some pretty hot litigation down in Hades since I was here last. The city of Cimmeria has been suing the State of Hades for ten years back dog-taxes."

"For what?" I cried.

"Unpaid dog-taxes for ten years," Boswell explained. "We have just as much government below in our cities as you have, and I will say for Hades that our cities are better run than yours."

"I suppose that is due to the fact that when a man gets to Hades he immediately becomes a reformer," I suggested, with a wink at the machine, which somehow or other did not seem to appreciate the joke.

"Possibly," observed Boswell. "Whatever the reason, however, the fact remains that Cimmeria is a well-governed city, and, what is more, it isn't afraid to assert its rights even as against old Apollyon himself."

"It's safe enough for a corporation," said I. "Much safer for a corporation which has no soul, than for an individual who has. You can't torture a city—"

"Oh, can't you!" laughed Boswell. "Humph. Apollyon can make it as hot for a city as he can for an individual. It is evident that you never heard of Sodom and Gomorrah—which is surprising to me, since your jokes about Lot's wife being too fresh and getting salted down, would seem to indicate that you had heard something about the punishment those cities underwent."

"You are right, Bozzy," I said. "I had forgotten. But tell me about the dog-tax. Does the State own a dog?"

"Does it?" roared Boswell. "Why, my dear fellow, where were you brought up and educated. Does the State own a dog!"

"That's what I asked you," I put in, meekly. "I may be very ignorant, unless you mean the kind that we have in our legislatures, called the watch-dogs of the treasury, or, perhaps, the dogs of war. But I never thought any city would be crazy enough to make the government take out a license for them."

"Never heard of a beast named Cerberus, I suppose?" said Boswell.

"Yes, I have," I answered. "He guards the gates to the infernal regions."

"Well—he's the bone of contention," said Boswell. "You see, about ten years ago the people of Cimmeria got rather tired of the condition of their streets. They were badly paved. They were full of good intentions, but the citizens thought they ought to have something more lasting, so they voted to appropriate an enormous sum for asphalting. They didn't realize how sloppy asphalt would become in that climate, but after the asphalt was put down they found out, and a Beelzebub of a time of it they had.

"Pegasus sprained his off hind leg by slipping on it, Bucephalus got into it with all four feet and had to be lifted out with a derrick, and every other fine horse we had was more or less injured, and the damage suits against the city were enormous. To remedy this, the asphalting was taken up and a Nicholson wood pavement was put down. This was worse than the other. It used to catch fire every other night, and, finally, to protect their houses, the people rose up *en masse* and ripped it all to pieces.

"This necessitated a third new pavement, of Belgian blocks, to pay for which the already overburdened city of Cimmeria had to issue bonds to an enormous amount, all of which necessitated an increase of taxes. Naturally, one of the first taxes to be imposed was a dog-tax, and it was that which led to this lawsuit, which, I regret to say, the city has lost, although Judge Blackstone's decision was eminently fair."

"Wouldn't the State pay?" I asked.

"Yes—on Cerberus as one dog," said Boswell. "The city claimed, however, that Cerberus was more than that, and endeavoured to collect on three dogs—one license for each head. This the State declined to pay, and out of this grew further complications of a distressing nature. The city sent its dog-catchers up to abscond with the dog, intending to cut off two of its heads, and return the balance as being as much of the beast as the State was entitled to maintain on a single license. It was an unfortunate move, for when Cerberus himself took the situation in, which he did at a glance, he nabbed the dog-catcher by the coat-tails with one pair of jaws, grabbed hold of his collar with another, and shook him as he would a rat, meanwhile chewing up other portions of the unfortunate official with his third set of teeth. The functionary was then carried home on a stretcher, and subsequently sued the city for damages, which he recovered.

"Another man was sent out to lure the ferocious beast to the pound with a *lasso*, but it worked no better than the previous attempt. The *lasso* fell all right tight about one of the animal's necks, but his other two heads immediately set to work and gnawed the rope through, and then set off after the dog-catcher, overtaking him at the very door of the pound. This time he didn't do any biting, but lifting the dog-catcher up with his various sets of teeth, fastened to his collar, coat-tails, and feet respectively, carried him yelling like a trooper to the end of the wharf and dropped him into the Styx.

"The result of this was nervous prostration for the dog-catcher, another suit for damages for the city, and a great laugh for the State authorities. In fact," Boswell added, confidentially, "I think perhaps the reason why the Prime-minister hasn't got Apollyon to hang the whole city government has been due to the fun they've got out of seeing Cerberus and the city fighting it out together. There's no doubt about it that he is a wonderful dog, and is quite capable of taking care of himself."

"But the outcome of the case?" I asked, much interested.

"Defeat for the city," said Boswell. "Failing to enforce its authority by means of its servants, the city undertook to recover by due process of law. The dog-catchers were powerless; the police declined to act on the advice of the commissioners, since dog-catching was not within their province; and the fire department averred that it was designed for the putting out of fires and not for extinguishing fiery canines like Cerberus. The dog, meanwhile, to show his contempt for the city, chewed the license-tag off the neck upon which it had been placed, and dropped it into a smelting-pot inside the gates of the infernal regions that was reserved to bring political prisoners to their senses, and, worse than all, made a perfect nuisance of himself by barking all day and baying all night, rain or shine."

"Papers in a suit at law were then served on Mazarin and the other members of Apollyon's council, the causes of complaint were recited, and damages for ten years back taxes on two dogs, plus the amounts recovered from the city by the two injured dog-catchers, were demanded. The suit was put upon the calendar, and Apollyon himself sat upon the bench with Judge Blackstone, before whom the case was to be tried.

"On both sides the arguments were exceedingly strong. Coke appeared for the city and Catiline for the State. After the complaint was read, the attorney for the State put in his answer, that the State's contention was that the ordinance had been complied with, that Cerberus was only one dog, and that the license had been paid; that the license having been paid, the dog-catchers had no right to endeavour to abduct the animal, and that having done so they did it at their own peril; that the suit ought to be dismissed, but that for the fun of it the State was perfectly willing to let it go on.

"In rebuttal the plaintiff claimed that Cerberus was three dogs to all intents and purposes, and the first dog-catcher was called to testify. After giving his name and address he was asked a few questions of minor importance, and then Coke asked:

"'Are you familiar with dogs?'

"'Moderately,' was the answer. 'I never got quite so intimate with one as I did with him.'

"'With whom?' asked Coke.

"'Cerberus,' replied the witness.

"'Do you consider him to be one dog, two dogs or three dogs?'

"'I object!' cried Catiline, springing to his feet. 'The question is a leading one.'

"'Sustained,' said Blackstone, with a nervous glance at Apollyon, who smiled reassuringly at him.

"'Ah, you say you know a dog when you see one?' asked Coke.

"'Yes,' said the witness, 'perfectly.'

"'Do you know two dogs when you see them, or even three?' asked Coke.

"'I do,' replied the witness.

"'And how many dogs did you see when you saw Cerberus?' asked Coke, triumphantly.

"'Three, anyhow,' replied the witness, with feeling, 'though afterwards I thought there was a whole bench-show atop of me.'

"'Your witness,' said Coke.

"A murmur of applause went through the court-room, at which Apollyon frowned; but his face cleared in a moment when Catiline rose up.

"'My cross-examination of this witness, your honour, will be confined to one question.' Then turning to the witness he said, blandly: 'My poor friend, if you considered Cerberus to be three dogs anyhow, why did you in your examination a moment since refer to the avalanche of caninity, of which you so affectingly speak, as him?'

"'He is a him,' said the witness.

"'But if there were three, should he not have been a them?'

"Coke swore profanely beneath his breath, and the witness squirmed about in his chair, confused and broken, while both Judge Blackstone and Apollyon smiled broadly. Manifestly the point of the defence had pierced the armour of the plaintiff.

"'Your witness for redirect,' said Catiline.

"'No thanks,' retorted Coke; 'there are others,' and, motioning to his first witness to step down, he called the second dog-catcher.

"'What is your business?' asked Coke, after the usual preliminary questions.

"'I'm out of business. Livin' on my damages,' said the witness.

"'What damages?' asked Coke.

"'Them I got from the city for injuries did me by that there—I should say them there—dorgs, Cerberus.'

"'Them there what?' persisted Coke, to emphasize the point.

"'Dorgs,' said the witness, convincingly—'D-o-r-g-s.'

"'Why s?' queried Coke. 'We may admit the r, but why the s?'

"'Because it's the pullural of dorg. Cerberus ain't any single-headed commission,' said the witness, who was something of a ward politician.

"'Why do you say that Cerberus is more than one dog?'

"'Because I've had experience,' replied the witness. 'I've seen the time when he was everywhere all at once; that's why I say he's more than one dorg. If he'd been only one dorg he couldn't have been anywhere else than where he was.'

"'When was that?'

"'When I *lassoed* him.'

"'Him?' remonstrated Coke.

"'Yes,' said the witness. 'I only caught one of him, and then the other two took a hand.'

"'Ah, the other two,' said Coke. 'You know dogs when you see them?'

"'I do, and he was all of 'em in a bunch,' replied the witness.

"'Your witness,' said Coke.

"'My friend,' said Catiline, rising quietly. 'How many men are you?'

"'One, sir,' was the answer.

"'Have you ever been in two places at once?'

"'Yes, sir.'

"'When was that?'

"'When I was in jail and in London all at the same time.'

"'Very good; but were you in two places on the day of this attack upon you by Cerberus?'

"'No, sir. I wish I had been. I'd have stayed in the other place.'

"'Then if you were in but one place yourself, how do you

know that Cerberus was in more than one place?'

"'Well, I guess if you—'

"'Answer the question,' said Catiline.

"'Oh, well—of course—'

"'Of course,' echoed Catiline. 'That's it, your honour; it is only "of course,"—and I rest my case. We have no witnesses to call. We have proven by their own witnesses that there is no evidence of Cerberus being more than one dog.'

"You ought to have heard the cheers as Catiline sat down," continued Boswell. "As for poor Coke, he was regularly knocked out, but he rose up to sum up his case as best he could. Blackstone, however, stopped him right at the beginning.

"'The counsel for the plaintiff might as well sit down,' he said, 'and save his breath. I've decided this case in favour of the defendant long ago. It is plain to everyone that Cerberus is only one dog, in spite of his many talents and manifest ability to be in several places at once, and inasmuch as the tax which is sued for is merely a dog-tax and not a poll-tax, I must render judgment for the defendants, with costs. Next case.'

"And the city of Cimmeria was thrown out of court," concluded Boswell. "Interesting, eh?"

"Very," said I. "But how will this affect Blackstone? Isn't he a City Judge?"

"No," replied Boswell; "he was, but his term expired this morning, and this afternoon Apollyon appointed him Chief Justice of the Supreme Court of Hades."

8:. A HAND-BOOK TO HADES

"Boswell," said I, the other night, as the machine began to click nervously. "I have just received a letter from an unknown friend in Hawaii who wants to know how the prize-fight between Samson and Goliath came out that time when Kidd and his pirate crew stole the House-Boat on the Styx."

"Just wait a minute, please," the machine responded. "I am very busy just now mapping out the itinerary of the first series of the Boswell Personally Conducted Tours you suggested some time ago. I laid that whole proposition before the Entertainment Committee of the Associated Shades, and they have resolved unanimously to charter the Ex-*Great Eastern* from the Styx Navigation Company, and return to the scenes of their former glory, devoting a year to it."

"Going to take their wives?" I asked.

"I don't know," Boswell replied. "That is a matter outside of the jurisdiction of the committee and must be decided by a full vote of the club. I hope they will, however. As manager of the enterprise I need assistance, and there are some of the men who can't be managed by anybody except their wives, or mothers-in-law, anyhow. I'll be through in a few minutes. Meanwhile let me hand you the latest product of the Boswell press."

With this the genial spirit produced from an invisible pocket a red-covered book bearing the delicious title of *Baedeker's Hades: A Hand-book for Travellers,* which has entirely superseded, according to the advertisement on the fly-leaves, such books as Virgil and Dante's *Inferno* as the best guide to the lower regions, as well it might, for it appeared on perusal to have been prepared with as much care as one of the more material guide-books of the same publisher, which so greatly assist travellers on this side of the Stygian River.

Some time, if Boswell will permit, I shall endeavour to have this little volume published in this country since it contains many valuable hints to the man of a roving disposition, or for the stay-at-home, for that matter, for all roads lead to Hades. For instance, we do not find in previous guide-books, like Dante's *Inferno,* any references whatsoever to the languages it is well to know before taking the Stygian tour; to the kind of money needed, or its quantity *per capita*; no allusion to the necessity of passports is found in Dante or Virgil; custom-house requirements are ignored by these authors; no statements as to the kind of clothing needed, the quality of the hotels—nor indeed any real information of vital importance to the traveller is to be found in the older books.

In *Baedeker's Hades,* on the other hand, all these subjects are exhaustively treated, together with a very comprehensive series of chapters on "Stygian Wines," "Climate," and "Hellish Art"— the expression is not mine—and other topics of essential interest.

And of what suggestive quality was this little book. Who would ever have guessed from a perusal of Dante that as Hades is the place of departed spirits so also is it the ultimate resting-place of all other departed things. What delightful anticipations are there in the idea of a visit to the Alexandrian library, now suitably housed on the south side of Apollyon Square, Cimmeria, in a building that would drive the trustees of the Boston Public Library into envious despair, even though living Bacchantes are found daily improving their minds in the recesses of its commodious alcoves!

What joyous feelings it gives one to think of visiting the navy-yards of Tyre and finding there the ships concerning the whereabouts of which poets have vainly asked questions for ages! Who would ever dream that the question of the balladist, himself an able dreamer concerning classic things, "Where are the Cities of Old Time," could ever find its answer in a simple guide-book telling us where Carthage is, where Troy and all the lost cities of antiquity!

Then the details of amusements in this wonderful country— who could gather aught of these from the Italian poet? The theatres of Gehenna, with *Hamlet* produced under the joint direction of Shakespeare and the Prince of Denmark himself, the great Zoo of Sheolia, with Jumbo, and the famous woolly horse of earlier days, not to mention the long series of menageries which have passed over the dark river in the ages now forgotten; the hanging gardens of Babylon, where the picnicking element of Hades flock week after week, chuting the chutes, and clambering joyously in and out of the Trojan Horse, now set up in all its majesty therein, with bowling-alleys on its roof, elevators in its legs, and the original Ferris-wheel in its head; the freak museums in the densely populated sections of the large cities, where Hop o' my Thumb and Jack the Giant Killer are exhibited day after day alongside of the great ogres they have killed; the opera-house, with Siegfried himself singing, supported by the real Brunhild and the original, *bona fide* dragon Fafnir, running of his own motive power, and breathing actual fire and smoke without the aid of a steam-engine and a plumber to connect him therewith before he can go out upon the stage to engage Siegfried in deadly combat.

For the information contained in this last item alone, even if the book had no other virtue, it would be worthy of careful perusal from the opening paragraph on language, to the last, dealing with the descent into the Vitriol Reservoir at Gehenna. The account of the feeding of Fafnir, to which admission can be had on payment of ten *oboli*, beginning with a *puree* of kerosene, followed by a half-dozen cartridges on the half-shell, an *entree* of nitro-glycerine, a solid roast of cannel-coal, and a salad of gun-cotton, with a mayonnaise dressing of alcohol and a pinch of powder, topped off with a *demi-tasse* of benzine and a box of matches to keep the fires of his spirit going, is one of the most moving things I have ever read, and yet it may be said without fear of contradiction that until this guide-book was prepared very few of the Stygian tourists have imagined that there was such a sight to be seen.

I have gone carefully over Dante, Virgil, and the works of Andrew Lang, and have found no reference whatsoever in the pages of any of these talented persons to this marvellous spectacle which takes place three times a day, and which I doubt not results in a performance of Siegfried for the delectation of the music lovers of Hades, which is beyond the power of the human mind to conceive.

The hand-book has an added virtue, which distinguishes it from any other that I have ever seen, in that it is anecdotal in style at times where an anecdote is available and appropriate. In connection with this same Fafnir, as showing how necessary it is for the tourist to be careful of his personal safety in Hades, it is related that upon one occasion the keeper of the dragon having taken a grudge against Siegfried for some unintentional slight, fed Fafnir upon Roman-candles and a sky-rocket, with the result that in the fight between the hero and the demon of the wood the Siegfried was seriously injured by the red, white, and blue balls of fire which the dragon breathed out upon him, while the sky-rocket flew out into the audience and struck a young man in the top gallery, knocking him senseless, the stick falling into a grand-tier box and impaling one of the best known social lights of Cimmeria.

"Therefore," adds the astute editor of the hand-book, "on Siegfried nights it were well if the tourist were to go provided with an asbestos umbrella for use in case of an emergency of a similar nature."

In that portion of the book devoted to the trip up the river Styx the legends surpass any of the Rhine stories in dramatic interest, because, according to Commodore Charon's excursion system, the tourist can step ashore and see the chief actors in them, who for a consideration will give a full-dress rehearsal of the legendary acts for which they have been famous. The sirens of the Stygian Lorelei, for instance, sit on an eminence not far above the city of Cimmeria, and make a profession of luring people ashore and giving away at so much per head locks of their hair for remembrance' sake, all of which makes of the Stygian trip a thing of far greater interest than that of the Rhine.

It had been my intention to make a few extracts from this portion of the volume showing later developments in the legends of the Drachenfels, and others of more than ordinary interest, but I find that with the departure of Boswell for the night the treasured hand-book disappeared with him; but, as I have already stated, if I can secure his consent to do so I will someday have the book copied off on more material substance than that employed in the original manuscript, so that the useful little tome may be printed and scattered broadcast over a waiting and appreciative world. I may as well state here, too, that I have taken the precaution to have the title *Baedeker's Hades* and its contents copyrighted, so that any pirate who recognizes the value of the scheme will attempt to pirate the work at his peril.

233

Hardly had I finished the chapter on the legends of the Styx when Boswell broke in upon me with: "Well, how do you like it?"

"It's great," I said. "May I keep it?"

"You may if you can," he laughed. "But I fancy it can't withstand the rigors of this climate any more than an unfireproof copy of one of your books could stand the caniculars of ours."

His words were soon to be verified, for as soon as he left me the book vanished, but whether it went off into thin air or was repocketed by the departing Boswell I am not entirely certain.

"What was it you asked me about Samson and Goliath?" Boswell observed, as he gathered up his manuscript from the floor beside the Enchanted Typewriter. "Whether they'd ever been in Honolulu?"

"No," I replied. "I got a letter from Hawaii the other day asking for the result of the prize-fight the day Kidd ran off with the house-boat."

"Oh," replied Boswell. "That? Why, ah, Samson won hands down, but only because they played according to latter-day rules. If it had been a regular knock-out fight, like the contests in the old days of the ring when it was in its prime, Goliath could have managed him with one hand; but the Samson backers played a sharp game on the Philistine by having the most recently amended Queensbury rules adopted, and Goliath wasn't in it five minutes after Samson opened his mouth."

"I don't think I understand," said I.

"Plain enough," explained Boswell. "Goliath didn't know what the modern rules were, but he thought a fight was a fight under any rules, so, like a decent chap, he agreed, and when he found that it was nothing but a talking-match he'd got into he fainted. He never was good at expressing himself fluently. Samson talked him down in two rounds, just as he did the other Philistines in the early days on earth."

I laughed. "You're slightly off there," I said. "That was a stand-up-and-be-knocked-down fight, wasn't it? He used the jaw-bone of an ass?"

"Very true," observed Boswell, "but it is evident that it is you who are slightly off. You haven't kept up with the higher criticism. It has been proven scientifically that not only did the whale not swallow Jonah, but that Samson's great feat against the Philistines was comparable only to the achievements of your modern senators. He talked them to death."

"Then why jawbone of an ass?" I cried.

"Samson was an ass," replied Boswell. "They prove that by the temple episode, for you see if he hadn't been one he'd have got out of the building before yanking the foundations from under it. I tell you, old chap, this higher criticism is a great thing, and as logical as death itself."

And with this Boswell left me.

I sincerely hope that the result of the fight will prove as satisfactory to my friend in Hawaii as it was to me; for while I have no particular admiration for Samson, I have always rejoiced to hear of the discomfitures of Goliath, who, so far as I have been able to ascertain, was not only not a gentleman, but, in addition, had no more regard for the rights of others than a member of the New York police force or the editor of a Sunday newspaper with a thirst for sensation.

9: Sherlock Holmes Again

I had intended asking Boswell what had become of my copy of the *Baedeker's Hades* when he next returned, but the output of the machine that evening so interested me that the handbook was entirely forgotten. If there ever was a hero in this world who could compare with D'Artagnan in my estimation for sheer ability in a given line that hero was Sherlock Holmes. With D'Artagnan and Holmes for my companions I think I could pass the balance of my days in absolute contentment, no matter what woeful things might befall me.

So it was that, when I next heard the tapping keys and dulcet bell of my Enchanted Typewriter, and, after listening intently for a moment, realized that my friend Boswell was making a copy of a Sherlock Holmes Memoir thereon for his next Sunday's paper, all thought of the interesting little red book of the last meeting flew out of my head. I rose quickly from my couch at the first sounding of the gong.

"Got a Holmes story, eh?" I said, walking to his side, and gazing eagerly over the spot where his shoulder should have been.

"I have that, and it's a winner," he replied, enthusiastically. "If you don't believe it, read it. I'll have it copied in about two minutes."

"I'll do both," I said. "I believe all the Sherlock Holmes stories I read. It is so much pleasanter to believe them true. If they weren't true they wouldn't be so wonderful."

With this I picked up the first page of the manuscript and shortly after Boswell presented me with the balance, whereon I read the following extraordinary tale:

A MYSTERY SOLVED
A WONDERFUL ACHIEVEMENT IN FERRETING
From Advance Sheets of
MEMOIRS I REMEMBER
BY
SHERLOCK HOLMES, ESQ.
Ferreter Extraordinary by Special Appointment
to his Majesty Apollyon

WHO THE LADY WAS!

It was not many days after my solution of the Missing Diamond of the *Nizam* of Jigamaree Mystery that I was called upon to take up a case which has baffled at least one person for some ten or eleven centuries. The reader will remember the mystery of the missing diamond—the largest known in all history, which the *Nizam* of Jigamaree brought from India to present to the Queen of England, on the occasion of her diamond jubilee. I had been dead three years at the time, but, by a special dispensation of his Imperial Highness Apollyon, was permitted to return *incog* to London for the jubilee season, where it so happened that I put up at the same lodging-house as that occupied by the *Nizam* and his suite.

We sat opposite each other at *table d'hôte*, and for at least three weeks previous to the losing of his treasure the Indian prince was very morose, and it was very difficult to get him to speak. I was not supposed to know, nor, indeed, was anyone else, for that matter, at the lodging-house, that the *Nizam* was so exalted a personage. He like myself was travelling *incog* and was known to the world as Mr. Wilkins, of Calcutta—a very wise precaution, inasmuch as he had in his possession a gem valued at a million and a half of dollars. I recognized him at once, however, by his unlikeness to a wood-cut that had been appearing in the American Sunday newspapers, labelled with his name, as well as by the extraordinary lantern which he had on his bicycle, a lantern which to the uneducated eye was no more than an ordinary lamp, but which to an eye like mine, familiar with gems, had for its crystal lens nothing more nor less than the famous stone which he had brought for her Majesty the Queen, his imperial sovereign.

There are few people who can tell diamonds from plate-glass under any circumstances, and Mr. Wilkins, otherwise the *Nizam*, realizing this fact, had taken this bold method of secreting his treasure. Of course, the moment I perceived the quality of the man's lamp I knew at once who Mr. Wilkins was, and I determined to have a little innocent diversion at his expense.

"It has been a fine day, Mr. Wilkins," said I one evening over the *pate*.

"Yes," he replied, wearily. "Very—but somehow or other I'm depressed tonight."

"Too bad," I said, lightly, "but there are others. There's that poor Nizam of Jigamaree, for instance—poor devil, he must be the bluest brown man that ever lived."

Wilkins started nervously as I mentioned the prince by name.

"Wh-why do you think that?" he asked, nervously fingering his butter-knife.

"It's tough luck to have to give away a diamond that's worth three or four times as much as the Koh-i-noor," I said. "Suppose

237

you owned a stone like that. Would you care to give it away?"

"Not by a damn sight!" cried Wilkins, forcibly, and I noticed great tears gathering in his eyes.

"Still, he can't help himself, I suppose," I said, gazing abruptly at his scarf-pin. "That is, he doesn't *know* that he can. The Queen expects it. It's been announced, and now the poor devil can't get out of it—though I'll tell you, Mr. Wilkins, if I were the *Nizam* of Jigamaree, I'd get out of it in ten seconds."

I winked at him significantly. He looked at me blankly.

"Yes, sir," I added, merely to arouse him, "in just ten seconds! Ten short, beautiful seconds."

"Mr. Postlethwaite," said the *Nizam*—Postlethwaite was the name I was travelling under—"Mr. Postlethwaite," said the *Nizam*—otherwise Wilkins—"your remarks interest me greatly." His face wreathed with a smile that I had never before seen there. "I have thought as you do in regard to this poor Indian prince, but I must confess I don't see how he can get out of giving the Queen that diamond. Have a cigar, Mr. Postlethwaite, and, waiter, bring us a triple magnum of champagne. Do you really think, Mr. Postlethwaite, that there is a way out of it? If you would like a ticket to Westminster for the ceremony, there are a half-dozen."

He tossed six tickets for seats among the crowned heads across the table to me. His eagerness was almost too painful to witness.

"Thank you," said I, calmly pocketing the tickets, for they were of rare value at that time. "The way out of it is very simple."

"Indeed, Mr. Postlethwaite," said he, trying to keep cool. "Ah—are you interested in rubies, sir? There are a few which I should be pleased to have you accept"—and with that over came a handful of precious stones each worth a fortune. These also I pocketed as I replied:

"Why, certainly; if I were the *Nizam*," said I, "I'd lose that diamond."

A shade of disappointment came over Mr. Wilkins's face.

"Lose it? How? Where?" he asked, with a frown.

"Yes. Lose it. Any way I could. As for the place where it should be lost, any old place will do as long as it is where he can find it again when he gets back home. He might leave it in his other clothes, or—"

"Make that two triple magnums, waiter," cried Mr. Wilkins, excitedly, interrupting me. "Postlethwaite, you're a genius, and if you ever want a house and lot in Calcutta, just let me know and they're yours."

You never saw such a change come over a man in all your life. Where he had been all gloom before, he was now all smiles and jollity, and from that time on to his return to India Mr. Wilkins was as happy as a school-boy at the beginning of vacation. The next day the diamond was lost, and whoever may have it at this moment, the British Crown is not in possession of the Jigamaree gem.

But, as my friend Terence Mulvaney says, that is another story. It is of the mystery immediately following this concerning which I have set out to write.

I was sitting one day in my office on Apollyon Square opposite the Alexandrian library, smoking an absinthe cigarette, which I had rolled myself from my special mixture consisting of two parts tobacco, one part *hasheesh*, one part of opium dampened with a liqueur glass of absinthe, when an excited knock sounded upon my door.

"Come in," I cried, adopting the usual formula.

The door opened and a beautiful woman stood before me clad in most regal garments, robust of figure, yet extremely pale. It seemed to me that I had seen her somewhere before, yet for a time I could not place her.

"Mr. Sherlock Holmes?" said she, in deliciously musical tones, which, singular to relate, she emitted in a fashion suggestive of a recitative passage in an opera.

"The same," said I, bowing with my accustomed courtesy.

"The ferret?" she sang, in *staccato* tones which were ravishing to my musical soul.

I laughed. "That term has been applied to me, *madame*," said I, chanting my answer as best I could. "For myself, however, I prefer to assume the more modest title of detective. I can work with or without clues, and have never yet been baffled. I know who wrote the Junius letters, and upon occasions have been known to see through a stone wall with my naked eye. What can I do for you?"

"Tell me who I am!" she cried, tragically, taking the centre of the room and gesticulating wildly.

"Well—really, *madame*," I replied. "You didn't send up any card—"

"Ah!" she sneered. "This is what your vaunted prowess amounts to, eh? Ha! Do you suppose if I had a card with my name on it I'd have come to you to inquire who I am? I can read a card as well as you can, Mr. Sherlock Holmes."

"Then, as I understand it, *madame*," I put in, "you have suddenly forgotten your identity and wish me to—"

"Nothing of the sort. I have forgotten nothing. I never knew for certain who I am. I have an impression, but it is based only on hearsay evidence," she interrupted.

For a moment I was fairly puzzled. Still I did not wish to let her know this, and so going behind my screen and taking a capsule full of cocaine to steady my nerves, I gained a moment to think. Returning, I said:

"This really is child's play for me, *madame*. It won't take more than a week to find out who you are, and possibly, if you have any clews at all to your identity, I may be able to solve this mystery in a day."

"I have only three," she answered, and taking a piece of swan's-down, a lock of golden hair, and a pair of silver-tinsel tights from her portmanteau she handed them over to me.

My first impulse was to ask the lady if she remembered the name of the asylum from which she had escaped, but I fortunately refrained from doing so, and she shortly left me, promising to return at the end of the week.

For three days I puzzled over the clews. Swan's-down, yellow hair, and a pair of silver-tinsel tights, while very interesting no doubt at times, do not form a very solid basis for a theory establishing the identity of so regal a person as my visitor. My first impression was that she was a vaudeville artist, and that the exhibits she had left me were a part of her make-up. This I was forced to abandon shortly, because no woman with the voice of my visitor would sing in vaudeville. The more ambitious stage was her legitimate field, if not grand opera itself.

At this point she returned to my office, and I of course reported progress. That is one of the most valuable things I learned while on earth—when you have done nothing, report progress.

"I haven't quite succeeded as yet," said I, "but I am getting at it slowly. I do not, however, think it wise to acquaint you with my present notions until they are verified beyond peradventure. It might help me somewhat if you were to tell me who it is you think you are. I could work either forward or backward on that hypothesis, as seemed best, and so arrive at a hypothetical truth anyhow."

"That's just what I don't want to do," said she. "That information might bias your final judgment. If, however, acting on the clews which you have, you confirm my impression that I am such and such a person, as well as the views which other people have, then will my status be well defined and I can institute my suit against my husband for a judicial separation, with back alimony, with some assurance of a successful issue."

I was more puzzled than ever.

"Well," said I, slowly, "I of course can see how a bit of swan's-down and a lock of yellow hair backed up by a pair of silver-tinsel tights might constitute reasonable evidence in a suit for separation, but wouldn't it—ah—be more to your purpose if I should use these data as establishing the identity of—er—somebody else?"

"How very dense you are," she replied, impatiently. "That's precisely what I want you to do."

"But you told me it was your identity you wished proven," I put in, irritably.

"Precisely," said she.

"Then these bits of evidence are—yours?" I asked, hesitatingly. One does not like to accuse a lady of an undue liking for tinsel.

"They are all I have left of my husband," she answered with a sob.

"Hum!" said I, my perplexity increasing. "Was the—ah—the gentleman blown up by dynamite?"

"Excuse me, Mr. Holmes," she retorted, rising and running the scales. "I think, after all, I have come to the wrong shop. Have you Hawkshaw's address handy? You are too obtuse for a detective."

My reputation was at stake, so I said, significantly:

"Good! Good! I was merely trying one of my disguises on you, *madame*, and you were completely taken in. Of course no one would ever know me for Sherlock Holmes if I manifested such dullness."

"Ah!" she said, her face lighting up. "You were merely deceiving me by appearing to be obtuse?"

"Of course," said I. "I see the whole thing in a nutshell. You married an adventurer; he told you who he was, but you've never been able to prove it; and suddenly you are deserted by him, and on going over his wardrobe you find he has left nothing but these articles: and now you wish to sue him for a separation on the ground of desertion, and secure alimony if possible."

It was a magnificent guess.

"That is it precisely," said the lady. "Except as to the extent of his 'leavings.' In addition to the things you have he gave my small brother a brass bugle and a tin sword."

"We may need to see them later," said I. "At present I will do all I can for you on the evidence in hand. I have got my eye on a gentleman who wears silver-tinsel tights now, but I am afraid he is not the man we are after, because his hair is black, and, as far as I have been able to learn from his valet, he is utterly unacquainted with swan's-down."

We separated again and I went to the club to think. Never

in my life before had I had so baffling a case. As I sat in the cafe sipping a cocaine cobbler, who should walk in but Hamlet, strangely enough picking particles of swan's-down from his black doublet, which was literally covered with it.

"Hello, Sherlock!" he said, drawing up a chair and sitting down beside me. "What you up to?"

"Trying to make out where you have been," I replied. "I judge from the swan's-down on your doublet that you have been escorting Ophelia to the opera in the regulation cloak."

"You're mistaken for once," he laughed. "I've been driving with Lohengrin. He's got a pair of swans that can do a mile in 2.10—but it makes them moult like the devil."

"Pair of what?" I cried.

"Swans," said Hamlet. "He's an eccentric sort of a duffer, that Lohengrin. Afraid of horses, I fancy."

"And so drives swans instead?" said I, incredulously.

"The same," replied Hamlet. "Do I look as if he drove squab?"

"He must be queer," said I. "I'd like to meet him. He'd make quite an addition to my collection of freaks."

"Very well," observed Hamlet. "He'll be here to-morrow to take luncheon with me, and if you'll come, too, you'll be most welcome. He's collecting freaks, too, and I haven't a doubt would be pleased to know you."

We parted and I sauntered homeward, cogitating over my strange client, and now and then laughing over the idiosyncrasies of Hamlet's friend the swan-driver. It never occurred to me at the moment however to connect the two, in spite of the link of swan's-down. I regarded it merely as a coincidence. The next day, however, on going to the club and meeting Hamlet's strange guest, I was struck by the further coincidence that his hair was of precisely the same shade of yellow as that in my possession. It was of a hue that I had never seen before except at performances of grand opera, or on the heads of fool detectives in musical burlesques. Here, however, was the real thing growing luxuriantly from the man's head.

"Ho-ho!" thought I to myself. "Here is a fortunate encounter; there may be something in it," and then I tried to lead him on.

"I understand, Mr. Lohengrin," I said, "that you have a fine span of swans."

"Yes," he said, and I was astonished to note that he, like my client, spoke in musical numbers. "Very. They're much finer than horses, in my opinion. More peaceful, quite as rapid, and amphibious. If I go out for a drive and come to a lake they trot quite as well across its surface as on the highways."

"How interesting!" said I. "And so gentle, the swan. Your wife, I presume—"

Hamlet kicked my shins under the table.

"I think it will rain to-morrow," he said, giving me a glance which if it said anything said shut up.

"I think so, too," said Lohengrin, a lowering look on his face. "If it doesn't, it will either snow, or hail, or be clear." And he gazed abstractedly out of the window.

The kick and the man's confusion were sufficient proof. I was on the right track at last. Yet the evidence was unsatisfactory because merely circumstantial. My piece of down might have come from an opera cloak and not from a well-broken swan, the hair might equally clearly have come from some other head than Lohengrin's, and other men have had trouble with their wives. The circumstantial evidence lying in the coincidences was strong but not conclusive, so I resolved to pursue the matter and invite the strange individual to a luncheon with me, at which I proposed to wear the tinsel tights. Seeing them, he might be forced into betraying himself.

This I did, and while my impressions were confirmed by his demeanour, no positive evidence grew out of it.

"I'm hungry as a bear!" he said, as I entered the club, clad in a long, heavy ulster, reaching from my shoulders to the ground, so that the tights were not visible.

"Good," said I. "I like a hearty eater," and I ordered a luncheon of ten courses before removing my overcoat; but not one morsel could the man eat, for on the removal of my coat his eye fell upon my silver garments, and with a gasp he wellnigh fainted. It was clear. He recognized them and was afraid, and in consequence lost his appetite. But he was game, and tried to laugh it off.

"Silver man, I see," he said, nervously, smiling.

"No," said I, taking the lock of golden hair from my pocket and dangling it before him. "Bimetallist."

His jaw dropped in dismay, but recovering himself instantly he put up a fairly good fight.

"It is strange, Mr. Lohengrin," said I, "that in the three years I have been here I've never seen you before."

"I've been very quiet," he said. "Fact is, I have had my reasons, Mr. Holmes, for preferring the life of a hermit. A youthful indiscretion, sir, has made me fear to face the world. There was nothing wrong about it, save that it was a folly, and I have been anxious in these days of newspapers to avoid any possible revival of what might in some eyes seem scandalous."

I felt sorry for him, but my duty was clear. Here was my man—but how to gain direct proof was still beyond me. No further admissions could be got out of him, and we soon parted.

Two days later the lady called and again I reported progress.

"It needs but one thing, *madame*, to convince me that I have found your husband," said I. "I have found a man who might be connected with swan's-down, from whose luxuriant curls might have come this tow-coloured lock, and who might have worn the silver-tinsel tights—yet it is all *might* and no certainty."

"I will bring my small brother's bugle and the tin sword," said she. "The sword has certain properties which may induce him to confess. My brother tells me that if he simply shakes it at a cat the cat falls dead."

"Do so," said I, "and I will try it on him. If he recognizes the sword and remembers its properties when I attempt to brandish it at him, he'll be forced to confess, though it would be awkward if he is the wrong man and the sword should work on him as it does on the cat."

The next day I was in possession of the famous toy. It was not very long, and rather more suggestive of a pancake-turner than a sword, but it was a terror. I tested its qualities on a swarm of gnats in my room, and the moment I shook it at them they fluttered to the ground as dead as door-nails.

"I'll have to be careful of this weapon," I thought. "It would be terrible if I should brandish it at a motor-man trying to get one of the Gehenna Traction Company's cable-cars to stop and he should drop dead at his post."

All was now ready for the demonstration. Fortunately the following Saturday night was club night at the House-Boat, and we were all expected to come in costume. For dramatic effect I wore a yellow wig, a helmet, the silver-tinsel tights, and a doublet to match, with the brass bugle and the tin sword properly slung about my person. I looked stunning, even if I do say it, and much to my surprise several people mistook me for the man I was after. Another link in the chain! *Even the public unconsciously recognized the value of my deductions. They called me Lohengrin!*

And of course it all happened as I expected. It always does. Lohengrin came into the assembly-room five minutes after I did and was visibly annoyed at my make-up.

"This is a great liberty," said he, grasping the hilt of his sword; but I answered by blowing the bugle at him, at which he turned livid and fell back. He had recognized its soft cadence. I then hauled the sword from my belt, shook it at a fly on the wall, which immediately died, and made as if to do the same at Lohengrin, whereupon he cried for mercy and fell upon his knees.

"Turn that infernal thing the other way!" he shrieked.

"Ah!" said I, lowering my arm. "Then you know its properties?"

"I do—I do!" he cried. "It used to be mine—I confess it!"

"Then," said I, calmly putting the horrid bit of zinc back into my belt, "that's all I wanted to know. If you'll come up to my office some morning next week I'll introduce you to your wife," and I turned from him.

My mission accomplished, I left the festivities and returned to my quarters where my fair client was awaiting me.

"Well?" she said.

"It's all right, Mrs. Lohengrin," I said, and the lady cried aloud with joy at the name, for it was the very one she had hoped it would be. "My man turns out to be your man, and I turn him over therefore to you, only deal gently with him. He's a pretty decent chap and sings like a bird."

Whereon I presented her with my bill for 5000 *oboli*, which she paid without a murmur, as was entirely proper that she should, for upon the evidence which I had secured the fair plaintiff, in the suit for separation of Elsa *vs.* Lohengrin on the ground of desertion and non-support, obtained her decree, with back alimony of twenty-five *per cent.* of Lohengrin's income for a trifle over fifteen hundred years.

How much that amounted to I really do not know, but that it was a large sum I am sure, for Lohengrin must have been very wealthy. He couldn't have afforded to dress in solid silver-tinsel tights if he had been otherwise. I had the tights assayed before returning them to their owner, and even in a country where free coinage of tights is looked upon askance they could not be duplicated for less than $850 at a ratio of 32 to 1.

10: GOLF IN HADES

"Jim," said I to Boswell one morning as the type-writer began to work, "perhaps you can enlighten me on a point concerning which a great many people have questioned me recently. Has golf taken hold of Hades yet? You referred to it some time ago, and I've been wondering ever since if it had become a fad with you."

"Has it?" laughed my visitor; "well, I should rather say it had. The fact is, it has been a great boon to the country. You remember my telling you of the projected revolution led by Cromwell, and Caesar, and the others?"

"I do, very well," said I, "and I have been intending to ask you how it came out."

"Oh, everything's as fine and sweet as can be now," rejoined

Boswell, somewhat gleefully, "and all because of golf. We are all quiet along the Styx now. All animosities are buried in the general love of golf, and every one of us, high or low, autocrat and revolutionist, is hobnobbing away in peace and happiness on the links. Why, only six weeks ago, Apollyon was for cooking Bonaparte on a waffle iron, and yesterday the two went out to the Cimmerian links together and played a mixed foursome, Bonaparte and Medusa playing against Apollyon and Delilah."

"Dear me! Really?" I cried. "That must have been an interesting match."

"It was, and up to the very last it was nip-and-tuck between 'em," said Boswell. "Apollyon and Delilah won it with one hole up, and they got that on the put. They'd have halved the hole if Medusa's back hair hadn't wiggled loose and bitten her caddie just as she was holeing out."

"It is a remarkable game," said I. "There is no sensation in the world quite equal to that which comes to a man's soul when he has hit the ball a solid clip and sees it sail off through the air towards the green, whizzing musically along like a very bird."

"True," said Boswell; "but I'm rather of the opinion that it's a safer game for shades than for you purely material persons."

"I don't see why," I answered.

"It is easy to understand," returned Boswell. "For instance, with us there is no resistance when by a mischance we come into unexpected contact with the ball. Take the experience of Diogenes and Solomon at the St. Jonah's Links week before last. The Wiseman's Handicap was on. Diogenes and Simple Simon were playing just ahead of Solomon and Montaigne. Solomon was driving in great form. For the first time in his life he seemed able to keep his eye on the ball, and the way he sent it flying through the air was a caution. Diogenes and Simple Simon had both had their second stroke and Solomon drove off. His ball sailed straight ahead like a missile from a catapult, flew in a beeline for Diogenes, struck him at the base of his brain, continued on through, and landed on the edge of the green."

"Mercy!" I cried. "Didn't it kill him?"

248

"Of course not," retorted Boswell. "You can't kill a shade. Diogenes didn't know he'd been hit, but if that had happened to one of you material golfers there'd have been a sickening end to that tournament."

"There would, indeed," said I. "There isn't much fun in being hit by a golf-ball. I can testify to that because I have had the experience," and I called to mind the day at St. Peterkin's when I unconsciously stymied with my material self the celebrated Willie McGuffin, the Demon Driver from the Hootmon Links, Scotland. McGuffin made his mark that day if he never did before, and I bear the evidence thereof even now, although the incident took place two years ago, when I did not know enough to keep out of the way of the player who plays so well that he thinks he has a perpetual right of way everywhere.

"What kind of clubs do you Stygians use?" I asked.

"Oh, very much the same kind that you chaps do," returned Boswell. "Everybody experiments with new fads, too, just as you do. Old Peter Stuyvesant, for instance, always drives with his wooden leg, and never uses anything else unless he gets a lie where he's got to."

"His wooden leg?" I roared, with a laugh. "How on earth does he do that?"

"He screws the small end of it into a square block shod like a brassey," explained Boswell, "tees up his ball, goes back ten yards, makes a run at it and kicks the ball pretty nearly out of sight. He can put with it too, like a dream, swinging it sideways."

"But he doesn't call that golf, does he?" I cried.

"What is it?" demanded Boswell.

"I should call it football," I said.

"Not at all," said Boswell. "Not a bit of it. He hasn't any foot on that leg, and he has a golf-club head with a shaft to it. There isn't any rule which says that the shaft shall not look like an inverted nine-pin, nor do any of the accepted authorities require that the club shall be manipulated by the arms. I admit it's bad form the way he plays, but, as Stuyvesant himself says, he never did travel on his shape."

"Suppose he gets a cuppy lie?" I asked, very much interested at the first news from Hades of the famous old Dutchman.

"Oh, he does one of two things," said Boswell. "He stubs it out with his toe, or goes back and plays two more. Munchausen plays a good game too. He beat the colonel forty-seven straight holes last Wednesday, and all Hades has been talking about it ever since."

"Who is the colonel?" I asked, innocently.

"Bogey," returned Boswell. "Didn't you ever hear of Colonel Bogey?"

"Of course," I replied, "but I always supposed Bogey was an imaginary opponent, not a real one."

"So he is," said Boswell.

"Then you mean—"

"I mean that Munchausen beat him forty-seven up," said Boswell.

"Were there any witnesses?" I demanded, for I had little faith in Munchausen's regard for the eternal verities, among which a golf-card must be numbered if the game is to survive.

"Yes, a hundred," said Boswell. "There was only one trouble with 'em." Here the great biographer laughed. "They were all imaginary, like the colonel."

"And Munchausen's score?" I queried.

"The same, naturally. But it makes him king-pin in golf circles just the same, because nobody can go back on his logic," said Boswell. "Munchausen reasoned it out very logically indeed, and largely, he said, to protect his own reputation. Here is an imaginary warrior, said he, who makes a bully, but wholly imaginary, score at golf. He sends me an imaginary challenge to play him forty-seven holes. I accept, not so much because I consider myself a golfer as because I am an imaginer—if there is such a word."

"Ask Dr. Johnson," said I, a little sarcastically. I always grow sarcastic when golf is mentioned.

"Dr. Johnson be—" began Boswell.

"Boswell!" I remonstrated.

"Dr. Johnson be it, I was about to say," clicked the typewriter, suavely; but the ink was thick and inclined to spread. "Munchausen felt that Bogey was encroaching on his preserve as a man with an imagination."

"I have always considered Colonel Bogey a liar," said I. "He joins all the clubs and puts up an ideal score before he has played over the links."

"That isn't the point at all," said Boswell. "Golfers don't lie. Realists don't lie. Nobody in polite—or say, rather, accepted—society lies. They all imagine. Munchausen realizes that he has only one claim to recognition, and that is based entirely upon his imagination. So when the imaginary Colonel Bogey sent him an imaginary challenge to play him forty-seven holes at golf—"

"Why forty-seven?" I asked.

"An imaginary number," explained Boswell. "Don't interrupt. As I say, when the imaginary colonel—"

"I must interrupt," said I. "What was he colonel of?"

"A regiment of perfect caddies," said Boswell.

"Ah, I see," I replied. "Imaginary in his command. There isn't one perfect caddy, much less a regiment of the little reprobates."

"You are wrong there," said Boswell. "You don't know how to produce a good caddy—but good caddies can be made."

"How?" I cried, for I have suffered. "I'll have the plan patented."

"Take a flexible brassey, and at the ninth hole, if they deserve it, give them eighteen strokes across the legs with all your strength," said Boswell. "But, as I said before, don't interrupt. I haven't much time left to talk with you."

"But I must ask one more question," I put in, for I was growing excited over a new idea. "You say give them eighteen strokes across the legs. Across whose legs?"

"Yours," replied Boswell. "Just take your caddy up, place him across your knees, and spank him with your brassey. Spank isn't a good golf term, but it is good enough for the average caddy; in fact, it will do him good."

"Go on," said I, with a mental resolve to adopt his prescription.

"Well," said Boswell, "Munchausen, having received an imaginary challenge from an imaginary opponent, accepted. He went out to the links with an imaginary ball, an imaginary bagful of fanciful clubs, and licked the imaginary life out of the colonel."

"Still, I don't see," said I, somewhat jealously, perhaps, "how that makes him king-pin in golf circles. Where did he play?"

"On imaginary links," said Boswell.

"Poh!" I ejaculated.

"Don't sneer," said Boswell. "You know yourself that the links you imagine are far better than any others."

"What is Munchausen's strongest point?" I asked, seeing that there was no arguing with the man—"driving, approaching, or putting?"

"None of the three. He cannot put, he foozles every drive, and at approaching he's a consummate ass," said Boswell.

"Then what can he do?" I cried.

"Count," said Boswell. "Haven't you learned that yet? You can spend hours learning how to drive, weeks to approach, and months to put. But if you want to win you must know how to count."

I was silent, and for the first time in my life I realized that Munchausen was not so very different from certain golfers I have met in my short day as a golfiac, and then Boswell put in:

"You see, it isn't lofting or driving that wins," he continued. "Cups aren't won on putting or approaching. It's the man who puts in the best card who becomes the champion."

"I am afraid you are right," I said, sadly, "but I am sorry to find that Hades is as badly off as we mortals in that matter."

"Golf, sir," retorted Boswell, sententiously, "is the same everywhere, and that which is dome in our world is directly in line with what is developed in yours."

"I'm sorry for Hades," said I; "but to continue about golf—

do the ladies play much on your links?"

"Well, rather," returned Boswell, "and it's rather amusing to watch them at it, too. Xanthippe with her Greek clothes finds it rather difficult; but for rare sport you ought to see Queen Elizabeth trying to keep her eye on the ball over her ruff! It really is one of the finest spectacles you ever saw."

"But why don't they dress properly?"

"Ah," sighed Boswell, "that is one of the things about Hades that destroys all the charm of life there. We are but shades."

"Granted," said I, "but your garments can—"

"Our garments can't," said Boswell. "Through all eternity we shades of our former selves are doomed to wear the shadows of our former clothes."

"Then what the devil does a poor dress-maker do who goes to Hades?" I cried.

"She makes over the things she made before," said Boswell. "That's why, my dear fellow," the biographer added, becoming confidential—"that's why some people confound Hades with— ah—the other place, don't you know."

"Still, there's golf!" I said; "and that's a panacea for all ills. *you* enjoy it, don't you?"

"Me?" cried Boswell. "Me enjoy it? Not on all the lives in Christendom. It is the direst drudgery for me."

"Drudgery?" I said. "Bah! Nonsense, Boswell!"

"You forget—" he began.

"Forget? It must be you who forget, if you call golf drudgery."

"No," sighed the genial spirit. "No, *I* don't forget. I remember."

"Remember what?" I demanded.

"That I am Dr. Johnson's caddy!" was the answer. And then came a heartrending sigh, and from that time on all was silence. I repeatedly put questions to the machine, made observations to it, derided it, insulted it, but there was no response.

It has so continued to this day, and I can only conclude the story of my Enchanted Typewriter by saying that I presume golf has taken the same hold upon Hades that it has upon this world, and that I need not hope to hear more from that attractive region until the game has relaxed its grip, which I know can never be.

Hence let me say to those who have been good enough to follow me through the realms of the Styx that I bid them an affectionate farewell and thank them for their kind attention to my chronicles. They are all truthful; but now that the source of supply is cut off I cannot prove it. I can only hope that for one and all the future may hold as much of pleasure as the place of departed spirits has held for me.

Mr. Munchausen

In order that there may be no misunderstanding as to the why and the wherefore of this collection of tales it appears to me to be desirable that I should at the outset state my reasons for acting as the medium between the spirit of the late Baron Munchausen and the reading public. In common with a large number of other great men in history Baron Munchausen has suffered because he is not understood. I have observed with wondering surprise the steady and constant growth of the idea that Baron Munchausen was not a man of truth; that his statements of fact were untrustworthy, and that as a realist he had no standing whatsoever.

Just how this misconception of the man's character has arisen it would be difficult to say. Surely in his published writings he shows that same lofty resolve to be true to life as he has seen it that characterises the work of some of the high Apostles of Realism, who are writing of the things that will teach future generations how we of today ordered our goings-on. The note of veracity in Baron Munchausen's early literary venturings rings as clear and as true certainly as the similar note in the charming studies of Manx Realism that have come to us of late years from the pen of Mr. Corridor Walkingstick, of Gloomster Abbey and London.

We all remember the glow of satisfaction with which we read Mr. Walkingstick's great story of the love of the clergyman John Stress, for the charming little heroine, Glory Partridge. Here was

255

something at last that rang true. The picture was painted in the boldest of colours, and, regardless of consequences to himself, Mr. Walkingstick dared to be real when he might have given rein to his imagination. Mr. Walkingstick was, thereupon, lifted up by popular favour to the level of an apostle—nay, he even admitted the soft impeachment—and now as a moral teacher he is without a rival in the world of literature.

Yet the same age that accepts this man as a moral teacher, rejects Baron Munchausen, who, in different manner perhaps, presented to the world as true and lifelike a picture of the conditions of his day as that given to us by Mr. Walkingstick in his deservedly popular romance, *Episcopolians I have Met*. Of course I do not claim that Baron Munchausen's stories in bulk or in specified instances, have the literary vigour that is so marked a quality of the latter-day writer, but the point I do wish to urge is that to accept the one as a veracious chronicler of his time and to reject the other as one who indulges his pen in all sorts of grotesque vagaries, without proper regard for the facts, is a great injustice to the man of other times.

The question arises, why is this? How has this wrong upon the worthy realist of the eighteenth century been perpetrated? Is it an intentional or an unwitting wrong? I prefer to believe that it is based upon ignorance of the Baron's true quality, due to the fact that his works are rarely to be found within the reach of the public: in some cases, because of the failure of librarians to comprehend his real motives, his narratives are excluded from Public and Sunday-School libraries; and because of their extreme age, they are not easily again brought into vogue.

I have therefore, accepted the office of intermediary between the Baron and the readers of the present day, in order that his later work, which, while it shows to a marked degree the decadence of his literary powers, may yet serve to demonstrate to the readers of my own time how favourably he compares with some of the literary idols of today, in the simple matter of fidelity to fact. If these stories which follow shall serve to rehabilitate Baron Munchausen as a lover and practitioner of the arts of

Truth, I shall not have made the sacrifice of my time in vain. If they fail of this purpose I shall still have the satisfaction of knowing that I have tried to render a service to an honest and defenceless man.

Meanwhile I dedicate this volume, with sentiments of the highest regard, to that other great realist

Mr. Corridor Walkingstick

of

Gloomster Abbey   J. K. B.

1

I ENCOUNTER THE OLD GENTLEMAN

There are moments of supreme embarrassment in the lives of persons given to veracity,—indeed it has been my own unusual experience in life that the truth well stuck to is twice as hard a proposition as a lie so obvious that no one is deceived by it at the outset. I cannot quite agree with my friend, Caddy Barlow, who says that in a tight place it is better to lie at once and be done with it than to tell the truth which will need forty more truths to explain it, but I must confess that in my forty years of absolute and conscientious devotion to truth I have found myself in holes far deeper than any my most mendacious of friends ever got into.

I do not propose, however, to desert at this late hour the Goddess I have always worshipped because she leads me over a rough and rocky road, and whatever may be the hardships involved in my wooing I intend to the very end to remain the ever faithful slave of Mademoiselle Veracity. All of which I state here in prefatory mood, and in order, in so far as it is possible for me to do so, to disarm the incredulous and sniffy reader who may be inclined to doubt the truth of my story of how the manuscript of the following pages came into my possession. I am quite aware that to some the tale will appear absolutely and intolerably impossible. I know that if any other than I told it to me I should not believe it.

Yet despite these drawbacks the story is in all particulars, essential and otherwise, absolutely truthful. The facts are briefly these: It was not, to begin with, a dark and dismal evening. The snow was not falling silently, clothing a sad and gloomy world in a mantle of white, and over the darkling moor a heavy mist was not rising, as is so frequently the case.

There was no soul-stirring moaning of bitter winds through the leafless boughs; so far as I was aware nothing soughed within twenty miles of my bailiwick; and my dog, lying before a blazing log fire in my library, did not give forth an occasional growl of apprehension, denoting the presence or approach of an uncanny visitor from other and mysterious realms: and for two good reasons. The first reason is that it was midsummer when the thing happened, so that a blazing log fire in my library would have been an extravagance as well as an anachronism. The second is that I have no dog. In fact there was nothing unusual, or un-canny in the whole experience.

It happened to be a bright and somewhat too sunny July day, which is not an unusual happening along the banks of the Hudson. You could see the heat, and if anything had soughed it could only have been the mercury in my thermometer. This I must say clicked nervously against the top of the glass tube and manifested an extraordinary desire to climb higher than the length of the tube permitted. Incidentally I may add, even if it be not believed, that the heat was so intense that the mercury actually did raise the whole thermometer a foot and a half above the mantel-shelf, and for two mortal hours, from midday until two by the Monastery Clock, held it suspended there in midair with no visible means of support.

Not a breath of air was stirring, and the only sounds heard were the expanding creaks of the beams of my house, which upon that particular day increased eight feet in width and as-sumed a height which made it appear to be a three instead of a two storey dwelling. There was little work doing in the house. The children played about in their bathing suits, and the only other active factor in my life of the moment was our hired man who was kept busy in the cellar pouring water on the furnace coal to keep it from spontaneously combusting.

We had just had luncheon, burning our throats with the iced tea and with considerable discomfort swallowing the simmering cold roast fillet, which we had to eat hastily before the heat of the day transformed it into smoked beef. My youngest boy Willie perspired so copiously that we seriously thought of sending for a plumber to solder up his pores, and as for myself who have spent three summers of my life in the desert of Sahara in order to rid myself of nervous chills to which I was once unhappily subject, for the first time in my life I was impelled to admit that it was intolerably warm. And then the telephone bell rang.

"Great Scott!" I cried, "Who in thunder do you suppose wants to play golf on a day like this?"—for nowadays our telephone is used for no other purpose than the making or the breaking of golf engagements.

"Me," cried my eldest son, whose grammar is not as yet on a par with his activity. "I'll go."

The boy shot out of the dining room and ran to the telephone, returning in a few moments with the statement that a gentleman with a husky voice whose name was none of his business wished to speak with me on a matter of some importance to myself.

I was loath to go. My friends the book agents had recently acquired the habit of approaching me over the telephone, and I feared that here was another nefarious attempt to foist a thirty-eight volume tabloid edition of *The World's Worst Literature* upon me. Nevertheless I wisely determined to respond.

"Hello," I said, placing my lips against the rubber cup. "Hello there, who wants 91162 Nepperhan?"

"Is that you?" came the answering question, and, as my boy had indicated, in a voice whose chief quality was huskiness.

"I guess so," I replied facetiously;—"It was this morning, but the heat has affected me somewhat, and I don't feel as much like myself as I might. What can I do for you?"

"Nothing, but you can do a lot for yourself," was the astonishing answer. "Pretty hot for literary work, isn't it?" the voice added sympathetically.

"Very," said I. "Fact is I can't seem to do anything these days but perspire."

"That's what I thought; and when you can't work ruin stares you in the face, eh? Now I have a manuscript—"

"Oh Lord!" I cried. "Don't. There are millions in the same fix. Even my cook writes."

"Don't know about that," he returned instantly. "But I do know that there's millions in my manuscript. And you can have it for the asking. How's that for an offer?"

"Very kind, thank you," said I. "What's the nature of your story?"

"It's extremely good-natured," he answered promptly.

I laughed. The twist amused me.

"That isn't what I meant exactly," said I, "though it has some bearing on the situation. Is it a Henry James dandy, or does it bear the mark of Caine? Is it realism or fiction?"

"Realism," said he. "Fiction isn't in my line."

"Well, I'll tell you," I replied; "you send it to me by post and I'll look it over. If I can use it I will."

"Can't do it," said he. "There isn't any post-office where I am."

"What? "I cried. "No post-office? Where in Hades are you?"

"Gehenna," he answered briefly. "The transportation between your country and mine is all one way," he added. "If it wasn't the population here would diminish."

"Then how the deuce am I to get hold of your stuff?" I demanded.

"That's easy. Send your stenographer to the 'phone and I'll dictate it," he answered.

The novelty of the situation appealed to me. Even if my new found acquaintance were some funny person nearer at hand than Gehenna trying to play a practical joke upon me, still it might be worthwhile to get hold of the story he had to tell. Hence I agreed to his proposal.

"All right, sir," said I. "I'll do it I'll have him here tomorrow morning at nine o'clock sharp. What's your number? I'll ring you up."

"Never mind that," he replied. "I'm merely a tapster on your wires. I'll ring you up as soon as I've had breakfast and then we can get to work."

"Very good," said I. "And may I ask your name?"

"Certainly," he answered. "I'm Munchausen."

"What? The Baron?" I roared, delighted.

"Well—I used to be Baron," he returned with a tinge of sadness in his voice, "but here in Gehenna we are all on an equal footing. I'm plain Mr. Munchausen of Hades now. But that's a detail. Don't forget Nine o'clock. Goodbye."

"Wait a moment, Baron," I cried. "How about the royalties on this book?"

"Keep 'em for yourself," he replied. "We have money to burn over here. You are welcome to all the earthly rights of the book. I'm satisfied with the returns on the *Asbestos Edition*, already in its 468th thousand. Goodbye."

There was a rattle as of the hanging up of the receiver, a short sharp click and a ring, and I realised that he had gone.

The next morning in response to a telegraphic summons my stenographer arrived and when I explained the situation to him he was incredulous, but orders were orders and he remained. I could see, however, that as nine o'clock approached he grew visibly nervous, which indicated that he half believed me anyhow, and when at nine to the second the sharp ring of the 'phone fell upon our ears he jumped as if he had been shot.

"Hello," said I again. "That you, Baron?"

"The same," the voice replied. "Stenographer ready?"

"Yes," said I.

The stenographer walked to the desk, placed the receiver at his ear, and with trembling voice announced his presence. There was a response of some kind, and then more calmly he remarked,

"Fire ahead, Mr. Munchausen," and began to write rapidly in shorthand.

Two days later he handed me a typewritten copy of the following stories. The reader will observe that they are in the form of interviews, and it should be stated here that they appeared originally in the columns of the Sunday edition of the *Gehenna Gazette*, a publication of Hades which circulates wholly among the best people of that country, and which, if report saith truly, would not print a line which could not be placed in the hands of children, and to whose columns such writers as Chaucer, Shakespeare, Ben Jonson, Jonah and Ananias are frequent contributors.

Indeed, on the statement of Mr. Munchausen, all the interviews herein set forth were between himself as the principal and the Hon. Henry B. Ananias as reporter, or were scrupulously edited by the latter before being published.

2

The Sporting Tour of Mr. Munchausen

"Good morning, Mr. Munchausen," said the interviewer of the *Gehenna Gazette* entering the apartment of the famous traveller at the Hotel Deville, where the late Baron had just arrived from his sporting tour in the Blue Hills of Cimmeria and elsewhere.

"The interests of truth, my dear Ananias," replied the Baron, grasping me cordially by the hand, "require that I should state it as my opinion that it is not a good morning. In fact, my good friend, it is a very bad morning. Can you not see that it is raining cats and dogs without?"

"Sir," said I with a bow, "I accept the spirit of your correction but not the letter. It is raining indeed, sir, as you suggest, but having passed through it myself on my way hither I can personally testify that it is raining rain, and not a single cat or canine has, to my knowledge, as yet fallen from the clouds to the parched earth, although I am informed that down upon the coast an elephant and three cows have fallen upon one of the summer hotels and irreparably damaged the roof."

Mr. Munchausen laughed.

"It is curious, Ananias," said he, "what sticklers for the truth you and I have become."

"It is indeed, Munchausen," I returned. "The effects of this climate are working wonders upon us. And it is just as well. You and I are outclassed by these twentieth century prevaricators concerning whom late arrivals from the upper world tell such strange things. They tell me that lying has become a business and is no longer ranked among the Arts or Professions."

"Ah me!" sighed the Baron with a retrospective look in his eye, "lying isn't what it used to be, Ananias, in your days and mine. I fear it has become one of the lost arts."

"I have noticed it myself, my friend, and only last night I observed the same thing to my well beloved Sapphira, who was lamenting the transparency of the modern lie, and said that lying today is no better than the truth. In our day a prevarication had all of the opaque beauty of an opalescent bit of glass, whereas today in the majority of cases it is like a great vulgar plate-glass window, through which we can plainly see the ugly truths that lie behind. But, sir, I am here to secure from you not a treatise upon the lost art of lying, but some idea of the results of your sporting tour. You fished, and hunted, and golfed, and doubtless did other things. You, of course, had luck and made the greatest catch of the season; shot all the game in sight, and won every silver, gold and pewter golf mug in all creation?"

"You speak truly, Ananias," returned Mr. Munchausen. "My luck was wonderful—even for one who has been so singularly fortunate as I. I took three tons of speckled beauties with one cast of an ordinary horse whip in the Blue Hills, and with nothing but a silken line and a minnow hook landed upon the deck of my steam yacht a whale of most tremendous proportions; I shot game of every kind in great abundance, and in my golf there was none to whom I could not give with ease seven holes in every nine and beat him out."

"Seven?" said I, failing to see how the ex-Baron could be right

"Seven," said he complacently. "Seven on the first, and seven on the second nine; fourteen in all of the eighteen holes."

"But," I cried, "I do not see how that could be. With fourteen holes out of the eighteen given to your opponent even if you won all the rest you still would be ten down."

"True, by ordinary methods of calculation," returned the Baron, "but I got them back on a technicality, which I claim is a new and valuable discovery in the game. You see it is impossible to play more than one hole at a time, and I invariably proved to the Greens Committee that in taking fourteen holes at once my opponent violated the physical possibilities of the situation. In every case the point was accepted as well taken, for if we allow golfers to rise above physical possibilities the game is gone. The integrity of the Card is the soul of Golf," he added sententiously.

"Tell me of the whale," said I, simply. "You landed a whale of large proportions on the deck of your yacht with a simple silken line and a minnow hoof

"Well it's a tough story," the Baron replied, handing me a cigar. "But it is true, Ananias, true to the last word. I was fishing for eels. Sitting on the deck of *The Lyre* one very warm afternoon in the early stages of my trip, I baited a minnow hook and dropped it overboard. It was the roughest day at sea I had ever encountered. The waves were mountain high, and it is the sad fact that one of our crew seated in the main-top was drowned with the spray of the dashing billows.

"Fortunately for myself, directly behind my deck chair, to which I was securely lashed, was a powerful electric fan which blew the spray away from me, else I too might have suffered the same horrid fate. Suddenly there came a tug on my line. I was half asleep at the time and let the line pay out involuntarily, but I was wide-awake enough to know that something larger than an eel had taken hold of the hook. I had hooked either a Leviathan or a derelict. Caution and patience, the chief attributes of a good angler were required I hauled the line in until it was taut.

"There were a thousand yards of it out, and when it reached the point of tensity, I gave orders to the engineers to steam closer to the object at the other end. We steamed in five hundred yards, I meanwhile hauling in my line. Then came another tug and I let out ten yards. 'Steam closer,' said I. 'Three hundred yards sou sou-west by nor'-east,' The yacht obeyed on the instant. I called the Captain and let him feel the line. 'What do you think it is?' said I.

"He pulled a half dozen times. 'Feels like a snag,' he said, 'but seein' as there ain't no snags out here, I think it must be a fish.' 'What kind?' I asked. I could not but agree that he was better acquainted with the sea and its denizens than I. 'Well,' he replied, 'it is either a sea serpent or a whale.' At the mere mention of the word whale I was alert. I have always wanted to kill a whale. 'Captain,' said I, 'can't you tie an anchor onto a hawser, and bait the flukes with a boa constrictor and make sure of him?' He looked at me contemptuously. 'Whales eats fish,' said he, 'and they don't bite at no anchors. Whales has brains, whales has.' 'What shall we do?' I asked. 'Steam closer,' said the Captain, and we did so."

Munchausen took a long breath and for the moment was silent

"Well?" said I.

"Well, Ananias," said he. "We resolved to wait. As the Captain said to me, 'Fishin' is waitin'' So we waited. 'Coax him along,' said the Captain. 'How can we do it?' I asked. 'By kindness,' said he. 'Treat him gently, persuasive-like and he'll come.' We waited four days and nobody moved and I grew weary of coaxing. 'We've got to do something,' said I to the Captain. 'Yes,' said he, 'Let's make him move. He doesn't seem to respond to kindness.' 'But how?' I cried. 'Give him an electric shock,' said the Captain. 'Telegraph him his mother's sick and maybe it'll move him.'

"'Can't you get closer to him?' I demanded, resenting his facetious manner. 'I can, but it will scare him off,' replied the Captain. So we turned all our batteries .on the sea. The dynamo shot forth its bolts and along about four o'clock in the afternoon there was the whale drawn by magnetic influence to the side of *The Lyre*. He was a beauty, Ananias,' Munchausen added with enthusiasm. "You never saw such a whale. His back was as broad as the deck of an ocean steamer and in his length he exceeded the dimensions of *The Lyre* by sixty feet."

"And still you got him on deck?" I asked,—I, Ananias, who can stand something in the way of an exaggeration.

"Yes," said Munchausen, lighting his cigar, which had gone out. "Another storm came up and we rolled and rolled and rolled, until I thought *The Lyre* was going to capsize."

"But weren't you seasick?" I asked.

"Didn't have a chance to be," said Munchausen. "I was thinking of the whale all the time. Finally there came a roll in which we went completely under, and with a slight pulling on the line the whale was landed by the force of the wave and laid squarely upon the deck."

"Great Sapphira!" said I. "But you just said he was wider and longer than the yacht!"

"He was," sighed Munchausen. "He landed on the deck and by sheer force of his weight the yacht went down under him. I swam ashore and the whole crew with me. The next day Mr. Whale floated in strangled. He'd swallowed the thousand yards of line and it got so tangled in his tonsils that it choked him to death. Come around next week and I'll give you a couple of pounds of whale-bone for Mrs. Ananias, and all the oil you can carry."

I thanked the old gentleman for his kind offer and promised to avail myself of it, although as a newspaper man it is against my principles to accept gifts from public men.

"It was great luck, Baron," said I. "Or at least it would have been if you hadn't lost your yacht"

"That was great luck too," he observed nonchalantly. "It cost me ten thousand dollars a month keeping that yacht in commission. Now she's gone I save all that. Why it's like finding money in the street, Ananias. She wasn't worth more than fifty thousand dollars, and in six months I'll be ten thousand ahead."

I could not but admire the cheerful philosophy of the man, but then I was not surprised. Munchausen was never the sort of man to let little things worry him.

"But that whale business wasn't a circumstance to my catch of three tons of trout with a single cast of a horsewhip in the Blue Hills," said the Baron after a few moments of meditation, during which I could see that he was carefully marshalling his facts.

"I never heard of its equal," said I. "You must have used a derrick."

"No," he replied suavely. "Nothing of the sort It was the simplest thing in the world. It was along about five o'clock in the afternoon when with my three guides and my valet I drove up the winding roadway of Great Sulphur Mountain on my way to the Blue Mountain House where I purposed to put up for a few days. I had one of those big mountain wagons with a covered top to it such as the pioneers used on the American plains, with six fine horses to the fore. I held the reins myself, since we were in the midst of a terrific thunderstorm and I felt safer when I did my own driving.

"All the flaps of the leathern cover were let down at the sides and at the back, and were securely fastened. The roads were unusually heavy, and when we came to the last great hill before the lake all but I were walking, as a measure of relief to the horses. Suddenly one of the horses balked right in the middle of the ascent, and in a moment of impatience I gave him a stinging flick with my whip, when like a whirlwind the whole six swerved to one side and started on a dead run upward. The jolt and the unexpected swerving of the wagon threw me from my seat and I landed clear of the wheels in the soft mud of the roadway, fortunately without injury.

"When I arose the team was out of sight and we had to walk the remainder of the distance to the hotel. Imagine our surprise upon arriving there to find the six panting steeds and the wagon standing before the main entrance to the hotel dripping as though they had been through the Falls of Niagara, and, would you believe it, Ananias, inside that leather cover of the wagon, packed as tightly as sardines, were no less than three thousand trout, not one of them less than a pound and some of them getting as high as four. The whole catch weighed a trifle over six thousand pounds."

"Great Heavens, Baron," I cried. "Where the dickens did they come from?"

"That's what I asked myself," said the Baron easily. "It seemed astounding at first glance, but investigation showed it after all to be a very simple proposition. The runaways after reaching the top of the hill turned to the left, and clattered on down toward the bridge over the inlet to the lake. The bridge broke beneath their weight and the horses soon found themselves struggling in the water. The harness was strong and the wagon never left them. They had to swim for it, and I am told by a small boy who was fishing on the lake at the time that they swam directly across it, pulling the wagon after them. Naturally with its open front and confined back and sides the wagon acted as a sort of drag-net and when the opposite shore was gained, and the wagon was pulled ashore, it was found to have gathered in all the fish that could not get out of the way."

The Baron resumed his cigar, and I sat still eyeing the ample pattern of the drawing-room carpet

"Pretty good catch for an afternoon, eh?" he said in a minute.

"Yes," said I. "Almost too good. Baron. Those horses must have swam like the dickens to get over so quickly. You would think the trout would have had time to escape."

"Oh I presume one or two of them did," said Munchausen. "But the majority of them couldn't. The horses were all fast, record-breakers anyhow. I never hire a horse that isn't"

And with that I left the old gentleman and walked blushing back to the office. I don't doubt for an instant the truth of the Baron's story, but somehow or other I feel that in writing it my reputation is in some measure at stake.

Note—Mr. Munchausen, upon request of the Editor of the *Gehenna Gazette* to write a few stories of adventure for his Imp's page, conducted by Sapphira, contributed the tales which form the substance of several of the following chapters.

3

THREE MONTHS IN A BALLOON

Mr. Munchausen was not handsome, the Imps liked him very much, he was so full of wonderful reminiscences, and was always willing to tell anybody that would listen, all about himself. To the Heavenly Twins he was the greatest hero that had ever lived. Napoleon Bonaparte, on Mr. Munchausen's own authority, was not half the warrior that he, the late Baron had been, nor was Caesar in his palmiest days, one-quarter so wise or so brave. How old the Baron was no one ever knew, but he had certainly lived long enough to travel the world over, and stare every kind of death squarely in the face without flinching. He had fought Zulus, Indians, tigers, elephants—in fact, everything that fights, the Baron had encountered, and in every contest he had come out victorious.

He was the only man the children had ever seen that had lost three legs in battle and then had recovered them after the fight was over; he was the only visitor to their house that had been lost in the African jungle and wandered about for three months without food or shelter, and best of all he was, on his own confession, the most truthful narrator of extraordinary tales living. The youngsters had to ask the Baron a question only, any one, it mattered not what it was—to start him off on a story of adventure, and as he called upon the Twins' father once a month regularly, the children were not long in getting together a collection of tales beside which the most exciting episodes in history paled into insignificant commonplaces.

"Uncle Munch," said the Twins one day, as they climbed up into the visitor's lap and disarranged his necktie, "was you ever up in a balloon?"

"Only once," said the Baron calmly. "But I had enough of it that time to last me for a lifetime."

"Was you in it for long?" queried the Twins, taking the Baron's watch out of his pocket and flinging it at Cerberus, who was barking outside of the window.

"Well, it seemed long enough," the Baron answered, putting his pocket-book in the inside pocket of his vest where the Twins could not reach it "Three months off in the country sleeping all day long and playing tricks all night seems a very short time, but three months in a balloon and the constant centre of attack from every source is too long for comfort.

"Were you up in the air for three whole months?" asked the Twins, their eyes wide open with astonishment

"All but two days," said the Baron. "For two of those days we rested in the top of a tree in India. The way of it was this: I was always, as you know, a great favourite with the Emperor Napoleon, of France, and when he found himself involved in a war with all Europe, he replied to one of his courtiers who warned him that his army was not in condition: 'Any army is prepared for war whose commander-in-chief numbers Baron Munchausen among his advisers. Let me have Munchausen at my right hand and I will fight the world.' So they sent for me and as I was not very busy I concluded to go and assist the French, although the allies and I were also very good friends.

"I reasoned it out this way: In this fight the allies are the stronger. They do not need me. Napoleon does. Fight for the weak, Munchausen, I said to myself, and so I went. Of course, when I reached Paris I went at once to the Emperor's palace and remained at his side until he took the field, after which I remained behind for a few days to put things to rights for the Imperial family. Unfortunately for the French, the King of Prussia heard of my delay in going to the front, and he sent word to his forces to intercept me on my way to join Napoleon at all hazards, and this they tried to do. When I was within ten miles of the Emperor's headquarters, I was stopped by the Prussians, and had it not been that I had provided myself with a balloon for just such an emergency, I should have been captured and confined in the King's palace at Berlin, until the war was over.

"Foreseeing all this, I had brought with me a large balloon

packed away in a secret section of my trunk, and while my bodyguard was fighting with the Prussian troops sent to capture me, I and my valet inflated the balloon, jumped into the car and were soon high up out of the enemy's reach. They fired several shots at us, and one of them would have pierced the balloon had I not, by a rare good shot, fired my own rifle at the bullet, and hitting it squarely in the middle, as is my custom, diverted it from its course, and so saved our lives.

"It had been my intention to sail directly over the heads of the attacking party and drop down into Napoleon's camp the next morning, but unfortunately for my calculations, a heavy wind came up in the night and the balloon was caught by a northerly blast, and blown into Africa, where, poised in the air directly over the desert of Sahara, we encountered a dead calm, which kept us stalled up for two miserable weeks."

"Why didn't you come down?" asked the Twins, "wasn't the elevator running?"

"We didn't dare," explained the Baron, ignoring the latter part of the question. "If we had we'd have wasted a great deal of our gas, and our condition would have been worse than ever. As I told you we were directly over the centre of the desert. There was no way of getting out of it except by long and wearisome marches over the hot, burning sands with the chances largely in favour of our never getting out alive. The only thing to do was to stay just where we were and wait for a favouring breeze. This we did, having to wait four mortal weeks before the air was stirred."

"You said two weeks a minute ago, Uncle Munch," said the Twins critically.

"Two? Hem! Well, yes it was two, now that I think of it. It's a natural mistake," said the Baron stroking his moustache a little nervously. "You see two weeks in a balloon over a vast desert of sand, with nothing to do but whistle for a breeze, is equal to four weeks anywhere else. That is, it seems so. Anyhow, two weeks or four, whichever it was, the breeze came finally, and along about midnight left us stranded again directly over an Arab encampment near Wady Haifa. It was a more perilous position really, than the first, because the moment the Arabs caught sight of us they began to make frantic efforts to get us down. At first we simply laughed them to scorn and made faces at them, because as far as we could see, we were safely out of reach. This enraged them and they apparently made up their minds to kill us if they could. At first their idea was to get us down alive and sell us as slaves, but our jeers changed all that, and what should they do but whip out a lot of guns and begin to pepper us.

"'I'll settle them in a minute,' I said to myself, and set about loading my own gun. Would you believe it, I found that my last bullet was the one with which I had saved the balloon from the Prussian shot?"

"Mercy, how careless of you. Uncle Munch!" said one of the Twins. "What did you do?"

"I threw out a bag of sand ballast so that the balloon would rise just out of range of their guns, and then, as their bullets got to their highest point and began to drop back, I reached out and caught them in a dipper. Rather neat idea, eh? With these I loaded my own rifle and shot every one of the hostile party with their own ammunition, and when the last of the attacking Arabs dropped I found there were enough bullets left to fill the empty sand bag again, so that the lost ballast was not missed. In fact, there were enough of them in weight to bring the balloon down so near to the earth that our anchor rope dangled directly over the encampment, so that my valet and I, without wasting any of our gas, could climb down and secure all the magnificent treasures in rugs and silks and rare jewels these robbers of the desert had managed to get together in the course of their dep-redations.

"When these were placed in the car another breeze came up, and for the rest of the time we drifted idly about in the heavens waiting for a convenient place to land. In this manner we were blown hither and yon for three months over land and sea, and finally we were wrecked upon a tall tree in India, whence we escaped by means of a convenient elephant that happened to come our way, upon which we rode triumphantly into Calcutta. The treasures we had secured from the Arabs, unfortunately, we had to leave behind us in the tree, where I suppose they still are. I hope someday to go back and find them."

Here Mr. Munchausen paused for a moment to catch his breath. Then he added with a sigh, "course, I went back to France immediately, but by the time I reached Paris the war was over, and the Emperor was in exile. I was too late to save him, though I think if he had lived some sixty or seventy years longer I should have managed to restore his throne, and Imperial splendour to him."

The Twins gazed into the fire in silence for minute or two. Then one of them asked:

"But what did you live on all that time, Uncle Munch?"

"Eggs," said the Baron. "Eggs and occasionally fish. My servant had had the foresight when getting the balloon ready to include, among the things put into the car, a small coop in which were six pet chickens I owned, and without which I never went anywhere. These laid enough eggs every day to keep us alive. The fish we easily when our balloon stood over the sea, baiting our anchor with pieces of rubber gas pipe used to inflate the balloon, and which looked very much like worms."

"But the chickens?" said the Twins. "What did they live on?"

The Baron blushed. "I am sorry you asked that question," he said, his voice trembling somewhat. "But I'll answer it if you promise never to tell anyone. It was the only time in my life that I ever practised an intentional deception upon any living thing, and I have always regretted it, although our very lives depended upon it."

"What was it, Uncle Munch?" asked the Twins, awed to think that the old warrior had ever deceived anyone.

"I took the eggshells and ground them into powder, and fed them to the chickens. The poor creatures supposed it was cornmeal they were getting," confessed the Baron. "I know it was mean, but what could I do?"

273

"Nothing," said the Twins softly. "And we don't think it was so bad of you after all. Many another person would have kept them laying eggs until they starved, and then he'd have killed them and eaten them up. You let them live."

"That may be so," said the Baron, with a smile that showed how relieved his conscience was by the Twins' suggestion. "But I couldn't do that you know, because they were pets. I had been brought up from childhood with those chickens."

Then the Twins, jamming the Baron's hat down over his eyes, climbed down from his lap and went to their play, strongly of the opinion that, though a bold warrior, the Baron was a singularly kind, soft-hearted man after all.

4

SOME HUNTING STORIES

The Heavenly Twins had been off in the mountains during their summer holiday, and in consequence had seen very little of their good old friend, Mr. Munchausen. He had written them once or twice, and they had found his letters most interesting, especially that one in which he told how he had killed a moose up in Maine with his Waterbury watch spring, and I do not wonder that they marvelled at that, for it was one of the most extraordinary happenings in the annals of the chase. It seems, if his story is to be believed, and I am sure that none of us who know him has ever had any reason to think that he would deceive intentionally; it seems, I say, that he had gone to Maine for a week's sport with an old army acquaintance of his, who had now become a guide in that region.

Unfortunately his rifle, of which he was very fond, and with which his aim was unerring, was in some manner mislaid on the way, and when they arrived in the woods they were utterly without weapons; but Mr. Munchausen was not the man to be daunted by any such trifle as that, particularly while his friend had an old army musket, a relic of the war, stored away in the attic of his woodland domicile.

"Th' only trouble with that ar musket," said the old guide,

"ain't so much that she won't shoot straight, nor that she's got a kick onto her like an unbroke mule. What I'm most afeard 'on about your shootin' with her ain't that I think she'll bust neither, for the fact is we ain't got nothin' for to bust her with, seein' as how ainmynition is skeerce. I got powder, an' I got waddin', but I ain't got no shot."

"That doesn't make any difference," the Baron replied. "We can make the shot. Have you got any plumbing in the camp? If you have, rip it out, and I'll melt up a water-pipe into bullets."

"No, sir," retorted the old man. "Plumbin' is one of the things I came here to escape from."

"Then," said the Baron, "I'll use my watch for ammunition. It is only a three-dollar watch and I can spare it."

With this determination, Mr. Munchausen took his watch to pieces, an ordinary time-piece of the old-fashioned kind, and, to make a long story short, shot for several days with the component parts of that useful affair rammed down into the barrel of the old musket. With the stem-winding ball he killed an eagle; with pieces of the back cover chopped up to a fineness of medium-sized shot he brought down several other birds, but the great feat of all was when he started for moose with nothing but the watch-spring in the barrel of the gun.

Having rolled it up as tight as he could, fastened it with a piece of twine, and rammed it well into the gun, he set out to find the noble animal upon whose life he had designs. After stalking the woods for several hours, he came upon the tracks which told him that his prey was not far off, and in a short while he caught sight of a magnificent creature, his huge antlers held proudly up and his great eyes full of defiance.

For a moment the Baron hesitated. The idea of destroying so beautiful an animal seemed to be abhorrent to his nature, which, warrior-like as he is, has something of the tenderness of a woman about it. A second glance at the superb creature, however, changed all that, for the Baron then saw that to shoot to kill was necessary, for the beast was about to force a fight in which the hunter himself would be put upon the defensive.

"I won't shoot you through the head, my beauty," he said, softly, "nor will I puncture your beautiful coat with this load of mine, but I'll kill you in a new way."

With this he pulled the trigger. The powder exploded, the string binding the long black spring into a coil broke, and immediately the strip of steel shot forth into the air, made directly toward the neck of the rushing moose, and coiling its whole sinuous length tightly about the doomed creature's throat strangled him to death.

As the Twins' father said, a feat of that kind entitled the Baron to a high place in fiction at least, if not in history itself. The Twins were very much wrought up over the incident, particularly, when one too-smart small imp who was spending the summer at the same hotel where they were said that he didn't believe it, but he was an imp who had never seen a cheap watch, so how should he know anything about what could be done with a spring that cannot be wound up by a great strong man in less than ten minutes?

As for the Baron he was very modest about the achievement, for when he first appeared at the Twins' home after their return he had actually forgotten all about it, and, in fact, could not recall the incident at all, until Diavolo brought him his own letter, when, of course, the whole matter came back to him.

"It wasn't so very wonderful, anyhow," said the Baron. "I should not think, for instance, of bragging about any such thing as that. It was a simple affair all through."

"And what did you do with the moose's antlers?" asked Angelica. "I hope you brought 'em home with you, because I'd like to see 'em."

"I wanted to," said the Baron, stroking the Twins' soft brown locks affectionately. "I wanted to bring them home for your father to use as a hat rack, dear, but they were too large. When I had removed them from the dead animal, I found them so large that I could not get them out of the forest, they got so tangled up in the trees. I should have had to clear a path twenty feet wide and seven miles long to get them even as far as my friend's hut, and after that they would have had to be carried thirty miles through the woods to the express office."

"I guess it's just as well after all," said Diavolo. "If they were as big as all that, Papa would have had to build a new house to get 'em into."

"Exactly," said the Baron. "Exactly. That same idea occurred to me, and for that reason I concluded not to go to the trouble of cutting away those miles of trees. The antlers would have made a very expensive present for your father to receive in these hard times."

"It was a good thing you had that watch," the Twins observed, after thinking over the Baron's adventure. "If you hadn't had that you couldn't have killed the moose."

"Very likely not," said the Baron, "unless I had been able to do as I did in India thirty years ago at a man hunt."

"What?," cried the Twins. "Do they hunt men in India?"

"That all depends, my dears," replied the Baron. "It all depends upon what you mean by the word they. Men don't hunt men, but animals, great wild beasts sometimes hunt them, and it doesn't often happen that the men escape. In the particular man hunt I refer to I was the creature that was being hunted, and I've had a good deal of sympathy for foxes ever since. This was a regular fox hunt in a way, although I was the fox, and a herd of elephants were the huntsmen."

"How queer," said Diavolo, unscrewing one of the Baron's shirt studs to see if he would fall apart.

"Not half so queer as my feelings when I realised my position," said the Baron with a shake of his head. "I was frightened half to death. It seemed to me that I'd reached the end of my tether at last. I was studying the fauna and flora of India, in a small Indian village, known as ah—what was the name of that town! Ah—something like Rathabad—no, that isn't quite it—however, one name does as well as another in India. It was a good many miles from Calcutta, and I'd been living there about three months. The village lay in a small valley between two ranges of hills, none of them very high. On the other side of the westerly hills was a great level stretch of country upon which herds of elephants used to graze. Out of this rose these hills, very precipitously, which was a very good thing for the people in the valley, else those elephants would have come over and played havoc with their homes and crops.

"To me the plains had a great fascination, and I used to wander over them day after day in search of new specimens for my collection of plants and flowers, never thinking of the danger I ran from an encounter with these elephants, who were very ferocious and extremely jealous of the territory they had come through years of occupation to regard as their own. So it happened, that one day, late in the afternoon, I was returning from an expedition over the plains, and, as I had found a large number of new specimens, I was feeling pretty happy. I whistled loudly as I walked, when suddenly coming to a slight undulation in the plain what should I see before me but a herd of sixty-three elephants, some eating, some thinking, some romping, and some lying asleep on the soft turf.

"Now, if I had come quietly, of course, I could have passed them unobserved, but as I told you I was whistling. I forget what the tune was, The *Marsellaise* or *Die Wacht Am Rhein*, or maybe Tommie Atkins, which enrages the elephants very much, being the national anthem of the British invader. At any rate, whatever the tune was it attracted the attention of the elephants, and then their sport began. The leader lifted his trunk high in the air, and let out a trumpet blast that echoed back from the cliff three miles distant. Instantly every elephant was on the alert Those that had been sleeping awoke, and sprang to their feet. Those that had been at play stopped in their romp, and under the leadership of the biggest brute of the lot they made a rush for me. I had no gun; nothing except my wits and my legs with which to defend myself, so I naturally began to use the latter until I could get the former to work.

"It was nip and tuck. They could run faster than I could, and I saw in an instant that without stratagem I could not hope to reach a place of safety. As I have said, the cliff, which rose straight up from the plain like a stone-wall, was three miles away, nor was there any other spot in which I could find a refuge. It occurred to me as I ran that if I ran in circles I could edge up nearer to the cliff all the time, and still keep my pursuers at a distance for the simple reason that an elephant being more or less unwieldy cannot turn as rapidly as a man can, so I kept running in circles. I could run around my short circle in less time than the enemy could run around his larger one, and in this manner I got nearer and nearer my haven of safety, the bellowing beasts snorting with rage as they followed.

"Finally, when I began to see that I was tolerably safe, another idea occurred to me, which was that if I could manage to kill those huge creatures the ivory I could get would make my fortune. But how! That was the question. Well, my dearly beloved Imps, I admit that I am a fast runner, but I am also a fast thinker, and in less than two minutes I had my plan arranged. I stopped short when about two hundred feet from the cliff, and waited until the herd was fifty feet away. Then I turned about and ran with all my might up to within two feet of the cliff, and then turning sharply to the left ran off in that direction. The elephants, thinking they had me, redoubled their speed, but failed to notice that I had turned, so quickly was that movement executed.

"They failed likewise to notice the cliff, as I had intended. The consequence was the whole sixty-three of them rushed head first, bang! with all their force, into the rock. The hill shook with the force of the blow and the sixty-three elephants fell dead. They had simply butted their brains out."

Here the Baron paused and pulled vigorously on his cigar, which had almost gone out.

"That was fine," said the Twins.

"What a narrow escape it was for you. Uncle Munch," said Diavolo.

"Very true," said the great soldier rising, as a signal that his story was done. "In fact you might say that I had sixty-three narrow escapes, one for each elephant."

"But what became of the ivory?" asked Angelica.

"Oh, as for that!" said the Baron, with a sigh, "I was disappointed in that. They turned out to be all young elephants, and they had lost their first teeth. Their second teeth hadn't grown yet I got only enough ivory to make one paper cutter, which is the one I gave your father for Christmas last year."

Which may account for the extraordinary interest the Twins have taken in their father's paper-cutter ever since.

5

THE STORY OF JANG

"Did you ever own a dog, Baron Munchausen?" asked the reporter of the *Gehenna Gazette*, calling to interview the eminent nobleman during Dog Show Week in Cimmeria.

"Yes, indeed I have," said the Baron, "I fancy I must have owned as many as a hundred dogs in my life. To be sure some of the dogs were iron and brass, but I was just as fond of them as if they had been made of plush or lamb's wool. They were so quiet, those iron dogs were; and the brass dogs never barked or snapped at any one."

"I never saw a brass dog," said the reporter. "What good are they?"

"Oh they are likely to be very useful in winter," ;he Baron replied. "My brass dogs used to guard my fireplace and keep the blazing logs from rolling out into my room and setting fire to the rug the Khan of Tartary gave me for saving his life from a herd of Antipodes he and I were hunting in the Himalaya Mountains."

"I don't see what you needed dogs to do that for," said the reporter. "A fender would have done just as well, or a pair of andirons," he added.

"That's what these dogs were," said the Baron. "They were fire dogs and fire dogs are andirons."

Ananias pressed his lips tightly together, and into his eyes came a troubled look. It was evident that, revolting as the idea was to him, he thought the Baron was trying to deceive him. Noting his displeasure, the Baron inwardly resolving to be careful how he handled the truth, hastened on with his story.

"But dogs were never my favourite animals," he said. "With my pets I am quite as I am with other things. I like to have pets that are entirely different from the pets of other people, and that is why in my day I have made companions of such animals as the sangaree, and the camomile, and the—ah—the two-horned piccolo. I've had tame bees even in fact my bees used to be the wonder of Siam, in which country I was stationed for three years, having been commissioned by a British company to make a study of its climate with a view to finding out if it would pay the company to go into the ice business there. Siam is, as you have probably heard, a very warm country, and as ice is a very rare thing in warm countries these English people thought they might make a vast fortune by sending tug-boats up to the Arctic Ocean, and with them capture and tow icebergs to Siam, where they might be cut up and sold to the people at tremendous profit.

"The scheme was certainly a good one, and I found many of the wealthy Siamese quite willing to subscribe for a hundred pounds of ice a week at ten dollars a pound, but it never came to anything because we had no means of preserving the icebergs after we got them into the Gulf of Siam. The water was so hot that they melted before we could cut them up, and we nearly got ourselves into very serious trouble with the coast people for that same reason. An iceberg, as you know, is a huge affair, and when a dozen or two of them had melted in the Gulf they added so to the quantity of water there that fifty miles of the coast line were completely flooded, and thousands of valuable fish, able to live in warm water only, were so chilled that they got pneumonia, and died.

"You can readily imagine how indignant the Siamese fishermen were with my company over the losses they had to bear, but their affection for me personally was so great that they promised not to sue the company if I would promise not to let the thing occur again. This I promised, and all went well But about the bees, it was while I was living in Bangkok that I had them, and they were truly wonderful. There was hardly anything those bees couldn't do after I got them tamed."

"How did you tame them, Baron?" asked Ananias.

"Power of the eye, my boy," returned the Baron. "I attracted their attention first and then held it Of course, I tried my plan on one bee first. He tamed the rest. Bees are very like children. They like to play stunts—I think it is called stunts, isn't it, when one boy does something, and all his companions try to do the same thing?"

"Yes," said Ananias, "I believe there is such a game, but I shouldn't like to play it with you."

"Well, that was the way I did with the bees," said Mr. Munchausen. "I tamed the king bee, and when he had learned all sorts of funny little tricks, such as standing on his head and humming tunes, I let him go back to the swarm. He was gone a week, and then he came back, he had grown so fond of me—as well he might, because I fed him well, giving him a large basket of flowers three times a day. Back with him came two or three thousand other bees, and whatever Jang did they did."

"Who was Jang?" asked Ananias.

"That was the first bee's name. King Jang. Jang is Siamese for Billie, and as I was always fond of the name, Billie, I called him Jang. By and by every bee in the lot could hum the Star Spangled Banner and Yankee Doodle as well as you or I could, and it was grand on those soft moonlight nights we had there, to sit on the back porch of my *pagoda* and listen to my bee orchestra discoursing sweet music. Of course, as soon as Jang had learned to hum one tune it was easy enough for him to learn another, and before long the bee orchestra could give us any bit of music we wished to have. Then I used to give musicales at my house and all the Siamese people, from the king down asked to be invited, so that through my pets my home became one of the most attractive in all Asia.

"And the honey those bees made! It was the sweetest honey you ever tasted, and every morning when I got down to breakfast there was a fresh bottleful ready for me, the bees having made it in the bottle itself over night. They were the most grateful pets I ever had, and once they saved my life. They used to live in a hive I had built for them in one corner of my room and I could go to bed and sleep with every door in my house open, and not be afraid of robbers, because those bees were there to protect me.

"One night a lion broke loose from the Royal Zoo, and while trotting along the road looking for something to eat ho saw my front door wide open. In he walked, and began to sniff. He sniffed here and he sniffed there, but found nothing but a pot of anchovy paste, which made him thirstier and hungrier than ever. So he prowled into the parlour, and had his appetite further aggravated by a bronze statue of the Emperor of China I had there. He thought in the dim light it was a small-sized human being, and he pounced on it in a minute.

"Well, of course, he couldn't make any headway trying to eat a bronze statue, and the more he tried the more hungry and angry he got. He roared until he shook the house and would undoubtedly have awakened me had it not been that I am always a sound sleeper and never wake until I have slept enough. Why, on one occasion, on the Northern Pacific Railway, a train I was on ran into and completely telescoped another while I was asleep in the smoking car, and although I was severely burned and hurled out of the car window to land sixty feet away on the prairie, I didn't wake up for two hours. I was nearly buried alive because they thought I'd been killed, I lay so still.

"But to return to the bees. The roaring of the lion disturbed them, and Jang buzzed out of his hive to see what was the matter just as the lion appeared at my bedroom door. The intelligent insect saw in a moment what the trouble was, and he sounded the alarm for the rest of the bees, who came swarming out of the hive in response to the summons, Jang kept his eye on the lion meanwhile, and just as the prowler caught sight of your mid peacefully snoring away on the bed, dreaming his boyhood, and prepared to spring upon me, Jang buzzed over and sat down upon his back, putting his sting where it would do the most

283

good.

"The angry lion, who in a moment would have fastened his teeth upon me, turned with a yelp of pain, and the bite which was to have been mine wrought havoc with his own back. Following Jang's example, the other bees ranged themselves in line over the lion's broad shoulders, and stung him until he roared with pain. Each time he was stung would whisk his head around like a dog after a flea, and bite himself, until finally he had literally chewed himself up, when he fainted from sheer exhaustion, and I was saved. You can imagine m surprise when next morning I awakened to find dying lion in my room."

"But, Baron," said Ananias. "I don't understand one thing about it. If you were fast asleep while all this was happening how did you know that Jang did those things?"

"Why, Jang told me himself," replied the Baron calmly.

"Could he talk?" cried Ananias in amazement

"Not as you and I do," said the Baron. "Of course not, but Jang could spell. I taught him how. You see I reasoned it out this way. If a bee can be taught to sing a song which is only a story in music, why can't he be taught to tell a story in real words. It was worth trying anyhow, and I tried. Jang was an apt pupil. He was the most intelligent bee I ever met, and it didn't take me more than a month to teach him his letters, and when he once knew his letters it was easy enough to teach him how to spell. I got a great big sheet and covered it with twenty-six squares, and in each of these squares I painted a letter of the alphabet, so that finally when Jang came to know them, and wanted to tell me anything he would fly from one square to another until he had spelled out whatever he wished to say.

"I would follow his movements closely, and we got so after awhile that we could converse for hours without any trouble whatsoever. I really believe that if Jang had been a little heavier so that he could push the keys down far enough he could have managed a typewriter as well as anybody, and when I think about his wonderful mind and delicious fancy I deeply regret that there never was a typewriting machine so delicately made that a bee of his weight could make it go. The world would have been very much enriched by the stories Jang had in his mind to tell, but it is too late now. He is gone forever."

"How did you lose Jang, Baron?" asked Ananias, with tears in his eyes.

"He thought I had deceived him," said the Baron, with a sigh. "He was as much of a stickler for truth as I am. An American friend of mine sent me a magnificent parterre of wax flowers which were so perfectly made that I couldn't tell them from the real. I was very proud of them, and kept them in my room near the hive. When Jang and his tribe first caught sight of them they were delighted and they sang as they had never sung before just to show how pleased they were Then they set to work to make honey out of them. They must have laboured over those flowers for two months before I thought to tell them that they were only wax and not at all real.

"As I told Jang this, I unfortunately laughed, thinking that he could understand the joke of the thing as well as I, but I was mistaken. All that he could see was that he had been deceived, and it made him very angry. Bees don't seem to have a well-developed sense of humour. He cast a reproachful glance at me and returned to his hive and on the morning of the third day when I waked up they were moving out. They flew to my lattice and ranged themselves along the slats and waited for Jang. In a moment he appeared and at a given signal they buzzed out of my sight, humming a farewell dirge as they went. I never saw them again."

Here the Baron wiped his eyes.

"I felt very bad about it," he went on, "and resolved then never again to do anything which even suggested deception, and when several years later I had my crest designed I had a bee drawn on it, for in my eyes my good friend the bee, represents three great factors of the good and successful life—Industry, Fidelity, and Truth."

Whereupon the Baron went his way, leaving Ananias to think it over.

285

6
He Tells the Twins of Fireworks

There was a great noise going on in the public square of Cimmeria when Mr. Munchausen sauntered into the library at the home of the Heavenly Twins.

"These Americans are having a great time of it celebrating their Fourth of July," said he, as the house shook with the explosion of a bomb. "They've burnt powder enough already to set ten revolutions revolving, and they're going to outdo themselves tonight in the park. They've made a bicycle out of the two huge pin-wheels, and they're going to make Benedict Arnold ride a mile on it after it's lit."

The Twins appeared much interested. They too had heard much of the celebration and some of its joys and when the Baron arrived they were primed with questions.

"Uncle Munch," they said, helping the Baron to remove his hat and coat, which they threw into a corner so anxious were they to get to work, "do you think there's much danger in little boys having fire-crackers and rockets and pin-wheels, or in little girls having torpeters?"

"Well, I don't know," the Baron answered, warily. "What does your venerable Dad say about it?"

"He thinks we ought to wait until we are older, but we don't," said the Twins.

"Torpeters never sets nothing afire," said Angelica.

"That's true," said the Baron, kindly; "but after all your father is right. Why do you know what happened to me when I was a boy?"

"You burnt your thumb," said the Twins, ready to make a guess at it.

"Well, you get me a cigar, and I'll tell you what happened to me when I was a boy just because my father let me have all the fireworks I wanted, and then perhaps you will see how wise your father is in not doing as you wish him to," said Mr. Munchausen.

286

The Twins readily found the desired cigar, after which Mr. Munchausen settled down comfortably in the hammock, and swinging softly to and fro, told his story.

"My dear old father," said he, "was the most indulgent man that ever lived. He'd give me anything in the world that I wanted whether he could afford it or not, only he had an original system of giving which kept him from being ruined by indulgence of his children. He gave me a Rhine steamboat once without its costing him a cent I saw it, wanted it, was beginning to cry for it, when he patted me on the head and told me I could have it, adding, however, that I must never take it away from the river or try to run it myself. That satisfied me.

"All I wanted really was the happiness of feeling it was mine, and my dear old daddy gave me permission to feel that way. The same thing happened with reference to the moon. He gave it to me freely and ungrudgingly. He had received it from his father, he said, and he thought he had owned it long enough. Only, he added, as he had about the steamboat, I must leave it where it was and let other people look at it whenever they wanted to, and not interfere if I found any other little boys or girls playing with its beams, which I promised and have faithfully observed to this day.

"Of course from such a parent as this you may very easily see everything was to be expected on such a day as the Tenth of August which the people in our region celebrated because it was my birthday. He used to let me have my own way at all times, and it's a wonder I wasn't spoiled. I really can't understand how it is that I have become the man I am, considering how I was indulged when I was small.

"However, like all boys, I was very fond of celebrating the Tenth, and being a more or less ingenious lad, I usually prepared my own fireworks and many things happened which might not otherwise have come to pass if I had been property looked after as you are. The first thing that happened to me on the Tenth of August that would have a great deal better not have happened, was when I was—er—how old are you Imps?"

"Sixteen," said they. "Going on eighteen."

"Nonsense," said the Baron. "Why you're not more than eight"

"Nope—we're sixteen," said Diavolo. "I'm eight and Angelica's eight and twice eight is sixteen."

"Oh," said the Baron. "I see. Well, that was exactly the age I was at the time. Just eight to a day."

"Sixteen we said," said the Twins.

"Yes," nodded the Baron. "Just eight, but going on towards sixteen. My father had given me ten *thalers* to spend on noises, but unlike most boys I did not care so much for noises as I did for novelties. It didn't give me any particular pleasure to heap a giant cracker go off with a bang. What I wanted to do most of all was to get up some kind of an exhibition that would please the people and that could be seen in the daytime instead of at night when everybody is tired and sleepy. So instead of spending my money on fire-crackers and torpedoes and rockets, I spent nine *thalers* of it on powder and one *thaler* on putty blowers.

"My particular object was to make one grand effort and provide passers-by with a free exhibition of what I was going to call 'Munchausen's Grand Geyser Cascade.' To do this properly I had set my eye upon a fish pond not far from the town hall. It was a very deep pond and about a mile in circumference, I should say. Putty blowers were then selling at five for a pfennig and powder was cheap as sand owing to the fact that the powder makers, expecting a war, had made a hundred times as much as was needed, and as the war didn't come off, they were willing to take almost anything they could get for it. The consequence was that the powder I got was sufficient in quantity to fill a rubber bag as large as five sofa cushions.

"This I sank in the middle of the pond, without telling anybody what I intended to do, and through the putty blowers, sealed tightly together end to end, I conducted a fuse, which I made myself, from the powder bag to the shore My idea was that I could touch the thing off, you know, and that about sixty square feet of the pond would fly up into the air and then fall gracefully back again like a huge fountain. If it had worked as I expected everything would have been all rights but it didn't. I had too much powder, for a second after I had lit the fuse there came a muffled roar and the whole pond in a solid mass, fish and all, went flying up into the air and disappeared.

"Everybody was astonished, not a few were very much frightened. I was scared to death but I never let on to any one that I was the person that had blown the pond off. How high the pond went I don't know, but I do know that for a week there wasn't any sign of it, and then most unexpectedly out of what appeared to be a clear sky there came the most extraordinary rain-storm you ever saw. It literally poured down for two days, and, what I alone could understand, with it came trout and sunfish and minnows, and most singular to all but myself an old scow that was recognised as the property of the owner of the pond suddenly appeared in the sky falling toward the earth at a fearful rate of speed.

"When I saw the scow coming I was more frightened than ever because I was afraid it might fall upon and kill some of our neighbours. Fortunately, however, this possible disaster was averted, for it came down directly over the sharp-pointed lightning-rod on the tower of our public library and stuck there like a piece of paper on a file.

"The rain washed away several acres of finely cultivated farms, but the losses on crops and fences and so forth were largely reduced by the flush that came with the storm. One farmer took a rake and caught three hundred pounds of trout, forty pounds of sun-fish, eight turtles, and a minnow in his potato patch in five minutes. Others were almost as fortunate, but the damage was sufficiently large to teach me that parents cannot be too careful about what they let their children do on the day they celebrate."

"And weren't you ever punished?" asked the Twins.

"No, indeed," said the Baron. "Nobody ever knew that I did it because I never told them. In fact you are the only two persons who ever heard about it, and you mustn't tell, because there an still a number of farmers around that region who would sue me for damages in case they knew that I was responsible for the accident."

"That was pretty awful," said the Twins. "But we don't want to blow up ponds so as to get cascadeses, but we do want torpeters. Torpeters aren't any harm, are they, Uncle Munch?"

"Well, you can never tell. It all depends on the torpedo. Torpedoes are sometimes made carelessly," said the Baron. "They ought to be made as carefully as a druggist makes pills. So many pebbles, so much paper, and so much saltpetre and sulphur, or whatever else is used to make them go off. I had a very unhappy time once with a carelessly made torpedo. I had two boxes full. They were those tin-foil torpedoes that little girls are so fond of, and I expected they would make quite a lot of noise, but the first ten I threw down didn't go off at all. The eleventh for some reason or other, I never knew exactly what, I hurled with all my force against the side of my father's barn, and my, what a surprise it was!

"It smashed in the whole side of the barn and sent seven bales of hay, and our big farm plough bounding down the hillside into the town. The hay-bales smashed down fences; one of them hit a cow-shed on its way down, knocked the back of it to smithereens and then proceeded to demolish the rear end of a small crockery shop that fronted on the main street It struck the crockery shop square in the middle of its back and threw down fifteen dozen cups and saucers, thirty-two water pitchers, and five china busts of Shakespeare. The din was frightful—but I couldn't help that. Nobody could blame me, because I had no means of knowing that the man who made the torpedoes was careless and had put a solid ball of dynamite into one of them. So you see, my dear Imps, that even torpedoes are not always safe."

"Yes," said Angelica. "I guess I'll play with my dolls on my birthday. They never goes off and blows things up."

"That's very wise of you," said the Baron.

"But what became of the plough, Uncle Munch?" said Diavolo.

"Oh, the plough didn't do much damage," replied Sir. Munchausen. "It simply furrowed its way down the hill, across the main street, to the bowling green. It ploughed up about one hundred feet of this before it stopped, but nobody minded that much because it was to have been ploughed and seeded again anyhow within a few days. Of course the furrow it made in crossing the road was bad, and to make it worse the share caught one of the water pipes that ran under the street, and ripped it in two so that the water burst out and flooded the street for a while, but one hundred and sixty thousand dollars would have covered the damage."

The Twins were silent for a few moments and then they asked:

"Well, Uncle Munch, what kind of fireworks are safe anyhow?"

"My experience has taught me that there are only two kinds that are safe," replied their old friend. "One is a Jack-o'-lantern and the other is a cigar, and as you are not old enough to have cigars, if you will put on your hats and coats and go down into the garden and get me two pumpkins, I'll make each of you a Jack-o'-lantern. What do you say?"

"We say yes," said the Twins, and off they went, while the Baron taming over in the hammock, and arranging a pillow comfortably under his head, went to sleep to dream of more birthday recollections in case there should be a demand for them later on.

7

SAVED BY A MAGIC LANTERN

When the Sunday dinner was over, the Twins, on Mr. Munchausen's invitation, climbed into the old warrior's lap, Angelica kissing him on the ear, and Diavolo giving his nose an affectionate tweak.

"Ah!" said the Baron. "That's it!"

"What's what. Uncle Munch?" demanded Diavolo.

"Why that," returned the Baron. "I was wondering what it was I needed to make my dinner an unqualified success. There was something lacking, but what it was, we have had so much, I could not guess until you two Imps kissed me and tweaked my nasal feature. Now I know, for really a feeling of the most blessed contentment has settled upon my soul."

"Don't you wish *you* had two youngsters like us. Uncle Munch?" asked the Twins.

"Do I wish I had? Why I have got two youngsters like you," the Baron replied. "I've got 'em right here too."

"Where?" asked the Twins, looking curiously about them for the other two.

"On my knees, of course," said he. "You are mine. Your papa gave you to me—and you are as like yourselves as two peas in a pod."

"I—I hope you aren't going to take us away from here," said the Twins, a little ruefully. They were very fond of the Baron, but they didn't exactly like the idea of being given away.

"Oh no—not at all," said the Baron. "Your father has consented to keep you here for me and your mother has kindly volunteered to look after you. There is to be no change, except that you belong to me, and, *vice versa*, I belong to you."

"And I suppose, then," said Diavolo, "if you belong to us you've got to do pretty much what we tell you to?"

"Exactly," responded Mr. Munchausen. "If you should ask me to tell you a story I'd have to do it, even if you were to demand the full particulars of how I spent Christmas with Mtulu, King of the Taafe Eatars, on the upper Congo away down in Africa—which is a tale I have never told anyone in all my life."

"It sounds as if it might be interesting," said the Twins. "Those are real candy names, aren't they?"

"Yes," said the Baron. "Taafe sounds like taffy and Mtulu is very suggestive of chewing gum. That's the curious thing about the savage tribes of Africa. Their names often sound as if they might be things to eat instead of people. Perhaps that is why they sometimes eat each other—though, of course, I won't say for sure that that is the real explanation of cannibalism."

"What's cannon-ballism?" asked Angelica.

"He didn't say cannon-ballism," said Diavolo, scornfully. "It was candy-ballism."

"Well—you've both come pretty near it," said the Baron, "and we'll let the matter rest there, or I won't have time to tell you how Christmas got me into trouble with King Mtulu."

The Baron called for a cigar, which the Twins lighted for him and then he began.

"You may not have heard," he said, "that some twenty or thirty years ago I was in command of as expedition in Africa. Our object was to find Late Majolica, which we hoped would turn up half way between Lollokolela and the Clebungo Mountaina Lollokolela was the furthermost point to which civilisation had reached at that time, and was directly in the pathway to the Clebungo Mountains, which the natives said were full of gold and silver mines and scattered all over which were reputed to be caves in which diamonds and rubies and other gems of the rarest sort were to be found in great profusion. No white man had ever succeeded in reaching this marvellously rich range of hills for the reason that after leaving Lollokolela there was, as far as was known, no means of obtaining water, and countless adventurous spirits had had to give up because of the overpowering thirst which the climate brought upon them.

"Under such circumstances it was considered by a company of gentlemen in London to be well worth their while to set about the discovery of a lake, which they decided in advance to call Majolica, for reasons best known to themselves; they probably wanted to jar somebody with it And to me was intrusted the mission of leading the expedition. I will confess that I did not want to go for the very good reason that I did not wish to be eaten alive by the savage tribes that infested that region, but the company provided me with a close fitting suit of mail, which I wore from the time I started until I returned.

"It was very fortunate for me that I was so provided, for on three distinct occasions I was served up for state dinners and each time successfully resisted the carving knife and as a result, was thereafter well received, all the chiefs looking upon me as one who bore a charmed existence."

Here the Baron paused long enough for the Twins to reflect upon and realise the terrors which had beset him on his way to Lake Majolica, and be it said that if they had thought him brave before they now deemed him a very hero of heroes.

"When I set out," said the Baron, "I was accompanied by ten Zanzibaris and a thousand tins of condensed dinners."

"A thousand what, Uncle Munch?" asked Jack, his mouth watering.

"Condensed dinners," said the Baron, "I had a lot of my favourite dinners condensed and put up in tins. I didn't expect to be gone more than a year and a thousand dinners condensed and tinned, together with the food I expected to find on the way, elephant meat, rhinoceros steaks, and tiger chops, I thought would suffice for the trip. I could eat the condensed dinners and my followers could have the elephant's meat, rhinoceros steaks, and tiger chops—not to mention the bananas and other fruits which grow wild in the African jungle.

"It was not long, however, before I made the discovery that the Zanzibaris, in order to eat tigers, need to learn first how to keep tigers from eating them. We went to bed late one night on the fourth day out from Lollokolela, and when we waked up the next morning every mother's son of us, save myself had been eaten by tigers, and again it was nothing but my coat of mail that saved me. There was eighteen tigers' teeth sticking into the sleeve of the coat, as it was. You can imagine my distress at having to continue the search for Lake Majolica alone. It was then that I acquired the habit of talking to myself, which has kept me young ever since, for I enjoy my own conversation hugely, and find myself always a sympathetic listener.

"I walked on for days and days, until finally, on Christmas Eve, I reached King Mtulu's palace. Of course your idea of a palace is a magnificent five-storey building with beautiful carvings all over the front of it, marble stair-cases and handsomely painted and gilded ceilings. King Mtulu's palace was nothing of the sort, although for that region it was quite magnificent, the walls being decorated with elephants' tusks, crocodile teeth and many other treasures such as delight the soul of the Central African.

"Now as I may not have told you. King Mtulu was the fiercest of the African chiefs, and it is said that up to the time when I outwitted him no white man had ever encountered him and lived to tell the tale. Consequently, when without knowing it on this sultry Christmas Eve, laden with the luggage and the tinned dinners and other things I had brought with me I stumbled upon the bloodthirsty monarch I gave myself up for lost

"'Who comes here to disturb the royal peace?' cried Mtulu, savagely, as I crossed the threshold.

"'It is I, your highness,' I returned, my face blanching, for I recognized him at once by the ivory ring he wore in the end of his nose.

"'Who is I?' retorted Mtulu, picking up his battle axe and striding forward.

"A happy thought struck me then. These folk are superstitious. Perhaps the missionaries may have told these uncivilised creatures the story of Santa Claus. I will pretend that I am Santa Claus. So I answered, 'Who is I, O Mtulu, Bravest of the Taafe Chiefs? I am Santa Claus, the Children's Friend, and bearer of gifts to and for all.'

"Mtulu gazed at me narrowly for a moment and then he beat lightly upon a *tom-tom* at his side. Immediately thirty of the most villainous-looking natives, each armed with a club, appeared.

"'Arrest that man,' said Mtulu, 'before he goes any farther. He is an impostor.'

"'If your majesty pleases,' I began.

"'Silence!' he cried, 'I am fierce and I eat men, but I love truth. The truthful man has nothing to fear from me, for I have been converted from my evil ways and since last New Year's day I have eaten only those who have attempted to deceive me. You will be served raw at dinner tomorrow night. My respect for your record as a man of courage leads me to spare you the torture of the frying-pan. You are Baron Munchausen. I recognized you the moment you turned pale. Another man would have blushed.'

"So I was carried off and shut up in a mud hovel, the interior walls of which were of white, a fact which strangely enough, preserved my life when later I came to the crucial moment. I had brought with me, among other things, for my amusement solely, a magic lantern. As a child, I had always been particularly fond of pictures, and when I thought of the lonely nights in Africa, with no books at hand, no theatres, no cotillions to enliven the monotony of my life, I resolved to take with me my little magic-lantern as much for company as for anything else.

"It was very compact in form. It folded up to be hardly larger than a wallet containing a thousand one dollar bills, and the glass lenses of course could be carried easily in my trousers pockets. The views, instead of being mounted on glass, were put on a substance not unlike glass, but thinner, called gelatine. All of these things I carried in my vest pockets, and when Mtulu confiscated my luggage the magic lantern and views of course escaped his notice.

"Christmas morning came and passed and I was about to give myself up for lost, for Mtulu was not a king to be kept from eating a man by anything so small as a suit of mail, when I received word that before dinner my captor and his suite were going to pay me a formal parting call. Night was coming on and as I sat despondently awaiting the king's arrival, I suddenly bethought me of a lantern slide of the British army, standing and awaiting the command to fire, I happened to have with me. It was a superb view—lifelike as you please. Why not throw that on the wall and when Mtuln enters he will find me apparently with a strong force at my command, thought I.

"It was no sooner thought than it was done and my life was saved. Hardly was that noble picture reflected upon the rear wall of my prison when the door opened and Mtulu, followed by his suite, appeared. I rose to greet him, but apparently he saw me not. Mute with terror he stood upon the threshold gazing at that terrible line of soldiers ready as he thought to sweep him and his men from the face of the earth with their death-dealing bullets.

"'I am your slave,' he replied to my greeting, kneeling before me, 'I yield all to you.'

"'I thought you would,' said I. 'But I ask nothing save the discovery of Lake Majolica, If within twenty-four hours Lake Majolica is not discovered I give the command to fire!' Then I turned and gave the order to carry arms, and lo! by a quick change of slides, the army appeared at a carry. Mtulu gasped with terror, but accepted my ultimatum. I was freed, Lake Majolica was discovered before ten o'clock the next morning, and at five o'clock I was on my way home, the British army reposing quietly in my breast pocket. It was a mighty narrow escape!"

"I should say so," said the Twins. "But Mtuln must have been awful stupid not to see what it was."

"Didn't he see through it when he saw you put the army in your pocket?" asked Diavolo.

"No," said the Baron, "that frightened him worse than ever, for you see he reasoned this way. If I could carry an army in my pocket-book, what was to prevent my carrying Mtulu himself and all his tribe off in the same way! He thought I was a marvellous man to be able to do that."

"Well, we guess he was right," said the Twins, as they climbed down from the Baron's lap to find an atlas and search the map of Africa for Lake Majolica. This they failed to find and the Baron's explanation is unknown to me, for when the Imps returned, the warrior had departed.

8

AN ADVENTURE IN THE DESERT

"The editor has a sort of notion, Mr. Munchausen," said Ananias, as he settled down in the big armchair before the fire in the Baron's library, "that he'd like to have a story about a giraffe. Public taste has a necky quality about it of late."

"What do you say to that, Sapphira?" asked the Baron, politely turning to Mrs. Ananias, who had called with her husband. "Are you interested in giraffes?"

"I like lions better," said Sapphira. "They roar louder and bite more fiercely."

"Well, suppose we compromise," said the Baron, "and have a story about a poodle dog. Poodle dogs sometimes look like lions, and as a rule they are as gentle as giraffes."

"I know a better scheme than that," put in Ananias. "Tell us a story about a lion and a giraffe, and if you feel disposed throw in a few poodles for good measure. I'm writing on space this year."

"That's so," said Sapphira, wearily. "I could say it was a story about a lion and Ananias could call it a giraffe story, and we'd each be right"

"Very well," said the Baron, "it shall be a story of each, only I must have a cigar before I begin. Cigars help me to think, and the adventure I had in the Desert of Sahara with a lion, a giraffe, and a slippery elm tree was so long ago that I shall have to do a great deal of thinking in order to recall it"

So the Baron went for a cigar, while Ananias and Sapphira winked enviously at each other and lamented their lost glory. In a minute the Baron returned with the weed, and after lighting it, began his story.

"I was about twenty years old when this thing happened to me," said he. "I had gone to Africa to investigate the sand in the Desert of Sahara for a Sand Company in America. As you may already have heard, sand is a very useful thing in a great many ways, more particularly however in the building trades. The Sand Company formed for the purpose of supplying sand to everybody that wanted it, but land in America at that time was so very expensive that there was very little profit in the business. People who owned sand banks and sand lots asked outrageous prices for their property; and the seashore people were not willing to part with any of theirs because they needed it in their hotel business.

"The great attraction of a seaside hotel is the sand on the

298

beach, and of course the proprietors weren't going to sell that. They might better even sell their brass bands. So the Sand Company thought it might be well to build some steamships, load them with oysters, or mowing machines, or historical novels, or anything else that is produced in the United States, and in demand elsewhere; send them to Egypt, sell the oysters, or mowing machines, or historical novels, and then have the ships fill up with sand from the Sahara, which they could get for nothing, and bring it back in ballast to the United States."

"It must have cost a lot!" said Ananias.

"Not at all," returned the Baron. "The profits on the oysters and mowing machines and historical novels were so large that all expenses both ways were more than paid, so that when it was delivered in America the sand had really cost less than nothing. We could have thrown it all overboard and still have a profit left. It was I who suggested the idea to the President of the Sand Company—his name was Bartlett, or—ah—Mulligan—or some similar well-known American name, I can't exactly recall it now. However, Mr. Bartlett, or Mr. Mulligan, or whoever it was, was very much pleased with the idea and asked me if I wouldn't go to the Sahara, investigate the quality of the sand, and report; and as I was temporarily out of employment I accepted the commission.

"Six weeks later I arrived in Cairo and set out immediately on a tour of the desert I went alone because I preferred not to take any one into my confidence, and besides one can always be more independent when he has only his own wishes to consult. I also went on foot, for the reason that camels need a great deal of care—at least mine would have, if I'd had one, because I always like to have my steeds well groomed whether there is any one to see them or not. So to save myself trouble I started off alone on foot.

"In twenty-four hours I travelled over a hundred miles of the desert, and the night of the second day found me resting in the shade of a slippery elm tree in the middle of an oasis, which after much suffering and anxiety I had discovered. It was a beautiful moonlight night and I was enjoying it hugely. There were no mosquitoes or insects of any kind to interfere with my comfort No insects could have flown so far across the sands. I have no doubt that many of them have tried to get there, but up to the time of my arrival none had succeeded, and I felt as happy as though I were in Paradise.

"After eating my supper and taking a draught of the delicious spring water that purled up in the middle of the oasis, I threw myself down under the elm tree, and began to play my violin, without which in those days I never went anywhere."

"I didn't know you played the violin," said Sapphira. "I thought your instrument was the trombone—plenty of blow and a mighty stretch."

"I don't—now," said the Baron, ignoring the sarcasm. "I gave it up ten years ago—but that's a different story. How long I played that night I don't know, but I do know that lulled by the delicious strains of the music and soothed by the soft sweetness of the atmosphere I soon dropped off to sleep. Suddenly I was awakened by what I thought to be the distant roar of thunder. 'Humph!' I said to myself. 'This is something new. A thunder storm in the Desert of Sahara is a thing I never expected to see, particularly on a beautifully clear moonlight night'—for the moon was still shining like a great silver ball in the heavens, and not a cloud was anywhere to be seen.

"Then it occurred to me that perhaps I had been dreaming, so I turned over to go to sleep again. Hardly had I closed my eyes when a second ear-splitting roar came bounding over the sands, and I knew that it was no dream, but an actual sound that I heard. I sprang to my feet and looked about the horizon and there, a mere speck in the distance, was something—for the moment I thought a cloud, but in another instant I changed my mind, for glancing through my telescope I perceived it was not a cloud but a huge lion with the glitter of hunger in his eye.

"What I had mistaken for the thunder was the roar of this savage beast. I seized my gun and felt for my cartridge box only to discover that I had lost my ammunition and was there alone, unarmed, in the great desert, at the mercy of that savage creature, who was drawing nearer and nearer every minute and giving forth the most fearful roars you ever heard. It was a terrible moment and I was in despair.

"'It's all up with you, Baron,' I said to myself, and then I caught sight of the tree. It seemed my only chance. I must climb that. I tried, but alas! As I have told you it was a slippery elm tree, and I might as well have tried to climb a greased pole. Despite my frantic efforts to get a grip upon the trunk I could not climb more than two feet without slipping back. It was impossible. Nothing was left for me to do but to take to my legs, and I took to them as well as I knew how. My, what a run it was, and how hopeless. The beast was gaining on me every second, and before me lay mile after mile of desert. 'Better give up and treat the beast to a breakfast. Baron,' I moaned to myself. 'When there's only one thing to do, you might as well do it and be done with it. Your misery will be over the more quickly if you stop right here.'

"As I spoke these words, I slowed up a little, but the frightful roaring of the lion unnerved me for an instant, or rather nerved me on to a spurt, which left the lion slightly more to the rear— and which resulted in the saving of my life; for as I ran on, what should I see about a mile ahead but another slippery elm tree, and under it stood a giraffe who had apparently fallen asleep while browsing among its upper branches, and filling its stomach with its cooling cocoanuts.

"The giraffe had its back to me, and as I sped on I formed my plan. I would grab hold of the giraffe's tail; haul myself up onto his back; climb up his neck into the tree, and then give my benefactor a blow between the eyes which would send him flying across the desert before the lion could come along and get up into the tree the same way I did.

"The agony of fear I went through as I approached the long-necked creature was something dreadful. Suppose the giraffe should be awakened by the roaring of the lion before I got there and should rush off himself to escape the fate that awaited me?

I nearly dropped, I was so nervous, and the lion was now not more than a hundred yards away. I could hear his breath as he came panting on.

"I redoubled my speed; his pants came closer, closer, until at length after what seemed a year, I reached the giraffe, caught his tail, raised myself up to his back, crawled along his neck and dropped fainting into the tree just as the lion sprang upon the giraffe's back and came on toward me. What happened then I don't know, for as I have told you I swooned away; but I do know that when I came to, the giraffe had disappeared and the lion lay at the foot of the tree dead from a broken neck."

"A broken neck?" demanded Sapphira.

"Yes," returned the Baron. "A broken neck! From which I concluded that as the lion reached the nape of the giraffe's neck, the giraffe had waked up and bent his head toward the earth, thus causing the lion to fall head first to the ground instead of landing as he had expected in the tree with me."

"It was wonderful," said Sapphira, scornfully.

"Yes," said Ananias, "but I shouldn't think a lion could break his neck falling off a giraffe. perhaps it was one of the slippery elm cocoanuts that fell on him."

"Well, of course," said the Baron, rising, "that would all depend upon the height of the giraffe. Mine was the tallest one I ever saw."

"About how tall?" asked Ananias.

"Well," returned the Baron, thoughtfully, as if calculating, "did you ever see the Eiffel Tower?"

"Yes," said Ananias.

"Well," observed the Baron, "I don't think my giraffe was more than half as tall as that"

With which estimate the Baron bowed his guests out of the room, and with a placid smile on his face, shook hands with himself.

"Mr. and Mrs. Ananias are charming people," he chuckled, "but amateurs both—deadly amateurs."

9

DECORATION DAY IN THE CANNIBAL ISLANDS

"Uncle Munch," said Diavolo as he clambered up into the old warrior's lap, "I don't suppose you could tell us a story about Decoration Day could you?"

"I think I might try," said Mr. Munchausen, puffing thoughtfully upon his cigar and making a ring with the smoke for Angelica to catch upon her little thumb. "I might try—but it will all depend upon whether you want me to tell you about Decoration Day as it is celebrated in the United States, or the way a band of missionaries I once knew in the Cannibal Islands observed it for twenty years or more."

"Why can't we have both stories?" said Angelica. "I think that would be the nicest way. Two stories is twice as good as one."

"Well, I don't know," returned Mr. Munchausen. "You see the trouble is that in the first instance I could tell you only what a beautiful thing it is that every year the people have a day set apart upon which they especially honour the memory of the noble fellows who lost their lives in defence of their country. I'm not much of a poet and it takes a poet to be able to express how beautiful and grand it all is, and so I should be afraid to try it.

"Besides it might sadden your little hearts to have me dwell upon the almost countless number of heroes who let themselves be killed so that their fellow-citizens might live in peace and happiness. I'd have to tell you about hundreds and hundreds of graves scattered over the battle fields that no one knows about, and which, because no one knows of them, are not decorated at all, unless Nature herself is kind enough to let a little dandelion or a daisy patch into the secret, so that they may grow on the green grass above these forgotten, unknown heroes who left their homes, were shot down and never heard of afterwards."

"Does all heroes get killed?" asked Angelica.

"No," said Mr. Munchausen. "I and a great many others lived through the wars and are living yet."

"Well, how about the missionaries?" said Diavolo. "I didn't know they had Decoration Day in the Cannibal Islands."

"I didn't either until I got there," returned the Baron. "But they have and they have it in July instead of May. It was one of the most curious things I ever saw and the natives, the men who used to be cannibals, like it so much that if the missionaries were to forget it they'd either remind them of it or have a celebration of their own. I don't know whether I ever told you about my first experience with the cannibals—did I?"

"I don't remember it, but if you had I would have," said Diavolo.

"So would I," said Angelica. "I remember most everything you say, except when I want you to say it over again, and even then I haven't forgotten it."

"Well, it happened this way," said the Baron. "It was when I was nineteen years old. I sort of thought at that time I'd like to be a sailor, and as my father believed in letting me try whatever I wanted to do I took a position as first mate of a steam brig that plied between San Francisco and Nepaul; taking San Francisco canned tomatoes to Nepaul and bringing Nepaul pepper back to San Francisco, making several dollars both ways. Perhaps I ought to explain to you that Nepaul pepper is red, and hot; not as hot as a furnace fire, but hot enough for your papa and myself when we order oysters at a club and have them served so cold that we think they need a little more warmth to make them palatable and digestible.

"You are not yet old enough to know the meaning of such words as palatable and digestible, but some day you will be and then you'll know what your Uncle means. At any rate it was on the return voyage from Nepaul that the water tank on the *Betsy S.* went stale and we had to stop at the first place we could to fill it up with fresh water. So we sailed along until we came in sight of an Island and the Captain appointed me and two sailors a committee of three to go ashore and see if there was a spring anywhere about.

"We went, and the first thing we knew we were in the midst

of a lot of howling, hungry savages, who were crazy to eat us. My companions were eaten, but when it came to my turn I tried to reason with the chief. 'Now see here, my friend,' said I, 'I'm perfectly willing to be served up at your breakfast, if I can only be convinced that you will enjoy eating me. What I don't want is to have my life wasted!'

"'That's reasonable enough,' said he. 'Have you got a sample of yourself along for me to taste?' 'I have,' I replied, taking out a bottle of Nepaul pepper, that by rare good luck I happened to have in my pocket. 'That is a portion of my left foot powdered. It will give you some idea of what I taste like,' I added. 'If you like that, you'll like me. If you don't, you won't.'"

"That was fine," said Diavolo. "You told pretty near the truth, too. Uncle Munch, because you are hot stuff yourself, ain't you?"

"I am so considered, my boy," said Mr. Munchausen. "The chief took a teaspoonful of the pepper down at a gulp, and let me go when he recovered. He said he guessed I wasn't quite his style, and he thought I'd better depart before I set fire to the town. So I filled up the water bag, got into the row-boat, and started back to the ship, but the *Betsy S.* had gone and I was forced to row all the way to San Francisco, one thousand, five hundred and sixty-two miles distant The captain and crew had given us all up for lost. I covered the distance in six weeks, living on water and Nepaul pepper, and when I finally reached home, I told my father that, after all, I was not so sure that I liked a sailor's life.

"But I never forgot those cannibals or their island, as you may well imagine. They and their home always interested me hugely and I resolved if the fates ever drove me mat way again, I would go ashore and see how the people were get- ting on. The fates, however, were a long time in drawing me that way again, for it was not until July, ten years ago that I reached there the second time. I was off on a yachting trip, with an English friend, when one afternoon we dropped anchor off that Cannibal Island.

"'Let's go ashore,' said I. 'What for?' said my host; and then I told him the story and we went, and it was well we did so, for it was then and there that I discovered the new way the missionaries had of celebrating Decoration Day.

"No sooner had we landed than we noticed that the Island had become civilised. There were churches, and instead of tents and mud-hovels, beautiful residences appeared here and there, through the trees. 'I fancy this isn't the island,' said my host. 'There aren't any cannibals about here.' I was about to reply indignantly, for I was afraid he was doubting the truth of my story, when from the top of a hill, not far distant, we heard strains of music. We went to see whence it came, and what do you suppose we saw? Five hundred villainous looking cannibals marching ten abreast along a fine street, and, cheering them from the balconies of the houses that fronted on the highway, were the missionaries and their friends and their children and their wives.

"'This can't be the place, after all,' said my host again.

"'Yes it is,' said I, 'only it has been converted. They must be celebrating some native festival.' Then as I spoke the procession stopped and the head missionary followed by a band of beautiful girls, came down from a platform and placed garlands of flowers and beautiful wreaths on the shoulders and heads of those reformed cannibals. In less than an hour every one of the huge black fellows was covered with roses and pinks and: flowers of all kinds, and then they started on parade again. It was a fine sight, but I couldn't stand what it was all done for until that night, when I dined with the head missionary—and what do you suppose it was?"

"I give it up," said Diavolo, "maybe the missionaries thought the cannibals didn't have clothes on."

"I guess I can't guess," said Angelica.

"They were celebrating Decoration Day," said Mr. Munchausen. "They were strewing flowers on the graves of departed missionaries."

"You didn't tell us about any graves," said Diavolo.

"Why certainly I did," said the Baron. "The cannibals themselves were the only graves poor departed missionaries ever had.

Every one of those five hundred savages was the grave of a missionary, my dears, and having been converted, and taught that it was not good to eat their fellow-men, they did all in their power afterwards to show their repentance, keeping alive the memory of the men they had treated so badly by decorating themselves on memorial day—and one old fellow, the savagest looking, but now the kindest-hearted being in the world, used always to wear about his neck a huge sign, upon which he had painted in great black letters:

Here Lies
John Thomas Wilkins.
Sailor.
Departed This Life. May 24th, 1861.
He Was a Man of Splendid Taste.

"The old cannibal had eaten Wilkins and later when he had been converted and realised that he himself was the grave of a worthy man, as an expiation he devoted his life to the memory of John Thomas Wilkins, and as a matter of fact, on the Cannibal Island Decoration Day he would lie flat on the floor all the day, groaning under the weight of a hundred potted plants, which he placed upon himself in memory of Wilkins."

Here Mr. Munchausen paused for breath, and the twins went out into the garden to try to imagine with the aid of a few practical experiments how a cannibal would look with a hundred potted plants adorning his person.

10

Mr. Munchausen's Adventure With a Shark

> HERE LIES
>
> JOHN THOMAS WILKINS,
>
> SAILOR.
>
> DEPARTED THIS LIFE, MAY 24TH, 1861.
>
> HE WAS A MAN OF SPLENDID TASTE.

This was the card sent by the reporter of the *Gehenna Gazette*, and Mrs. Ananias to Mr. Munchausen upon his return from a trip to mortal realms concerning which many curious reports have crept into circulation. Owing to a rumour persistently circulated at one time, Mr. Munchausen had been eaten by a shark, and it was with the intention of learning, if possible, the basis for the rumour that Ananias and Sapphira called upon the redoubtable Baron of other days.

Mr. Munchausen graciously received the callers and asked what he could do for them. "Our readers, Mr. Munchausen," explained Ananias, "have been much concerned over rumours of your death at the hands of a shark."

"Sharks have no hands," said the Baron quietly.

"Well—that aside," observed Ananias. "Were you killed by a shark?"

"Not that I recall," said the Baron. "I may have been, but I don't remember it Indeed I recall only one adventure with a shark. That grew out of my mission on behalf of France to the Czar of Russia. I carried letters once from the King of France to his Imperial Coolness the Czar."

"What was the nature of the letters?" asked Ananias.

"I never knew," replied the Baron. "As I have said, it was a secret mission, and the French Government never took me into its confidence. The only thing I know about it is that I was sent to St Petersburg, and I went, and in the course of time I made myself much beloved of both the people and his Majesty the Czar. I am the only person that ever lived that was liked equally by both, and if I had attached myself permanently to the Czar, Russia would have been a different country today."

"What country would it have been, Mr. Munchausen," asked Sapphira innocently, "Germany or Siam?"

"I can't specify, my dear *madame*," the Baron replied. "It wouldn't be fair. But, at any rate, I went to Russia, and was treated warmly by everybody, except the climate, which was, as it is at all times, very freezing. That's the reason the Russian people like the climate. It is the only thing the *Czar* can't change by Imperial decree, and the people admire its independence and endure it for that reason. But as I have said, everybody was pleased with me, and the *Czar* showed me unusual attention. He gave fetes in my honour. He gave the most princely dinners, and I met the very best people in St. Petersburg, and at one of these dinners I was invited to join a yachting party on a cruise around the world.

"Well, of course, though a landsman in every sense of the word, I am fond of yachting, and I immediately accepted the invitation. The yacht we went on was the *Boomski Zboomah*, belonging to Prince—er—now what was that Prince's name! Something like—er—Sheeroff or Jibski—or—er—well, never mind that. I meet so many princes it is difficult to remember their names. We'll say his name was Jibski."

"Suppose we do," said Ananias, with a jealous grin. "Jibski is such a remarkable name. It will look well in print."

"All right," said the Baron, "Jibski be it The yacht belonged to Prince Jibski, and she was a beauty. There was a stateroom and a steward for everybody on board, and nothing that could contribute to a man's comfort was left unattended to. We set sail on the 23rd of August, and after cruising about the North coast of Europe for a week or two, we steered the craft south, and along about the middle of September we reached the Amphibian Islands, and anchored. It was here that I had my first and last experience with sharks. If they had been plain, ordinary sharks I'd have had an easy time of it, but when you get hold of these Amphibian sharks you are likely to get yourself into twenty-three different kinds of trouble."

"My!" said Sapphira. "All those? Does the number include being struck by lightning?"

"Yes," the Baron answered, "And when you remember that there are only twenty-four different kinds altogether you can see what a peck of trouble an Amphibian shark can get you into. I thought my last hour had come when I met with him. You see when we reached the Amphibian Islands, we naturally thought we'd like to go ashore and pick the cocoanuts and raisins and other things that grow there, and when I got upon dry land again I felt strongly tempted to go down upon the beautiful little beach in the harbour and take a swim. Prince Jibski advised me against it, but I was set upon going. He told me the place was full of sharks, but I wasn't afraid because I was always a remarkably rapid swimmer, and I felt confident of my ability, in case I saw a shark coming after me, to swim ashore before he could possibly catch me, provided I had ten yards start

"So in I went leaving my gun and clothing on the beach. Oh, it was fun! The water was quite warm, and the sandy bottom of the bay was deliciously so pleasant to the feet. I suppose I must sported in the waves for ten or fifteen mi before the trouble came. I had just turned somersault in the water, when, as my head came to the surface, I saw directly in front of an unmistakable fin of a shark, and to my unspeakable dismay not more than five feet away. As I told you, if it had been ten yards away I should had no fear, but five feet meant another story altogether.

"My heart fairly jumped into my mouth. It would have sunk into my boots if I had had them on, but I hadn't, so it leaped upward into my mouth as I turned to swim ashore, by which time the shark had reduced the distance between us by one foot. I feared that all was up with me, and was trying to think of an appropriate set of last words, when Prince Jibski, noting my peril, fired one of the yacht's cannon in our direction.

"Ordinarily this would have been useless, for the yacht's cannon was never loaded with anything but a blank charge, but in this instance it was better than if it had been loaded with ball and shot, for not only did the sound of the explosion attract the attention of the shark and cause him to pause for a moment, but also the wadding from the gun dropped directly upon my back, so showing that Prince Jibski's aim was not as good as it might have been. Had the cannon been loaded with a ball or a shell, you can very well understand how it would have happened that yours truly would have been killed then and there."

"We should have missed you," said Ananias sweetly.

"Thanks," said the Baron. "But to resume. The shark's pause

gave me the start I needed, and the heat from the burning wadding right between my shoulders caused me to redouble my efforts to get away from the shark and it, so that I never swam faster in my life, and was soon standing upon the shore, jeering at my fearful pursuer, who, strange to say, showed no inclination to stop the chase now that I was, as I thought, safely out of his reach.

"I didn't jeer very long I can tell you, for in another minute I saw why the shark didn't stop chasing me, and why Amphibian sharks are worse than any other kind. That shark had not only fin like all other sharks to swim with, but he had likewise three pairs of legs that he could use on land quite as well as he could use the fins in the water. And then began the prettiest chase you ever saw in your life. As he emerged from the water I grabbed up my gun and ran. Round and round the island we tore, I ahead, he thirty or forty yards behind, until I got to a place where I could stop running and take a hasty shot at him. Then I aimed, and fired.

"My aim was good, but struck one of the huge creature's teeth, broke it off short, and bounded off to one side. This made him more angry than ever, and he redoubled his efforts to catch me. I redoubled mine, until I could get another shot at him. The second shot, like the first, struck the creature in the teeth, only this time it was more effective. The bullet hit his jaw lengthwise, and knocked every tooth on that side of his head down his throat. So it went. I ran. He pursued. I fired; he lost his teeth, until finally I had knocked out every tooth he had, and then, of course, I wasn't afraid of him, and let him come up with me.

"With his teeth he could have ground me to atoms at one bite. Without them he was as powerless as a bowl of currant jelly, and when he opened his huge jaws, as he supposed to bite me in two, he was the most surprised looking fish you ever saw on land or sea to discover that the effect his jaws had upon my safety was about as great as had they been nothing but two feather bed mattresses."

"You must have been badly frightened, though," said Ananias.

"No," said the Baron. "I laughed in the poor disappointed thing's face, and with a howl of despair, he rushed back into the sea again. I made the best time I could back to the yacht for fear he might return with assistance."

"And didn't you ever see him again Baron?" asked Sapphira.

"Yes, but only from the deck of the yacht as we were weighing anchor," said Mr. Munchausen. "I saw him and a dozen others like him doing precisely what I thought they would do, going ashore to search me out so as to have a little cold Munch for dinner. I'm glad they were disappointed, aren't you?"

"Yes, indeed," said Ananias and Sapphira, but not warmly.

Ananias was silent for a moment, and then walking over to one of the bookcases, he returned in a moment, bringing with him a huge atlas.

"Where are the Amphibian Islands, Mr. Munchausen?" he said, opening the book. "Show them to me on the map. I'd like to print the map with my story."

"Oh, I can't do that," said the Baron, "because they aren't on the map any more. When I got back to Europe and told the map-makers about the dangers to man on those islands, they said that the interests of humanity demanded that they be lost So they took them out of all the geographies, and all the cyclopaedias, and all the other books, so that nobody ever again should be tempted to go there; and there isn't a schoolteacher or a sailor in the world today who could tell you where they are"

"But, you know, don't you?" persisted Ananias.

"Well, I did," said the Baron; "but, really I have had to remember so many other things that I have forgotten that. All that I know is that they were named from the fact that they were infested by Amphibious animals, which are animals that can live on land as well as on water."

"How strange!" said Sapphira.

"It's just too queer for anything," said Ananias, "but on the whole I'm not surprised."

And the Baron said he was glad to hear it

11

THE BARON AS A RUNNER

The Twins had been on the lookout for the Baron for at least an hour, and still he did not come, and the little Imps were beginning to fed blue over the prospect of getting the usual Sunday afternoon story. It was past four o'clock, and for as long a time as they could remember the Baron had never failed to arrive by three o'clock. All sorts of dreadful possibilities came up before their mind's eye. They pictured the Baron in accidents of many sorts. They conjured up visions of him lying wounded beneath the ruins of an apartment house, or something else equally heavy that might have fallen upon him on his way from his rooms to the station, but that he was more than wounded they did not believe, for they knew that the Baron was not the sort of man to be killed by anything killing under the sun.

"I wonder where he can be?" said Angelica, uneasily to her brother, who was waiting with equal anxiety for their common friend.

"Oh, he's all right!" said Diavolo, with a confidence he did not really feel. "He'll turn up all right, and even if he's two hours late he'll be here on time according to his own watch. Just you wait and see."

And they did wait and they did see. They waited for ten minutes, when the Baron drove up, smiling as ever, but apparently a little out of breath. I should not dare to say that he was really out of breath, but he certainly did seem to be so, for he panted visibly, and for two or three minutes after his arrival was quite unable to ask the Imps the usual question as to their very good health. Finally, however, the customary courtesies of the greeting were exchanged, and the decks were cleared for action.

"What kept you. Uncle Munch?" asked the Twins, as they took up their usual position on the Baron's knees.

"What what?" replied the warrior. "Kept me? Why, am I late?"

"Two hours," said the Twins. "Dad gave you up and went out

for a walk."

"Nonsense," said the Baron. "I'm never that late."

Here he looked at his watch.

"Why I do seem to be behind time. There must be something wrong with our time-pieces. I can't be two hours late, you know."

"Well, let's say you are on time, then," said the Twins. "What kept you?"

"A very funny accident on the railroad," said the Baron lighting a cigar. "Queerest accident that ever happened to me on the railroad, too. Our engine ran away."

The Twins laughed as if they thought the Baron was trying to fool them.

"Really," said the Baron. "I left town as usual on the two o'clock train, which, as you know, comes through in half an hour, without a stop. Everything went along smoothly until we reached the Vitriol Reservoir, when much to the surprise of everybody the train came to a standstill. I supposed there was a cow on the track, and so kept in my seat for three or four minutes as did everyone else. Finally the conductor came through and called to the brakeman at the end of our car to see if his brakes were all right.

"'It's the most unaccountable thing,' he said to me. 'Here's this train come to a dead stop and I can't see why. There isn't a brake out of order on any one of the cars, and there isn't any earthly reason why we shouldn't go ahead.'

"'Maybe somebody's upset a bottle of glue on the track,' said I. I always like to chaff the conductor, you know, though as far as that is concerned, I remember once when I was travelling on a South American Railway our train was stopped by highwaymen, who smeared the tracks with a peculiar sort of gum. They'd spread it over three miles of track, and after the train had gone lightly over two miles of it the wheels stuck so fast ten engines couldn't have moved it. That was a terrible affair."

"I don't think we ever heard of that, did we?" asked Angelica.

"I don't remember it," said Diavolo.

"Well, you would have remembered it, if you had ever heard of it," said the Baron "It was too dreadful to be forgotten—not for us, you know, but for the robbers. It was one of the Imperial trains in Brazil, and if it hadn't been for me the Emperor would have been carried off and held for ransom. The train was brought to a standstill by this gluey stuff, as I have told you, and the desperadoes boarded the cars and proceeded to rifle us of our possessions. The Emperor was in the ear back of mine, and the robbers made directly for him, but fathoming their intention I followed close upon their heels.

"You are our game,' said the chief robber, tapping the Emperor on the shoulder, as he entered the Imperial car.

"'Hands off,' I cried throwing the ruffian to one side.

"He scowled dreadfully at me, the Emperor looked surprised, and another one of the robbers requested to know who was I that I should speak with so much authority. 'Who am I?' said I, with a wink at the Emperor. 'Who am I? Who else but Baron Munchausen of the Bodenwerder National Guard, ex-friend of Napoleon of France, intimate of the Mikado of Japan, and famed the world over as the deadliest shot in two hemispheres.'

"The *desperadoes* paled visibly as I spoke, and after making due apologies for interfering with the train, fled shrieking from the car. They had heard of me before.

"'I thank you, sir,' began the Emperor, as the would-be assassins fled, but I cut him short 'They must not be allowed to escape,' I said, and with that I started in pursuit of the desperate fellows, overtook them, and glued them with the gum they had prepared for our detention to the face of a precipice that rose abruptly from the side of the railway, one hundred and ten feet above the level. There I left them. We melted the glue from the tracks by means of our steam heating apparatus, and were soon booming merrily on our way to Rio Janeiro when I was fêted and dined continuously for weeks by the people, though strange to say the Emperor's behaviour toward me was very cool."

"And did the robbers ever get down?" asked the Twins.

"Yes, but not in a way they liked," Mr. Munchausen replied. "The sun came out, and after a week or two melted the glue that held them to the precipice, whereupon they fell to its base and were shattered into pieces so small there wasn't an atom of them to be found when a month later I passed that way again on my return trip."

"And didn't the Emperor treat you well, Uncle Munch?" asked the Imps.

"No—as I told you he was very cool towards me, and I couldn't understand it, then, but I do now," said the Baron. "You see he was very much in need of ready cash, the Emperor was, and as the taxpayers were already growling about the expenses of the Government he didn't dare raise the money by means of a tax. So he arranged with the *desperadoes* to stop the train, capture him, and hold him for ransom. Then when the ransom came along he was going to divide up with them. My sudden appearance, coupled with my determination to rescue him, spoiled his plan, you see, and so he naturally wasn't very grateful. Poor fellow, I was very sorry for it afterward, because he really was an excellent ruler, and his plan of raising the money he needed wasn't a bit less honest than most other ways rulers employ to obtain revenue for State purposes."

"Well, now, let's get back to the runaway engine," said the Twins. "You can tell us more about South America after you get through with that. How did the engine come to run away?"

"It was simple enough," said the Baron. "The engineer, after starting the train came back into the smoking car to get a light for his pipe, and while he was there the coupling-pin between the engine and the train broke, and off skipped the engine twice as fast as it had been going before. The relief from the weight of the train set its pace to a mile a minute instead of a mile in two minutes, and there we were at a dead stop in front of the Vitriol Station with nothing to move us along. When the engineer saw what had happened he fainted dead away, because you know if a collision had occurred between the runaway engine and the train ahead he would have been held responsible."

"Couldn't the fireman stop the engine?" asked the Twins.

"No. That is, it wouldn't be his place to do it, and these railway fellows are queer about that sort of thing," said the Baron. "The engineers would go out upon a strike if the railroad were to permit a stoker to manage the engine, and besides that the stoker wouldn't undertake to do it at a stoker's wages, so there wasn't any help to be looked for there. The conductor happened to be nearsighted, and so he didn't find out that the engine was missing until he had wasted ten or twenty minutes examining the brakes, by which time, of course, the runaway was miles and miles up the track.

"Then the engineer came to, and began to wring his hands and moan in a way that was heartrending. The conductor, too, began to cry, and all the brakemen left the train and took to the woods. They weren't going to have any of the responsibility for the accident placed on their shoulders. Whether they will ever turn up again I don't know. But I realised as soon as anybody else that something had to be done, so I rushed into the telegraph office and telegraphed to all the station masters between the Vitriol Reservoir and Cimmeria to clear the track of all trains, freight, local, or express, or somebody would be hurt, and that I myself would undertake to capture the runaway engine.

"This they all promised to do, whereupon I bade goodbye to my fellow-travellers, and set off up the track myself at full speed. In a minute I strode past Sulphur Springs, covering at least eight ties at a stretch. In two minutes I thundered past Lava Hurst, where I learned that the engine had twenty miles start of me. I made a rapid calculation mentally—I always was strong in mental arithmetic, which showed that unless I was tripped up or got side-tracked somewhere I might overtake the runaway before it reached Noxmere.

"Redoubling my efforts, my stride increased to twenty ties at a jump, and I made the next five miles in two minutes. It sounds impossible, but really it isn't so. It is hard to run as fast as that at the start, but when you have got your start the impetus gathered in the first mile's run sends you along faster in the second, and so your speed increases by its own force until finally you go like the wind. At Gasdale I had gained two miles on the engine, at Sneakskill I was only fifteen miles behind, and upon my arrival at Noxmere there was scarcely a mile between me and the fugitive. Unfortunately a large crowd had gathered at Noxmere to see me pass through, and some small boy had brought a dog along with him and the dog stood directly in my path. If I ran over the dog it would kill him and might trip me up.

"If I jumped with the impetus I had theft was no telling where I would land. It was a hard point to decide either way, but I decided in favour of the jump, simply to save the dog's life, for I love animals. I landed three miles up the road and ahead of the engine, though I didn't know that until I had run ten miles farther on, leaving the engine a hundred yards behind me at every stride It was at Miasmatica that I discovered my error and then I tried to stop. It was almost in vain; I dragged my feet over the ties, but could only slow down to a three-minute gait. Then I tried to turn around and slow up running backward; this brought my speed down ten minutes to the mile, which made it safe for me to run into a haystack at the side of the railroad just this side of Cimmeria.

"Then, of course, I was all right I could sit down and wait for the engine, which came booming along forty minutes later. As it approached I prepared to board it, and in five minutes was in full control. That made it easy enough for me to get back here without further trouble. I simply reversed the lever, and back we came faster than I can describe, and just one hour and a half from the time of the mishap the runaway engine was restored to its deserted train and I reached your station here in good order. I should have walked up, but for my weariness after that exciting run, which as you see left me very much out of breath, and which made it necessary for me to hire that worn-out old hack instead of walking up as is my wont."

"Yes, we see you are out of breath," said the Twins, as the Baron paused, "Would you like to lie down and take a rest?"

"Above all things," said the Baron. "I'll take a nap here until

318

your father returns," which he proceeded at once to do.

While he slept the two Imps gazed at him curiously, Angelica, a little suspiciously.

"Bub," said she, in a whisper, "do you think that was a true story?"

"Well, I don't know," said Diavolo. "If anybody else than Uncle Munch had told it, I wouldn't have believed it But he hates untruth. I know because he told me so."

"That's the way I feel about it," said Angelica. "Of course, he can run as fast as that, because he is very strong, but what I can't see is how an engine ever could run away from its train."

"That's what stumps me," said Diavola

12

Mr. Munchausen Meets His Match

(Reported by Henry W. Ananias for the *Gehenna Gazette*.)

When Mr. Munchausen, accompanied by Ananias and Sapphira, after a long and tedious journey from Cimmeria to the cool and wooded heights of the Blue Sulphur Mountains, entered the portals of the hotel where the greater part of his summers are spent, the first person to greet him was Beelzebub Sandboy,—the curly-headed Imp who acted as "Head Front" of the Blue Sulphur Mountain House, his eyes a-twinkle and his swift running feet as ever ready for a trip to any part of the hostelry and back.

Beelzy, as the Imp was familiarly known, as the party entered, was in the act of carrying a half-dozen pitchers of iced-water upstairs to supply thirsty guests with the one thing needful and best to quench that thirst, and in his excitement at catching sight once again of his ancient friend the Baron, managed to drop two of the pitchers with a loud crash upon the office floor. This, however, was not noticed by the powers that ruled. Beelzy was not perfect, and as long as he smashed less than six pitchers a day on an average the management was disposed not to complain.

"There goes my friend Beelzy," said the Baron, as the pitchers fell. "I am delighted to see him. I was afraid he would not be here this year since I understand he has taken up the study of theology."

"Theology?" cried Ananias. "In Hades?"

"How foolish," said Sapphira. "We don't need preachers here."

"He'd make an excellent one," said Mr. Munchausen. "He is a lad of wide experience and his fish and bear stories are wonderful. If he can make them gee, as he would put it, with his doctrines he would prove a tremendous success. Thousands would flock to hear him for his bear stories alone. As for the foolishness of his choice, I think it is a very wise one. Everybody can't be a stoker, you know."

At any rate, whatever the reasons for Beelzebub's presence, whether he had given up the study of theology or not, there he was plying his old vocation with the same perfection of carelessness as of yore, and apparently no farther along in the study of theology than he was the year before when he bade Mr. Munchausen "goodbye forever" with the statement that now that he was going to lead a pious life the chances were he'd never meet his friend again.

"I don't see why they keep such a careless boy as that," said Sapphira, as Beelzy at the first landing turned to grin at Mr. Munchausen, emptying the contents of one of his pitchers into the lap of a nervous old gentleman in the office below.

"He adds an element of excitement to a not over-exciting place," explained Mr. Munchausen. "On stormy days here the men make bets on what fool thing Beelzy will do next He blacked all the russet shoes with stove polish one year, and last season in the rush of his daily labours he filled up the watercooler with soft coal instead of ice. He's a great bell-boy, is my friend Beelzy."

A little while later when Mr. Munchausen and his party had been shown to their suite, Beelzy appeared in their drawing-room and was warmly greeted by Mr. Munchausen, who introduced him to Mr. and Mrs. Ananias.

"Well," said Mr. Munchausen, "you're here again, are you?"

"No, indeed," said Beelzy. "I ain't here this year. I'm over at the Coal-Yards shovellin' snow. I'm my twin brother that died three years before I was born."

"How interesting," said Sapphira, looking at the boy through her lorgnette.

Beelzy bowed in response to the compliment and observed to the Baron:

"You ain't here yourself this season, be ye?"

"No," said Mr. Munchausen, drily. "I've gone abroad. You've given up theology I presume?"

"Sorter," said Beelzy. "It was lonesome business and I hadn't been at it more'n twenty minutes when I realised that bein' a missionary ain't all jam and buckwheats. It's kind o' dangerous too, and as I didn't exactly relish the idea o' bein' et up by Samoans an' Feejees I made up my mind to give it up an' stick to bell-boyin' for another season any how; but I'll see you later, Mr. Munchausen. I've got to hurry along with this iced-water. It's overdue now, and we've got the kickinest lot o' folks here this year you ever see. One man here the other night got as mad as hookey because it took forty minutes to soft bile an egg. Said two minutes was all that was necessary to bile an egg softer'n mush, not understanding anything about the science of eggs in a country where hens feeds on pebbles."

"Pebbles?" cried Mr. Munchausen. "What, do they lay Roc's eggs?"

Beelzy grinned.

"No, sir—they lay hen's eggs all right, but they're as hard as Adam's aunt."

"I never heard of chickens eating pebbles," observed Sapphira with a frown. "Do they really relish them?"

"I don't know, Ma'am," said Beelzy, "I ain't never been on speakin' terms with the hens, Ma'am, and they never volunteered no information. They eat 'em just the same. They've got to eat something and up here on these mountains there ain't anything but gravel for 'em to eat That's why they do it. Then when it comes to the eggs, on a diet like that, cobblestones ain't in it with 'em for hardness, and when you come to bile 'em it takes a week to get 'em soft, an' a steam drill to get 'em open— an' this feller kicked at forty minutes! Most likely he's swearin' around upstairs now because this iced-water ain't came; and it ain't more than two hours since he ordered it neither."

"What an unreasonable gentleman," said Sapphira.

"Ain't he though!" said Beelzy. "And he ain't over liberal neither. He's been here two weeks now and all the money I've got out of him was a five-dollar bill I found on his bureau yesterday morning. There's more money in theology than there is in him."

With this Beelzebub grabbed up the pitcher of water, and bounded out of the room like a frightened fawn. He disappeared into the dark of the corridor, and a few moments later was evidently tumbling head over heels up stairs, if the sounds that greeted the ears of the party in the drawing- room meant anything.

The next morning when there was more leisure for Beelzy the Baron inquired as to the state of his health.

"Oh it's been pretty good," said he. "Pretty good. I'm all right now, barrin' a little gout in my right foot, and ice-water on my knee, an' a crick in my back, an' a tired feelin' all over me generally. Ain't had much to complain about. Had the measles in December, and the mumps in February; an' along about the middle o' May the whoopin' cough got a holt of me; but as it saved my life I oughtn't to kick about that."

Here Beelzy looked gratefully at an invisible something— doubtless the recollection in the thin air of his departed case of whooping cough, for having rescued him from an untimely grave.

"That is rather curious, isn't it?" queried Sapphira, gazing intently into the boy's eyes. "I don't exactly understand how the whooping cough could save anybody's life, do you, Mr. Munchausen?"

"Beelzy, this lady would have you explain the situation, and I must confess that I am myself somewhat curious to learn the details of this wonderful rescue," said Mr. Munchausen.

"Well, I must say," said Beelzy, with a pleased smile at the very great consequence of his exploit in the lady's eyes, "if I was a-goin' to start out to save people's lives generally I wouldn't have thought a case o' whoopin' cough would be of much use savin' a man from drownin', and I'm sure if a feller fell out of a balloon it wouldn't help him much if he had ninety dozen cases o' whoopin' cough concealed on his person; but for just so long as I'm the feller that has to come up here every June, an' shoo the bears out o' the hotel, I ain't never goin' to be without a spell of whoopin' cough along about that time if I can help it. I wouldn't have been here now if it hadn't been for it"

"You referred just now," said Sapphira, "to shooing bears out of the hotel. May I inquire what useful function in the *ménage* of a hotel a bear-shooer performs?"

"What useful what?" asked Beelzy.

"Function—duty—what does the duty of a bear-shooer consist in?" explained Mr. Munchausen. "Is he a blacksmith who shoes bears instead of horses?"

"He's a bear-chaser," explained Beelzy, "and I'm it," he added. "That, Ma'am, is the function of a bear-shoer in the menagerie of a hotel."

Sapphira having expressed herself as satisfied, Beelzebub continued.

"You see this here house is shut up all winter, and when everybody's gone and left it empty the bears come down out of the mountains and use it instead of a cave. It's more cosier and less windier than their dens. So when the last guest has gone, and all the doors are locked, and the band gone into winter quarters, down come the bears and take possession. They generally climb through some open window somewhere. They divide up all the best rooms accordin' to their position in bear society and settle down to a regular hotel life among themselves."

"But what do they feed upon?" asked Sapphira.

"Oh they'll eat anything when they're hungry," said Beelzy. "Sofa cushions, parlour rugs, hotel registers—anything they can fasten their teeth to. Last year they came in through the *cupola*, burrowin' down through the snow to get at it, and there they stayed enjoyin' life out o' reach o' the wind and storm, snug's bugs in rugs. Year before last there must ha' been a hundred of 'em in the hotel when I got here, but one by one I got rid of 'em. Some I smoked out with some cigars Mr. Munchausen gave me the summer before; some I deceived out, gettin' 'em to chase me through the winders, an' then doublin' back on my tracks an' lockin' 'em out. It was mighty wearin' work.

"Last June there was twice as many. By actual tab I shooed two hundred and eight bears and a panther off into the mountains. When the last one as I thought disappeared into the woods I searched the house from top to bottom to see if there was any more to be got rid of. Every blessed one of the five hundred rooms I went through, and not a bear was left that I could see. I can tell you, I was glad, because there was a partickerly ugly run of 'em this year, an' they gave me a pile o' trouble. They hadn't found much to eat in the hotel, an' they was disappointed and cross. As a matter of fact, the only things they found in the place they could eat was a piano stool and an old hair trunk full o' paper-covered novels, which don't make a very hearty meal for two hundred and eight bears and a panther."

"I should say not," said Sapphira, "particularly if the novels were as light as most of them are nowadays."

"I can't say as to that," said Beelzy. "I ain't got time to read 'em and so I ain't any judge. But all this time I was sufferin' like hookey with awful spasms of whoopin' cough. I whooped so hard once it smashed one o' the best echoes in the place all to flinders, an' of course that made the work twice as harder. So, naturally, when I found there warn't another bear left in the hotel, I just threw myself down anywhere, and slept. My! how I slept. I don't suppose anything ever slept sounder'n I did. And then it happened."

Beelzy gave his trousers a hitch and let his voice drop to a stage whisper that lent a wondrous impressiveness to his narration.

"As I was a-layin' there unconscious, dreamin' of home and father, a great big black hungry bruin weighin' six hundred and forty-three pounds, that had been hidin' in the bread oven in the bakery, where I hadn't thought of lookin' for him, came saunterin' along, hummin' a little tune all by himself, and lickin' his chops with delight at the idee of havin' me raw for his dinner. I lay on unconscious of my danger, until he got right up dose, an' then I waked up, an' openin' my eyes saw this great black savage thing gloatin' over me an' tears of joy runnin' out of his mouth as he thought of the choice meal he was about to have. He was sniffin' my bang when I first caught sight of him."

"Mercy!" cried Sapphira, "I should think you'd have died of fright."

"I did," said Beelzy, politely, "but I came to life again in a minute. 'Oh Lor!' says I, as I see how hungry he was. 'This here's the end o' me;' at which the bear looked me straight in the eye, licked his chops again, and was about to take a nibble off my right ear when 'Whoop!' I had a spasm of whoopin'. Well, Ma'am, I guess you know what that means. There ain't nothin' more uncanny, more terrifyin' in the whole run o' human noises, barrin' a German Opery, than the whoop o' the whoopin' cough.

"At the first whoop Mr. Bear jumped ten feet and fell over backwards onto the floor; at the second he scrambled to his feet and put for the door, but stopped and looked around hopin' he was mistaken, when I whooped a third time. The third did the business. That third whoop would have scared Indians. It was awful. It was like a tornado blowin' through a fog-horn with a megaphone in front of it. When he heard that, Mr. Bear turned on all four of his heels and started on a scoot up into the woods that must have carried him ten miles before I quit coughin'.

"An' that's why, Ma'am, I say that when you've got to shoo bears for a livin', an attack o' whoopin' cough is a useful thing to have around."

Saying which, Beelzy departed to find Number 433's left boot which he had left at Number 334's door by some odd mistake.

"What do you think of that, Mr. Munchausen?" asked Sapphira, as Beelzy left the room.

"I don't know," said Mr. Munchausen, with a sigh. "I'm inclined to think that I am a trifle envious of him. The rest of us are not in his class."

13

WRIGGLETTO

It was in the afternoon of a beautiful summer day, and Mr. Munchausen had come up from the simmering city of Cimmeria to spend a day or two with Diavolo and Angelica and their venerable parents. They had all had dinner, and were now out on the back *piazza* overlooking the magnificent river Styx, which flowed from the mountains to the sea, condescending on its way thither to look in upon countless insignificant towns which had grown up on its banks, among which was the one in which Diavolo and Angelica had been born and lived all their lives. Mr. Munchausen was lying comfortably in a hammock, collecting his thoughts.

Angelica was somewhat depressed, but Diavolo was jubilant and all because in the course of a walk they had had that morning Diavolo had killed a snake.

"It was fine sport," said Diavolo. "He was lying there in the sun, and I took a stick and put him out of his misery in two minutes."

Here Diavolo illustrated the process by whacking the Baron over his waistcoat with a small *malacca* stick he carried.

"Well, I didn't like it," said Angelica. "I don't care for snakes, but somehow or other it seems to me we'd ought to have left him alone. He wasn't hurting anybody off there. If he'd come walking on our place, that would have been one thing, but we went walking where he was, and he had as much right to take a sun-bath there as we had."

"That's true enough," put in Mr. Munchausen, resolved after Diavolo's whack, to side against him. "You've just about hit it,

Angelica. It wasn't polite of you in the first place, to disturb his snake-ship in his nap, and having done so, I can't see why Diavolo wanted to kill him."

"Oh, pshaw!" said Diavolo, airily. "What's snakes good for except to kill? I'll kill 'em every chance I get. They aren't any good."

"All right," said Mr. Munchausen, quietly. "I suppose you know all about it; but I know a thing or two about snakes myself that do not exactly agree with what you say. They are some good sometimes, and, as a matter of fact, as a general rule, they are less apt to attack you without reason than you are to attack them. A snake is rather inclined to mind its own business unless he finds it necessary to do otherwise. Occasionally too you'll find a snake with a truly amiable character. I'll never forget my old pet Wriggletto, for instance, and as long as I remember him I can't help having a warm corner for snakes in my heart."

Here Mr. Munchausen paused and puffed thoughtfully on his cigar as a far-away half-affectionate look came into his eye.

"Who was Wriggletto?" asked Diavolo, transferring a half dollar from Mr. Munchausen's pocket to his own.

"Who was he?" cried Mr. Munchausen. "You don't mean to say that I have never told you about Wriggletto, my pet boa-constrictor, do you?"

"You never told me," said Angelica. "But I'm not everybody. Maybe you've told some other little Imps."

"No, indeed!" said Mr. Munchausen. "You two are the only little Imps I tell stories to, and as far as I am concerned, while I admit you are not everybody you are somebody and that's more than everybody is. Wriggletto was a boa-constrictor I once knew in South America, and he was without exception, the most remarkable bit of a serpent I ever met. Genial, kind, intelligent, grateful and useful, and, after I'd had him a year or two, wonderfully well educated. He could write with himself as well as you or I can with a pen. There's a recommendation for you. Few men are all that—and few boa-constrictors either, as far as that goes. I admit Wriggletto was an exception to the general run of serpents, but he was all that I claim for him, nevertheless."

"What kind of a snake did you say he was?" asked Diavolo.

"A boa-constrictor," said Mr. Munchausen, "and I knew him from his childhood, I first encountered Wriggletto about ten miles out of Para on the River Amazon. He was being swallowed by a larger boa-constrictor, and I saved his life by catching hold of his tail and pulling him out just as the other was getting ready to give the last gulp which would have taken Wriggletto in completely, and placed him beyond all hope of ever being saved."

"What was the other boa doing while you were saving Wriggletto?" asked Diavolo, who was fond always of hearing both sides to every question, and whose father, therefore, hoped he might someday grow up to be a great judge, or at least serve with distinction upon a jury.

"He couldn't do anything," returned Mr. Munchausen. "He was powerless as long as Wriggletto's head stuck in his throat and just before I got the smaller snake extracted I killed the other one by cutting off his tail behind his ears. It was not a very dangerous rescue on my part as long as Wriggletto was likely to be grateful. I must confess for a minute I was afraid he might not comprehend all I had done for him, and it was just possible he might attack me, but the hug he gave me when he found himself free once more was reassuring. He wound himself gracefully around my body, squeezed me gently and then slid off into the road again, as much as to say 'Thank you, sir, you're a brick.'

"After that there was nothing Wriggletto would not do for me. He followed me everywhere I went from that time on. He seemed to learn all in an instant that there were hundreds of little things to be done about the house of an old bachelor like myself which a willing serpent could do, and he made it his business to do those things: like picking up my collars from the floor, and finding my studs for me when they rolled under the bureau, and a thousand and one other little services of a like nature, and when you, Master Diavolo, try in future to say that snakes are only good to kill and are of no use to any one, you must at least make an exception in favour of Wriggletto."

"I will," said Diavolo, "But you haven't told us of the other useful things he did for you yet."

"I was about to do so," said Mr. Munchausen. "In the first place, before he learned how to do little things about the house for me, Wriggletto acted as a watch-dog and you may be sure that nobody ever ventured to prowl around my house at night while Wriggletto slept out on the lawn. Para was quite full of conscienceless fellows, too, at that time, any one of whom would have been glad to have a chance to relieve me of my belongings if they could get by my watch-snake. Two of them tried it one dark stormy night, and Wriggletto when he discovered them climbing in at my window, crawled up behind them and winding his tail about them crept down to the banks of the Amazon, dragging them after him. There he tossed them into the river, and came back to his post once more."

"Did you see him do it, Uncle Munch?" asked Angelica.

"No, I did not. I learned of it afterwards. Wriggletto himself said never a word. He was too modest for that," said Mr. Munchausen. "One of the robbers wrote a letter to the Para newspapers about it, complaining that any one should be allowed to keep a reptile like that around, and suggested that anyhow people using snakes in place of dogs should be compelled to license them, and put up a sign at their gates:

BEWARE OF THE SNAKE!

"The man never acknowledged, of course, that he was the robber,—said that he was calling on business when the thing happened,—but he didn't say what his business was, but I knew better, and later on the other robber and he fell out, and they confessed that the business they had come on was to take away a few thousand gold coins of the realm which I was known to have in the house locked in a steel chest

"I bought Wriggletto a handsome silver collar after that, and it was generally understood that he was the guardian of my place, and robbers bothered me no more. Then he was finer than a cat for rats. On very hot days he would go off into the cellar, where it was cool, and lie there with his mouth wide open and his eyes shut, and catch rats by the dozens. They'd run around in the dark, and the first thing they'd know they'd stumble into Wriggletto's mouth; and he swallowed them and licked his chops afterwards, just as you or I do when we've swallowed a fine luscious oyster or a clam.

"But pleasantest of all the things Wriggletto did for me—and he was untiring in his attentions in that way—was keeping me cool on hot summer nights. Para as you may have heard is a pretty hot place at best, lying in a tropical region as it does, but sometimes it is awful for a man used to the Northern climate, as I was. The act of fanning one's self, so far from cooling one off, makes one hotter than ever. Maybe you remember how it was with the elephant in the poem:

'Oh my, oh dear!' the elephant said,
'It is so awful hot!
I've fanned myself for seventy weeks,
And haven't cooled a jot.'

"And that was the way it was with me in Para on hot nights. I'd fan and fan and fan, but I couldn't get cool until Wriggletto became a member of my family, and then I was all right. He used to wind his tail about a huge palm-leaf fan I had cut in the forest, so large that I couldn't possibly handle it myself, and he'd wave it to and fro by the hour, with the result that my house was always the breeziest place in Para."

"Where is Wriggletto now?" asked Diavolo.

"Heigho!" sighed Mr. Munchausen. "He died, poor fellow, and all because of that silver collar I gave him. He tried to swallow a *jibola* that entered my house one night on wickedness intent, and while Wriggletto's throat was large enough when he stretched it to take down three *jibolas*, with a collar on which wouldn't stretch he couldn't swallow one. He didn't know that, unfortunately, and he kept on trying until the *jibola* got a quarter way down and then he stuck. Each swallow, of course, made the collar fit more tightly and finally poor Wriggletto choked himself to death.

"I felt so badly about it that I left Para within a month, but meanwhile I had a suit of clothes made out of Wriggletto's skin, and wore it for years, and then, when the clothes began to look worn, I had the skin retanned and made over into shoes and slippers. So you see that even after death he was useful to me. He was a faithful snake, and that is why when I hear people running down all snakes I tell the story of Wriggletto."

There was a pause for a few moments, when Diavolo said, "Uncle Munch, is that a true story you've been giving us?"

"True?" cried Mr. Munchausen. "True? Why, my dear boy, what a question! If you don't believe it, bring me your atlas, and I'll show you just where Para is."

Diavolo did as he was told, and sure enough, Mr. Munchausen did exactly as he said he would, which Diavolo thought was very remarkable, but he still was not satisfied.

"You said he could write as well with himself as you or I could with a pen. Uncle Munch," he said. "How was that?"

"Why that was simple enough," explained Mr. Munchausen. "You see he was very black, and thirty-nine feet long and re- markably supple and slender. After a year of hard study he learned to bunch himself into letters, and if he wanted to say anything to me he'd simply form himself into a written sentence. Indeed his favourite attitude when in repose showed his wonderful gift in chirography as well as his affection for me. If you will get me a card I will prove it"

Diavolo brought Mr. Munchausen the card and upon it he drew the following:

"There," said Mr. Munchausen. "That's the way Wriggletto always used to lie when he was at rest His love for me was very affecting."

14

THE POETIC JUNE-BUG, TOGETHER WITH SOME REMARKS ON THE GILLYHOOLY BIRD

"Uncle Munch," said Diavolo one afternoon as a couple of bicyclers sped past the house at breakneck speed, "which would you rather have, a bicycle or a horse?"

"Well, I must say, my boy, that is a difficult question to answer," Mr. Munchausen replied after scratching his head dubiously for a few minutes. "You might as well ask a man which he prefers, a hammock or a steam-yacht. To that question I should reply that if I wanted to sell it, I'd rather have a steam-yacht, but for a pleasant swing on a cool *piazza* in midsummer or under the apple-trees, a hammock would be far preferable. Steam-yachts are not much good to swing in under an apple tree, and very few *piazzas* that I know of are big enough—"

"Oh, now, you know what I mean. Uncle Munch," Diavolo retorted, tapping Mr. Munchausen upon the end of his nose, for a twinkle in Mr. Munchausen's eye seemed to indicate that he was in one of his chaffing moods, and a greater tease than Mr. Munchausen when he felt that way no one has ever known. "I mean for horseback riding, which would you rather have?"

"Ah, that's another matter," returned Mr. Munchausen, calmly. "Now I know how to answer your question. For horseback riding I certainly prefer a horse; though, on the other hand, for bicycling, bicycles are better than horses. Horses make very poor bicycles, due no doubt to the fact that they have no wheels."

Diavolo began to grow desperate.

"Of course," Mr. Munchausen went on, "all I have to say in this connection is based merely on my ideas, and not upon any personal experience. I've been horseback riding on horses, and bicycling on bicycles, but I never went horseback riding on a bicycle, or bicycling on horseback. I should think it might be

exciting to go bicycling on horseback, but very dangerous. It is
hard enough for me to keep a bicycle from toppling over when
I'm riding on a hard, straight, level well-paved road, without experimenting with my wheel on a horse's back. However if you
wish to try it someday and will get me a horse with a back as big
as Trafalgar Square I'm willing to make the effort.

Angelica giggled. It was lots of fun for her when Mr. Munchausen teased Diavolo, though she didn't like it quite so much
when it was her turn to be treated that way. Diavolo wanted to
laugh too, but he had too much dignity for that, and to conceal
his desire to grin from Mr. Munchausen he began to hunt about
for an old newspaper, or a lump of coal or something else he
could make a ball of to throw at him.

"Which would you rather do, Angelica," Mr. Munchausen
resumed, "go to sea in a balloon or attend a dumb-crambo party
in a chicken-coop?"

"I guess I would," laughed Angelica.

"That's a good answer," Mr. Munchausen put in. "It is quite
as intelligent as the one which is attributed to the Gillyhooly
bird. When the Gillyhooly bird was asked his opinion of giraffes,
he scratched his head for a minute and said,

'The question hath but little wit
That you have put to me,
But I will try to answer it
With prompt candidity.

The automobile is a thing
That's pleasing to the mind;
And in a lustrous diamond ring
Some merit I can find.

Some persons gloat o'er French Chateaux;
Some dote on lemon ice;
While others gorge on mixed gateaux.
Yet have no use for mice.

I'm very fond of oyster-stew,
I love a patent-leather boot,

But after all, 'twixt me and you,
The fish-ball is my favourite fruit.'

"Hoh" jeered Diavolo, who, attracted by the allusion to a kind of bird of which he had never heard before, had given up the quest for a paper ball and returned to Mr. Munchausen's side, "I don't think that was a very intelligent answer. It didn't answer the question at all."

"That's true, and that is why it was intelligent," said Mr. Munchausen. "It was noncommittal. Some day when you are older and know less than you do now, you will realise, my dear Diavolo, how valuable a thing is the reply that answereth not."

Mr. Munchausen paused long enough to let the lesson sink in and then he resumed.

"The Gillyhooly bird is a perfect owl for wisdom of that sort," he said. "It never lets anybody know what it thinks; it never makes promises, and rarely speaks except to mystify people. It probably has just as decided an opinion concerning giraffes as you or I have, but it never lets anybody into the secret."

"What is a Gillyhooly bird, anyhow?" asked Diavolo.

"He's a bird that never sings for fear of straining his voice; never flies for fear of wearying his wings; never eats for fear of spoiling his digestion; never stands up for fear of bandying his legs and never lies down for fear of injuring his spine," said Mr. Munchausen. "He has no feathers, because, as he says, if he had, people would pull them out to trim hats with, which would be painful, and he never goes into debt because, as he observes himself, he has no hope of paying the bill with which nature has endowed him, so why run up others?"

"I shouldn't think he'd live long if he doesn't eat?" suggested Angelica.

"That's the great trouble," said Mr. Munchausen. "He doesn't live long. Nothing so ineflfahly wise as the Gillyhooly bird ever does live long. I don't believe a Gillyhooly bird ever lived more than a day, and that, connected with the fact that he is very ugly and keeps himself out of sight, is possibly why no one has ever seen one. He is known only by hearsay, and as a matter of fact, besides ourselves, I doubt if anyone has ever heard of him."

Diavolo eyed Mr. Munchausen narrowly.

"Speaking of Gillyhooly birds, however, and to be serious for a moment," Mr. Munchausen continued flinching nervously under Diavolo's unyielding gaze; "I never told you about the poetic June-bug that worked the typewriter, did I?"

"Never heard of such a thing," cried Diavolo. "The idea of a June-bug working a typewriter."

"I don't believe it," said Angelica, "he hasn't got any fingers."

"That shows all you know about it," retorted Mr. Munchausen. "You think because you are half-way right you are all right However, if you don't want to hear the story of the June-bug that worked the typewriter, I won't tell it My tongue is tired, anyhow."

"Please go on," said Diavolo. "I want to hear it"

"So do I," said Angelica. "There are lots of stories I don't believe that I like to hear—*Jack the Giant-killer* and *Cinderella*, for instance."

"Very well," said Mr. Munchausen. "I'll tell it, and you can believe it or not, as you please. It was only two summers ago that the thing happened, and I think it was very curious. As you may know, I often have a great lot of writing to do and sometimes I get very tired holding a pen in my hand. When you get old enough to write real long letters you'll know what I mean. Your writing hand will get so tired that sometimes you'll wish some wizard would come along smart enough to invent a machine by means of which everything you think can be transferred to paper as you think it, without the necessity of writing.

"But as yet the only relief to the man whose hand is worn out by the amount of writing he has to do is the use of the typewriter, which is hard only on the fingers. So to help me in my work two summers ago I bought a typewriting machine, and put it in the great bay-window of my room at the hotel where I was stopping. It was a magnificent hotel, but it had one draw-back—it was infested with June-bugs. Most summer hotels are afflicted with mosquitoes, but this one had June-bugs instead,

335

and all night long they'd buzz and butt their heads against the walls until the guests went almost crazy with the noise.

"At first I did not mind it very much. It was amusing to watch them, and my friends and I used to play a sort of game of chance with them that entertained us hugely. We marked the walls off in squares which we numbered and then made little wagers as to which of the squares a specially selected June-bug would whack next. To simplify the game we caught the chosen June-bug and put some powdered charcoal on his head, so that when he butted up against the white wall he would leave a black mark in the space he hit. It was really one of the most exciting games of that particular kind that I ever played, and many a rainy day was made pleasant by this diversion.

"But after awhile like everything else June-bug Roulette as we called it began to pall and I grew tired of it and wished there never had been such a thing as a June-bug in the world. I did my best to forget them, but it was impossible. Their buzzing and butting continued uninterrupted, and toward the end of the month they developed a particularly bad habit of butting the electric call button at the side of my bed. The consequence was that at all hours of the night, hall-boys with iced-water, and house-maids with bath towels, and porters with kindling-wood would come knocking at my door and routing me out of bed—summoned of course by none other than those horrible butting insects. This particular nuisance became so unendurable that I had to change my room for one which had no electric bell in it

"So things went, until June passed and July appeared. The majority of the nuisances promptly got out but one especially vigorous and athletic member of the tribe remained. He became unbearable and finally one night I jumped out of bed either to kill him or to drive him out of my apartment forever, but he wouldn't go, and try as I might I couldn't hit him hard enough to kill him. In sheer desperation I took the cover of my type-writing machine and tried to catch him in that.

"Finally I succeeded, and, as I thought, shook the heedless

creature out of the window promptly slamming the window shut so that he might not return; and then putting the typewriter cover back over the machine, I went to bed again, but not to sleep as I had hoped. All night long every second or two I'd hear the typewriter click. This I attributed to nervousness on my part. As far as I knew there wasn't anything to make the typewriter click, and the fact that I heard it do so served only to convince me that I was tired and imagined that I heard noises.

"The next morning, however, on opening the machine I found that the June-bug had not only not been shaken out of the window, but had actually spent the night inside of the cover, butting his head against the keys, having no wall to butt with it, and most singular of all was the fact that, consciously or unconsciously, the insect had butted out a verse which read:

'I'm glad I haven't any brains,
For there can be no doubt
I'd have to give up butting
If I had, or butt them out.'

"Mercy! Really?" cried Angelica.

"Well I can't prove it," said Mr. Munchausen, "by producing the June-bug, but I can show you the hotel, I can tell you the number of the room; I can show you the typewriting machine, and I have recited the verse. If you're not satisfied with that I'll have to stand your suspicions."

"What became of the June-bug?" demanded

"He flew off as soon as I lifted the top of the machine," said Mr. Munchausen. "He had all the modesty of a true poet and did not wish to be around while his poem was being read."

"It's queer how you can't get rid of June-bugs, isn't it, Uncle Munch," suggested Angelica.

"Oh. we got rid of 'em next season all right," said Mr. Munchausen. "I invented a scheme that kept them away all the following summer. I got the landlord to hang calendars all over the house with one full page for each month. Then in every room we exposed the page for May and left it that way all summer.

337

When the June-bugs arrived and saw these, they were fooled into believing that June hadn't come yet, and off they flew to wait. They are very inconsiderate of other people's comfort," Mr. Munchausen concluded, "but they are rigorously bound by an etiquette of their own. A self respecting June-bug would no more appear until the June-bug season is regularly open than a gentleman of high society would go to a five o'clock tea munching fresh-roasted peanuts. And by the way, that reminds me I happen to have a bag of peanuts right here in my pocket."

Here Mr. Munchausen, transferring the luscious goobers to Angelica, suddenly remembered that he had something to say to the Imps' father, and hurriedly left them.

"Do you suppose that's true, Diavolo?" whispered Angelica as their friend disappeared.

"Well it might happen," said Diavolo, "but I've a sort of notion that it's 'maginary like the Gillyhooly bird. Gimme a peanut."

15

A LUCKY STROKE

"Mr. Munchausen," said Ananias, as he and the famous warrior drove off from the first hole at the Missing Links, "you never seem to weary of the game of golf. What is its precise charm in your eyes,—the health-giving qualities of the game or its capacity for bad lies?"

"I owe my life to it," replied the Baron. "That is to say to my precision as a player I owe one of the many preservations of my existence which have passed into history. Furthermore it is ever varying in its interest. Like life itself it is full of hazards and no man knows at the beginning of his stroke what will be the requirements of the next. I never told you of the bovine lie I got once while playing a match with Bonaparte, did I?"

"I do not recall it," said Ananias, foozling his second stroke into the stone wall.

"I was playing with my friend Bonaparte, for the Cosmopolitan Championship," said Munchausen, "and we were all even at

338

the thirty-sixth hole. Bonaparte had sliced his ball into a stubble field from the tee, whereat he was inclined to swear, until by an odd mischance I drove mine into the throat of a bull that was pasturing on the fair green two hundred and ninety-eight yards distant. 'Shall we take it over?' I asked. 'No,' laughed Bonaparte, thinking he had me. 'We must play the game. I shall play my lie. You must play yours.'

"'Very well,' said I. 'So be it Golf is golf, bull or no bull.' And off we went It took Bonaparte seven strokes to get on the green again, which left me a like number to extricate my ball from the throat of the unwelcome bovine. It was a difficult business, but I made short work of it Tying my red silk handkerchief to the end of my brassey I stepped in front of the great creature and addressing an imaginary ball before him made the usual swing back and through stroke. The bull, angered by the fluttering red handkerchief, reared up and made a dash at me. I ran in the direction of the hole, the bull in pursuit for two hundred yards. Here I hid behind a tree while Mr. Bull stopped short and snorted again.

"Still there was no sign of the ball, and after my pursuer had quieted a little I emerged from my hiding place and with the same club and in the same manner played three. The bull surprised at my temerity threw his head back with an angry toss and tried to bellow forth his wrath, as I had designed he should, but the obstruction in his throat prevented him. The ball had stuck in his pharynx. Nothing came of his spasm but a short hacking cough and a wheeze—then silence. 'I'll play four,' I cried to Bonaparte, who stood watching me from a place of safety on the other side of the stone wall.

"Again I swung my red-flagged brassey in front of the angry creature's face and what I had hoped for followed. The second attempt at a bellow again resulted in a hacking cough and a sneeze, and lo the ball flew out of his throat and landed dead to the hole. The caddies drove the bull away. Bonaparte played eight, missed a putt for a nine, stymied himself in a ten, holed out in twelve and I went down in five."

"Jerusalem!" cried Ananias. "What did Bonaparte say?"

"He delivered a short, quick nervous address in Corsican and retired to the club-house where he spent the afternoon drowning his sorrows in Absinthe high-balls. 'Great hole that, Bonaparte,' said I when his geniality was about to return. 'Yes,' said he. 'A regular lu-lu, eh?' said I. 'More than that, Baron,' said he. 'It was a Waterlooloo.' It was the first pun I ever heard the Emperor make."

"We all have our weak moments," said Ananias drily, playing nine from behind the wall. "I give the hole up," he added angrily.

"Let's play it out anyhow," said Munchausen, playing three to the green.

"All right," Ananias agreed, taking a ten and rimming the cup.

Munchausen took three to go down, scoring six in all.

"Two up," said he, as Ananias putted out in eleven.

"How the deuce do you make that out? This is only the first hole," cried Ananias with some show of heat.

"You gave up a hole, didn't you?" demanded Munchausen.

"Yes."

"And I won a hole, didn't I?"

"You did—but—"

"Well that's two holes. Fore!" cried Munchausen.

The two walked along in silence for a few minutes, and the Baron resumed.

"Yes, golf is a splendid game and I love it, though I don't think I'd ever let a good canvas-back duck get cold while I was talking about it When I have a canvas-back duck before me I don't think of anything else while it's there. But unquestionably I'm fond of golf, and I have a very good reason to be. It has done a great deal for me, and as I have already told you, once it really saved my life."

"Saved your life, eh?" said Ananias.

"That's what I said," returned Mr. Munchausen, "and so of course that is the way it was."

"I should admire to hear the details," said Ananias. "I presume you were going into a decline and it restored your strength and vitality."

"No," said Mr. Munchausen, "it wasn't that way at all. It saved my life when I was attacked by a fierce and ravenously hungry lion. If I hadn't known how to play golf it would have been farewell forever to Mr. Munchausen, and Mr. Lion would have had a fine luncheon that day, at which I should have been the turkey and cranberry sauce and mince pie all rolled into one."

Ananias laughed.

"It's easy enough to laugh at my peril now," said Mr. Munchausen, "but if you'd been with me you wouldn't have laughed very much. On, the contrary, Ananias, you'd have ruined what little voice you ever had screeching."

"I wasn't laughing at the danger you were in." said Ananias. "I don't see anything funny in that. What I was laughing at was the idea of a lion turning up on a golf course. They don't have lions on any of the golf courses that I am familiar with."

"That may be, my dear Ananias," said Mr. Munchausen, "but it doesn't prove anything. What you are familiar with has no especial bearing upon the ordering of the Universe. They had lions by the hundreds on the particular links I refer to. I laid the links out myself and I fancy I know what I am talking about. They were in the desert of Sahara. And I tell you what it is," he added, slapping his knee enthusiastically, "they were the finest links I ever played on. There wasn't a hole shorter than three miles and a quarter, which gives you plenty of elbow room, and the fair green had all the qualities of a first class billiard table, so that your ball got a magnificent roll on it"

"What did you do for hazards?" asked Ananias.

"Oh we had 'em by the dozen," replied Mr. Munchausen. "There weren't any ponds or stone walls, of course, but there were plenty of others that were quite as interesting. There was the Sphynx for instance; and for bunkers the pyramids can't be beaten. Then occasionally right in the middle of a game a caravan ten or twelve miles long, would begin to drag its interminable length across the middle of the course, and it takes mighty nice work with the lofting iron to lift a ball over a caravan without hitting a camel or killing an Arab, I can tell you.

"Then finally I'm sure I don't know of any more hazardous hazard for a golf player—or for anybody else for that matter—than a real hungry African lion out in search of breakfast, especially when you meet him on the hole furthest from home and have a stretch of three or four miles between him and assistance with no revolver or other weapon at hand. That's hazard enough for me and it took the best work I could do with my brassey to get around it.

"You always were strong at a brassey lie," said Ananias.

"Thank you," said Mr. Munchausen. "There are few lies I can't get around. But on this morning I was playing for the Mid-African Championship. I'd been getting along splendidly. My record for fifteen holes was about seven hundred and eighty-three strokes, and I was flattering myself that I was about to turn in the best card that had ever been seen in a medal play contest in all Africa, My drive from the sixteenth tee was a simple beauty. I thought the ball would never stop, I hit it such a tremendous whack. It had a flight of three hundred and eighty-two yards and a roll of one hundred and twenty more, and when it finally stopped it turned up in a mighty good lie on a natural tee, which the wind had swirled up.

"Calling to the monkey who acted as my caddy—we used monkeys for caddies always in Africa, and they were a great success because they don't talk and they use their tails as a sort of extra hand,—I got out my brassey for the second stroke, took my stance on the hardened sand, swung my club back, fixed my eye on the ball and was just about to carry through, when I heard a sound which sent my heart into my boots, my caddy galloping back to the club house, and set my teeth chattering like a pair of castanets. It was unmistakable, that sound.

"When a hungry lion roars you know precisely what it is the moment you hear it, especially if you have heard it before. It doesn't sound a bit like the miauing of a cat; nor is it suggestive of the rumble of artillery in an adjacent street There is no mistaking it for distant thunder, as some writers would have you believe. It has none of the gently mournful quality that characterises the soughing of the wind through the leafless branches of the autumnal forest, to which a poet might liken it; it is just a plain lion-roaring and nothing else, and when you hear it you know it.

"The man who mistakes it for distant thunder might just as well be struck by lightning there and then for all the chance he has to get away from it ultimately. The poet who confounds it with the gentle soughing breeze never lives to tell about it. He gets himself eaten up for his foolishness. It doesn't require a Daniel come to judgment to recognise a lion's roar on sight.

"I should have perished myself that morning if I had not known on the instant just what were the causes of the disturbance. My nerve did not desert me, however, frightened as I was. I stopped my play and looked out over the sand in the direction whence the roaring came, and there he stood a perfect picture of majesty, and a giant among lions, eyeing me critically as much as to say, 'Well this is luck, here's breakfast fit for a king!' but he reckoned without his host. I was in no mood to be served up to stop his ravening appetite and I made up my mind at once to stay and fight. I'm a good runner, Ananias, but I cannot beat a lion in a three mile sprint on a sandy soil, so fight it was. The question was how. My caddy gone, the only weapons I had with me were my brassey and that one little *gutta percha* ball, but thanks to my golf they were sufficient

"Carefully calculating the distance at which the huge beast stood, I addressed the ball with unusual care, aiming slightly to the left to overcome my tendency to slice, and drove the ball straight through the lion's heart as he poised himself on his hind legs ready to spring upon me. It was a superb stroke and not an instant too soon, for just as the ball struck him he sprang forward, and even as it was landed but two feet away from where I stood, but, I am happy to say, dead.

"It was indeed a narrow escape, and it tried my nerves to

the full, but I extracted the ball and resumed my play in a short while, adding the lucky stroke to my score meanwhile. But I lost the match,—not because I lost my nerve, for this I did not do, but because I lifted from the lion's heart. The committee disqualified me because I did not play from my lie and the cup went to my competitor. However, I was satisfied to have escaped with my life. I'd rather be a live runner-up than a dead champion any day."

"A wonderful experience," said Ananias. "Perfectly wonderful. I never heard of a stroke to equal that."

"You are too modest, Ananias," said Mr. Munchausen drily. "Too modest by half. You and Sapphira hold the record for that, you know."

"I have forgotten the episode," said Ananias.

"Didn't you and she make your last hole on a single stroke?" demanded Munchausen with an inward chuckle.

"Oh—yes," said Ananias grimly, as he recalled the incident. "But you know we didn't win any more than you did."

"Oh, didn't you?" asked Munchausen.

"No," replied Ananias. "You forget that Sapphira and I were two down at the finish."

And Mr. Munchausen played the rest of the game in silence. Ananias had at last got the best of him.

LEONAUR

ALSO FROM LEONAUR
AVAILABLE IN SOFTCOVER OR HARDCOVER WITH DUST JACKET

MR MUKERJI'S GHOSTS *by S. Mukerji*—Supernatural tales from the British Raj period by India's Ghost story collector.

KIPLINGS GHOSTS *by Rudyard Kipling*—Twelve stories of Ghosts, Hauntings, Curses, Werewolves & Magic.

Lightning Source UK Ltd.
Milton Keynes UK
13 October 2010

161201UK00001B/36/P